# SUFFER THE CHILDREN

In London a paedophile is brutally murdered in his own home, and to protect other known offenders the police must haul the families of their victims down to the station for questioning. And for DI Will Wagstaffe, better known as Staffe, it's just another day, because nothing is simple, least of all Staffe's personal life. There's heartache from Sylvie, his estranged lover, and the dark shadow of Jessop, his ex-partner and mentor. And as he digs for answers in the grime of the city, there's also pressure from his boss and the newspapers who are gunning for him. Everywhere he turns the boundaries between right and wrong have been blurred, but the main question remains: just how far would you go to protect your children?

ADAM CREED

# SUFFER THE CHILDREN

*Complete and Unabridged*

# CHARNWOOD
Leicester

First published in Great Britain in 2009 by
Faber and Faber Limited
London

First Charnwood Edition
published 2009
by arrangement with
Faber and Faber Limited
London

British Library CIP Data

Creed, Adam.
    Suffer the children.
    1. Police- -England- -London- -Fiction.
    2. Child molesters- -Crimes against- -Fiction.
    3. London (England)- -Fiction. 4. Detective and
    mystery stories. 5. Large type books.
    I. Title
    823.9'2–dc22

    ISBN 978–1–84782–915–3

Published by
F. A. Thorpe (Publishing)
Anstey, Leicestershire

Set by Words & Graphics Ltd.
Anstey, Leicestershire
Printed and bound in Great Britain by
T. J. International Ltd., Padstow, Cornwall

This book is printed on acid-free paper

Adam Creed was born in Salford and read PPE at Balliol College, Oxford, before working for Flemings in the City. He abandoned his career to study writing at Sheffield Hallam University, following which he wrote in Andalucia then returned to England to work with writers in prison. He is now Head of Writing at Liverpool John Moores University and Project Leader of Free to Write. He has a wife and two beautiful daughters.

For Georgina

# Acknowledgements

I would like to thank Clive, Pat and the Parva Lads from prison; Susan and the Paul Hamlyn Foundation; Aileen, Dave and Jenny from Liverpool; Dave, Patricia, Pat and Terry from probation, as well as everyone at Arch, Adelaide House, Southwood and Walton; Eduardo and the village folk of Yegen; Livewire in Kenmare; Tony from the Bridge; Patrick, Rob and Jake from Conville and Walsh; and Walter, Katherine, Angus and Lee from the stuff of dreams. I am particularly grateful to Edmund Cusick, poet, for his grace, loyalty and inspiration.

# Monday Afternoon

Staffe raises his head as high as he can, sucks in the Underground air. He is pushed from behind and his chest rubs up against the head of a raven-haired woman as they shuffle towards the escalator. She curses in an eastern tongue and he wants to apologise, but knows it isn't warranted, nor will it accomplish anything.

Judgement is scheduled for 14.00. He tries to push into the left-hand line but there is no gap. A group of teenage malevolents jostles through against the flow, leaving a sweet pall of solvents. He holds his breath as he takes a half step on to the moving escalator, waits, then breathes deep, and pictures Judge Burns; the events of the past two days in court. His nerves tighten and Staffe tries to calm his rushing blood. He makes sure the case papers are wedged tight into the pit of his arm and does up the collar of his shirt. The top button presses against his Adam's apple as he swallows. He tightens his tie right up.

Staffe says a silent mantra, reaffirms that this is what he chose for himself. 'This is my life. Be the best you can. This is my life. Be the best you can.' He replays his responses to cross-examination from the morning and picks through Judge Burns's summing-up for hints that the evidence they have garnered might prevail. He places a hand on his heart, feels the original of a secret witness statement in his breast pocket.

The world comes down to meet him, it seems, and the ticket barriers appear. They form a line between him and the white daylight beyond. News-sellers stand like bookends at the gateway to Chancery Lane.

The line of people clatters like dominoes and he has to shuffle forward with tiny steps and the raven-haired woman curses again. His phone vibrates in his trouser pocket and he fumbles for it, trying not to drop the pile of precious papers. By the time he manages to get the phone up to his ear, the ringing ceases. The screen shows *Marie*, the name of his sister. He knows it will be trouble, but also knows he has to focus on the job in hand.

The screen tells him, too, that it is 13.56. He puts his ticket into the machine and goes through, holding a firm, straight line. The smells of drains and bodies and newsprint fade quickly. The sound of chatter and curses and dragged luggage softens as he walks out on to the pavement. The bright day blisters the backs of his eyes and when he blinks, the arch silhouette of the Tube entrance burns purple and yellow on his eyelids.

Staffe steps into the traffic which is stood still, and weaves a way towards the other side of the street where there is more space. He feels a whisper of breeze on his face and looks down towards the law courts, the Thames beyond. The traffic shifts and right beside him a horn blares and as he skips quickly to the kerbside, St Bride's peals the hour. He knows if he runs, he will sweat all afternoon.

Staffe wipes a palm down the thigh of his charcoal-grey suit and looks up into Judge Burns's eyes. Burns shuffles the papers, narrows his eyes as if he is giving the sentencing serious consideration, but it is plain to Staffe that the decision is already made.

The courtroom air is tight and the trapped heat of summer stifles, just a line of small, rectangular and reinforced windows pulled open three feet below the high ceiling. The jury and the press hold their breath. The defendant, Jadus Golding, nineteen, is don of the Dalston e.Gang. He smirks, leaning against the dock rails with a pimp slouch.

Yesterday, three members of Golding's e.Gang had been ejected from the court whilst Sohan Kelly had given his evidence. 'Blat-blat-blat,' they had shouted. 'You dead motherfucker.' Jabbing fingers at him, pointing imaginary Glocks. 'You snitching bitch, man, fuckin' grass, kissing white man's ass.' Kelly had looked across to Staffe and then hung his head. The e.Gang had turned their attentions from Sohan Kelly to Staffe, smiles on their faces — as if no law could touch them.

Staffe takes a deep breath, touches Sohan Kelly's original statement in his pocket. Trails of sweat run from behind each ear, into his collar. He swallows and the top button of his shirt presses against his throat. Judge Burns avoids the eyes of the defendant and his family as he speaks. ' . . . Jadus Golding,' says Burns, looking down, 'I sentence you to seven years.'

The family stands, raging. Golding's father spits towards the judge then spits again at Staffe, hitting him on the shoulder.

Today, Sohan Kelly is at home, preparing his flight into hiding. Staffe had told him it was best if he didn't come into court, best if he kept his head down, maybe went to Mumbai to stay with friends on his mother's side. He said he couldn't get the visa. Staffe's boss, Pennington, said he would sort it.

'Fucking kill you, Wagstaffe,' shouts Jadus Golding.

'You won't need to,' shouts his father.

Staffe looks across at them. He is an officer of the law. What should he fear from people like this? He prays that Sohan Kelly is long gone, taking his dubious truth with him.

★　★　★

As the afternoon draws to a close, Staffe gets up from his worn, leather captain's chair and runs a hand through his tousled hair. He should get it cut, but nowadays it pays not to look like a copper. He leans towards the fan and takes air on his face, summons thanks to whoever might be up there, for another small victory of good over bad: a seven year tariff for a small-time gangster who thought that pulling a gun on a post office manager could redesign his life for the better. The post office manager is a basket case now, having to sell his bad dream.

Staffe makes a pile of the witness statements,

forensic reports and charge sheets. He takes Sohan Kelly's original statement, folded time and again, from the inside pocket of his jacket. He has considered ripping it up, time and again, but slips it in with the rest of the papers and lifts the whole lot high, drops them on top of the filing cabinet. He wipes his unclean palms down over his hips and looks at the stack of papers, takes them down again. He removes Sohan Kelly's original statement and puts it back in his jacket pocket.

He presses the intercom. 'You got a minute, Pulford?'

'Be straight in, sir,' comes the tinny reply.

Staffe opens his drawer and takes out the airline ticket. It's been a long time coming, but finally he's getting to meet Muñoz. Tomorrow morning he'll be on flight 729 to Bilbao. It's well over three years since his last proper holiday and the best part of three years since Sylvie. They were supposed to have gone to Corsica for two weeks. Staffe had cancelled it, which he had done before. But he wouldn't be given the chance again.

There's a knock at the door and Staffe calls: 'Come in.' He closes his eyes, imagines a sea breeze sweeping across a Basque promenade; a week of no telephones.

'Off tomorrow, sir,' says Pulford.

Staffe opens his eyes, sees his detective sergeant closing the door behind him. Pulford's suit is sharp and his hair is trim, glistening with fresh wax. When he enters the room, he brings a scent of freshness with him. He doesn't carry fat and his face is unravaged, a tinge of redness in his cheeks. Of the two of them, Pulford seems more the part than his inspector. 'His time will come,' thinks Staffe. 'I'm afraid there's quite a bit of tidying up, Pulford.'

'That's what I'm here for, sir. Is it the Golding case? Seven years, eh? That's a result.'

Staffe thinks about what Golding and his father had threatened. He feels bad that he is happy to be heading for a foreign shore. 'He'll be out in three and a half and his crew will still be at it while he's away. They'll put his share to one side for when he gets out. Life goes on.'

'You told me to enjoy the successes when they come along.'

'You don't have to take your own advice, Sergeant,' says Staffe, breaking out into a laugh.

'Is that advice?' says Pulford, trying to keep a straight face.

They laugh together and Staffe sits back in the captain's chair, rocking. He points to the pile of paperwork. 'Let's just say I'm letting you bask in the success. You can think about it while you're writing that lot up.' Staffe slips the airline ticket into the empty inside pocket of his suit jacket.

'Good job you managed to get a statement out of that Kelly guy, get him to testify.'

'That smart-arsed barrister of Golding's might just appeal, so make an inventory and get everything properly filed away. Leave the door open.' He watches Pulford struggle out of the room, feels something of himself go with him.

The heat is stifling and the desktop fan simply shifts the hot air from one part of Staffe's office

6

to another. In the city it seems there's nowhere to hide from the beating sun and the trapped fumes. It comes up from the Underground, comes down from the cloudless skies.

A shape appears in the doorway. DC Josie Chancellor looks dishevelled. Her skirt is all creased around her lap and the top three buttons of her shirt are undone.

'I hear you're actually taking some leave, sir.'

'I don't know why everyone's so interested. It's only a week.'

'Congratulations on the Golding case.'

'It was a team effort. You should be congratulating yourself, Chancellor.'

Josie closes the door and makes her way into the room. She rests her bottom on the edge of his desk, crosses her legs at the ankle. 'You were after him long before I arrived. I heard about the threats, in court.'

'It's nothing.' Staffe feels his heart hitch up. He's been threatened before and doesn't know why he should be so bothered by this one. Maybe he's getting too old for this game.

'What did you get him on in the end?'

'Conspiracy with intent.'

'Thanks to Sohan Kelly. You look as though you could do with a drink.'

'I'd love to.'

'But you won't.'

'We could get something to eat,' he says.

'I need to change.'

'You look fine to me.'

'Haven't you got to pack for your holiday?'

'I travel light.' He stands up, takes his suit

jacket from off the back of his chair, slings it over his shoulder.

'You should wear suits more often, Staffe. You look good.'

'And you . . . ' He looks towards the closed door, rubs his fingers into the hollow where his head meets his neck, wet from the long hot day.

'Yes?'

' . . . you look just great.'

'How do you know what a girl wants to hear?'

'I don't. I just tell the truth. You know that.'

Josie gives him a knowing look. 'That's the best and worst of you, sir.'

★  ★  ★

Karl Colquhoun steps over the off-cuts of wood and tramps through the sawdust. If he closes his eyes, he can imagine walking in a forest undergrowth. He punches in the security code to the staff toilet and pushes open the door. It smells the way you'd expect a men's toilet in a builders' merchants to smell.

Karl presses down the cold tap with the ball of his hand. He waits for it to run cold and paddles the water on to his face, then the back of his neck. He can hear the tin voice of a radio over the tannoy. It's a roadshow somewhere by the sea and reminds him of the last time he and Leanne went to Margate. He shouldn't have gone. By law.

There's another twenty minutes until the afternoon break and he'd love to have his tea out the back with the rest of the boys, taking in the breeze that comes up off the dual carriageway, but he won't. He needs to keep himself to himself. He's been here nearly a year, but now the word is out. Karl leans on the basin, looks into the smeared mirror. He squints, sees a young and pure him looking back. He closes his eyes, pictures himself and Leanne in a quiet corner of the beach: waves collapsing, then the rolling lull of pebbles rattling, wet. Gulls free and squawking in a vast blue sky.

He opens his eyes and sees himself for what he is. He straightens up. Tonight, he will take Leanne down to the Thames where, at low tide, there's a kind of beach.

Then he remembers they're not talking, haven't been properly since they came back from Margate. She loves him, for sure. She tells him every day but she's just not herself right now.

A loud rap at the door startles him and he calls, 'Won't be a minute.' Then there's the duller sound of a hard fist, banging.

'The fuckin' frag's in there.' It's Denness's voice. 'Jackin' off.' Ross Denness is new at Marvitz Builders Merchants, arriving last week with Karl's whole history to hand — on account of the fact that he is a cousin of Leanne's. It took Denness less than a day to start telling everyone that Karl is the reason Leanne has had to give up her kids to the social.

The Karl in the mirror is a frightened man — looking older than his years. He'll be moving on soon, now Denness has let the cat out of the bag. He'll put an advert in the papers out north. They won't know him from Adam up in Golders

9

Green and Muswell Hill. The plan is to go back to doing what he does best: cabinetmaking, French polishing. The money is good, so long as he can tide himself over until word gets round and his first raft of invoices get paid.

For the rest of the afternoon, he bags up sawdust, and then slopes away without saying goodbye. Nobody has ever proved that Karl Colquhoun interfered with the kids from his first marriage, or with Leanne's. Even so, he's made sure there'll be no further heartbreak because he's had the snip and Leanne, at the age of twenty-four, got herself sterilised.

Karl gets the 73 back home and goes upstairs, sits right at the back on the left-hand side, watches East London pass him by on his route back towards the City. An office gent sits in front, smelling of booze and wearing a handmade suit. He makes Karl want to heave. He should get up, switch to another seat, but he can't move. His muscles are slack. One by one, he weighs up exactly who is on this deck of the bus. His breathing is tight, his head light. He leans forward and stares at the floor but the sweet fumes of booze get thicker. He breathes through his mouth and counts down from five hundred and as soon as he can feel his legs again, he summons all his strength, stands. Staring at the floor, he makes his way down the stairs and gets off, a stop early.

On the walk back to the Limekiln estate, he goes to the halal shop to get milk and antiperspirant. While he is queuing, the whiff of booze hits him again but when he's paid and turns to see who's wearing it, nobody is there. Karl's heart stops, then beats double time and won't slow down. His fingers tremble and his stomach feels empty.

He walks quickly back to the Limekiln estate, head bowed, all the way up to the urine-stained, concrete deck of the Limekiln tower, accompanied by the sound of barking dogs. Why do people keep killer animals in a tower block, he wonders, picking up a used syringe and putting it in his pocket before a child comes across it. He just wants to be inside, to lock the door behind him and wait for Leanne to come home. They won't go out tonight. The river can wait.

He pulls out his key and his watch beeps. It makes him jump. It is precisely four. He slips his key in, but before he can turn it, Karl is startled by a pungent whiff of drink. He feels a shadow on him and his skin prickles. His muscles go slack and, again, he can't move. The shadow gets darker, colder, and as he turns round, he sees a looming, masked figure. Wide, piercing eyes, blood-red lips. He closes his eyes and raises his hands to protect himself but he is too late and hears a dull, cracking noise. A searing pain shoots though his skull, down into his neck. His legs give way and he falls heavily on the Limekiln concrete, his skin ripping on the floor. Somebody laughs. A bully's laugh.

Karl wants to curl up and let the dark come, for it all to be over, but he forces himself to look up. He sees a hand on the key to the door. He reaches into his pocket for the syringe but a searing pain jags up and down along his arm. He

11

looks at the leg of the person who clubbed him and bites into his own lip, forcing his hand into his pocket. He can feel the syringe and takes a grip, eases his hand out of the pocket. He breathes in as much air as he can and sizes up the leg. You can kill someone by sliding air into their blood. But just as he pulls his arm back to stab into the leg, it shifts and he feels a vast thud to his balls. It forces all the air out of him and now the dark comes for him.

* * *

When he comes round, Karl is looking at the ceiling of his bedroom. He can't move and there's something metal in his mouth. He can't move his jaw or tongue and his insides feel raw. He tastes blood. Someone in a white mask, with black eyes and blood-red lips, holds a whisky bottle aloft.

As they get closer, the blood-red lips make the shape of a smile. He strains to close his mouth but all he can do, as the whisky is poured and poured, is shut his eyes tight, feel the liquid burn him all the way down into his stomach.

With each swallow, he cries another soundless sob, drowned by the spirit. He suddenly feels rough hands on his midriff, down the waistband of his jeans. They tug them down, rip his shirt open.

The person in the mask shows him the bottle with one hand. In the other, a long, thin, glinting sharp blade. Karl's bowels subside as he feels the cold steel on him, hears someone say: 'This is from the children.'

Karl fears that this is not the moment he will die. He fears the last breaths will be long and drawn out. As the white-hot line is drawn around his balls, he sees one last thing — a silver gleam, getting bigger and bigger in his sight. He tries to close his eyes, but fingers force one eye open and the blade comes impossibly big until it obscures all the light and touches him. As he waits for the pain he knows his heart does not beat when it should. You don't hear it until it is gone. The blood inside him runs up against itself and a choir bellows out. He prays for it to cease.

★   ★   ★

Staffe looks across at Josie and smiles. They are in the kitchen of the house in Kilburn that he has just finished renovating.

'You're not eating,' she says, putting her knife and fork together on the empty plate.

'I'd rather cook than eat.'

'You're a people pleaser,' she laughs. 'Who'd have thought it?'

'Try telling that to Jadus Golding.'

'Not pleasing our Jadus doesn't make you a bad person.'

Staffe spears a scallop with his fork and runs it through the beurre blanc sauce.

She stops eating and takes a slug of wine, watching him. 'You've got big hands,' she says. 'Big fingers.'

'My fingers are too big and I'm too old,' he says.

'I like your fingers, Staffe.'

13

'Do you want some more wine,' he says, picking up the bottle, offering to pour.

'I think I've had enough.' She leans across and picks up her car keys from the middle of the table, spins them round on her index finger like a gunslinger with a revolver.

'You can stay,' he says. 'It's only early.'

'You don't mean that, and anyway . . . '

'What?'

'Just have a good holiday.' She has a soft, smudged smile. 'Sir.'

Staffe scrapes the plates into the bin, rinses them and when he hears the front door slam he goes through to the living room. He watches Josie skip down the steps and make her way towards the gap in the beech trees. Somehow, she must know he's watching her go because she twiddles a wave with her fingers without looking, fixing her tights with the other hand, then slams the gate shut as she shouts at the kids to stop playing kerbie in the road.

★ ★ ★

Tanya Ford can't get out of the house quick enough. She did her citizenship homework the minute she got in and has been changing in and out of outfits ever since. The 'look' is half fairy-tale princess: half street-corner slut. As soon as the door-bell rings, she scampers downstairs and out, linking arms with her best friend and calling back to her mother 'Don't worry' as she is told not to be late, to be careful.

'I love you, Tan,' calls her mother and Tanya

14

wants to call back that she loves her, too. But she doesn't, just twiddles her fingers and blows a kiss. Her friend giggles.

When they get to the corner of the road, Tanya folds the waistband of her skirt down, once, twice, meticulously. She applies her lipstick and starts texting, feeling the slow rush of love that's in the air.

★ ★ ★

Guy Montefiore tips 5 per cent. He always tips 5 per cent. It brings the fare to twelve eighty-five and he waits for the change to come back through, asks for a receipt. The cabbie huffs and puffs, saying he can't find a pen.

As he waits, Guy thinks about his daughter. Thomasina is fourteen going on nineteen and he worries about how she is getting on with her mother, picking up bad habits. He grimaces and exhales, blows the thought away.

His mobile phone signals that it has received a text message and he begins to palpitate. 'Forget the receipt,' he says as he opens the door and climbs out. 'You should carry a pen. It's a tool of your trade.' He slams the door, harder than necessary. But her words appear on the screen and his fury subsides. He begins to compose a response. A smile comes to his face.

He wonders whether the summer will ever burn itself out. He prefers the shorter days of autumn and winter. The longer nights suit him — he doesn't have to wait two, three hours after work before there's the darkness to shield him.

15

But the trouble with the long nights is that his loves are tucked up in bed, not out and about.

Not any old love. It's got to be perfect. The way it never is for most people.

Guy knows her name and her movements, knows her favourite pop star and who her best friends are. He's been watching so long now he can even guess what she'll be wearing. Monday night, youth club night, dressing like a tart because that's what her friends do. It's not because she wants to be with a boy. She's not like that. No, Tanya simply wants to belong, and soon she will. Soon, she will be loved and she will be able to love back. The first time.

Guy lets himself in the back door of the church hall, turning sideways and shuffling along between the rows of junk waiting to be collected. There is a dull light from the reinforced glass pane above the fire door but he can do this in the dark.

He passes the tiny kitchen and takes a deep breath, feels a swell in his loins. He presses the door to the stairs that go below and the sound of music comes up. The bass vibrates, buzzes up along his legs as he goes down into the dark, running his hand along the rough, unpainted bricks, feeling for the overalls. He takes them off the hook at the bottom of the stairs and undresses himself. He folds his clothes the best he can. They were, when all is said and done, made to touch him just so — at considerable expense.

Guy laments that Tanya has never, knowingly, seen him at his best, but feels a surge at the thought that soon — so very, very soon — that will change.

He makes his way towards the chinks of light that come through the gaps in the stage. As he goes, the music gets louder. He distills the sounds: a hundred teenagers dancing, giggling, scurrying, the deeper voice of a young alpha male as the song peters to an end, demanding what the next one should be. For a moment it is just the soft flesh of voices. Guy stops, mid-step, and holds his breath until the next song cranks up. He crouches down in the usual spot, stage left. It's where the gap in the sections that make up the stage is greatest. It's also where she stands. Thank God she's such a creature of habit.

Guy presses his face to the painted wood and for the first time in twenty-three hours, looking up from just above the level of the dance floor, he sees her. She's wearing his favourite skirt and a cut-off, silky top that is new. He should be annoyed with her. It shows too much.

Tanya's legs are impossibly smooth and they have tanned to the colour of milky coffee. Her tummy has the tiniest pod of puppy fat, her hips haven't quite spread wide yet. She pivots, hand pointing out at someone he can't see in a gesture of ironic drama. Someone nudges her and her skirt swirls as she turns to see. He can see the finest down in the hollow of the small of her back.

His breathing is deeper, shorter, he feels the knot in the pit of his stomach tighten. Weak in the legs, he falls back on his haunches, lies all the

17

way back for a moment and lets the music wash over him. He can smell the wood of the bare boards. In the dark, he pictures her dancing, her friends drifting away, slowly, one by one, until she's all on her own.

⋆   ⋆   ⋆

It takes Staffe fifteen minutes to pack: two T-shirts and two long-sleeved shirts; two pairs of shorts and a pair of Dockers. He'll travel in his jeans and an old linen jacket. Eight pairs of boxers and socks and Douglass's *History of ETA*. And he's done. He checks his phone, sees the missed call from his sister, Marie, and he tries her but there's no response. He leaves a message to say he's going away and he hopes Harry is fine. He deliberates, says, 'And you, too.'

Staffe first went to Bilbao twenty years ago, to identify what remained of his parents. His sister was off the rails and somewhere in the Far East so he was left to cope on his own. He made the arrangements to bring them back home. He gave up on university and as soon as his share of the proceeds of their estate came through, he bought a flat in South Ken, for cash. A year later, he took out a mortgage to buy another. Then the compensation came through. Funny, how you can measure the value of two people; put a price on what it might be worth to not have a full complement of parents.

In the ensuing months and years, young Staffe drank too much and made friends too readily,

18

took recreational drugs too much and too often. He got up later and later — and sometimes not at all. And he charmed the birds down from the trees the way he always could — a gift that deserted him for only the briefest period of his mourning. And the lovers became part of his mourning, so an analyst had once told him. Gradually, after he joined the Force, he dropped his vices, one by one.

Three years ago, when he lost Jessop, his partner in the Force, Staffe went back to the Basque country to resume the process of finding whoever left that bomb in the seafront restaurant. Sylvie had left him, too, and he felt as if there was nothing but empty space all around him.

He swore to build up the evidence piece by piece. He would gain a conviction and he would gift the killer justice rather than retribution. In his dreams, he asks the killer to seek forgiveness and, on his parents' behalf, he grants it. In his darkest moments, he cannot see a way to do this.

The renovated house smells of fresh plaster and varnished woodwork, new carpets, too. It is too big for him, far too much space. He calls Rosa but there is no response. He decides to go out anyway and makes his way upstairs for what has become a ritual. In the bathroom, he takes out his running gear from the Adidas bag and turns on the shower. The water jets down, hard on his scalp and shoulders; he takes the heat up a notch so it's almost scalding him and he scrubs and scrubs with the soap. The smell of coal tar gets thicker and thicker, the steam gets more and more dense. This evening, he will run out to Kentish Town and through Islington into the City. Rosa lives in the Barbican. There is a chance, he thinks in more optimistic snatches, that she knows where he's coming from.

\* \* \*

Looking up at her place, it is plain that Rosa has company. Staffe's lungs are bursting and he is dripping with sweat, happy to be at rest. He goes into the piazza and leans against a raised flower bed. He breathes deep and his chest burns. He runs his hand around his neck and feels the dirt coming away. As the evening comes slowly on, he thinks of Rosa, the first time.

Sylvie had been gone a couple of months and his partner, Jessop, had been shipped out to the Met. Staffe got an assault call — not really his bag, but he was in the area.

Rosa was in her flat, the one he is looking up at now. It was a neighbour who called but Rosa, crying, didn't want to press charges. Staffe held her and said she didn't have to and as she drew back her head to kiss him 'thank you', he saw her bruised eye up close. To this day, he doesn't know why, but he held on to her, a hand on each hip. Her body felt so soft, even through her clothes. 'Let me take you out,' he said. 'Help you forget this.'

'I don't think you know what I do,' she said.

'I think I do. And I don't think I care,' he said.

He took her out for dinner and afterwards they went to a place of his in Belsize Park. He told her she was like one of Goya's women. Later, he had to explain it was young Goya. He showed her and it made them laugh. That first night, they listened to Miles Davis and Bessie Smith and he made her real hot chocolate and he held her and nothing happened. When she went to the bathroom, he rifled through her diary and clocked the name of the guy who was down for that evening. He wanted to go out and beat him to a pulp. But he didn't.

'You all right? You don't look all right,' she had said when she came back. 'You look sad.'

'Don't I always?' he had said.

'Not to me.' She pulled him towards her and began kissing him. He let her, for a while; then he said, 'I love somebody.'

'You deserve to,' she said.

Three days later, Staffe found out where Rosa's client worked and went through his police history. The man worked as a money broker and Staffe guessed his employers didn't know what their young gun had done in his past. So he told them. He felt bad about it for as long as it took him to remember the bruises on Rosa's face.

A middle-aged man comes out on to the deck in front of Rosa's flat. He'll have come straight from work — for a happy hour. Staffe makes his way up there, passes the man on the stairs. He smells expensive, has a kindly smile and a wedding ring. He knocks on Rosa's door and her face lights up. She kisses him and ushers him in, and they talk, not much more — the way it has always been — and when he gets back to the renovated house in Kilburn, he draws the new

21

curtains against the still bright mid-evening sun and lays back on his sofa, listening to the children playing in the street. He closes his eyes and incants a mantra that lulls him into sleep.

★　★　★

He dozes briefly and fitfully, tossing and turning through visions of Sohan Kelly and Jadus Golding — his family and gang with their smug threats. 'We'll kill you, Kelly. We'll kill you, Wagstaffe!'

And he wakes to the telephone rattle and rubs his eyes. It is still light and he leans down, reaches for the old Bakelite phone — an SOC freebie that was never called as evidence. He could have returned it to its owner but the owner never made it back from intensive care. There was no next of kin.

'Yes!' he snaps.

'Sir?' says Pulford.

Staffe hears his DS anew — the voice sounding older, more grave than in the flesh.

'It's bad, sir. Bad.' His breathing is short.

'Bad?' says Staffe.

'I've never seen anything like it.'

Pulford is a graduate trainee, resented by practically all his colleagues, and even though Staffe can't be sure he'll last any kind of distance, he resists the temptation to hold a person's intelligence against them. 'What is it?'

'I didn't know whether I should call you.'

'Well you did.'

'I can refer it to Pennington.'

'I said 'what is it'!'

'A murder, sir.' Staffe pictures Pulford pacing, his ruddy cheeks gone pale, grey. 'No. More an execution.'

'Where?'

'On the Limekiln estate.'

'Put me through to Janine.'

'You're supposed to be . . . '

'Just do it!'

Staffe imagines the walk to the scene of crime, up through a guard of honour of ten-to fourteen-year-olds taking time out from running crystal meth and crack. It's the very bottom rung on the most rickety ladder. One or two will get to have the Subaru Impreza and drink Cristal, have someone else running bags for them. Most will end up using, going down the line, falling by the wayside for ever. It's as easy as a slow, soft squeeze on the trigger of a gun that's slipped into your hand by a man with a smile on his face.

As he waits to be put through he stands up, kicks the bed, forgetting his feet are bare. 'Shit!'

'What?'

'Janine? You're on the Limekiln?' He thinks he can hear her swallow before she speaks.

'Been here an hour or so. You're supposed to be on holiday.' There's a quiver in her voice.

'I'll be there in quarter of an hour.'

Staffe washes his face and under his arms, then throws on a button-down shirt. He picks up his packed bag and feels himself switch on as the setting Kilburn sun spears into the hall through the stained-glass panel of the front door. It's a

Victorian house and the door is a perfect match. He got it years ago from a reclamation yard up in Southgate. He was with Sylvie when he bought it.

Staffe's heart sags and he says 'No' out loud to himself. He can't quite stop all the sadness. He wants to have been a better man. He shrugs, even though he's alone. He's been alone too long not to value himself as an audience.

He pulls the heavy front door closed behind him and wishes the kids weren't still playing kerbie in the road. He thinks about telling them to watch themselves but says nothing. Sometimes your spirit is too frail to take casual profanities from the nine-year-old loved ones of your neighbours.

Round the back, up the narrow lane that his house backs on to, he slips the big fat key into the big fat padlock that tries to ward off evil spirits from his lock-up. He takes two steps back, bringing the doors with him, looking at his two cars. It's a night for the crap one. It's almost always a night for the crap one.

There's an ingrained pall of long-ago cigarettes in the old Peugeot and as he twists the ignition key, Staffe feels a burning yen for a long, slow, drag on a Rothmans. The diesel engine coughs up like a one-lung smoker. The radio comes on of its own accord and he turns it up a notch. Stravinsky, he thinks, and the violins scratch away over the long slow swoon of brass and wind. He thinks it's the Firebird. He doesn't mind Stravinsky but he wishes it was Grieg. Something smoother for a night like this. He

24

pictures himself on a Basque waterfront. All alone, watching the Atlantic swell.

*　*　*

Janine is outside the victim's flat when Staffe gets to the Limekiln. The victim is Karl Colquhoun: thirty-six years old with two conditional discharges. Round here, that makes him an angel.

As Staffe approaches Janine, walking along the decked, concrete access, it looks as if she might be taking in the sunset, leaning on the rusted railing and peering out over the quadrangle of the Limekiln. The crime-scene tape is out: more a curtain going up on a new drama than a shield to keep folk away. The people have come, hanging around in groups. It's like a bear pit and Staffe thinks what a sick joke it is that it takes something like this to bring a community together.

Staffe leans out and calls down to the uniformed officers to disperse the growing crowd. The officers shrug. They move towards the cluster of small groups and Staffe waits for a reaction, half expecting something to flare. But it doesn't. One or two women move forward, out of the groups and up to the officers. They start talking, gesturing up to the fifth floor, snarling.

'What the hell's going on, Janine?'

She shakes her head, says nothing and nods towards a door. Two uniformed officers are standing by it. Their faces are ashen. These are men who've seen most of the worst that London can muster.

'I'll take a look. You can talk me through it in

a minute, hey?' he says, putting a hand on her shoulder. He lets it rest, comfortable. He takes a step towards her, whispers into her hair, 'Take your time.'

'Thanks, Staffe. I'll be all right in a minute.'

He runs his hand down her back, feels the hollow of its small with the ball of his thumb. He smiles. Her eyes go soft, damp and they each remember a happy time that should have lasted longer. Staffe remembers her eyes, wild and wide, the unlikely words that came out of her thin mouth.

'Staffe,' she says.

'Yes.'

She takes a hold of his hand, looking around to make sure they're not seen. 'Nothing.' She squeezes his hand.

Staffe takes a deep one, makes his way in.

'Where is Pulford?'

'He's gone back to the station. It hit him hard, poor love.' She says it without irony.

'It's not his first.'

'You'll see when you get there.'

Everywhere, there are signs that the usual people have attended to the usual necessaries. The evidence is bagged and sitting on the plastic-looking oval dining table. But nobody's here. No one's stayed longer than necessary.

A brown Formica display unit matches the dining table. Its veneered ply shelves shoulder school pictures of two different kids. The kids aren't smiling. Most school photographers can cun a smile from the shyest or most miserable of children. And now Staffe feels it. A cold shiver

26

runs up his spine. His scalp pinches. Not a happy home, this. Not by any stretch.

The hallway to the bedrooms is papered with big dark flowers and as he opens the first door the smell hits him. A deep, sweet smell which catches at the top of his throat. He takes a big stride in, clocking the feet splayed at the foot of the bed, trainers still on, a piece of pink gum between heel and sole in the hollow that never rubs clean. Karl Colquhoun's trousers are ruched round his ankles and a brown crust has formed all around the leg flesh. It spreads on to the unmade bed. Blood, still red, is streaked down Karl's thighs, thickest around his groin.

Then Staffe sees it. His hand instinctively takes a hold of his mouth and nose. He wants to gag but hears Janine rustling up behind him.

'The human eyeball is spherical,' she says. 'The testicle measures 2.5 centimetres by 5 centimetres but it's oval. That's why it's protruding,' says Janine. 'They would have had to sever the optic nerve, which is half a centimetre thick. It would require some kind of blade or a pair of scissors. Same with the vas deferens.'

'His balls?'

She nods. 'It would require significant force. A decent blade.'

'And someone who knew what they were doing?' Staffe pretends to be observing the body but he focuses on infinity.

'Either that or a quick learner. A strong stomach, for sure.'

'Wouldn't there be two of them — one to hold him down?'

27

'We'll have to wait for the autopsy but my guess is he was paralytic. There's an empty litre of Scotch by the bed,' says Janine. She sounds tired. 'There's swelling to the jaw, I'd guess it is fractured.'

Staffe forces himself to look back at the body; he needs to see it in situ. He focuses on the man's face, feeling himself about to heave but he swallows it away and squints. He suddenly feels as if he is connected somehow to this awful situation. He knows this man. He's sure he does.

He grabs a pair of gloves and pulls them on, goes into the lounge and rummages through the drawers in the sideboard, eventually finds a photograph of Karl Colquhoun. He's right. This man has been in Staffe's house. The best part of a year ago, he had gone down to Staffe's flat in Queens Terrace, South Ken. Not only that, Staffe had made him cups of tea while he repaired the marquetry on a Cobb writing table. Karl Colquhoun did a wonderful job. He was painstaking and uncompromising. A craftsman. You'd think he had something to offer a civilised society.

Staffe goes back to the bedroom and looks down at Karl Colquhoun. The man this happened to, the way they did it . . . he is no ordinary victim. Perhaps no kind of victim at all — in some people's eyes. He turns his back and walks through the flat, nods at the uniformed officer on the door, who says, 'Sir, shall I lock the place down?'

Staffe nods and thinks of the warmer clime that awaits him with the far older and political

28

crime that killed his parents — supposedly a crime of reason. And he wonders whether that makes it better or worse than the brutal slaying of Karl Colquhoun, no angel, perhaps. Regardless, he'll chase them down. It's what he does.

Walking down the stairwell, the sounds of his own footsteps echo against others coming up at him. As he passes them, they look down, and at level two the smell of aerosol paint is thick and new. Even while the police are here, they're tagging the place. The chemicals catch in his throat and Staffe takes the last few flights two steps at a time and runs out into the courtyard, gulping at the air.

'Someone's in a hurry.'

Pennington is leaning against the old Peugeot. He pushes himself off the rusted car and dusts himself down, adjusts the knot of his tie. He looks more like an accountant than a chief inspector. He is wiry, with dark, sheened hair that has more than a hint of Just For Men. As always, he wears a double-breasted suit. He shoots his cuffs. 'Didn't expect to see you here, Staffe.'

'I'm off in the morning, sir. First thing.'

'Couldn't resist a look, eh, Inspector?' Pennington puts a hand on his Seamaster watch, takes a studied look at the time. 'We *can* manage without you.' He fixes Staffe with a lame smile.

'I just thought, what with Rimmer off on the long sick.'

'Stress. Ha!' Pennington looks past Staffe and up, towards the Limekiln tower. He talks as if he is being recorded. 'Don't you think that if the

29

word didn't exist, the condition would never arise.' He mimics a whine. ''I'm all stressed out.'' He looks straight at Staffe, slit eyes. 'Well, everybody's stressed, unless they do fuck all. It's what keeps us going. It's good for us!'

'Some more than others, perhaps. Sir.'

'You don't get stressed, though, do you, Staffe? No chance of that! You get yourself on holiday. How long's it been? Two years? Longer?'

He nods. 'You don't want me to stay, sir?'

'I'd have thought that with the Golding episode you'd see the advantage in keeping a low profile. A bit of sun on your back.'

'And what about Sohan Kelly? Will he be feeling the sun on his back? I hear he's about to be magicked off to India but there's trouble with his visa.'

'Kelly's taken care of. He needn't concern you.'

'But he does, sir.'

'He got us our conviction.'

Staffe feels Kelly's original statement, safe in his pocket. He wants to know exactly what kind of a hold Pennington has over Sohan — to make him change the evidence the way he did. 'And what did it get him?'

Pennington gives Staffe a look that could kill. He takes a step closer and lowers his voice. 'You know that bastard Golding — and all the bastards he runs with — had it coming. And you know that poor sod of a postmaster will be a quivering wreck for all his days. Kelly was your witness, Staffe. Your witness. I'll get him away from here, don't you worry. Bloody visas!'

Staffe can't say anything; can't remind Pennington it was his idea to conjure up Sohan Kelly. He looks Pennington in the eye. 'I've never believed that ends justify the means, sir.'

'For fuck's sake, Staffe' — Pennington is talking through his teeth now — 'I'm not going to have another ethical debate. I'm telling you, what's done is done. And by Christ, justice has been done.'

'Not my kind of justice, sir.'

'There's no place in Jadus Golding's world for philosophers. Remember, Golding did it! And what's more, Wagstaffe, the buck stops with you.' Pennington jabs a finger at Staffe, pulls himself up short from actually touching the chest.

'Don't I know it, sir. Don't I know it.'

Pennington plays with his cuffs again, calming himself. 'So. You get yourself off, Staffe. Leave us to take care of this.' He nods up at the Limekiln tower. 'It's a done deal by the looks of things. The wife's gone missing. Odds on it's her. Open. Shut.'

'And if it's not?'

'Then we'll gather the evidence. The way we always do.'

'You're short-handed.'

'There's always the Met if we're struggling.'

'The Met!'

Pennington turns sideways, takes a step away. 'Get yourself off, Staffe. Trust me, we can survive without you.'

Staffe makes his way into the night. As he walks towards his car, Pennington's Jag purrs

31

past, red lights fading to nothing and just as he is left all alone, with the Limekiln tower looming like a monster in the dark sky, he hears a bang! And glass falls to ground from the street light above. The street goes dead, dead dark. Staffe stops in his tracks, fears the worst. He clenches his fists in readiness. For what?

He looks behind him and up at the dark tower, then he hears something. He peers into the dark, sees a moving shape by his car. He knows he can't take a backward step, so he walks slowly towards his car, watching his steps. Catcalls ring out from inside the Limekiln. Dogs bark. Closer, Staffe is sure he can hear breathing, heavy. As he gets to the car he hears something behind him and he spins round, calls out, 'Who's there!' He flicks on his pocket Maglite and casts a sharp beam out into the night. Nothing. He checks up and down the street. When he turns to his car, the beam illuminates a fresh violation. The letter *J* is key-carved into the car door. 'J,' he says aloud. 'Jadus bloody Golding,' he whispers to himself.

Opposite, two figures in baseball caps and hoods drawn down, look out at him from a boarded shop doorway. They could be anybody. A car speeds by. Anybody could be in it, carrying anything. In the City, there's too many people, too many vehicles. The headlight swoop seems to show that the hooded youths in the doorway are smiling.

★　★　★

32

Back in his suit, Guy Montefiore is inconspicuous. In this part of Fulham the worlds of City and Media rub shoulders with white trash.

He switches back and forth, avoids the one or two streets that butt up from the big estates. He makes the smallest detour to pick up some tonic water from Oddbins and as he comes back out on to the street, a man in a flight jacket on the opposite side of the road turns quickly away. Guy checks around him. It doesn't feel as if he's being watched and he knows, as one who watches, what to look for.

He doesn't have to wait long when he gets to Tanya's street. Tanya Ford uncouples her arm from her friend and they kiss on both cheeks. Tanya skips up the steps to her tiny townhouse and the door opens before she can knock. She is loved, but she didn't see Guy. She never does.

Within ten minutes, Guy is delving into his Gieves & Hawkes trouser pocket and sticking his key into a million quids' worth of late Victorian terraced house. He kicks off his shoes and goes into the study that used to be the family room. He dials Thomasina's number. As it rings — and usually it rings and rings and rings before she picks up — he tucks the phone into the crook of his shoulder and makes a middling G & T, takes a sip and shoos the cat off his armchair with the tip of a toe.

'I want to speak to Thomasina,' he says to the male that answers. Some dirty bastard her mother has dragged home.

'Is that her dad? They said to say you can't.'

'Who are you?' Guy's heart goes double fast.

'Fuck off. I'm her boyfriend.'

'Her boyfriend? Whose boyfriend? Not Thomasina's.'

But it's dead.

# Tuesday Morning

Staffe has locked down the Kilburn flat and given Josie a key so she can take in the mail and water the plants.

The Tube doors slide shut and Staffe feels a tiny pocket of emptiness — a single air bubble can close down an entire heating system. Last night, when he got back from the Limekiln estate, visions of Jadus Golding tampered with his sleep again and now he feels tired, shakes open the *Guardian*, trying to get the mind clean, working in straight lines again, but he sees the front page of somebody else's *News*. The headline is:

**SELF-HELP MURDER.**

He squints at the strapline that runs beneath an old photograph of Karl Colquhoun.

**A Crime That's Not a Crime?**
**More pages 4 and 5.**

He takes a hold of the *News* and tugs it down to see a wide-eyed young Asian man looking up, afraid. 'It's OK. I'm police. Can I borrow your paper?'

The young man nods, folds it neatly and hands it across.

Staffe accepts it, says, 'Sorry. Here, have this,'

handing him the *Guardian*.

According to the *News*, Colquhoun's murder is a crime of passion. His wife, apparently, has had to give her children up because of what Karl did to his kids from a previous marriage; and if the wife did it, could that make her more saint than sinner? She would be doing society a favour.

Staffe rereads the report but his mind is distracted by the very opposite kind of a killing: as cold-blooded and indiscriminate as they come. He closes his eyes, tries to picture his coming together with Santi Extbatteria in Spain. The train builds speed on its way towards Heathrow as the distance between stations grows. It rocks from side to side and the more Staffe thinks about what happened to his parents, the closer his eyes clench, tight shut. His stomach churns and his mouth slowly fills with fluid. He swallows. He wants to be sick. He wants to get off but knows he can't.

★   ★   ★

DCI Pennington scans the room to check on the team at his disposal. The temporary incident room at Leadengate Station is undersized and packed tight. 'I want you, Johnson, to stay bang on top of this. Report directly to me and keep them at it. With a bit of luck, this should be done and dusted within a week.' Pennington looks around the room. 'Where is DS Pulford?'

'On his PlayStation,' calls out one of the DCs. The laughter spreads.

'Very funny. Now, where is he?'

The room falls silent.

'Well find out. I want everyone keyed into this. Done and dusted, I say. Done and dusted.'

Johnson had been off on the sick for a week but he soon got better when he heard Staffe was on his way to Spain, that Pennington needed someone to ride shotgun. Now, he stands tall, leaning against the open door, red hair receding, his sleeves rolled up showing thick, pale forearms, freckled like a salmon. He is struggling to keep the smile off when he feels a tug on the tail of his jacket.

'You're better, Johnson.'

He turns round, hisses, 'Bloody hell! What are you doing here?'

'Thought I'd keep an eye out.'

'You heard the DCI. It's practically done and dusted.'

'In which case I can take my leave next week. And anyway, where *is* Pulford?' says Staffe, leaning against the far wall, obscured from Pennington's line of vision.

'You heard. On his PlayStation.'

'I know you know, Johnson, so why don't you just tell me.'

'He's chasing down the wife. Leanne Colquhoun.'

'And he's taken a counsellor, or at least a WPC?' says Staffe.

All Johnson can do is shrug.

'You bloody idiots.'

'She's got a sister, down Southend.'

'And Pulford's got a warrant?'

Johnson shakes his head, feels like he's at

school again. But just as Staffe prepares to unleash a full onslaught, Johnson sees his attention wane. It's DI Wagstaffe's turn to play the schoolboy as Pennington gets wind of him.

'Staffe!' booms the DCI. 'What the hell . . . '

*　*　*

In Staffe's office, Pennington stands dead still in front of the window, pushes out his narrow, pigeon chest and furrows his brow. 'I thought we agreed you should take some time away. Especially after the Golding case.'

'It can wait, sir.'

'I had this under control, you know. I told you — we can survive without you.'

Staffe wants to say, *I know your game. You're pushing for commissioner and if you can put a front-page crime to bed without your senior DI then that's all to the good. You ambitious bastard!* But all he says is, 'I know, sir.' He remembers the first time he ever met Pennington. Staffe was a DC and had just been taken under DS Jessop's hard-nosed wing. Jessop and Pennington had both gone for the DI post and Pennington had won. His knife was sharper. Jessop and Staffe would be together for fifteen years and even though Jessop made DI, Pennington would always be a step ahead.

Pennington turns his back, signifying their meeting is over, and Staffe's heart sinks as he reminds himself that Pulford has gone chasing after their only suspect without any backup. All he can hope is that Pulford draws a blank.

DS David Pulford puts the unmarked Vectra through its paces, driving it a gear higher than you'd drive your own as he cuts down off the A127, following the estuary alongside the reclaimed land they've taken from silt to make money.

He tries not to think of the bollocking he might get, for not waiting for the warrant. He left a message for Carly Kellerman, Leanne Colquhoun's caseworker, and then had driven out of London as though it was he who was fleeing the scene, not Leanne Colquhoun. Nobody had seen Leanne come home to the Limekiln from her job at Surrey Racing, but around six thirty she had run off the estate screaming like a banshee.

From what Pulford has gleaned so far about Karl Colquhoun, he's led the kind of life that takes the 'victim' out of 'murder victim'. 'Give the wife a medal not a prison sentence. What's a mother to do, to protect her kids?' — is the way it sounds to most.

Pulford knows the case could be an opportunity for him, but he quickly chastises himself for wanting to profit from such things, even though he, too, is something of a victim. He realises exactly what they think of him at Leadengate CID: a fast-tracked graduate who's already a detective sergeant, even though (some say) he knows jack shit and has only taken four years to learn it. He had three years drinking and screwing, playing on his Playstation and watching *Countdown* while better men, men like

Johnson, were getting their hands well and truly dirty, pushing back crime in the city's sordid corners.

The satnav directs him on to a new-build brownfield estate down by the wide brown river. It's designed for the aspirationalists, for thirty-somethings busting both balls to try to get ahead. It's not where you'd expect Leanne Colquhoun's sister to be. In other words, it's not Holloway.

Pulford knocks twice, loud, and takes a step back. He looks at the pretty face that appears by the jamb of the door and glances down at the photo. It could be a dolled-up Leanne, he's not sure.

'I'm here to . . . '

'Yes,' she says, 'we were expecting you. Leanne's upstairs. You'd better come in. Take your shoes off, if you don't mind.'

Pulford's heart skips one, two beats. Now he knows she's here, he might be in schtuck, might also be on to a good thing.

'She just wanted some time, you know.' She nods towards the living room and he goes through, wishing he had brought a WPC.

'I'm Detective Sergeant Pulford.'

'Karen Donnelly. I'm Leanne's sister, but you know that, don't you.' She sits down, looks out through the sliding, metal-framed patio doors that give on to ten by ten of new-laid decking, a tiny lawn beyond, then medium-brown fencing. 'She loved him, you know. Always did.'

'Colquhoun?' says Pulford, taking out his notebook, scribbling away.

'She did the worst thing, but she did it for him. It's a terrible thing, love.'

'She killed him for his own sake?'

'She let them take her children away,' says Karen Donnelly, staring to infinity. 'Love.'

'Did she tell you she killed him?'

She fixes a stare on Pulford, lets it burn into him. He flinches and looks away as she tells him, slowly, to 'Fuck off.'

'Did Leanne tell you how he died?'

Karen Donnelly shrugs.

'He can't have treated her well.'

Karen looks at him as though she might be about to confide but decides against it. She shakes her head.

'You'll have to come with me to the station. It's Leadengate, in the City.'

'Aha. Fancy crimes.'

'Nothing fancy about this one,' says Pulford, stopping himself from giving away any details of the cause of death.

'I've got to pick my children up from school at four. Then I have to make dinner. Then I've got to go to work.' She looks around her home. To Pulford, it seems as though she might resent it, the things she does to pay for it.

'What about Leanne's kids? Doesn't she want to see them?'

'Children. She's got children,' says Karen Donnelly. 'Goats have kids.'

'Don't ask her fuckin' nothin',' says Leanne Colquhoun, coming down the stairs. She looks younger than in the photograph, looks to Pulford as though a burden might have been lifted. 'We

41

can get my kids on the way. As long as it's all right with the fuckin' caseworker. I'd like to see them.'

Pulford looks at Karen who looks at the floor. She looks ashamed.

⋆　⋆　⋆

Staffe parks the knackered old Peugeot in the Kilburn lock-up alongside another vehicle, which is covered in a dirty dust sheet. He closes the heavy steel doors, fixes the padlock and looks up at the back of his house. Built to last by the Victorians. It was a good buy but it's not home and he thinks he might let it out, might move across to one of his better houses in a better neighbourhood — even though it isn't long since the scaffolding came down and the skips were towed to landfill. He stops this thought, though, wondering if he is thinking this because of Golding's threats. Has he suddenly allowed a nineteen-year-old gangster to turn him into a coward? But is it cowardly to lean away from a blow, to swerve a tackle?

There is a light on upstairs — even though it's daylight, even though he turned everything off. He goes to the fence, presses his face against it, peers through a knothole in the wood. He can see a shadow moving across the dining window.

He rushes round the front of the building and takes out his phone to call for back-up. A closer inspection of the front door shows no sign of forced entry. He puts the phone back in his pocket and is just about to put his key to the door when he hears a scream from inside the house.

It sounds like a woman but he can't be sure and Staffe stands, frozen. There is another scream, and the low murmur of someone crying. A raised voice — through an open window upstairs. He locked the house down, he's sure.

Staffe runs down the steps to the lower-ground floor and bounds back up, holding a spade that he keeps in a damp storeroom. He peers through the letter box, sees nothing but can smell recent cigarette smoke. He hasn't had so much as a drag on a Rothmans in three years.

He puts the key to the door again, hand shaking, and takes a deep breath, steps inside. The noise comes from upstairs and it is definitely a woman.

'Oh my God. Oh my God,' she says, as if she is pleading for mercy or for help.

As he goes up the stairs, spade in hand, Staffe hears someone crying and tracks the sounds to the back bedroom, where he had seen the light. He pauses, holds the spade out ahead of him and notices splatterings of blood on the carpet. There is a trail from the bathroom. He kicks open the door to the bedroom, rushes into the room and the howling of the woman within redoubles.

'What the hell! What the . . . '

'Marie?' he says.

Her hands are covered in blood; horror written right across her face.

Staffe looks at a child, curled on the floor and clutching his blood-smeared head, sobbing. 'What's happened. Who did this?'

'It's your fault,' says his sister. 'It's your fault, you idiot, Will.'

'Where did they go? Where are they!' Staffe is kneeling down by the child, taking him in his arms and saying, 'Harry, are you all right? Oh, Harry.'

'Of course he's all right,' she says. 'It's me that's cut.' She holds out her arm to show Staffe. 'I cut it on that bloody stupid shower screen of yours.'

'What are you doing here, Marie?'

'You said I could come any time. You gave me a key.'

'You could have let me know.'

'You're supposed to be on holiday. If you can call it that!' She looks daggers at him and sits on the edge of the bed, holding her bleeding arm. 'Oh shut up, Harry. Please!'

Staffe picks up his nephew from the floor and holds him to his chest then sits on the bed next to his sister, wraps an arm around her. Even though one is soaked in blood, the other in tears, he savours the moment, feels the relief course through his veins.

'It's nice to see you, Marie.'

'Oh yeah. Just great,' she says.

*   *   *

Young Harry is in Staffe's lounge bemoaning the fact that there is no Nickelodeon to be had from the small-screen TV. The best Staffe has managed is to dig out an old pack of cards and quickly teach him how to play pontoon. And now he has returned to the kitchen to patch up the boy's mother.

'You should go to hospital.'

'I'll be fine,' says Marie.

Staffe rolls her sleeve right up and looks at the wound. The glass shower screen cut the inside of her forearm but missed the vein by a centimetre or so. He cleans the cut and applies iodine which makes her flinch and as she scrunches her eyes, he takes a closer look at the fresh bruise higher up on her arm. When she opens her eyes, she catches him and rolls her sleeve down.

'My bet is there's another one on the other arm. Am I right?'

'Just concentrate on the cut, Will.'

'I always said he was a bastard.'

'And your life is just perfect.'

'You should report him. He'll do it to someone else.'

'Why do you always have to fight other people's battles?'

'You're my sister, for God's sake.'

'And what about you, Will? Who are you seeing?'

'My life's too complicated at the moment.'

'You live alone, Will. It's the most uncompli- cated situation a man could be in. Or is it this stupid quest of yours?'

'They were your parents, too, Marie.'

'It was twenty years ago, for God's sake. Don't you think they'd want you to move on?'

Staffe wants to tell her he has no choice, that he wants to move on, but he can predict where that conversation would go. 'I'm trying to do the right thing.'

'Do the right thing for yourself. Look at Sylvie.'

'No! Let's not look at Sylvie. And, anyway, at least I didn't run away when it happened.'

'I didn't run away, I travelled.'

'You blew your inheritance.'

'I spent it. I invested it in experiences. You know, Will, sometimes I really don't understand where you get your values from.'

He thinks about this, which makes him remember his father — always working, occasionally talking about what he was going to do with 'his time' when he retired. Would his father be proud of what he does? He'll never know. Staffe feels lost, gazes at his sister. 'What would he make of us? How we turned out?'

'Oh, Will. We have to live for ourselves.'

'And not the ghosts,' he says.

She shrugs, looks embarrassed. 'I've never asked you for anything, Will. Harry's going to school at the end of summer. You know if . . . '

Staffe wraps an arm around her, pulls her into the crook of his neck and speaks softly. 'I'd love you to stay. I wish you'd come years ago.'

'It's not to stay. We fight like cat and dog, Will. We always have.'

He lifts her sleeve and looks at the other bruise. 'I know.' He rocks, gently, holding his baby sister tighter and tighter and trying not to picture what a mess she must be in to accept his help after all these years.

'Why didn't you go away?' she says.

The thought occurs to Staffe that, after all these years, he might be afraid of catching up with Santi Extbatteria.

'Let's go and see how Harry is. Maybe I'll teach him to play poker.'

'I can see you're going to be a fine role model.'

As they go, they laugh. She fixes her face and he thinks that perhaps he really should move across town.

★ ★ ★

Leadengate Station is quieter than Staffe can remember. Every available officer is either out on the knock and search, or phoning down everybody who ever knew Karl Colquhoun. Pennington received the call from the commissioner and had to make a statement to the press.

Staffe makes his way towards the interview suites and hears the raised voices of his DSs: Johnson and Pulford, in the corridor.

'You should know to take support,' says Johnson.

'I didn't want her to get away.'

'It's not my fault you lack experience.' Johnson sees Staffe and he looks at his shoes.

'What the hell are you two firing off about?' Staffe slides the spyhole plate to the main interview room and sees Leanne Colquhoun. He frowns. 'What if she heard that, you idiots,' he says in a scolding whisper. He turns to Johnson. 'What do you know about Colquhoun's first wife?' he says to Johnson.

'Debra Bowker? She's moved out of the country, to Tenerife.'

'Get me her number. And find out how long

she has been there. I need the dates of all her visits since she left and double-check with the airlines.'

Johnson looks daggers at Pulford and Staffe can see that he is gutted to have lost out on this case. He puts a hand on Johnson's shoulder and ushers him down the corridor, saying as he goes, 'I know where you're coming from, Rick. But we're a DI down anyway at the moment, with Rimmer on the sick. This could be the biggest case we'll get in years and the press are all over it already. We've got to pull together.'

'Is that why you came back?' Even though there's venom in Johnson's voice, he has dark rings under his eyes. It seems to Staffe his DS should be at home resting.

Staffe looks back at the young Pulford, getting the breaks that Johnson thinks he deserves. 'If that's your attitude, you'll still be a DS when you pick up your pension. If you can't pitch in as part of a team . . . '

'You know damn well I can.'

'It's not what I'm seeing just lately.'

'I thought this was going to be my chance, boss. Never mind.' Johnson shoots Staffe a resigned look, gives a tired 'what the hell' raise of the eyebrows. 'But it'd be nice if you cut me some slack sometime. Just let me tell the muppet what a tosser he is every now and again.'

Staffe laughs and slaps Johnson on the shoulder, watches his DS make a weary way down the corridor. Johnson turns and calls, 'I'll get Bowker's co-ordinates for you, boss.'

'Good man,' calls Staffe, watching the

dishevelled Johnson go. He and Becky have three young children and he is all done in. Staffe looks back at Pulford, leaning against the wall, young and fresh; tall and thin with his hair cut in trendy mini quiffs. His suit is sharply tailored, no doubt paid for by his mum. Staffe takes a deep breath and goes back towards Pulford.

Staffe will not chastise Pulford for racing off after Leanne Colquhoun. He is pleased that the young pup came back with something to show his sceptics, despite riding roughshod through procedure.

He returns to the interview room, bends down to look through the spyhole at Leanne Colquhoun. She sits calmly on the far side of the desk, the bare bones of an attractive woman — not yet twenty-five, but all gone to seed. She's got her hair scraped into a severe, high-up ponytail; not enough eye makeup and too much lipstick. Her eyes are narrow and hard, her cheekbones high and sharp. The skin of her neck is tight and there are three lines on her forehead that don't go away when she stops scowling.

Staffe doesn't fancy her — not for this one, not as a murderer. But almost everyone else in the building does.

He can tell she hasn't been crying, even though only twenty-four hours ago she purport-edly returned from her afternoon shift down at Surrey Racing to find her lover lying on her bed, blood soaking the sheets from the accomplished butchery. Just thinking about it now makes Staffe feel sick.

Karl Colquhoun's heart probably stopped

49

beating from wave after wave of pain — not from the loss of blood from the fine cuts that were applied to the scrotum, but from the eyes. The killers knew what they were doing. They knew they would not be disturbed. There were no noticeable signs of entry, which doesn't help Leanne's cause.

A litre of supermarket-brand whisky had been forced upon Colquhoun and he may well have been passing in and out of consciousness before being tied to the bedposts. As well as semen, blood and excrement, the bed sheets showed residues of vomit. Everywhere, naturally, were the prints and DNA of Karl and Leanne Colquhoun. And nobody else.

Staffe ushers Pulford towards him, says, 'Tell me again, what exactly she said about Karl.'

'She loves him. Sorry, she *loved* him.'

'Did she mean it?'

'She said she didn't believe it had happened.'

Staffe looks at Leanne again, dragging on a cigarette so her cheeks sink in even further — gaunt like the victim of a Balkan war — and staring with clear grey eyes. You would never guess what she had seen — or done — in her own home so recently. And while the owner of the betting shop swears blind she didn't leave the office at all that afternoon, Staffe has discovered that to be a lie. Leanne Colquhoun had fled the Limekiln scene without her handbag. That is the kind of hurry she was in. In the handbag, there was a receipt for Ibuprofen from the Londis halfway between the Limekiln and Surrey Racing. The receipt was timed at 15.46 and

Janine's best guess for the likeliest time of death is 15.00 to 17.00.

'How come we're not getting stuck into her, sir?' says Pulford.

Staffe pulls away from the spyhole. 'You should know why. She's entitled to a solicitor.'

'She was happy enough to talk in the car.'

'The car you brought her back in without so much as a WPC or a counsellor. She's a grieving widow. Traumatised.'

'Traumatised, my arse.'

'Your arse should be in a sling.'

Pulford leans back against the wall and looks up at the flickering fluorescent light. 'Why did the bookie lie? You think he's giving her one? She claims to have loved Karl Colquhoun. Loved him so much she couldn't see her own kids? Yeah, right.'

Staffe taps the spyhole to the metal door. 'Tell me what you see.' He watches Pulford peer into the interview room, listens as the young graduate begins his summary verdict.

'I see a woman who feels no guilt for stopping years of abuse, of herself and her kids, and if you ask me she's done our job for us.'

'So now it's our job to castrate suspects is it?'

'You know what I mean.'

'And where's the evidence?'

'She lied about being in the betting shop. She fled the scene . . . '

' . . . the evidence that Karl Colquhoun interfered with his kids.'

'You've spoken to the caseworker, Carly Kellerman.'

'There's no evidence,' says Staffe. 'The CPS didn't have a case.'

'They took her kids away. That's a pretty good motive.'

'She loved him more than her own children. She chose him. How could a woman do that to a man she loved?'

'She'd hate herself, wouldn't she? She'd want to make amends.'

Staffe sighs, tries to make sense of everything he knows about Leanne Colquhoun: wife, mother. 'And even if he was messing with her kids, in this country we don't chop their bollocks off.'

'We leave it for somebody else to do, then we punish the wrong person.'

'We collect evidence and build the best case for the Crown. This is a civilised country. We don't always get the guilty man, but when we don't it's so we don't fill our jails with the innocent.'

'If he wasn't messing with her kids, why'd she do it?'

'Who says she did?'

'If she didn't, who did?'

'That's what we're going to find out.'

The door from reception clatters open and Staffe recognises who it is straight away — slightly fatter than last time they met and a little looser in the jowl.

Stanley Buchanan and Staffe started their careers on opposite sides of the same coin and at the same time. Buchanan looks jaded and gives a tut-tut shake of the head. Maybe it's dealing more with the guilty than the innocent all your life and trying to treat the two the same that drives poor Stanley to drink. Time was, Staffe and Stanley had that in common, too.

'The complaints are on file already, DI Wagstaffe, but I may as well tell you what I've told DCI Pennington.' He sits down next to Leanne Colquhoun and taps her twice on the shoulder. 'We'll have you out of here in two shakes of a lambkin's tail. Don't you worry, Leanne.' Staffe thinks this must be a good day for Stanley, maybe just the couple of large ones down the Old Doctor Butler's Head. 'This is a bereaved woman, a woman of impeccable standing without so much as a caution to her name. What possessed you to allow a young sergeant to press-gang this poor woman without a female officer or a counsellor in sight?'

'Very good, Stanley,' says Staffe.

'You can call me Mr Buchanan.'

'I didn't force my way in,' says Pulford.

'That's enough, Sergeant,' says Staffe.

'She fled the murder scene. She could have been trying to . . . '

'I said enough!'

Staffe turns to Leanne. 'Why didn't you call the police?'

She stares straight past him, says, 'I've got nothing to say to you.'

'You could tell us why you lied about being in the bookies all afternoon,' says Pulford.

She looks up at Pulford, gives him a patronising smile. 'I want to see my kids.'

Buchanan says, 'There are three witnesses who

53

say my client was only out of her place of work for ten minutes.'

'You can see the children soon, Leanne,' says Staffe. 'They're in the Phoenix Suite with the caseworker.'

Staffe pulls up a chair so he's sitting within a couple of feet of her. He waits for her to look at him and shoots Pulford a look to keep quiet.

Eventually, Leanne does look up at Staffe and he smiles with his eyes. He thinks he can see a softening in the hard creases of her face and he tunes into his softest voice, puts his forearm on the desk and leans ever so slightly forward. She looks away, then straight back at him when he says, 'I'd like you to tell me about when they took your children away. Is it the way it looks on the file? I just want to see it the way you see it. That's all. Then you can go.'

'Home?'

'We'll see.' He shoots the look at Pulford again. This is his case and he's not settling for the obvious.

'You don't have to answer that, Leanne. It's irrelevant,' says Buchanan.

She looks back at Staffe, makes the slightest of smiles, like faint parentheses at the corners of her mouth. 'He's got a history, Karl. Least that's what they say.' Leanne talks about Karl Colquhoun as if he's still around, not lying blue-grey on a slab nearby with his belly and chest butterflied for autopsy.

Staffe listens as much to how she's talking as to what she says. 'And they said he was . . . ?'

Leanne Colquhoun nods. Staffe can see she's

54

fighting back the tears. Is it pride? Is it because if she cries, it's an acceptance he is dead?

'Do you believe them? Do you think he did that to his other children?'

'I'll swear on my life he never touched a hair on *my* kids' heads.'

'And would you swear on his life too?'

She looks at Staffe, says, 'I love him. I love him so much.' And the face goes soft. 'Where does a woman like me find love in this world?' The creases in her forehead go smooth and she smiles. Her eyes are glassy and the tears come. And come.

★ ★ ★

The Phoenix Suite, a newly built specialist unit for holding victims of sexual offences, is just five minutes down the road from Leadengate Station and as Staffe approaches it, the Barbican shimmers in the summer heat.

He is immediately shown into a brightly decorated room with windows overlooking a jungle-style garden. Children's paintings adorn the walls and classical music is in the ether. From a Wendy house in the corner, a young woman in her early twenties appears on all fours.

'Hi, Will,' she says, standing up, dusting down her skirt.

'Hi, Carly.'

In the windows of the Wendy house, the faces of two children become suddenly miserable.

Carly Kellerman nods behind her and says, 'This is Calvin and Lee-Angelique.' Carly smiles brightly. Her hair is a bounty of rolling, golden curls.

'Hello,' says Staffe, crouching and overly cheery.

One look at Staffe is enough to tell them that their fun is dead.

Carly sits down at a low table and invites Staffe to take a child's seat. She beckons the children and turns off the smile, nods earnestly as Staffe begins to ask his questions, encouraging the children to answer.

Calvin is the younger, at six, but he does all the talking. Lee-Angelique is eight and simply stares at Staffe, her mouth turned down towards the floor.

'When was the last time you saw your mum?'

'Sunday. We see her every Sunday and she took us to Margate. It's the best place.'

'And what about Karl? Do you ever see him?'

At this, Lee-Angelique gets up from the table and goes back into the Wendy house.

'We never see him. Mum talks about him.'

Staffe looks at Calvin's hands, scrunched up into pudgy little fists.

'He can't come near us,' says Lee-Angelique from inside the Wendy house. 'That's what she said.'

'Shush, Lee-Ange,' says Calvin.

'But he came to the seaside.'

Calvin gets up and Carly tries to comfort him, saying, 'He didn't. You've got it wrong, Lee love.'

'And he touched me. He did.'

Calvin shrugs Carly off, goes to join his sister in the Wendy house. He pulls the door closed behind him.

'He can't have,' whispers Carly. 'They check. They can tell, you know,' and she looks down into her own lap, shakes her head slowly.

Calvin calls out from inside the Wendy house. 'Is Karl gone?'

'He's gone away,' says Staffe. 'He won't be coming back.'

Calvin lets a smile appear, showing the gaps between his teeth. Lee-Angelique is standing behind him, looking as though it will take much, much more to bring a smile to her face.

\* \* \*

'Take these down to secretarial and tell them it's important,' says Staffe, handing Pulford a tape of the interview with Leanne Colquhoun and his notes from the meeting with Carly Kellerman and the Colquhoun children. 'I'm going to have another word with Leanne Colquhoun.' He picks up his jacket from the back of the chair. It's suede and too young for him, he thinks. It was Sylvie's choice and, if truth be known, it probably wasn't just the jacket that was too young for him.

In the corridor, Staffe catches sight of Josie, walking away. He walks double-quick to catch up with her but there's no need. She stands by the coffee machine. As he approaches, she presses a button but nothing happens.

'It's out of order.'

'What exactly is out of order, sir?'

'I was wondering if maybe . . . ' He reaches his hand out, presses the flat of his palm on the wall

57

that she is leaning against.

'What?' She smiles. 'You know, I've heard you used to be a bit of a ladies' man, sir.'

'And I heard you should believe half of what you see . . . '

' . . . and nothing of what you hear,' she says, laughing. 'My dad used to say that. Maybe he's right.'

Staffe pushes himself up and away from the wall, runs a hand through his hair and takes a step back, tugs at his jacket. He's seen Pennington coming down the corridor and takes another step back.

'Wagstaffe, Chancellor,' says Pennington, the merest break in his stride.

'Sir,' says Josie.

'Your office, Wagstaffe. This Colquhoun debacle, a quick word, if you will.'

'Debacle, sir?' says Staffe, following the DCI into his office.

'Chancellor!' booms Pennington from the doorway to Wagstaffe's office, 'get Pulford and tell the clever dick to bring his university educated backside down here tout suite.'

Pennington takes the seat behind Staffe's desk. Turning the tables is his style. Before he got the move upstairs, Pennington was one of the canniest coppers Staffe had come across. He must have been, to always be one step ahead of Jessop. Pennington picks up a pen and taps a 10 × 8 photograph that he has placed on the desk in front of him, spins it around so Staffe can see it.

In black and white, the carnage of Karl Colquhoun's butchered body looks even more

58

grotesque. Staffe leans forward, then stands back. He squints, to get the detail without getting too close — as if it might be contagious. When it was taken, only one of the testicles has been placed into an eye socket. By the side of the bed, someone is leaning over his body, twisting to look into camera. They are wearing a peaked hood with eyes and a mouth cut out — a hurried imitation of the KKK or a religious penitent. Their eyes are heavily made up with kohl and the mouth, smiling manically, is daubed with dark lipstick. Long blonde hair flows from the bottom of the hood. The figure is wearing white gloves, spattered with blood.

'Is that Leanne Colquhoun?' says Staffe.

'I've got a bad feeling about this,' says Pennington. 'The last thing we want is publicity. You know what the commissioner is like. Sort this out fast, Staffe.' He leans forward, hands Staffe a piece of paper. It's a photocopy of a note that has been pasted together from a newspaper — the *News* — judging by the typeface.

## SEE JUSTICE DONE.

'What I don't get', says Pennington, 'is Karl Colquhoun has never even done time. There was that allegation three years ago, but nothing came of it. It's not a matter of public record, just a dead file down at the CPS. So if she didn't want him dead, who would? And want him dead the way he went. These are sadistic bastards. The question is, Staffe . . . ?'

This was a Pennington ploy.

'The question is, sir . . . ' Staffe is trying to not only deduce the profile of the likely murderer, but do it within the template of Pennington's own processes. 'The question is . . . Who would have suffered so much at the hands of Karl Colquhoun to feel the need . . . Feel compelled to replicate that suffering. Like a mirror, to hold it up to him.'

'I'm getting wind that you don't fancy the wife for this one, Staffe. And she's the only one that answers your question so far.'

'There's Debra Bowker, Karl Colquhoun's ex-wife. She's in Tenerife and according to Social Services she took her kids with her, away from Colquhoun.'

'How old are they?'

'They'll be ten and twelve now. And I'm trying to get hold of Leanne Colquhoun's ex, to see if he might have a motive.'

'Tick tock, Staffe. Tick tock.'

There's a knock at the door and before either Staffe or his boss can respond, Pulford strides in. He stands proud, legs apart, arms crossed. Anybody would guess he had come for a commendation. His expression changes the moment Pennington begins to speak, his voice scarily quiet.

'What makes you so special, DS Pulford, as to be able to swan roughshod over the simple rules that the rest of us mortals have to follow . . . '

'I fully support what DS Pulford did, sir,' says Staffe. Out of the corner of his eye he sees Pulford's head hang, like a scorned schoolboy. 'Given the urgency of this case, sir . . . '

'Don't be clever with me, Staffe. I want good

evidence that we can present to a court of law. Good evidence and admissible statements, Staffe.' Pennington gets up, puts Staffe's pen into his inside pocket and adjusts his tie.

He closes the door behind him, softly, and Pulford says, 'Thanks, sir.'

'Shut up, Pulford. Just bloody shut up.'

★  ★  ★

Stanley Buchanan smells of mint which is unable to mask all the drink. Leanne Colquhoun's eyes are red and it is clear that the truth is beginning to set in.

'I understand you took Calvin and Lee-Angelique to Margate last weekend,' says Staffe.

'It was nice weather. So what?'

'You took them there with your ex, did you? Calvin and Lee-Angelique's dad?'

'You got to be jokin'. He's a waste of space.'

'He never went? Must have been hard work for you on your own.'

'Not as much as if he'd gone fightin' or on the piss or trying to screw some slag.'

'He's got a temper, has he? Holds a grudge?'

'I'm better off without him, is all.'

'What's his name?'

'Rob. Rob Boxall.'

'But Karl was more of a help was he?'

'What do you mean?'

'No one would know, would they? Easy enough to slip away to the seaside.'

'You're out of order, DI Wagstaffe,' says Buchanan.

'Why would Lee-Angelique lie? She said Karl went with you.'

'You said I could see them.'

'I just need a few more questions answering.'

'DI Wagstaffe,' says Buchanan. 'That sounds like an inducement.'

But Staffe's watching Leanne. Her spirit is breaking and she murmurs into her lap, 'He's not like what they said. He's not.'

'Where can I find your ex — Rob?'

'Dalston, if he's not banged up. Try the Rag.'

'The Ragamuffin pub?'

She nods, sniffing the tears away. Staffe goes across to the desk, puts his finger on the 'stop' button of the tape machine. 'Last question, Leanne. Where did you stay in Margate?'

'The Old Dickens.'

'Sounds nice.'

'It's a shithole.' She looks up at Staffe, pleading. 'He didn't do nothing, my Karl. He never done nothing to my babies. It's all lies.' Leanne wrings her hands in her lap.

Staffe presses 'stop' and feels like a complete bastard. Even Stanley Buchanan gives him a look as if to say 'How low can you get?'

★　★　★

Leadengate incident room is practically empty, just a couple of uniformed officers sharing a joke by the water cooler and DI Rick Johnson at a desk, surrounded by paper, head in his hands. All the other uniformed officers are either on another knock and note around the Limekiln estate, or searching the bins and crannies in a four-hundred-yard radius.

Leadengate was built a hundred and twenty years ago and is unsuited to the technological rigours of twenty-first-century policing. The incident room is a cross between a local history society exhibition and a computer auction room. But Staffe knows the importance of having one hub, one place where all the information comes together.

If a case is going to be closed quickly, the key connection usually has to be established within four or five days of the crime. The skill is to be able to see that key connection — amidst the mountains of statements and data — for what it is.

But so far, evidence is in short supply. No one was seen trying to gain access to Karl and Leanne Colquhoun's flat. No one saw Leanne Colquhoun until she ran screaming on to the Limekiln access deck. There is no sign of the murder weapon, which is possibly a narrow-bladed Stanley. No sign of the gauze and other materials that were used to tether and gag Karl Colquhoun. And no eyes.

Staffe has read and reread the forensic report on the scene. It makes no sense to him. The scene was clean as a whistle, save the substances that leaked from Karl Colquhoun. Residues of cleaning solutions were found on all handles, chair backs, doorplates and the bedstead. And on top of that the killer had found the time to pose for, and possibly take, a photograph in the middle of the execution.

If he is asked to believe that Leanne Colquhoun did all this, Staffe cannot for the life of him determine why she would flee the scene, screaming, leaving behind a handbag which contained a receipt from a supermarket that placed her out of her workplace close to the time of death.

Staffe sits down next to Johnson and waits for him to look up.

'Any joy with Tenerife?'

'Debra Bowker claims not to have been back here for over a year. I'm running checks with all the airlines but my guess is she's telling the truth.'

'And what did she say when you told her Karl Colquhoun was dead?'

'All she said was the bastard never sent Christmas presents anyway.'

'Was she shocked?'

'I couldn't say. Maybe. I don't know.'

'If she wasn't shocked . . . '

'I know, sir. I'm sorry, it just didn't register.'

Staffe can see that Johnson is out on his feet. 'How's the new baby, Rick?'

'He's great, sir, but there's three of them now in that bloody flat and Becky has lost interest in even going out. But I can't afford anything bigger, no way.'

Staffe thinks about what kind of a mess Johnson is in. Becky Johnson used to be a lawyer, pulling in twice what her husband brought home. She went back to work after the first two were born, Sian and Ricky. But after the third, young Charlie, she gave up. Once, Johnson joked they'd be better off if he was the one at home. But he hadn't laughed. Staffe had asked why Becky hadn't gone back after Charlie but Johnson had looked daggers at him, said, 'Is that your business? You don't own me.'

'Get yourself off home,' Staffe says now. 'Give me Debra Bowker's number and I'll call her.'

'There's too much to do.'

'Take Becky and the kids down the park. And there's a favour you can do me. I'll call you later.' Staffe scrunches a note up and presses it into Johnson's hand, looks around furtively as he walks away.

When he reaches the door, Johnson calls out 'Sir!' looking at the twenty-pound note Staffe had slipped him.

'Get a takeaway. And put the kids to bed early.'

\*   \*   \*

Back in his office, Staffe picks up a copy of the photograph, reads the lettering.

### SEE JUSTICE DONE.

*See justice done* might mean 'kill the guilty'.
*See justice done* might mean 'protect the innocent'.
*See justice done*. Photograph it.

\*   \*   \*

The Kilburn house smells different. Marie has obviously burnt the lunch and been smoking her

65

roll-ups. Harry has left his computer games strewn over the living-room floor, but Staffe can't bring himself to be annoyed, possibly because of what he has in mind.

He quickly tidies up and opens the front windows and the doors on to the back garden to get a draught going, then gets down to business. Marie has left a note that she'll be back at six and will cook dinner, so Staffe texts her to say he'll be out. It is five o'clock now and he goes straight upstairs to the guest room. He sits on the floor and takes stock of how her suitcase is packed before he systematically goes through her things.

He tries not to feel bad about this. Marie has never asked him for help. They coped with the murder of their parents in different ways: Staffe went off the rails, but put his money into property and then joined the force. Within a few years Marie had blown her inheritance on travel, drugs and bad relationships before falling pregnant with Harry. The father, an out-of-work session musician, lasted less than a year.

Staffe picks a meticulous way through the suitcase, putting the clothes in one pile, her books and trinkets in another; it is not until he gets right to the bottom that he finds what he wants. A building society passbook shows that she has less than two hundred pounds. Her bank account is overdrawn. There is also a clutch of unpaid bills and he commits the billing address to memory — 26d St John's Road, Peckham. But there is nothing which bears the boyfriend's name. No joint names on any of her domestic contracts.

He sighs and goes to the window, looks up and down Shooters Hill to check she is not on her way back. He surveys her gypsy life in miniature and kneels by the small stack of books: Virginia Woolf, Angela Carter and Toni Morrison. He flicks through the pages and on the inside cover of *Beloved* he finds what he wants. Inscribed in a self-consciously flowery hand is the name. Paolo Di Venuto, Summer 2007. Despite his taste in books, Di Venuto has a penchant for roughing up his women.

Downstairs, a door slams and Staffe leaps up.

'Will!' calls Marie from downstairs.

'Shit,' he says to himself, quickly repacking the case as best he can in the order he recalls. Papers first, then books and clothes. He drops her bras and knickers and the hooks and eyes snag on each other, catch on his watch-strap. His hands begin to shake and he makes a mess of the penultimate layer, finishing off with singlet tops and a denim skirt.

She is coming up the stairs and Harry is clattering about in the room below.

'Will!'

He closes the suitcase, struggling with the lock as he hears her padding along the hallway. He slides the case back by the side of the bed and rushes to the window, begins to open it as the door is pushed open.

Marie frowns, hands on hips. 'What the hell!'

Staffe knows his only option is to fight fire with fire. 'For Christ's sake, Marie. Those roll-ups of yours stink the place out. Can't you smoke outside?'

'This is our room. I'd appreciate . . . '

'I'd appreciate it if you smoked outside. OK!'

'If you don't want us here, there's other places I could go.'

Staffe knows this is a lie. If there was anywhere, she'd be there. 'Look. You can stay as long as you want. You know that.' She is wearing a short-sleeved, Amnesty International T-shirt and he can see where the foundation make-up has faded, failing to cover her bruises. He walks across to her, trying to be cool. He puts his hands on her shoulders. She feels fragile. He kisses her on her forehead and says softly, into her hair, 'I'm sorry I came into your room. I won't do it again.'

She wraps her arms around his waist and he pats her back, the way he remembers his mother doing when they wouldn't go to sleep.

\* \* \*

Marvitz Builders Merchants, where Karl Colquhoun worked, is closing up for the day when Staffe gets there. Johnson should have done this visit, but Staffe needs a personal favour from his sergeant and this is his idea of recompense.

Staffe has brought a photograph of Karl Colquhoun but there was no need. The foreman of the timber section knows why he is there as soon as Staffe shows his warrant card.

'I was expecting a visit,' he says.

'Do you usually shut at this time?'

'This weather, there's only one place builders'll be. They get rained off in winter and sunned off on days like these. My boys'll be with them, no doubt.'

Staffe looks around the deserted bays, piles of sawdust and chippings all over the floor, the smell of resin sweet in the thick air.

'He was a good worker, Colquhoun. Wouldn't have left the place in a state like this.' The manager takes hold of a broom.

'How did he get on with your boys?' says Staffe.

'All right, till Ross Denness came.'

'Who's he?'

'A new lad. Knew Karl from the estate he lived on.'

'And where might I find our friend Denness?'

The manager has begun to sweep up and says, 'Pound to a penny he'll be in the Rag.'

'The Ragamuffin!'

'You know it?'

'No. But I know someone who does.'

\* \* \*

The landlord of the Ragamuffin points a gnarled, badly re-set finger in the direction of a tall, gangling late-twenties man with lank hair and a sneering smile.

Ross Denness is in the far corner of the pub, leaning against the pool table with a young girl rubbed up against him.

The Ragamuffin would have been a good boozer at some point, until they knocked all the vaults and tap rooms and snugs into one and painted the walls blue and replaced the last beer pump for yet another brand of premium lager. There are more girls than men, drinking alcopops and showing their backsides with impossibly low trousers or obscenely high skirts. The men strut round with their pumped-up chests and shaven heads and there is quite definitely something in the air.

Staffe sips his Diet Coke and watches Denness. The girl shows her face and looks barely sixteen. It's a thin line, he thinks, that separates Denness from his work colleague, Karl Colquhoun.

He gets the landlord's attention again and nods to the pool table. 'Monday afternoon. Was Denness in here?'

'He's in most every afternoon.'

'And Monday?'

'He was here. Got in about half four, five, I'd say.'

'For how long?'

The landlord laughs. 'Till shut. Same ole, unless he pulls.' He looks across at Denness. 'Reckon he'll be havin' an early one today. He's a boy!'

'And what about Rob? Rob Boxall.'

'Rob's not been in for ages.'

'He know Denness?' asks Staffe.

'You'd best ask him that.'

'I'm asking you.'

The landlord shrugs and picks up a glass from the glasswasher tray, starts to wipe it dry.

Across the room, Denness must have said something lewd as the girl puts the bottle of blue fluorescence in her mouth. She pretends to be offended and punches him in the chest. He falls backwards on the table and she moves up against him so his knee is between her thighs. When he comes back upright, he puts a hand up her practically non-existent thin white cotton skirt and she kisses him.

Staffe decides enough is enough and by the time he gets to the table their heads are circling manically. She clocks Staffe while she necks open-eyed with Denness, pushing his hand away from whatever base they call it in these parts.

'Ross,' says Staffe, tapping him on the shoulder.

'What the fuck . . . ?' Denness looks up, a smear of lipstick all around his stubbled mouth.

'I'm DI Wagstaffe, just wanted a few words.'

'If it's about that kid-fiddler Colquhoun, I say good riddance to bad shit.'

Staffe looks at the girl, says, 'Shouldn't you be doing your homework?'

'I've got ID,' she says, playing with her streaked hair extensions.

'I'm sure there's a story behind that, too. I could look into it, if you want.'

Denness is taller than Staffe and a couple of mates have come across, half laughing, half snarling, holding bottles. Staffe's heart beats fast and his palms begin to sweat. Even after twenty years in the game, there are places where the law doesn't wash, people it doesn't know how to touch any more. 'On your way,' he says to the girl.

She looks at Denness and he shrugs. As she

gathers up her handbag and cigarettes, Denness slaps her bottom. She laughs and runs her tongue around her lips.

'The fuck do you want?' says Denness. 'You done your job in the first place no one would have needed to top that piece a shit.'

'How do you know Colquhoun did what he was supposed to have done?' says Staffe.

'Everyone knew.'

'Knew what?'

'His last missus had to piss off out the country to keep him off his own kids and now they say his new missus can't see her own kids in case he starts giving them one. Fuckin' frag.'

'You seem to know a lot about the victim.'

'Victim?' says Denness. 'Give 'em a medal, I say. And, anyway, I worked with him, didn't I?'

'And you live round the corner from him.'

'So fuckin' what?'

'Do you know Leanne Colquhoun?'

He takes a swig from his bottle of Beck's and says, 'I know a lot of women. How d'you expect me to keep track?'

Denness is swaggering now and his mates are laughing, nudging closer still, forming a ring.

'What about Leanne's ex, Rob Boxall? You know him?'

Out of the corner of his eye, Staffe can see Denness's mates look away, drinking from their bottles.

'Don't ring no bells.'

'Just so you know, you're being watched. Put your filthy hands anywhere near that girl again and I'll have *you* for kiddie fiddling.'

'She's a woman, you muppet,' says Denness.

'That'll be your burden of proof,' says Staffe.

'The fuck you say?' says Denness, like he's wrestling with algebra.

Staffe has had enough. He turns on his heel and pushes his way out of the pub. When he gets to his car, he leans against the off-side wing, sees the girl in the bright white light of a fried chicken queue opposite. Ross Denness comes out of the Rag. The girl waves at him but Denness blanks her. He has a face like thunder and, putting his head down, he strides off up the high street.

Unsure whether to follow him, Staffe feels suddenly nervous, as if he might be under-equipped. But then a car blazes towards him. It blares its horn and swerves towards his car and Staffe has to throw himself on the bonnet. He rolls on to the pavement as the car screeches to a halt just yards away and a youth jumps out shouting, 'What the fuck!' Staffe gets up off the pavement, brushes himself down.

The youth from the car walks towards Staffe, leaning backwards and swaggering with his pelvis pushed out, low-slung baggy jeans and a sideways baseball cap. As he walks, he talks, jabbing two fingers towards Staffe as if he's holding a gun. 'You in the fuckin' road, man. What you doin'? We seen you, man. Know your game.'

Staffe takes a deep breath and reaches into his inside pocket for his warrant card. The youth flinches, reaches into his own back pocket and with a fizzing noise he releases the catch to a

73

flick knife. Staffe holds out his warrant card and says, 'I'm police, you fucking prick, now drop that knife and put your nose against the wall.'

He doesn't know how this will pan out, can't be sure he can pull it off. You never can be sure. And true enough, the ringleader looks back towards his mates in the car. Staffe knows he only has one chance. Four of them pile out of the car, so Staffe takes a step towards the youth and launches himself, going for the arm with the knife. He takes hold of the weapon and feels a bright seam of pain open up along his arm. He twists the youth's wrist and sees his face come towards him, snarling. Staffe shoves him into the wall, drops him to the floor.

The youth squeals and the blade drops to the pavement, metallic, smeared with Staffe's blood. Staffe puts his boot on the blade and stands back as the chav curls into a ball, saying, 'Fuckin' bully, I'll do you. Fuckin' bully, don't hit me no more.' The ringleader looks daggers at the four mates who have stopped dead in their tracks. Then, to the gathering crowd, he says, to no one in particular, 'You see that? You see that fuckin' copper pullin' a knife on me.'

Staffe bends down, picks up the knife and as he does he sees blood streaming off the ends of his fingers. His suede jacket is torn and the pain begins to kick and spread. He grimaces, blade in hand and the crowd takes a step back as he puts a foot on the youth's chest.

The teenage girl comes out of the fried chicken shop, shouting, 'He's been lookin' for a fight, that copper. Been in the Rag tryin' to start on my boyfriend, he was.' In the near distance a police siren winds up its wail and Staffe takes a deep breath, holds his wrist as tight as he can. He anticipates the allegations, the audience with Pennington and all the paperwork. He wishes he had gone to Bilbao and can practically smell the sea air as he watches the blood pool around his feet. He feels fainter and fainter as the adrenalin begins to abate.

# Tuesday Evening

'You should go to the hospital with this, sir,' says Josie, tying the bandage around Staffe's wrist.

'How did you get on with tracking Leanne's ex down?'

'Rob Boxall? He's doing two years in Bellmarsh for dealing MDMA and C meth. Been in since May, so he's off the hook.'

'You'd better get someone to pay him a visit, see if he knows Ross Denness?'

'Sure, sir.' Josie is examining Staffe's arm. Still holding his hand, she says, 'That youth outside the Rag . . . '

'What about him?'

'He's saying you went at him with the knife. His mates are backing him up. And so's that girl.'

'Have we got an ID on him?'

'We've got a couple.' Josie sits down on the opposite side of his desk and leans forward with her elbows on the desk, her face resting on the backs of her hands. She raises her eyebrows and says, 'He said to say, 'Jadus knows'.'

'What's that supposed to mean?'

Josie leans back in the chair. She looks at him long, hard, quizzical.

'What's wrong?'

'You should be on a beach or up a mountain and here you are with your arm all bandaged up and some gangland fatwa out on you. Let me buy you a drink.'

76

'I can't do that.'

'It's a case of you 'won't' do it, not 'can't'.'

'Thanks for the lecture.'

'Don't mention it,' she says, standing up and walking out of the office. As she gets to the door she leans back into the room, says, 'If anybody ever *needed* a drink . . . ' and she laughs.

Staffe gestures for Josie to close the door behind her; as she does, he dials Johnson's home number. 'Rick?' he says.

'Just going out for the takeaway, sir.'

'You can do me a favour,' says Staffe.

'Ahaa,' says Johnson.

'I want you to go down to Peckham, scare the living shit out of a lowlife called Paolo Di Venuto.'

'For doing what?'

'For being a bastard.'

'Can you be more precise?'

'He's seeing my sister. Scare him off with anything and everything you can think of: benefit fraud, immigration, dealing or possession. You'll get the drift when you see him. And see how he responds to an allegation of ABH. Just say you've had an anonymous complaint.'

'I don't suppose there's any point asking why I'm doing this?'

'26d St John's Road,' says Staffe, hanging up, punching in Debra Bowker's number in Tenerife. As it rings, he writes himself a note to get the 'see justice done' photograph remastered, to investigate its every detail, to get the Tech's take on the hood's material, any labelling on the clothes and match the hair in the photo to any

77

samples taken from the scene and from Leanne Colquhoun.

A woman answers the phone.

'Mrs Bowker? Debra Bowker?' says Staffe.

'Miss.'

'I'm DI Wagstaffe from Leadengate CID.'

'I spoke to one of your colleagues.'

Staffe leans back in his chair, puts his feet up on the bottom drawer of his desk. On the other end of the line, he can hear children playing. 'I just wanted to be sure about your movements over the past few weeks.'

'I told your colleague.' She sighs. 'Look. If I was you, I'd have me at the top of your list but I can assure you, I had nothing to do with it. Much as it would have pleased me to see the bastard suffer.'

'What do you know about Rob Boxall?'

'Nothing.'

'And what about Ross Denness, Mrs Bowker?'

'Miss!'

Staffe sits up, quickly. He scrawls a note — 'debra colquhoun. check passports and airlines'. 'I apologise. As a matter of interest, when did you stop being called Debra Colquhoun?'

'The minute I slammed the door on him.'

'But when did your divorce come through?'

'Ten months. Are we done?'

'If you remember anything, about Ross Denness, let me know.' In the background, a child screams out and Staffe says, 'We're done. For now.'

'How's his mum taken it? Maureen?' says

78

Debra. There is another child's scream in the background. 'I have to go. Give her my love if you speak to her. And tell her Danielle and Kimberley say 'hi'.'

Staffe buzzes through to the incident room and tells Josie to get on to the airlines again and check the name Debra Colquhoun. Then he tells her to pay Karl's mother a visit. 'Don't push her, just get her talking about Karl, and about the first wife too if you can. Softly, softly. And tell her that Danielle and Kimberley say 'hi'. Tell her they send their love.'

★ ★ ★

Josie knows that Maureen Colquhoun is sixty-one years old and has been widowed for three years. Her husband died of sclerosis of the liver, but they had been separated for some time. Karl Colquhoun was her only son.

Maureen shows Josie into the front room. It's a museum piece of how somebody on a budget might conjure a model of Edwardian comfort, with its fat, veneered furniture and a floral tapestry three-piece; a busy, patterned carpet of purples and greens, a whiff of Mr Sheen. She fusses over Josie, running off to make tea and coming back with biscuits on a doily'd plate, sitting on the edge of her chair, knees together and hands clasped.

'It is about Karl, Mrs Colquhoun.'

'Call me Maureen.'

'I'm very sorry, about what happened to him.' Mrs Colquhoun nods earnestly, hanging on to

Josie's every word. 'We're obviously trying our best to find out what happened. And one of the things is . . . well, I'd like to know what sort of a man he was, Maureen. What sort of a son he was.' Josie takes out her digital recorder, says, 'Do you mind if I tape us?'

Maureen shakes her head, slowly. She looks nonplussed. 'Does it matter what I say?'

Josie leans forward, holds Maureen's hands and says, 'Go on, tell me anything you want. About Karl or Debra or Leanne. Anything, Maureen.'

'They said he had been drinking. When the police came round they said that he had been killed and it was murder and when I asked who they thought it was, they didn't want to say but they said my son was inebriated. Well, I know that couldn't be. He's never touched a drop, not a drop. He's done wrong, I know he has, and there's things I can't turn a blind eye to no matter how I try, but I won't believe he'd been drinking. I won't.'

Josie thinks it curious that a mother might become so agitated about a son who drinks when he is also a father who very probably abused his own children. 'Do you miss the children, Maureen? Your grandchildren.'

'How do you know I don't see them?'

'They're in Tenerife.' Maureen's face goes tight and she purses her lips. A hard look comes easily to her eyes and she blinks something away. 'He didn't tell you, did he?'

'She took them all the way over there? Mary, mother of God. All the way over there.'

'They say 'hello', and send their love,' says Josie, watching Staffe's message exert its power on the smiling face of Maureen Colquhoun.

'Poor Debra. God bless her. Oh, those children. Those beautiful children!'

'You say Karl never drank.'

'Never a drop and nor would you. Nor would you if you'd had his father.' The smile has gone again now. 'It got out of hand, so terribly out of hand.' She lets go of Josie and puts her hands between her knees in a downturn prayer. 'He always said it was a sad man who drank in the house, but when I had Karl, he brought whisky into the house. He'd come home from the pub and drink the bottle, the whole bottle. And then he'd go upstairs. Karl would cry as soon as he smelt the stench of drink coming.'

'When you say he went upstairs, Maureen?'

'There's nothing I could do.'

'If someone really wanted to hurt Karl, to take him to a dark place, they would make him drunk. Is that right, Maureen?'

'Oh yes. That would be right.'

'And if someone got him drunk, against his will, they would have to know him quite well. Not many people knew about his past, Maureen? He didn't talk about it much?'

'Why would he talk about it?'

Josie wants to stay longer, wants to talk about normal things with Maureen but she decides she will send a counsellor round. It's something she agrees with Staffe about — there's nothing to be gained by playing the amateur psychologist.

The day is ending and the heat begins to lift away from London's tar and glass. Staffe puts down his mobile, registering what Josie has told him about Maureen Colquhoun and her son, the victim.

He switches back and forth from rat run to rat run, south and west to Queens Terrace. He remembers it, the first time. When he bought the flat, his mother and father were not long dead and the weekends there were long, bleak, lonely affairs.

Staffe double-parks and uses a beany hat on top of the dash to wedge a parking permit up against the windscreen. He flips the boot and takes out his thirty-year-old white plastic Adidas holdall. He feels the twinge of a sad and happy memory and closes his eyes, takes a deep breath and exhales in five equally measured orbs. Sometimes he thinks it's bullshit, but sometimes it works and now, turning the key in the door, he gets a nostalgic glow.

The Queens Terrace flat smells lived-in and although the tenant has left a few things and not hoovered or even put the last meal's dishes away, Staffe texts the managing agent to say they can return the tenant's deposit. He sits in the beaten-up old club chair in the bay window and leans back. He eyes up the cornice mouldings and the ceiling rose, thinks maybe it's time to move back into this one. It would certainly keep him and Marie from each other's throats. He thinks about young Harry being dragged from pillar to post.

Staffe goes through to the bathroom, takes out his running gear from the Adidas bag and runs the shower. It's what he's done since he first joined the Force: a hot shower first, to get him sweating. Then a run and a cold shower when he gets back. He remembers the first time Jessop came round, saw what he was doing. 'It's like an exorcism,' he had said. And he laughed.

The water jets down, hard on his scalp and shoulders and he turns the heat up a notch so it's almost scalding him. He scrubs and scrubs with the soap, the smell of coal tar getting thicker and thicker, the steam getting more and more dense. As he scrubs, he plaits over and over, in different orders, the events of the last few days.

★ ★ ★

Josie rations out a glass of Semillon Chardonnay from a box in the fridge and takes a peek at the roasting medley of peppers, courgettes and whole baby carrots, drizzled with olive oil and sucking up the essence of two bulbs of garlic. Her mouth waters and she sets out two pork chops, seasons them and checks her watch, skips across the room and kneels into the diminishing space where her CD player sits on the floor under the small window that juts into the angle of the roof.

It took a leap of faith and every scrimped and saved half-penny she could muster, but three years ago, with some help from her parents down in Hastings, Josie Chancellor bought this studio flat in the roof space of an old, unrefurbished house near Victoria. Even now, she just about covers the interest on the mortgage and once a quarter she feels her pulse race when she sees what kind of debt she is in with the Alliance & Leicester.

This is the first proper date she has had since she transferred to Leadengate six months ago and although it is David Pulford who is coming round, it's not him that she is thinking about. 'Believe nothing of what you hear and only half of what you see,' is what her father used to say. What would he make of DI Will Wagstaffe?

She sits on the floor with her feet tucked up under her bottom and sips from her glass, questioning her motives for saying 'yes' to Pulford so readily. She curses herself for being so stupid as to invite him round for a meal.

The intercom buzzes and she drains her glass, stooping as she stands so as not to bang her head on the sloping ceiling. She pauses by the intercom's crackling speaker, lets it buzz again. She sighs, then turns off the oven and puts the chops into a cereal bowl, puts a sideplate on top and places the covered meat in the fridge. The intercom buzzes a third time, long and hard, and she presses the button to receive.

'Hi, Josie, it's me,' says Pulford.

'Wait there.'

'What?'

'I didn't have a chance to get anything in. Let's go out.' She checks in her purse. Three pounds fifty, nothing in the bank, and two days till pay day.

Pounding away, from street to square and on to the Brompton Road, Staffe feels the sweat coming faster and faster. He closes his ears to everything but the shock of the road thudding up from his feet, along his thighs and up into his torso and fast-beating heart. He's too old for this, but he catches sight of the park on the other side of Knightsbridge and jaycanters through the traffic, up on to the sand-track bridleway. His muscles burn, his lungs roast. The sound gets duller, deeper.

He can see there is one truth that governs everything that happens under the blood-red sky of the city. He knows that this truth is stitched together by the actions of millions of people living alongside each other. Everything is connected and everything can be understood.

Even the clumsy or haphazard criminal will have a rationale. There will be a pattern to their behaviour. The trouble is: the more evidence you accumulate, the more obscured the reasons can become. Denness or Rob Boxall; Leanne or Debra Bowker. Or someone not yet uncovered. Whoever did it knew Karl Colquhoun's darkest secret.

Staffe looks up into the dusking expanse of the park. He takes a long, arcing U-turn by the Serpentine lake and heads back towards the Knightsbridge lights. He soon has the streets beneath him again, hammering down towards Victoria. After six, seven minutes he accelerates into a sprint, full pelt, and pulls himself up quickly, hands on hips.

His shins are splinting and the sweat comes thick and fast, prickling his scalp, shallowing in the small of his back. It has been three years since his last cigarette but Staffe feels a nicotine craving in his lungs, burning deep, so he straightens himself from his haunches, falls into a painful jog. He says 'per-se-vere, per-se-vere' over and again, feeling too old for this.

\* \* \*

In the sumptuous pastel interior of a classical Georgian building in Mayfair, Guy Montefiore declines the kind offer of another glass of champagne and attempts a swift exit from the offices of Synge and Co.

On his way out of the building, Guy sees old man Synge coming in off the street and he looks around the foyer for a corner to occupy, any refuge from an awkward conversation, but the old man has seen him. He waves out of politeness and sticks on an unconvincing smile as Synge comes in off the street.

'Hello there, Guy. So nice to see you.'

'Likewise, Patrick. Likewise.' Guy extends a hand, feels the force of the old man's powerful grasp.

'Everything fine?' says Patrick Synge with the tilted head of a confidant.

'*Everything*,' says Guy, summoning a stoic smile. Despite the pleasantries, their relationship is governed by contracts like Bibles, fees the size of operating theatres.

'Fine. Just fine. No more nonsense, hey?'

'Not a bit of it. Sorry, Patrick . . . ' Guy hasn't actually stopped moving, ' . . . I'm already late.'

'Don't let them work you too hard,' calls the old man as Guy slots into the revolving door.

Guy Montefiore makes his way through the arch by the Grapes and into Shepherd's Market. He veers right, away from the raucous apron of suited drinkers that spills into the small square.

He is completely unaware of a man twenty paces behind.

When he very first spied Montefiore, the man had expected a thin, balding, greasy fellow with a grey pallor and stained suits. What he got was younger, smarter, taller, broader — someone you might see getting out of a Merc in the tennis club car park, giving you a firm handshake.

He watches Montefiore hail a cab and climb in and the man lets him go. He knows where Montefiore will be headed and he takes his time getting his own cab. He isn't here to follow Montefiore — he knows him just about well enough, he thinks — but to test how close he can get.

'Whereabouts?' says the cabbie.

'South Ken, for starters. Go through the park.'

They make their way through the fag end of the rush-hour traffic and he sits right back, watches Hyde Park Corner and the top of Park Lane scroll by. This is the city he loves, yet it allows a man like Montefiore, and people just like him, to do the things he did and hold down a plum job.

87

Staffe can't get his breath, feels as if the life is being pushed out of him. He gulps at the air and braces himself for another onslaught, counts down, slowly from ten, then turns off the tap. The shower stops and he leans against the glass bricks. They were Sylvie's idea, but now they need repointing. The Queens Terrace flat needs some care. As the water drips to nothing and his head still pounds, he thinks he can hear someone calling out. He steps out naked and opens the door, drips across the bedroom floor as he calls, 'Who's there? Who's there!' He has goosebumps and hears it again. It can't be. Not after three years.

'Sylvie!'

He runs into the hallway, not sure where the voice is coming from. He slows himself down, breathes deep, and goes into the kitchen. Nobody is there but he can still hear something. There is water deep in his ears.

Going into the lounge, he realises what a fool he has been. The voice is coming from a radio alarm. Not his, the old tenant's. Why would they wish to be awakened at dusk? And because it is getting darker outside, he can see himself naked in the tall, twelve-paned Georgian windows. He kneels down so he can just see his head and chest. He feels foolish but doesn't want to move. A memory wraps its arms around him. He is happy and sad.

'It's like living in a bloody goldfish bowl!' Sylvie had shouted.

'I've nothing to fear from the world,' Staffe had said.

She hated it when he refused to draw the curtains. 'And that's the trouble, Will.' She crosses her arms underneath her breasts. 'That's the bloody trouble.'

They have been arguing all weekend and he is tired of it all. He is dehydrated but wants more to drink. He thinks she might have sneaked upstairs for a line but won't say anything because he knows he is in the wrong, regardless.

She says, 'You've nothing to fear from the world. It can't touch you.' She takes a step closer, breathes in deep. 'You've been with *him*. I can smell it on you.'

'It's my job for Christ's sake.'

'Draw the bloody curtains, Will.'

He looks at the floor, follows the pattern in the parquet.

'And tomorrow you'll be off on the wild goose chase, I suppose. That's our time. You promised.'

'They're my parents. Jesus! If I can't . . . '

'They've been dead fifteen years.'

'Nineteen.'

'I'm only twenty-six, Will. I was seven when they died. I'm too young to be playing second fiddle to old men and ghosts.'

'I'm too old for you.'

'Oh no. You're not having that. You're just too bloody . . . ' She is picking up her coat from the club chair by the window. She looks out of the window. 'People can see us, Will. All I wanted was for you to draw the curtains and take me out for the day tomorrow. You know what day it is?'

He knows. They had been together three years.

The phone rings and she stops in her tracks.

'Don't answer it, Will.'

'It's Jessop,' he says.

'You don't say.'

'He needs me.'

'He'll understand.'

'They're trying to get rid of him.'

'I want us to be together, Will. I really do.'

The phone stops ringing.

'I'm trying to be loyal. A friend. How can loyalty be a bad thing?'

She walks to the door, says, 'You're not being loyal, you're choosing, Will. You're choosing to be with them rather than me.'

Staffe watches her go, wants to follow, but the phone goes. She closes the door and he picks up.

'The bastards have done it, Staffe. They're sending me to the Met.' It sounds for all the world as though Jessop has been crying. The hardest man he knows.

'Can I call you back?' The front door slams.

'I can't go there. This place is my life. My fucking life! And they know it, Staffe. They want shut of me.'

Staffe watches Sylvie step off the pavement. She takes a stride out in front of a taxi and puts her hands on her hips to stop it. If you saw her, you'd stop too.

'Let's go for a drink, Staffe. I need to talk to someone.'

'What about Delores?'

'She's not here.'

Sylvie gets into the cab. She doesn't look back.

'You know this'll be good for you, don't you, Staffe? They'll make you up to DI. You'd better come see if the shoes fit.'

'I'll see you in the Scotsman's Pack.'

★ ★ ★

Above the rooftops, the sky is streaked a salmon colour. Opposite, a taxi is parked up. Its 'for hire' light is switched off. It must be on a pickup.

Staffe's mobile rings and he stands up, looks for it. Staffe can see himself naked in the window. He walks slowly out of the room, follows the tone and answers.

'You're not here,' says Marie. 'I said I'd cook.'

'I might not be back for a couple of nights.'

'You're pissed off with me already?'

Staffe can hear a crack in his sister's voice, suspects she has probably been drinking. 'There's a place I've got to take care of.'

'Part of your little empire.'

'I'll call you in the morning. It'll be nice for you and Harry to have some peace and quiet.'

'You said 'take care of', Will. You take care of people, not buildings.'

The phone light fades and Staffe calls Johnson to say not to bother with the visit to Peckham but his wife answers.

'Hi, Becky. Is Rick there?'

'He's out,' she says, sounding annoyed.

Staffe wants to tell her to keep an eye out for her man, that he's under pressure and not to think he doesn't love her, but he makes an excuse and hangs up before he somehow puts his foot in it.

He goes back into the lounge, watches the taxi

91

parked opposite. It has been waiting a long time. He looks down at the picture of Karl Colquhoun on the Cobb writing table that the murdered man had, through some twisted rope-burn of fate, repaired. The monochrome body is spattered with the dark grey of blood. To the right, the mad eyes of his killer. As he looks into the eyes, Staffe feels watched. His naked flesh pinches and goosebumps spread all the way up his arms, across his chest. He picks up the photo and switches the light off, peering out into the dark. Opposite, the taxi's lights turn on and it moves off. Staffe can't see if anyone had got in.

★   ★   ★

The Crown and Mitre suits the man's purpose perfectly. It's a young pub, half Anzac, half Jack the Lad and the Gents is between the two bars so he can come into one bar, have a drink, then go to the toilet and leave through the other bar looking sufficiently different. Now he wears a thin windcheater and a baseball cap taken out of the small day bag. He has a feeling about tonight.

Montefiore sits in the window of the Chat Noir, a down-at-heel French café run by an old couple from Lisbon. The girl, Tanya, is still just outside, standing with a group of other girls, all wearing the same type of short flared skirts. Some of them have pudgy legs, some have spindly pins like yearling fillies. The girls are watching the skater boys — dressed head to toe in baggy Ts and hoodies and low-slung wide denim jeans with fat trainers — take runs at the low rail outside the Sainsbury's. It's where the pavement is widest but still pedestrians have to step into the gutter to avoid them. If they complain, they are told to 'fuck off'. The old folk think if they don't, they'll get happy-slapped.

Tanya cringes as one of the boys skates off, balancing on one leg on his board, crouching as he goes alongside an old woman who has stepped down into the road to go past them. The boy is on the edge of the pavement so the old woman can't step back up off the road. A bus goes past, hoots its horn and makes the woman jump. The boy laughs.

The man's blood comes up a notch and he can feel his hands begin to tremble so he pops two 50 mill propranolol, to bring him back down.

This has to be precise, controlled and unemotional. He puffs out his cheeks, tries to shake off imaginings of Montefiore getting the girl on her own; the things he would do to her; the sounds she would make. Her life would be tattered and so too the lives of her brother and sister, her mother and father who — in the absence of a properly punished perpetrator — would be left by the state to do nothing but blame themselves. For the rest of their lives.

The gang of girls and boys finish their peacocking for the night. The groups separate from each other and part with shouted obscenities and giggles; V signs and the finger — inarticulate expressions of pubescent desire.

He walks past the Chat Noir, clocking the dark, moving shadow of Montefiore in the window, and follows the group of girls. They begin to splinter. Tanya and one other girl cross the road and huddle together, sharing a mobile phone. They link arms and slow right down. As he passes them, the man can see Tanya is texting. They giggle.

His head is light and he walks on, hands fidgeting. So long has he waited. No end of thwarted nights waiting on this monster Montefiore. And all the time, the man wishing the loathing — this need — would go away. And now, this could be the night.

Montefiore should be passing them now and the man crosses the road, not daring to look back in case he gives himself away. By the time he has weaved his way through the traffic, stopping outside an estate agent's and chancing a look, he can see the girls have doubled back towards the Chat Noir and are taking a turn off the High Street.

They are going the wrong way.

No sign of Montefiore. Nowhere.

★　★　★

Staffe sits cross-legged on the floor with the laptop balanced on his knees and clicks into his emails. As usual, he opens all but the most obvious junk in case it's Sylvie. She doesn't have her own account, but uses those of friends. She last emailed him six months ago to see how he was getting on. He didn't reply.

Eventually, he is left with two: one from Janine and one from Pepe Muñoz.

hi staffe, thought you'd like to know the hair in the photo is a wig and not a very good one. probably a costume hire job. we're checking all outlets within five miles of bank. the hood is home made and probably an old tablecloth. the photograph is digital and probably a mid-range camera of 5-6 mill. pixels. blow-ups of the eyes don't reveal any reflections of accomplice. the paper it was printed on is fuji heavyweight photopro. sorry nothing more. Jan x.

Staffe fires back a reply telling her to get someone to check stockists of the photo paper and cross reference it to the PC World on the same estate as Marvitz Builders Merchants — where Karl Colquhoun worked; where Denness still works.

As for Pepe Muñoz, Babelfish reveals the news to be better.

Senor Wagstaffe, I am sorry you are ill and can not make the trip. We have closed another caucus of ETA Bilbao and have two men with the name Extbatteria. They are 23 and 27 years and are brothers. I have more details and can arrange for you to speak with them. Tell me when you can come next time. Pepe M.

Staffe emails back to say 'yes', he does want to meet the Extbatteria brothers but can it wait? He presses 'send' and puts the laptop on the floor, lies back on the restored wooden boards and tunes into the passages of air entering and leaving his lungs, feeding his heart. He feels light, watching the colours and shapes on the back of his eyelids and paints the anticipated moment of his coming together with Santi Extbatteria, the fifty-two-year-old man who thought the world would be a better place if he blew up twenty-three diners in a seafront restaurant.

Staffe knows that ETA are downsizing operations, seeking to advance the Basque cause through negotiations not explosives. A part of him bitterly resents this. It means his parents' deaths were in vain. He tries not to curse Extbatteria and his two sons, tries not to get excited at the prospect of unearthing the veteran terrorist's exile.

★　★　★

Desire banks up within Montefiore. It presses down on him, makes his legs weak. How can there be such a thing as forbidden love? Love must always prevail — you can't resist.

A client once said to him when they were putting together a development site of played-out shops round the back of Waterloo Station, 'You get one chance, Guy. We all get one chance and it's just a case of recognising it — and taking it. It's not luck, it's meant to be.'

He focuses in on Tanya and her friend, huddled over the mobile phone between the swings and the copse of trees deep in the heart of the park. He presses 'send', watches his words beam themselves down to the girls, sees the effect he has. She makes his stomach slow summersault. This close, he could reach, almost touch.

He is sad because he knows the beginning is also the end. He has made a career out of being able to spot value and evaluate risk, so he makes his way to the copse of rowan trees, tiny berries bursting from bud. He waits for her friend to do as he has instructed. If Tanya is to meet Alex, the boy she thinks she loves, the friend has to go. Alex is shy. Alex wants Tanya all to himself. Alex is miles away playing five-a-side football underneath the Westway flyover. Alex doesn't have a new mobile, has never texted Tanya. Never will.

Guy puts a hand into his pocket, fingers the ribbing to his balaclava. His breath is short and he is hot around his neck and shoulders. He feels as though someone is about to put a hand upon him — feels as if he can't bear the suspense any longer, but doesn't want it to stop.

Tanya's friend gives her a coy wave goodbye. Between the trees he can see Tanya make a nervous smile with her top teeth tight over her bottom lip. She gives a tiny shrug of her narrow shoulders, turns, walks towards Montefiore with her head down, her shoulders turned in, as if she is ashamed of her young, beautiful body. Guy shuffles back into the copse, makes a hurried patrol of the perimeter, looking for anybody walking a dog or making a lovers' diversion.

There is nobody within a hundred yards.

He can hear her come into the trees but she stops. She calls his name. 'Alex?' It's little more than a whisper.

Guy crouches. He can see her bare legs

beneath the low canopy of trees. He puts his finger on the button, presses 'send' and listens to her gasp at its one vibrating ring.

'Alex,' she says again. 'You're here?'

'I'm here,' says Guy, into the wool of his balaclava. After he has said it, he moves swiftly to his left so she follows the sound of his voice towards an empty place. As he stalks, he removes a drugged rag from a sealed plastic envelope.

She moves awkwardly between the branches. Guy is behind her now.

'I can't see you, Alex.'

Montefiore holds his breath and takes a silent, final stride — barely able to move. His legs are jelly and his heart beats double time. He is ecstatic. He is sad. He reaches out, taps her on the shoulder, watches her turn slowly. Her eyes go wide and a scream gets stuck in her throat.

He feels as happy as he ever has in all his life. He moves swiftly forward and places one hand on the back of her head as if he is going to slowly, softly pull her towards him for a first kiss. Her mouth does open and, rather than put his mouth on hers, he reaches up with his other, gloved hand and he silences her with the soaked rag. He can smell the chloroform as he watches her wide eyes lid down in fine spasms, like butterfly wings.

Her hair is softer than you could ever dream and she's light in his grasp. He pulls the rag away quickly, wanting her to come round before he is done. He needs a response. He lays her down, easily; then lies alongside, looking around, beneath the canopy. He smiles to himself, happy to be alone with his love.

He pulls his balaclava off, nestles his face into the well of her jaw and neck. He inhales her, runs his hand along her thin, soft skin. He moves his head, kisses her jaw, kisses her closed eyes, kisses her closed mouth, makes it open by kissing her harder. He feels the soft cotton at the top of her legs and pushes her legs apart. He unzips himself and takes hold of her bottom. He feels a shadow on the back of his neck. He turns cold.

Guy twists to look up but he can't believe what he sees. At first he thinks it's a warped mirror, but then the mouth and eyes inside the balaclava shape a smile, and the figure talks.

'You're done, Guy.'

'It's not what . . .'

The man gives him a kick to his open flies and Montefiore squeals with pain.

'Don't hurt me,' says Montefiore, looking at the weapon in the man's hand. The blade glints.

'You're not in charge now, Guy. Put a foot wrong, and it will be Thomasina's turn.'

'No!'

And as if it were a full stop, the man kicks Montefiore again. While Montefiore writhes around in agony, the man says, 'You think I'm going to kill you?' And before Guy can respond, he puts the sole of his shoe on Guy's balls. Leans forward. 'But you'd be wrong. You might even say I'm going to do the opposite. But first, I'm coming to see you. Soon. And if you say a single word to anybody, fucking anybody! You'll look your daughter in the eye from the dock and then you'll die in prison. But not until she has. And you want to know how she'll die?'

'No!' says Guy, sobbing. 'I'll do it. Whatever you want, I'll do it.'

The man takes his foot off Guy, takes a step back and Guy zips up, gets to his feet. He looks down at Tanya. He loves her, still. She's the only one. All the others turned out to be tainted in the end. Dirty. Whores.

★ ★ ★

Staffe winces as he applies a dash of iodine to his wound. He presses a fresh dressing to the cut and slides between the sheets of the first bed he ever bought. He stares at the ceiling and an image of his mother and father comes to him, waving from on deck in Portsmouth harbour on their way to Spain. His father had taken early retirement after a life of nothing but work and they were going to walk in the Picos de Europa, after first going to visit Bilbao and Guernica. Young Will couldn't see the back of them quick enough.

He had smoked a joint on the drive back to their house in Thames Ditton, and when he had got home he went straight to the Angel and bought two grams of coke. At the end of the night he went back to his parents' house with his friends and partied for a week — until the police came knocking, not busting his spoiled white ass for drugs but to tell him he had, at the age of eighteen, been orphaned.

The pain is dull. He is so, so tired, but sleep has ebbed away from him. Could Colquhoun's murder be the work of a mercenary? Hired by

100

Debra Bowker? But why now? Why after all these years? Two wives. Two suspects. And Ross Denness?

And what did Golding mean by he 'knows'? Where is Sohan Kelly? What if the e.Gang get to Kelly? Should Staffe go and see him or is he best left alone?

Maybe Colquhoun's wasn't a professional killing. But they got in and got out without so much as a broken pane or the finest trace of DNA.

Far away in the white noise of low-grinding wagons beating the congestion by using unearthly hours, a siren sounds. It tails away, warps into the night. Staffe is drifting now, thinking of the children who suffered. A silence to be broken.

★　★　★

Johnson shows his warrant card to the minicab driver and tells him to: 'Fuckin' wait, unless you want someone to have a real good look over this piece of shit.'

There is no response from 26d so he buzzes the downstairs and is told that Paolo Di Venuto will probably be in the Golden Fleece.

'What's he look like?' says Johnson.

'Who are you?'

'Police. Bet you got something in your place. Maybe growin' a bit of weed. Cookin' up some C meth?' He takes a step back, looks up at the peering face at the curtains, holds up his warrant card and smiles.

The intercom crackles. 'Skinny fuck with long hair. He'll be in a jean jacket and a white vest. Combat shorts. Never fuckin' changes.'

Johnson checks his watch, can't afford to hang around, so he tells the minicab driver to wait up outside the pub. As he walks along the High Road, he works up a sweat and plots ahead to what might transpire. He feels weak and knows he should have sorted himself out before he came. He stops, hands on knees and gulps at the air, shakes himself down.

'The fuck you lookin' at!' he shouts at a couple of youths. One black, one white, both looking for trouble. But they stop dead when they see Johnson's face, look down at his big clenched fists. They cross the road, muttering, and he strides off, the blood flowing through him now as he pictures Di Venuto, pictures him beating up on Staffe's sister, pictures him turning her over, pulling off her pants, pressing her buttocks out, softening her up.

The Golden Fleece is fifty yards away. He should wait outside until they throw out but it looks like a place that locks in. He pictures the look on her face when he's done; hears the slap when she complains, a line of blood coming from the corner of her mouth, an eye swelling, the lies she'll make up to cover for him. He pushes open the door and it slams into the wall. Half a dozen at the bar turn round, the smiles off their faces. Johnson points to the dark one in the jean jacket and shorts second from left and says 'Di Venuto!' striding towards him as he watches the others shuffle away. One of them takes a hold of his bitch pop by the throat and Johnson says, 'Put the fuckin' bottle down or I'll shove it up your arse.'

He puts the bottle down.

Di Venuto opens his mouth to say something but he doesn't get the chance. Johnson kicks him in the balls and as he doubles over, he punches him in the neck, takes a hold of his hair and drags him outside. Patsy Cline sings them on their way and out to the street. Johnson stamps on his face and pulls him to his feet. 'You know what you done? You know what you fuckin' done!'

Di Venuto nods, blood pumping from a gash across his nose. Johnson can see the bone. His eyes will swell good. 'I'm gonna pay,' begs Di Venuto. 'I swear to fuckin' God I'm gonna pay!'

And Johnson laughs. God shining down on him. He won't know Staffe's sent him. He thinks this is over some drugs he's ripped off or a loan shark he's crossed.

Suddenly, Johnson feels weak again. The blood has dumped and he is no longer wired quite the same tight way. He needs to be gone — and quick — so he holds a hand up, beckons the minicab. He hasn't even got the strength to give Di Venuto a farewell slap.

As they drive off, he wonders if that was what Staffe had wanted, or will it just mean Di Venuto takes it out on someone else. If he does, he'll come back. Next time he'll be stronger.

★   ★   ★

Guy takes a draught of wine. His heart beats fast and his fingers tremble. This is the deepest night can be. It is at its most silent. Soon, the birds will sing and the newspaper boys will stir.

103

He hears the soft metal of the gate's latch and quickly drains the glass. He stands, looks at his watch. It is four minutes to three. He holds his breath, prays hard that the silence will stretch, that something will occur to him.

Two loud raps at the door.

All night, Montefiore has tried and failed to fathom an option that ends with him not answering the door. If the man was going to kill him, he would have done it in the park.

The man's portrait outline is shadowed in the door's stained glass and the threat to Thomasina resounds. The cartilage around his knees fails and he is short of breath, light in the head. He reaches out, shoots the bolt, unlocks the door, and pulls it ajar.

Somehow, in the sliced jag of a moment, as he sees the man in the open door, Montefiore knows he is done for. He tries to shut it back, but the man puts out a foot.

He cries out, for help, but before the gushing air can make a sound, his breath is cut dead by a fast and expert blow to the Adam's apple. Montefiore drops to his knees, makes himself into a ball and feels a rag on his face. He recognises the smell as he fades, slowly, away.

*   *   *

Montefiore is dead still. He is naked from the waist down to his Church's shoes, gagged with gauze, and streaks of blood run from his eyes down his cheeks.

The final touches are applied. The tiny video

camera is propped up so it takes in the whole of Guy Montefiore: his misshapen frame on the screen, bound up to a metal cross, made up from interlocking high-tensile aluminium tubes. The cross is, in turn, suspended from the ceiling by three lengths of rope. There were originally four. That was the hardest part: finding the main joists in the ceiling, something strong enough to screw into, to take Montefiore's weight.

Montefiore's thighs are bound to his chest with wagon lashes and he looks as if he is suspended in mid-air, jumping into a swimming pool. Bombing, they used to call it. Each of the three remaining ropes vary in length. Each rope has a number pinned to it: 1, 2, 3, 4.

Inside Montefiore, entering his body via the anus, is a five-foot length of two by two. The other end is securely attached to the floor by four screwed metal shelf brackets. He hangs from the cross which is in turn suspended by the various ropes.

Through the drumming of the pain, Montefiore hears a car outside. It changes gear, revs up and the engine cuts out. A door opens and shuts. Then another. He tries to slow the pain, breathes in deep. He pushes his tongue at the gauze, trying to fashion a pocket of air, some way that if he emptied his lungs, some sound might ensue. He can hear his neighbours coming up the path and he breathes in as much as he can. Pain shoots up through his body and he shakes his head as he screams, trying to will the sound out. It seems loud in his ears, but he watches as the figure in the hood smiles with its blood-red lips as it turns up the radio.

They both wait for the neighbours to open and close their front door. A finger presses 'record' on the video and Montefiore watches the figure advance towards him, cloaked in white — the penitent's hood showing only wild, black eyes and blood-red lips that make a smile as a hand grabs the rope. Montefiore feels himself shift and the wood grates against him, inside. He knows he can't take much more. He feels his eyes go moist, sticky. He can't see, just feels the thick liquid touching his cheeks. He tries to take a deep breath, prepare in some way but the pain is too much. He hears a grunt, then a swish and he jags down. He hears something tear, inside him. For a second his arms are slack and then as the tearing sound comes again, something in his head closes down.

★　★　★

The phone cuts into the night with a shrill tone.

'Who is it?' says Staffe, drowsy.

'No time to sleep, Staffe. Not if you're going to get to the bottom of this.' It is a woman's voice.

'Who is this?'

'48 Billingham Street, W8. We've got a fresh one for you.'

'What?'

The phone clicks dead.

Staffe calls 1471, gets the mobile number that has called him, then he rings Leadengate, asks for the incident response sergeant and is pleased to hear it is Jombaugh.

'I need backup down at 48 Billingham Street, Jom.'

'Never heard of it.'

'It's W8.'

'What are you doing, Staffe? That's Met country.' He's known Jombaugh ever since he was first a DC under Jessop's wing. Jombaugh used to be under that wing, too, but he got so he didn't want any more of the streets. He cared more about his family. It all but broke his heart when Jessop was moved to the Met.

'I got a personal call, at home, for Christ's sake.'

'You're not at home,' says Jombaugh. 'This number you've phoned from. It's not home.'

'What?' The penny drops. Whoever called him knows him too well. Who would know he was staying here tonight?

'What did they say when they called?'

' "We've got a fresh one for you." '

'That could mean anything.'

'It was a woman, Jom. And I don't think it is 'anything'. I reckon it's connected with the Limekiln.'

'I have to call the Met, sir.'

'The Met! Just give me two men.'

'It's what we have to do. I don't like it any more than you.'

'Well at least get me a warrant for entry and search. Send it down with Johnson.'

'Will, you shouldn't . . . '

But Staffe hangs up, figures he can get there before the Met do. He *has* to get there first.

There's no time to shave or clean his teeth, he

just gets into yesterday's clothes. He is running out the door when a shiver shoots right the way down him. He takes a breath, goes into the kitchen for his three-inch, steel-handled Sabatier paring knife.

★ ★ ★

Staffe switchbacks on to and across the Cromwell Road. He keeps the Peugeot in second all the way and as he pulls off the North End Road, he reckons he will have fifteen, twenty minutes before Johnson gets there — and the Met. He ushers a chant to slow his racing blood, clear his muggy head. He presses his right foot to the floor, listens to the engine roar and wail, all the way to Billingham. When he gets there, he slows it right down, parks silently and eases the door shut, runs softly to the house.

The curtains in the front room are drawn shut. Seemingly, no lights on inside. It is an early Victorian semi, two storeys plus a mansard attic conversion. To the side is a high gate that leads to the garden and Staffe takes hold of the top of the gate, heaves himself up, cocks a leg, and just gets the sole of his shoe on top. He levers himself up and launches himself down to the other side. Round the back, and seeing the place is locked tight, Staffe weighs up the best method of forcing his own entry. Small-paned French windows show into a dark dining room and in the sash window to the kitchen a tiny neon bud of green flashes on and off from the oven.

He has to be quick.

His eyes dart, see a key on the inside of the door of the French windows. He rummages in the dustbin and finds a sheet of newspaper and an old jar of honey. He smears what is left of the honey on a small piece of the newspaper and presses it on the pane of glass closest to the key. He finds a rock and takes a deep breath, then punches the glass with the rock. Most of the glass sticks to the sticky newspaper. He listens for a reaction from inside, listens to hear if anybody has arrived out front. Nothing. He picks the glass from the frame, reaches gingerly in and turns the key.

As he opens the door, the house seems to gasp. Moving through to the patterned Victorian tiles of the hallway, he gets gooseflesh. Four doors lead off the hall and all are open, bar one. He checks that all the rooms are empty before standing by the one closed door. He puts a hand on the doorknob and presses his ear to the beeswaxed wooden panel.

He turns the knob slowly and pushes the door open inch by inch. He can hear a scratching noise from within and puts his head into the gap, looks into the dark room. There is a smell of human faeces and an odd contraption. An odd contraption with . . . a body? A body on a cross!

'My God,' he says to himself. 'My God,' and he feels weak. His hand lets go of the doorknob and the door is pulled away from him and there's another louder, scratching noise and a rope snags, the body jagging down. A muffled groan merges with a sound from a butcher's backroom.

Staffe looks up at the body, sees the eyes bulge

above long streaks of dried blood down the face, the shape of upturned knife blades. He takes a step towards the suspended body, sees what has gone on. The man's trousers are gathered around his feet. He looks away as soon as he sees the wood, where it has gone, and he runs to the front door. It isn't bolted from the inside. On the street a police car pulls up, blue lights flashing but no siren. Two armed officers leap out of the back.

Staffe raises his arms, holds his warrant card aloft. 'I'm police. I'm police! Call an ambulance. Quick, tell them to be quick, for God's sake.'

# Wednesday Morning

Staffe sits in Montefiore's study, awaiting authorisation to turn on the victim's computer.

According to his bank statements, Guy Montefiore pulls in twelve grand a month from Sanders and Fitch, a Corporate Finance House of the old school variety. The statements reveal that he sends three thousand eight hundred every month to Helena Montefiore and three times a year he pays eleven thousand pounds to Benenden School. Blue blood runs through this family, but something far darker is weaved beneath its surface. Deep and dark.

Jombaugh telephones, saying Johnson is on his way to sort out the warrants, and to give Staffe the all-clear accessing Montefiore's computer. Staffe hangs up and watches the antivirus programs power up, then clicks his way into Guy Montefiore's recent programs, the last websites visited. Two are enough. Much more than enough for Staffe. He tries to blink away what he has just seen — photographic images of young girls and grown men and far, far worse than what he has witnessed in the flesh this week. He tries to steel himself to bring to justice the person who violated and tortured Guy Montefiore. The images of the young girls scroll up on the back of Staffe's closed eyes. Some hadn't reached puberty.

Josie Chancellor stands in the doorway of

Montefiore's study. 'These Met boys aren't too keen having us around. I had a hell of a time getting in here.'

He swivels in Montefiore's captain's chair, to and fro, turning his back on the casement windows: the leafy green street outside; lime-hued light hazing through the trees. 'What have you got?'

'Pennington wants to see you, now — 'Sooner if possible', he said.' She sits down opposite him on a low-slung leather chesterfield, crosses her legs and starts giving it to him. 'The initial read on the gag has come in. It's a different fabric to the Colquhoun murder.'

'But the same method was applied.'

'No. I've checked against the photos from the Limekiln and they're different knots. They're saying it's a different MO. A different person.'

'Or the same clever person.' His mobile begins to vibrate and *Home* appears on the screen.

'He's just called me, Will. He's just called and he's got himself into trouble.' Marie begins to cry.

'Who?'

'Paolo. I think I still love him, Will.'

'What kind of trouble?'

'Someone's beaten him up.'

'Shit!'

'What?'

Suddenly, Staffe questions his judgement.

'I told him to come round here. That's all right, isn't it, Will?'

'I have to go, Marie. Let's talk later.'

'He's on his way here. I knew you wouldn't mind.'

112

Staffe spins the chair back and lets out a loud sigh.

'What's wrong?' says Josie.

'Nothing. Everything's just bloody dandy,' he says, clicking the mouse to Montefiore's computer, un-minimising the young girls. They look lost, straight into the camera. The men don't even look as if they are enjoying it. Staffe's own problems suddenly fade and he begins to think what methods were employed to entice the girls. He reminds himself that this computer belongs to a victim. 'Different fabric, different knot. One they killed, one they let live.' He spins round to face Josie and sees Johnson has finally arrived, is standing next to her. 'The method of entry is the same.'

'We don't know anything about the method of entry,' says Johnson.

'Exactly. The victims let the torturers in. Did they know them?'

'Victims?' says Johnson. 'Have you heard what Montefiore has got up to in the past?'

'And they called me at home. It has to be the same person. They called me to put the last nail in, to cut the last rope to send that thing right up him.'

'He's going to make it. The hospital rang the station,' says Johnson. 'They didn't want him dead.'

'When can we talk to him?'

'Not for a while.'

'I can't believe the Met are saying it's not the same person,' says Staffe. 'It's just so they get the case.'

'And we're saying it's a serial case so we can keep it?'

Staffe gives Johnson his dirtiest look, holds it until Johnson can't stand it any more. He needs to talk to him about Paolo Di Venuto, but that will have to wait. Johnson looks away and Staffe stands, chest jutting out, 'I'm saying it is a serial crime because I believe it to be the case. There is sufficient evidence and my experience directs me to believe it. If you or anybody from the Met has a problem with that, then we can have it out with DCI Pennington. Otherwise, I'd thank you to do your best to gather the evidence. Do you get me, Johnson?'

He nods.

'Let's go see Pennington. You can tell me what you know about Montefiore.'

★　★　★

Johnson drives Staffe up to Leadengate, his sleeves rolled up and the tendons of his thick white arms taut. 'Oh, we got the trace on the phone that called you. It's Montefiore's mobile.'

'Shit.' There are a couple of specks of blood on Johnson's shirt and a sheen of sweat all over him — face, neck, arms. Staffe blames himself for his sergeant's state and twists in his seat to face him. 'You weren't exactly subtle last night, were you?'

'That greaseball down in Peckham? Jesus, man, he had it coming.'

Staffe could tell Johnson that, thanks to his efforts, the greaseball is now living in his house. But he's not one for dirty laundry in public. 'You

114

went a bit further than I wanted.'

'He started it, sir.'

'You didn't let him know who you were?'

'The prick thought a dealer or a loan shark had sent me.'

As they come out of the northern end of Hyde Park and shimmy along the one-ways round the back of Oxford Street, Staffe considers what his team has gleaned about Guy Montefiore: a history with the CPS — he was briefly suspected, three years ago, of assaulting a young girl called Sally Watkins.

Montefiore is as far along the social scale from Karl Colquhoun as you can get. So far apart, they'd almost meet the other side — which they have, in terms of the crimes alleged, the charges which the Crown never pressed. It seems they share common ground when it comes to the vengeances exacted upon them.

'The charges never pressed,' thinks Staffe. Two men, never brought to justice. Neither on the sex offenders register. 'Tell me what you know about the wife.'

A vein in Johnson's neck bulges. 'According to the statement she gave our WPC, she left him three years ago. They've got a young girl of their own. Thomasina. She was eleven then. God knows if they told her what he'd done to the Watkins girl.'

'How old was Sally Watkins when he did it?'

'Twelve. Except we can't say he did it, can we?' Johnson is practically spitting his words. 'Because the fucking CPS dropped it.'

'How did it get reported?'

'This is the weird thing,' says Johnson. 'Montefiore's wife fingered him. The Watkins mother and father went round to see her and she called the Met.'

'Jesus, we need to see her.'

'Within a month his QC had got the CPS to drop the charges.'

As they turn on to Leadengate, Staffe sees a large van parked up outside the station, a uniformed constable about to give it a ticket. 'For Christ's sake, Johnson, tell that bloody Boy Scout not to book that van.'

'Whose is it?'

'Mine, for the day. Which reminds me, there's something you can do to make up for last night.'

\* \* \*

'You should have waited,' says Pennington. He sits erect behind his own desk. Nothing but a laptop, a notebook and a phone to clutter his world. 'You knew Montefiore is in the Met's jurisdiction.'

'I was responding to an emergency.'

'The door was rigged and you went storming in ham-fisted. How does that look?'

Staffe knows that with Pennington you can't give an inch. 'They called me at home.'

'You could have walked into a trap.'

'I called Jombaugh and requested backup. I had cause to believe it was an emergency — especially after Colquhoun.'

Pennington takes pause, leans back in his chair and does a majorette's twirl with his pencil. 'The

116

Met beg to differ about the connection.'

'For Christ's sake, sir, the same people have to be involved with both.'

'You know the implications for our resources. We're not the Met.'

'You're worried about money, sir? Is this all a matter of budget?' He looks at Pennington, sees a hard-nosed detective reduced to playing accountant — shuffling resources. Every year the targets go up, the pay budget comes down. Unless you can get your Force to work harder for less, crime's going to have to crack itself.

'Will,' Pennington leans forward and as soon as he hears his Christian name, Staffe knows the DCI is about to test him, 'there's nothing to stop you keeping in touch with the Met on this one, if they run with it.'

'I need to talk to Montefiore. I have to be the first to speak to him and I need access to his wife and daughter. And I have to talk to Sally Watkins.' Staffe feels hot beneath the collar of his suede jacket. 'For Christ's sake, anyone can see these cases are practically identical. Meanwhile, we've got Leanne Colquhoun being held.'

'She's still a suspect. I've seen the statements and if Karl Colquhoun did go to Margate and touch up those poor kids, that's a bloody good motive — no matter whether she loved him or not.'

'How could she have got to Montefiore if she was in our custody?'

'As we speak, these are two separate cases. I'm asking you to liaise with the Met, Will.'

'Give me two weeks. Two weeks with full support.'

'I can't do that.'

'They called me at home. There's something personal going on here.'

Pennington nods.

'And . . . ' Staffe thinks about the ropes, numbered 1, 2, 3, 4. The last one to be cut was three. Could Montefiore be the third? That would mean Colquhoun was the second.

'Staffe?' says Pennington.

And if Colquhoun was the second . . . maybe they should be looking backwards for a pattern.

'Staffe! If they are playing you along — and quite frankly, I think that sounds a bit fanciful — why give them what they want?'

'I can't find Karl Colquhoun's killer unless I follow up on Montefiore. I'm sure of that.'

'I'm worried about you, Will.' He looks past Staffe to the door. Lowers his voice. 'Sohan Kelly's car was torched last night.'

'You said you had taken care of him.'

Pennington looks at Staffe's bandaged wrist, dirty from the morning's exertions, with petals of blood seeping through the lint. 'You should know better than to get involved.'

Staffe hears the van outside, tooting. He grimaces. 'You lined Sohan Kelly up, sir. You asked me to take his statement. He had already changed his statement by the time I interviewed him.' Instinctively, Staffe puts his hand on his heart, feels the folded, first statement through the suede. As he does, he sees the tear in his sleeve where the knife went into him yesterday.

Pennington makes a tight smile at Staffe and picks up the phone. He dials. 'Geoff, I've got my

118

DI here and we'd like to run with the Montefiore assault for a few days, if only to eliminate the case as a link to the Colquhoun murder.' He nods, says 'Hmm . . . hmm . . . but this is a critical time for us, too. We'll copy all the evidence to you, send transcripts. I can assure you, Geoff, we'll bend over backwards for you. Yes . . . yes, very funny.' He makes a fake laugh — which must work. 'Thanks, Geoff.' He puts the phone down and logs the conversation in his notebook, leans back, and says to Staffe, 'You've got a week and your liaison at the Met is Smethurst. You know Smethurst, don't you?'

'Yes, sir.'

'Just make sure you get something. This could cost me. And if it does, it will cost you too.'

'Thanks, sir.'

'I don't want your thanks, Staffe.' Pennington picks up a file, hands it to Staffe, readjusts his glasses to the end of his nose, and turns his attention to his laptop.

On the stairs down, Staffe opens the file and takes out the photograph of Karl Colquhoun's Ku Klux killer and reads the Imaging Notes, squints at the remastered enlargement of the supposed killer's face. According to Imaging, they have tried to extrapolate the width of the shoulders and hips, the hands, the shadows above the lips, but they cannot be sure whether it is a man or a woman.

Staffe sees Stanley Buchanan a flight below. He skips down to catch up and slaps Buchanan on the shoulder. 'Now then, Stanley,' he says. 'Tell me why we should release your client and make it good. I think we've held her long enough.'

'What the hell do you want, Staffe?'

'Justice, Stanley. Same old, same old.' He is about to dripfeed Buchanan the prompts to get Leanne released when Pulford comes in through reception.

'Can I have a word, sir?'

'I'm sorry, Stan. Wait here, will you?'

As they go outside, they get a blast of heat. Pulford says, 'It's Debra Bowker, sir. She did come back to England, according to Budjet Air. Except she travelled as Debra Colquhoun. So I checked with the Secretary of State and her old passport was sworn as lost. Sounds fishy, don't you think?'

'Clue up on the extradition procedures. Don't do anything yet, just be ready if we need to get her over here. And check the BA flight times from Tenerife into Heathrow.'

Pulford nods, clearly pleased with himself. 'Weird thing is, sir, she travelled alone. She left her kids in Tenerife. I've been looking at the case notes for her kids, Danielle and Kimberley.'

'I've seen them.'

'Both the girls said Karl Colquhoun touched their genitals 'too much' when he bathed them. He gave them baths until they were seven and nine years old. Danielle Colquhoun told her mother what was happening when Colquhoun started bathing the younger one alone. Sound familiar?'

'Just like Calvin and Lee-Angelique Colquhoun,' says Staffe.

'Except Debra Bowker went to the police.'

'How long was she here, on her last visit?'

'It was six weeks ago and she stayed for a week. So far, there's no evidence that she met up with Karl Colquhoun. Leanne Colquhoun called Bowker a 'fucking whore', sir. There's no love lost there.'

Staffe smiles, says, 'All the more reason to release them from their captivities, hey?' He slaps his hands and goes back in to see Stanley Buchanan.

★ ★ ★

'Thanks for doing this, lads,' says Staffe, taking his favourite armchair from Pulford who is standing on the tailgate of the van. It is a nineteenth-century American spoonback and the last item to be loaded off.

'You've got some fancy shit, if you don't mind me saying.' Johnson is sitting on the step at the front of the house in Queens Terrace. He looks tired and Staffe would love to be able to tell him to get himself home, but he knows the subtext. Johnson will be damned if he'll let Pulford get ahead — in any respect.

Staffe hands the chair to Johnson and stands back, drags his forearm across his sodden forehead, and looks up at the windows of his flat. He thinks of Sylvie and immediately claps his hands, shakes the thought away, shouting up to Pulford, 'Come on. Let's get down to the Villiers estate.'

'Sally Watkins?' says Pulford.

121

Staffe goes across to Johnson, lowers his voice, 'I need you at the station. I've got something I'd like you to do for me.' He ushers Johnson towards the house. 'Check back, see if any other similar crimes have taken place in the last two or three years.'

'Similar crimes? We'd remember.'

'Further afield. Check the Met, even Thames Valley.'

'What are you saying, sir?'

'Let's just see if there's anything in the past that might connect, that's all.'

'Are you taking this a bit personal, sir?'

'Let's just pretend I'm in charge, eh, Johnson? Just pretend that you're here to do as you're told.'

'It's just . . . '

'Yes, I know! This would have been your case if I'd taken my leave. And it would probably be in the hands of the Met already. But it's not, Johnson. It's mine. Now here' — he tosses the key to the van — 'take the van back to the compound. And Johnson . . . ?'

'Sir?'

'I want you to know I appreciate everything you do.'

Johnson forces a smile, far from heartfelt.

★ ★ ★

'How many houses you got, sir?' says Pulford as they park up outside the Kilburn lock-up.

'What kind of a question is that to ask your boss?' Staffe opens the lock-up door and pulls

122

the dust sheet off his other car.

'Jesus, sir!' says Pulford.

'You stay there and lock it straight up as soon as I pull out,' says Staffe, tossing Pulford the keys to the lock-up. Staffe fires up his pride and joy, his Series 3 E-Type. He knows exactly what kind of cliché it is, knows most people will think he uses it — like most men who've rounded forty would use it — to help attract the ladies, help somehow turn back the years or stem a receding hairline. Not Staffe, though. He loves this car because his father did.

With the top down and driving down to the Villiers estate along the A24, it's a breeze. Through Clapham South and Balham and Tooting, Staffe drives it without irony. When he sees the signs for the A3 and Guildford, he feels sad.

For the main part, the E-Type sat in his father's garage but occasionally, on Sundays, his dad would take young Will out for a spin — up the A3 to Kingston Hill. He always thought it strange that his dad didn't take his mother. She could look beautiful, with her headscarf and dark glasses. Like something from the movies. On the way back, they'd drive real slow through Richmond Deer Park. The closer they got to home, with the Thames like a silver ribbon running to Hampton Court, the less they spoke — as if they knew life was waiting for them.

As they draw on to Villiers Avenue, Pulford says, 'Don't you think the Peugeot would have been, I don't know . . . '

'More discreet? I don't want to be discreet,

Pulford. I want everyone on this estate to know we're here. I want them crawling all over my baby. And when I've finished talking to Sally Watkins, I want you to have worked out who knows what about her mum and dad. That's Tyrone and Linda and, as far as we can gather, the mother flew the nest a while ago.'

Staffe parks up at the bottom of the Bevin Tower, avoiding the broken glass. Pulford blows his cheeks out, says, 'You not going to put the top up?'

Staffe laughs, tosses the keys. He checks the address in his notebook and swings his suede jacket over his shoulder, looks up at the towering wall of concrete and glass, the lowest of the low living in the sky.

Sally Watkins lives on the sixth floor but Staffe doesn't bother with the lift. The way things are going, he won't get a run today and he takes the stairs two at a time, pauses to get some breath on the fourth and looks down, sees a gaggle of people already gathering around the E-Type. He smiles to himself: just as he thought, it's the dads that are coming to see, not the kids.

Tyrone Watkins lets him in and immediately Staffe can't imagine him doing what was done to Montefiore, but he dismisses the facts that Tyrone Watkins is gnarled and malnourished; is unshaven and looks as though he hasn't seen the light of day in months.

Tyrone runs a neat ship. There is nothing on the shelves. No books or CDs or DVDs. A cable TV guide is in the middle of the floor. It looks well-thumbed. Tyrone sits straight back down and rests a dead gaze on the gigantic plasma TV screen, watches somebody preparing a meal on a beach. Staffe can hear a TV elsewhere in the house, either that or a stereo.

'Nice TV, Mr Watkins.'

'You can get them bigger, now. When I got it, it was the biggest. Just about.'

'When was that?'

Watkins doesn't answer, he just looks a little bit more sad, and Staffe guesses he's had the TV three years. An attempt to distract his daughter Sally from what Montefiore did to her. Allegedly.

'Is Sally here?' says Staffe.

Tyrone says, 'She's sleeping. She's not seeing no one today. No one, you hear.' He squints up at Staffe. 'Who you say you were?'

'Police, Mr Watkins.'

'Aah. That's right.'

'I'm from City of London. Leadengate.' Staffe wonders where to go next, contemplates telling Watkins about Montefiore but decides against it.

'Where is your wife, Mr Watkins?' Staffe sits opposite Tyrone and sinks back into a leatherette armchair. From here he can see into the open-plan kitchen area, separated from the living room by a breakfast bar. Staffe looks around the room, can't see a dining table, guesses this is TV-dinner land. 'She's gone, right?'

'Said she was going to get cigarettes. She loved a smoke. I remember the first time we met, my mum said when I come home: 'You been smoking, Tyrone? You don't smoke, Tyrone,' she said. And I didn't. Never have. She could smell

125

Linda's smoke on me. My Sally smokes but I don't mind. It reminds me.' He looks lost, looks as though he has exhausted himself just by talking. 'Plenty else for her to die of, this day and age.'

He looks up at Staffe with cloudy eyes. 'You police, you say?' He points the remote control at the TV and watches the giant image change to a house overlooking a foreign sea.

'I'd like to find your wife, Mr Watkins.'

'Said she was going for cigarettes.' A middle-aged couple are being shown round a Croatian waterfront home.

Staffe waits for Tyrone's eyes to lid down. As soon as his head lolls back against the chair's high, winged back, Staffe makes his way quietly down the hallway, following the sound of R & B music.

He taps lightly on the door. It says: 'Sally's Room. Enter at Your Peril'. He taps again and presses the door open as softly as he can, pokes his head round.

It's a small room. The translucent pink curtains are drawn and the light is soft. An orange glow comes through a scarf that's draped over the shade of her bedside lamp.

Sally Watkins is sitting on her bed in a short denim skirt with her back against the wall and her long, coltish legs dangling halfway to the floor. She's made up and wearing a tight-buttoned, cropped blouse that shows her flat, teenage tummy, makes the most of her cleavage. Her hair looks done. When she clocks Staffe with big, glazed eyes, she shifts her position, makes a

126

smile, says, 'Aah. Not seen you before.'

'I'm with the police, Sally.'

'I've not done nothing wrong.'

'I'm looking for your mother.'

'Bit late, aren't you? She's been gone three year.' Sally Watkins laughs and sneers. It makes her pretty face look ugly for a moment.

Staffe wants her to cover her legs and stop sitting back on her bed like that, as if a grown man in her bedroom offers no threat. He looks around the room a second time: no posters or dolls or teddy bears.

'Where do you think she is, Sally? Does she have family?'

'I'm her family and she's not here.'

'Does she have a brother or a sister?'

'Me uncle Barry lives up north somewhere. I don't know.'

'And what's his second name?'

'Wilkins. It's like Watkins. Me dad used to joke it was too much the same, her name. I didn't used to get it. But I do now. He was always jokin', me dad. Always jokin'.' She looks away, out of the window at the tower block next door. Staffe follows the gaze and when he looks back at her, she's got a pillow over her legs.

'I know what happened, Sally. I might be able to help, if you want.'

'They let him get away with it. Said it was better for me if we did nowt. Well plenty happened, didn't it?'

'Do you go to school, Sally?'

'You havin' a laugh?'

'Do you have a job?'

'I get by,' she says. She tries to sneer again but doesn't quite have the heart.

'Your dad . . . is he ill?'

'He's good for nothin' without her. He doesn't have a clue apart from how to use that fuckin' remote.'

'Does he ever leave the house?'

'Never. I do all the shoppin', pick up his social an' that.'

'Was he in the house the day before yesterday — in the evening, during the night?'

'He's got fuckin' bedsores, man. Covered in 'em. Gross. Have a look if you don't believe me. He's only thirty-five. It's disgustin'.'

'I'd kill for a cup of tea,' says Staffe. He sits on the small stool in front of her dressing table, covered in make-up and brushes; straighteners, curling tongs and a hairdryer.

A car horn sounds outside and Sally jumps off the bed, peers out of the window. She presses her face up against the glass and says, 'Nice motor. Is it yours?'

'The E-Type? Yes.'

'I'll make you a cup of tea. How you take it? You don't look like a copper.'

'I'm CID.'

'CID? Fuckin' 'ell.'

As soon as she's gone, Staffe rifles the drawers. The first is all bras and knickers, way sexier than a fifteen-year-old should be wearing. Second drawer are T-shirts, pristinely ironed. Third drawer is tissues and condoms. A whole load of condoms, and lube.

The bottom drawer is a whole childhood in

miniature: a doll and a teddy bear; sugar sachets and matchbooks and some souvenir pencils from Chessington World of Adventure, Thorpe Park, Brighton Pier. There's a stack of photographs with an elastic band around, and a slim stack of letters still in their envelopes, all opened with a knife. The top postmark is six months ago. Middlesbrough.

Staffe is on his knees when the door creaks back open. He sees her milky white legs and his heart sinks.

'If you'd asked, I'd of told you. You didn't need to go snooping,' says Sally Watkins, standing in the door. 'The kettle's boiling.'

'Sorry,' says Staffe. He looks up, wants forgiveness.

She makes a smile without the sneer and says, 'I'm going to have a sandwich. You want one?'

'I'd love one, Sally. I'll come and give you a hand.'

She leads the way, saying as she goes, 'Looking for me mum, eh?'

In the kitchen, there's just two of everything: knives, forks, dessert spoons, teaspoons. He opens a wall cupboard and sees sad pairs of side plates, dinner plates, cereal bowls and mugs. All neatly stacked. The inside of the cupboard is spotless. A waft of bleach as he closes the door.

As Sally makes the tuna and mayonnaise sandwiches, he looks for a towel. In a drawer there is a pile of ironed tea towels and at the side of them is a photocopied A5 flyer that reads:

# VABBA
## MEETS LIFE HEAD ON
### Victims
### Against
### Being
### Buried
### Alive

VABBA. Staffe knows what they're getting at — the need to move on, to reclaim your life after being sinned against. But he can't see any amount of victim support working for Tyrone Watkins or Sally.

'Here you are. Tuna Marie Rose.' She hands him the sandwich. 'I put a bit of tomato puree in with the mayo. It makes it go pink. It's better with seafood, see. Me mum taught me to do it.'

'Sally . . . ?'

'You want to look at them letters, don't you?'

'Would you mind?'

'What you want my mum for? He done it again? That bastard done it again?'

'He might have.'

'I'll get the address. You don't have to read the letters, do you?'

Staffe wants to read the letters, realises they might hold clues as to what Linda Watkins has been doing. 'Not if you don't want,' he says, 'but they might help. It'll be just me reads them. I promise.'

She looks at him and smiles, says, 'I'll get them.' She takes a cigarette from a packet of a budget brand and lights it too deftly with a

130

Zippo lighter she pulls from the back pocket of her little denim skirt.

Staffe takes a bite of his tuna Marie Rose sandwich and chews, swallows it down against his will. Far too sweet. It's a kid's snack. He tears off a piece of kitchen roll and wraps the rest of the sandwich, puts it in his jacket pocket, waits for her to come back.

He finishes his tea and goes to the door, calls out, 'Sally, you OK?'

There's no sound, just the whiff of burning, getting stronger. A thin scarf of smoke plumes up from under the bathroom door and the toilet flushes. Sally Watkins appears, Zippo in hand and wearing a sad face. She hands him a scrap of paper and says, 'That's her address. Least it was last I heard.'

'You shouldn't have burnt the letters, Sally.'

'I can't trust you. I'm sorry, but I can't.'

'It's an obstruction to the course of justice.'

'What you going to do? Hang me? And, anyway, you couldn't prove there was anything in them letters that would've got justice.'

Staffe takes the scrap of paper with Linda Watkins's address and says, 'You can trust me, Sally. I wish you could believe that.'

'How d'you like the sandwich?'

'Best I've had in a long time,' says Staffe.

He makes his way out of the flat and down the stairs and by the time he gets to Pulford there's a gaggle of about thirty people milling around the E-Type. Some are drinking from cans; most are thirty, forty years old and you'd think that in a decent world men like these would be out working, shedding their bad juice through sweat and toil.

'What d'you get?' says Staffe to Pulford.

'Nobody's seen the mother since she left. Said she was a bit stuck up. Thought she was too good for the place. My guess is she got knocked up by Tyrone and had to settle for this.' He looks up at the tower, back down at the ne'er-do-wells, drifting back to where they came from.

'Let's not jump to any conclusions.'

'They reckon her daughter's not exactly a chip off the block, though.' Pulford gets in the car and Staffe starts the engine. He says under his breath, leaning across, 'She's on the game by the sound of things. Reckon the old man never leaves the flat. Like never.'

'In which case we can cross him off the list.'

'What about her? Sally?' says Pulford.

'Sally's going to need an alibi, I'm afraid.'

'You reckon she did it?'

'No. But what I do reckon is that her alibi's probably one of this lot here and they won't want to be owning up to it.' Staffe reaches into his pocket, pulls out the sandwich. 'Here, have some tuna Marie Rose à la Sally Watkins.'

'Where we going now?' says Pulford.

'Harrow on the Hill. Let's see how the other half live.'

'On the other side of the law.'

As they drive off to interview Helena Montefiore, Pulford chews away at the sandwich. When he's done, he says, 'This is great. You make it? It's better than that feta and shit you normally have.'

Staffe drives under the Westway and looks up to
Wormwood Scrubs.

'This isn't the way,' says Pulford.

'I have to meet Smethurst,' says Staffe.

'From the Met?'

He pulls off Scrubs Lane and parks the
E-Type up on a side street of Victorian cottages
that have front gardens piled high with
mattresses and dead white goods.

'Call the office and dictate a report on the
Watkins visit. Get it emailed across to Smethurst.
All they need to know is we're checking up Sally
Watkins's alibi and following a lead to the mother.
Get a doctor to go see the dad and verify the
bedsores; and see if a WPC can get Sally some
safe-sex counselling. And get the Met to send us
the Watkins file.'

'Shouldn't we pull Sally in if she's underage?'

Staffe ignores him, not knowing whether
Sally's lot would improve if they did prosecute
her. For the moment he has no evidence and it
would get ugly if he started digging around her
life. On the balance of probabilities, his instinct
dictates against charging her.

He looks up at the Fusilier. It's a bad joke of
Smethurst's that they're meeting here. He
knows Staffe of old, from when the Force had to
share a thrusting young DC Staffe with the
whisky bottle. Staffe readily agreed to the venue
— Smethurst isn't the sort of bloke to show your
weaknesses to.

The place hasn't changed a great deal over the

years: a rambling, tall-windowed corner pub that curves with the fork in the road, gets its windows rattled once a minute as the buses and wagons trundle by. The locals are sat in ones and twos all around the edge of the pub — drinkers, not socialisers.

Smethurst raises his pint as Staffe approaches, as if to say 'Same for you?' He has a drinker's nose and a sheen of sweat on his round face, blotched red and white.

'I'll have a Scotch and water,' says Staffe.

Smethurst raises his eyebrows as if to say 'Back on it again, are we?'

'I'll take a Laphroaig, and I'll do my own water,' he tells the barmaid. 'Give me a glassful.'

They take the drinks to a seat by the window where the conversation will be drowned out by the sound of traffic.

Staffe puts down the separate glasses of malt whisky and water. 'I've been to see Tyrone Watkins and his daughter. You'll be getting a report from my DS.'

'Johnson? How's he doing? A damn good copper, if you ask me. I had him as a DC a few years back.'

'No. Pulford.'

'That pup?'

'There's nothing wrong with Pulford,' says Staffe, taking a sip of the water and raising the malt to his lips. He lets it touch and — in the thick of everything that's been going on with Colquhoun and Montefiore; with Marie and the move to Queens Terrace — he can picture himself by a Highland burn with a beautiful

134

woman, drinking their way through the bottle and watching clouds go by.

'You're too loyal, Staffe. It's a fool's trait.'

'Then you're no fool, eh?'

'Funny fella. You still getting plenty?'

Smethurst would be the runt of any litter: pug nose in a pink bloated face and a squat body on short spindly legs. He's always been drowned in his clothes and his suit sleeves come right down over his hands. 'Not so many that I'm taking your share. Anyway, let's leave the wit and repartee for later, shall we? I suppose I should thank you for running with us on this one.'

'We'll be taking it on soon enough. Unless you've got it cracked already.'

'I've got a strong enough pull, don't you worry.'

'Why do you want Montefiore so badly, Staffe?'

'It connects with the Colquhoun murder we had last week. Both victims are child rapists, the first a familial abuser, the second an assault by penetration. Both were unprosecuted.'

'You get a photo for Montefiore too?'

'Photo!' Staffe feels his blood rush. 'How d'you know about the photo?'

'We know everything. Suspects?'

And here, Smethurst has him. He can't say Leanne Colquhoun because she was banged up the night of the Montefiore assault. And Debra Bowker is in Tenerife. 'We're checking alibis.'

'Not the Watkins girl?'

'Routine follow-up. You'd be doing the same. We've got a trail on the mother, but the father's clinically attached to his sofa.'

'And what would the mother's connection be to Karl Colquhoun?' asks Smethurst.

'To throw us off the scent, maybe.' Staffe doesn't believe this himself. He wants to be chasing the case down, not explaining himself to Smethurst.

'Montefiore was a pro job, and so was Colquhoun — from what I've heard. But if you're right and there's been two so close together, you can bet your skinny arse there'll be another.'

Staffe takes another sip of water, rests the Laphroaig up against his lips again. 'What if it's not 'two close together'? What if there are other cases? I know there's been nothing on our patch.' Staffe looks Smethurst in the eye, sees a flickering of life, like a faraway light through a thick sea fret. 'Have you had any vengeance killings or assaults? Say in the last, I don't know, two or three years?'

Smethurst stares out the window. It is years since they worked a case together. He lifts his glass, takes a good slug, puts it back on the table, scratches at his head. 'There was one, but it's a long time ago. And funnily enough, if I've got it right, it was your old mate, Jessop, worked on it, just before he was pensioned off. Wasn't my case and it got tied up pretty quick but they fucked this woman right over.'

'Woman?'

'Yeah. A foreign woman.' Smethurst scratches at his head again, downs the remains of his pint. 'Stensson. Lotte Stensson was her name. But like

I said, they got the bloke that did for her. He was the dad. She'd been having a go at boys and girls, for years they reckon. She was a classroom assistant in a junior school. Makes you wonder who's doing the best job — us or the ones we bang up.'

'We get it right more often than not.'

'Sometimes we get it wrong when we get it right.'

'This Lotte Stensson, she was known to us as a risk but the CPS never pushed, right?' says Staffe.

'She lost her job, but yeah, the CPS couldn't push it through. How d'you know that?' Staffe stands up. 'Hey, you getting 'em in? You've not drunk that. Hey, Staffe!' But Staffe is halfway to the door.

He looks back at Smethurst, calls, 'My young pup'll be in touch for those Stensson notes. I'll get 'em in next time, Smet.'

'Smet? No one calls me that any more.' And he smiles, as if he can remember a better time.

\* \* \*

'According to Helena Montefiore's statement,' says Pulford, 'The Watkins's had gone round hoping that Sally had been lying. They had all waited for Montefiore to come in from work. Apparently, the minute they saw him, they knew she wasn't lying.' Pulford refers to his notes and reads verbatim. 'Sally's mother gave Helena Montefiore a photograph of Sally, and . . . ' Pulford looks away from Staffe, ' . . . she saw a

137

photo of Montefiore's daughter on the mantelpiece. The child was with a pony and Linda Watkins took the photograph out of its frame, went up to Helena Montefiore and pushed her little finger through the picture. She made a hole at the top of the girl's legs and pushed the end of her finger through. Then she fainted.'

'What did Montefiore's wife do?'

'She's a diamond, sir. She called the police.'

Staffe drives up into Harrow. With its grand old school on top of the hill, the steeply inclined, winding high street and its half-timbered bank and tea rooms, you could, for a hundred and fifty yards, be in the Cotswolds. He swings the E-Type on to a gravel driveway.

The house is double-fronted, brilliant white, and Georgian. 'Not bad for a disaffected divorcee,' he thinks as Helena Montefiore opens the door. She stands in the porch, leaning against the stone portal with sunglasses perched in her perfect hair. She has finely arched eyebrows and full lips; sculpted cheekbones and plump breasts in a tight white cashmere sweater; a tiny brown suede skirt and kitten-heeled slingbacks. He smiles at her from the piping hot leather seat of his overheating classic. She smiles back and Staffe could swear she licks each corner of her lips with a tiny poke of her tongue. He blinks it away.

'You take this one, Pulford.'

'You sure?'

Staffe stops, ten feet short of Helena Montefiore, turns to Pulford and says, 'We're a team, right?'

138

'Thanks, sir.'

The drawing room is beautifully finished in a high French country style and, as Pulford runs through the circumstances of Helena's separation from her husband, Staffe takes stock of her willingness to talk, takes further stock of the period pieces. There is a walnut chiffonier and a late-eighteenth-century credenza he'd be more than happy to have.

'Nothing was ever proven, the Crown never prosecuted the allegations, Mrs Montefiore,' says Pulford. 'But you left him.'

'He's done it again, hasn't he?' She shows a hint of disgust in the faintest curling of her lips. 'Someone's given him what he had coming, have they?'

Pulford takes pause and Staffe thinks the young DS has lost his way. He prepares to take over, hones a question, but Pulford leans back, interlocks his hands on his chest, says, 'If that had happened, what feelings would you have towards the person who did it?'

Helena Montefiore looks out of the window, stares into the sun-fired green of the weeping willows that flank the driveway.

'I know what happened to the Watkins people afterwards. I made it my business to find out how they fared. I think it's a crying shame.' She looks at Pulford, then Staffe. 'I could understand and forgive whatever happened to Guy.' She flinches when she says his name.

'You've been well looked after.'

'He loved Thomasina. He loved her more than me and if you really want to know, he was a

139

better father than a husband.' She looks at Staffe.

'And he still sees Thomasina?'

'He's not allowed within a mile of her. He signed up for that. It broke Thomasina's heart. She loved him more than anything.' She sits down on the edge of a chaise longue, leaning forward with her elbows on her knees and her head bowed.

Staffe says, in his softest voice, 'We are going to have to speak to Thomasina, I'm afraid. I'd rather it was here.'

Helena Montefiore stands up, smooths down the suede of her short skirt, draws her hands across her bottom. At the door she pauses, turns. 'You think I might have done it, to Guy, don't you? You think he might have . . . you know, with Thomasina?'

'You couldn't do such a thing. Surely.'

'You'd be amazed.' She smiles. 'I didn't, of course. But you'd be amazed.'

'And Thomasina . . . ?'

She glazes over again, stares out to the weeping willows. 'I'm as sure as I can be. She does love him, you know. I can't take that away from her. You can't take love out of a girl's life. You never know how little she's going to find.'

Helena stands by the door, holds it open as if to indicate it is time for Pulford and Staffe to leave. 'You're not going to speak to her. I won't let him touch her, not in any way at all, you see. I've spoken to a silk — he's a family friend.'

In the hallway, Staffe sees a teenage girl at the top of the stairs, as if she was on her way down but had been frozen, perhaps caught in a spell. He says to Helena, under his breath, 'We'll need to know where you were, midnight till six in the morning.'

'I was here all night,' says Helena in a stage voice, looking up the stairs. 'Wasn't I, darling? Come on down, Thommi.'

Thomasina Montefiore has none of her mother's striking beauty. She still has puppy fat in her face and legs and around her tummy. Her hair is cut short and dyed jet-black and she's wearing a London's Burning Clash T-shirt. Staffe remembers seeing them at the Roundhouse when he was just thirteen. His dad had picked him up after the gig — a rare event.

'Mummy said you were police,' says Thomasina. 'You don't look like police.' She looks at Staffe, gives him a tight smile.

'I was here, wasn't I, darling?' says Helena. 'The policemen want to go, Thommi.'

'Yes,' says Thommi.

'We sleep together.'

Thommi raises her eyebrows and shoots a look out of the corner of her eye at her mother as if to say, 'It's her idea. She doesn't realise I'm a woman for crying out loud,' and Staffe makes an instant prayer that Guy Montefiore never laid a finger on his own little girl.

# Wednesday Evening

It is bumper to bumper all the way into the City. The sun and exhaust fumes take their toll as Pulford clicks off his mobile and blows out his cheeks. He looks at his notes in disbelief.

'What's up?' asks Staffe.

'That was Josie. She's checked up on Lotte Stensson.'

Staffe clocks the temperature gauge, reaching into the red.

'It was a bloke called Kashell who did for her. Nico Kashell. He's doing life up in Wakefield.'

'And his MO?'

Pulford's voice drops a few decibels, half an octave, too. He reads from his notes.

'He broke her fingers.'

'Her fingers! And that killed her?'

'He broke them one by one. Twenty-two of the twenty-eight phalanges were fractured. Then he broke both ulnas, both tibias,' Pulford swallows hard, sounding as though he might gag, 'and then the femurs.'

Staffe pulls the E-Type over to the side of the road, puts his hazards on and turns off the engine. 'Carry on.'

'They reckon it was the sheer pain that killed her. It brought on a coronary. The shinbones were shattered to bits.'

'And was she gagged?'

'Yes.'

'Gauze?'

'Yes.'

'In her own home?'

'Yes.'

'Jesus,' says Staffe.

'And there's more,' says Pulford. 'It was your mate took Kashell's statement. Jessop. But he got pulled off the case. There was a conflict 'cos he was involved in the CPS investigation, you know, into Kashell's daughter's allegations.'

The unrelenting sun beats down hard and Staffe feels a squeeze from his past.

'They're good people, Helena Montefiore and the Watkins,' says Pulford. 'And that poor sod Nico Kashell, wasting his life up in Wakefield jail.'

'And . . . ?'

'And all because we can't do our job properly. Not allowed to by the fucking CPS. They had that Stensson woman and they dropped the charges against Montefiore. They didn't even get that far with Karl Colquhoun because the social services never pressed criminal proceedings. And how many, how fucking many all around the country are there that no one gets to hear of? They'd think twice, maybe, if a couple of them have their dicks chopped off.'

'Are you suggesting that we catch these people and impale them on splintered lengths of wood? Or break every bone in their body? Maybe we could televise it.'

'Or a webcast? Do you know there's more than a million hits every day on child porn sites?'

143

Staffe can't help reconjure the awful images he saw on Guy Montefiore's computer. 'How d'you fancy a little road trip?' says Staffe. 'To see Nico Kashell. And then on to Middlesbrough. We need to have a word with Linda Watkins.'

Pulford looks at the E-Type's bonnet, steam beginning to rise. 'We're not going up there in this shit tip are we?'

'It's a classic,' says Staffe. In the distance, through the traffic, the horizon warps above the shimmering tarmac.

'It's a fucked classic,' says Pulford, and they laugh.

But Staffe feels the clock counting down. In less than a week he will be pulled off the Montefiore case. He calls the AA, chastising himself for not using the Peugeot, and Pulford phones in to Leadengate. The AA tell Staffe they'll be an hour and twenty minutes and he bites his lip, sees Pulford is agitated — angry and excited at the same time as he clicks his phone off.

'The Met have been on. A young girl, Tanya Ford, has just gone into Fulham nick, filed a complaint that she was sexually assaulted by a middle-aged man. A well-spoken, middle-aged man. It happened last night and less than a mile from Montefiore's house.'

'Is somebody interviewing the girl?'

'Josie says she'll call you when it's set up. The parents aren't keen.'

They wait in silence and Staffe thinks about Jessop, driven halfway to madness by the job. It's time to make a call on the past.

144

* ★ ★

A squad car collects them and all the way in, bare-chested men and skimpily clad women sit outside pubs, drinking their way through the long hot summer. It will be the weekend soon and Staffe will allow himself a drink. The way it's been for three years.

Three years keeps cropping up: three years since Linda and Tyrone Watkins still had a life together, when young Sally was drug free and not on the game. Nico Kashell free as a bird. Three years since Sylvie went.

The squad car drops Staffe by the gates of the park where Tanya Ford alleges she was assaulted and he leans up against the trunk of a yew tree, grateful for shade. It's not long before Josie arrives, wearing a cap-sleeved polo shirt and mid-thigh shorts.

'Don't you just love the summer,' she says. They walk towards the copse of trees and she tugs at his suede jacket. 'Don't you ever take this off?'

'I've moved into a place not far from here. You could come round for a bite.'

'I think this is where it happened.' She points to the copse of rowan trees.

'How is the girl?'

'Tanya Ford? In pieces, of course.'

'You reckon she's telling the truth, then?'

Josie nods and stops, lays down a bag and they each take out plastic mitts for their feet and don gloves. She bends down, hands Staffe a handful of bags, tags and some tweezers. 'Janine wasn't

145

happy, you know, you having first pop. She says we've got twenty minutes.'

'It happened right in the trees?'

'And get this . . . ' She ducks under the outlying, low canopy of trees, makes her way into the cooler, dark centre of the small wood where you can smell soil, ' . . . Tanya Ford says there were two men. She thinks they both wore balaclavas. Then they knocked her out with chloroform.'

They look down at the patched grass and soil and compacted twigs.

'You go that way,' says Josie.

In the distance, Staffe can hear children play, young adults, too, having a game of softball. Beneath the canopy, he can see Josie's tanned calves. Looking back down at his own feet and inching forward, he sees a rag at the foot of a tree. He bends down, reaches with his tweezers. He calls Josie and gently lifts the evidence. He sniffs it and holds it out to her. 'That's chloroform.'

Josie holds open a brown-paper evidence bag and he drops the rag into it. He clears his throat, looks around the copse. 'Montefiore sees Tanya here, all alone. He's either been following her or it's a lucky find. Either way, he's ready, so he grabs her, hits her with the chloroform. Then he gets disturbed?'

'What makes you say that?'

'What's the medical evidence on Tanya?'

'There was no penetration, according to the girl. She's a virgin.'

'But what did the medical say?'

'There was no medical. Her mother came with her. They wouldn't allow it. Like I said, they don't want to press charges. The father came in halfway through the interview, says they want to draw a veil over it.'

'Shit.'

'He's going to get away with it again, Staffe.'

'We've got the rag. His prints might be on it. We can do him for assault, even if we can't get him for a sexual.'

'Is he conscious yet?'

'In and out,' says Staffe. 'It'll be another twenty-four hours before we can interview him.'

'It's a funny state of affairs, hey? Waiting for a child molester to recover so we can interview him to find the person who attacked him.'

'How did you get on with Sally Watkins?' asks Staffe.

'She couldn't vouch for where she was the other night. I asked Johnson to go round, put some pressure on her.' Josie sounds sad. 'Montefiore used chloroform on her too. He knocked her out first . . . waited for her to come round before he did what he did.' She looks away, scratches her leg, says, 'Bloody flies.'

★ ★ ★

The man watches Staffe and Josie walk away across the park. He saw them find the chloroform rag but he knows he didn't touch it. He would love to be a fly on the wall when Montefiore tells them. He'd like to see Montefiore's face when he realises — by looking

147

into their eyes — that they might not be able to do enough to protect him from the next reprisal. Except this time there will be sufficient rope.

He lets them go, knows he can catch up with them later, and he wonders how long it will take Staffe to make the leap backwards. When they are completely gone from sight he takes a seat on a park bench, watches the children play. He takes out the photograph of Guy Montefiore, strung up on his ropes and on his second jolt down, and begins to compose the caption that will accompany it. He watches a young mother with three daughters trying to cross the road.

Under her guidance, the children look first one way then the other and she lets them on to the road on their own, following at a safe distance.

An idea comes and he jots down a line. He looks at it twice, thinks of the permutations, the double meanings and he smiles to himself, thinks 'that will do nicely'.

★ ★ ★

Staffe is crying.

'Just how many houses have you got, Staffe?' says Josie.

It's something he always does when he peels onions. 'This isn't a house. I've only got this floor.'

'The whole of my place would fit into your lounge.'

'I'd rather I didn't have it — the price it came at.'

148

'How d'you mean?'

'I got it with an inheritance.'

'Somebody close?'

'Would you open the wine?' says Staffe.

'It's not the weekend yet.'

'It's for the sauce. And a glass for you, of course.'

Josie pops the cork. 'You didn't answer me.'

'Most of them belong to the building society. They're not mine.'

'I bet you've had them long enough to have made a bit of coin.' She comes up to Staffe with her head tilted to one side. She leans on the counter next to him. 'I bet you're loaded, hey, Staffe?'

'I don't worry about money.'

'You worry about plenty, though.'

'Isn't it supposed to be good to care?' He smiles at her, lobs a lemon up for her to catch and says, 'Squeeze that and stop doing my head in.'

'You'd better watch out, Staffe. You might attract the wrong type of girl. You know, a gold-digger.' She reaches across him for the wine, pours herself a glass and says, 'Who died?'

'How did you get on with Maureen Colquhoun? Remind me what she said about her poor son?'

'If you ask me, he was abused as a child. And the main thing is, his father was a drunk. Colquhoun hated drink.'

'They force-fed him till he was paralytic.'

'And you know what that means?' says Josie. She takes a sip of wine.

149

'Whoever killed him knew all about his ghosts.'

'And what about your ghosts?'

Staffe turns to face her front on, pointing the tip of the chef's knife towards her. He says in a mock German accent, 'Vot exactly do you want to know, Chancellor?'

'Who was Sylvie?'

'I need the lemon juice. Can't you squeeze?'

'I'll try. It's got to be easier than getting blood out of a stone, that's for sure.'

★ ★ ★

The lounge is cluttered with tea chests and Josie and Staffe are sitting cross-legged on the floor, eating cheesecake with their fingers and drinking coffee.

'What did you make of Sally Watkins?' says Staffe.

'She's a strong enough girl — I suppose you'd have to call her a woman after what she's been through.'

'And what she does for a living. Do you think we should do something about that?'

'Prosecute her, after what she's been through? I can't see what good would come of giving her a criminal record.'

'It might discourage her,' says Staffe.

'Compare her lot to what that bastard Montefiore's got. And to think, he's the cause.'

'I wouldn't want his life, though. Would you?' Staffe stands up, goes to the window and looks out. There's a car opposite with a man in the

150

driver's seat. Staffe thinks he's seen it before and he wonders whether the woman opposite is having an affair. 'Can you imagine, having it all and still feeling hollow? Being so unable to control your desires that you lose your daughter — the person you love most in life.'

'To have everything and it not be enough,' says Josie.

'Do you think Sally could have done it?'

'It makes sense, to leave him half dead, having to carry on,' says Josie. 'That's what she's had to do.'

'And the same would apply to the mother.'

'And Debra Bowker or the Kashells.'

Staffe looks across at Josie, sitting amongst his half unpacked belongings with her hair loose and her legs tucked under her bottom. 'Don't mention Lotte Stensson or Nico Kashell to Pennington.' The car outside starts up its engine.

She shakes her head, slow. The wine bottle is almost empty and there's a smile painted on her face. Her eyes look soft. 'How come they phoned you here?' says Josie. 'How would they know you were here?'

The case is spinning and he knows it won't stop until he gets up to Wakefield and Middlesbrough.

Josie says, 'You know I looked at the Sally Watkins file. There's holes all over it. Missing interviews, evidence not logged.'

'Those bastards at the Met,' says Staffe. 'They've no right to obstruct our investigation.'

'I'm not saying they are, sir.'

'This case is beginning to drive me insane.'

151

'Why am I here, if we're not going to talk about the case?'

'We can have dinner, for crying out loud.'

'Without anything going on.'

'Is something going on?' He chances a smile.

'Would that be a good idea?'

'Good ideas aren't always a good idea.'

Josie stands, goes across to the mantelpiece and picks up a photograph of Sylvie. 'I don't think you're ready.' She puts the photograph back on the mantelpiece, kneels down next to him. He can smell wine on her and wonders whether he should draw the curtains, which makes him think of Sylvie.

The curtains. The goldfish bowl.

The car opposite. He leaps up and rushes out of the room, unlocks the front door and runs into the street in his stocking feet, taking the steps two at a time and vaulting over the gate but he's too late. The car has screeched away and his eyes can't adjust to the evening gloom. He curses and all along the street, lights go on, here and there. Curtains twitch.

Josie comes down the steps.

'Where are you going?' he says.

'Thanks for the meal.' She reaches up on tiptoes and, with a hand on his chest, kisses the corner of his mouth. 'Sometimes, you're a bit too weird for me.' She closes the gate behind her and wiggles her fingers without turning round. He watches her go round the corner.

*Sometimes?* he thinks.

He goes inside to his new home, to his past. He is angry with himself for letting the car get away but happy they are prepared to come so close. Then he shivers, but it's not cold. He can feel the last of the adrenalin seep away and all he's left with is the certain knowledge that they are coming to him just as fast as he is getting to them. Except they know what they're looking for.

# Thursday Morning

The jail gives off bad pheromones as you walk up to its towering gate.

Staffe and Pulford make their way past HMP Wakefield's visitor centre and its raggedy queue of young girls dressed to their kind of nines in low-slung hipster tracksuit bottoms that show what they're wearing underneath. Some of them carry babies on their hips like wise African women. Older women are pulled down by the life their husbands and lovers have chosen. Strange, to be in a men's jail surrounded by women.

An old-school officer shows them to the room for private visits. He says nothing and Staffe is reminded that he does only half the job. Once the police track a criminal down, it's over to the business of incarceration, rehabilitation. Every man in this jail will, one day, be released, to perhaps live next door to us or our mothers or our sisters. Staffe ponders what kind of beast we want to be moulded by these beefed-up pale faced prison officers, these textbook psychologists.

The room reeks of stale cigarettes and ingrained sweat. There is one window, way above head height and slightly open. Flies bash themselves against the reinforced glass. The tubular light hums.

A middle-aged man in grey sweats is brought

in. This is Nico Kashell and he isn't cuffed. He looks down at the table, the way people sit in church. The PO sits by the door, lights up a cigarette even though there's a sign that says 'No Smoking', and he reads the *Daily Mirror*.

Kashell is five-seven and ghostly white even though there's Mediterranean blood running through him. He is spindly under his baggy prison cloth and doesn't respond when Staffe says, 'Hello.'

'The man says hello, shithead,' says the PO. Without looking up.

'Hello,' says Kashell, without looking up.

It's official: most murderers do it just the once, responding to extraordinary circumstances. They don't steal to feed drug habits or habitually abuse to feed sex habits or beat people up for kicks.

'Tell me how it happened, Nico. Tell me about that night.'

'There's plenty paper tells you that.'

'How did you get into her flat?'

He shrugs.

'How did you keep her quiet, or know which bones to break first? Did you know which one would kill her?'

He looks up, briefly, and his big sad, brown eyes are unable to sustain malice. He says, 'What you here for? I got time to do.'

'There's been another, Nico. When you did what you did to Lotte Stensson, was someone else there to help? If there was . . . ' Staffe looks at the PO, immersed in tabloid revelations. He leans towards Kashell. ' . . . it could help you.

155

You know what I'm saying?'

'I don't see no one else doing my time here.'

'You confessed. That was the only evidence against you, Nico.' He wills Kashell to engage in some way but nothing happens, so he nods to Pulford and leans back.

'It would suit you, I suppose?' says Pulford. He stands up, goes round the back of Kashell, lets the silence stretch.

'What's that?'

'You doing time in here on your own, taking the punishment to protect your accomplice. And they carry on the good work.'

Kashell weighs Staffe up. He makes a thin smile but his eyes look dead. 'You're barking up the wrong tree. Nowhere near understanding.'

'Understanding what?' says Pulford.

Kashell says, to Staffe, 'What a father had to do.'

'But to kill like that?'

'It's what keeps you going, man. Can't you see that?' But Kashell looks towards Staffe, straight through him. It is as if he can't focus, has nothing behind the eyes. For all the world, it seems Nico has lost his own soul.

Staffe nods to Pulford who sits back down. 'I don't see that you've made your life much better. And your girl has lost you when she needs you most.'

'I'm punished,' says Kashell. His eyes are glazed and he sniffs, hard, looks up again. Staffe sees his Adam's apple move up and down. 'And you know what? That woman, even the way she got it, it's nowhere near enough.'

'You're not avenged, are you, Nico?'

Kashell's lip quivers but he doesn't cry. Feeling sorry for yourself is no way to do your time. He shakes his head. 'Not nearly, man. Not nearly.'

'We'll come back, Nico. Next time, you can tell us exactly what you did that night, hey? Is there anything we can do for you, in the meantime?'

'Bring back Lotte Stensson?'

'So you can do it again?'

He shakes his head. 'No, man. You just don't get it, do you?'

'You can leave us, Sergeant,' says Staffe.

Pulford stands, befuddled, and Staffe waits patiently to have Kashell to himself, bar the smoking PO. He lowers his voice to barely a whisper. 'I know how you feel, Nico. Really I do.'

'How can you?'

'Trust me. Does a part of you wish you hadn't done it? Do you sometimes wish you had gone the other way — tried to forgive her?'

Nico plays with his fingers, as though he has invisible worry beads.

'It's a design fault,' says Staffe, 'that the anger comes first, the pity later. It's too late for some, isn't it, Nico?'

'How do you know this?'

'Somebody murdered my parents.'

'And have you caught up with them?'

'Not yet.'

'What will you do?'

'I pray I can forgive them.'

'I hope your prayers find their answer, Inspector.'

On the journey up the A1 to Middlesbrough, Staffe says, 'I'm not convinced Kashell could do that to Stensson.'

'You think they're copying him? Maybe it's someone who's done time with Kashell and been released.'

Staffe looks across to Pulford and smiles. 'Call the station. Get them to liaise with prison probation and check everyone who's been released from Wakefield in the last three months and living in London. And add a filter — anyone who shared a wing with Kashell. And make sure they weren't banged up again by the time Karl Colquhoun was killed.'

'There is a problem, though, sir. How would they know to go for Colquhoun or Montefiore? They were never prosecuted.'

'We need to find out why — exactly why — the CPS didn't push Lotte Stensson's prosecution,' says Staffe.

'She was a classroom assistant. It's bad for the government.'

'I don't buy that. But if that is the case, we need to dig it out.' Staffe pulls the Peugeot out into the fast lane, turning his thoughts to Linda Watkins and what kind of a basket case they are about to uncover in Middlesbrough.

He wonders whether, had Linda Watkins got hold of Montefiore and fashioned the most grizzly of tortures, she would have been at all placated by such revenge. Or would she be left wanting some other resolution — just like Nico Kashell.

Staffe's phone rings, shows *Pennington*.

'You sitting down, Staffe?'

'You could say that.'

'We've received another photograph,' says Pennington. 'Montefiore. Just as he's going down on to the wood.'

'Jesus! And the message? Is there a message?'

'It says, 'Road Safety: is that all you're good for? Look left, look right. Look ahead, look back.' I want you here as soon as, Staffe. Sooner!'

'Sir? Sir? I think my battery . . . Can you hear . . . ?' And Staffe hangs up. Always hang up when you're speaking, someone once told him. It might even have been Pennington. He turns his phone off and replays the words of the latest message — the reference to an impotent police force reduced to hoodwinking motorists. He wishes he was better at crosswords, the way his father had been.

If only you could go back in time.

*Go back*, he thinks. *Look left, look right. Look ahead, look back.* Is he being told to look back — at Kashell? Is he being told to look all round? He checks his mirrors, sees a speed camera flashing.

★ ★ ★

Linda Watkins has unblemished, alabaster skin and a thick tousle of shiny dark hair, expensively cut. She is tall and slim, elegant in a dark-grey, woollen trouser suit with a short, tailored jacket and hipster trousers. You'd never guess that she had a daughter on the game or had settled for a man who watches cable TV all day on the Villiers estate.

She speaks in measured, calm tones. 'If truth be known, I am surprised it has taken you this long to check up on me, not that I have done anything illegal, of course. Even in this day and age, I'm sure a woman is still entitled to leave her husband.'

Staffe picks up on her finely crafted sentences. 'And your daughter,' he says.

'You have probably come with your own conclusions as to what sort of person that makes me. I'll put the kettle on, shall I?'

She stands to one side and shows Staffe and Pulford into the front sitting room of her Edwardian semi. It has stripped floors and waxed doors with porcelain handles and finger plates. The walls are cream and there is a display of dried flowers in the fireplace. Staffe can't see a stereo but he can hear a jazz ballad being sung somewhere. Peggy Lee, he thinks. *Black Coffee*.

Pulford raises his eyebrows at Staffe when Linda goes out of the room. Staffe mooches around the living room. Watercolours hang: Mediterranean harbours, Swiss villages and English dales, but no photographs. Not a sign of Sally Watkins.

Linda comes back in, saying, 'Am I what you expected?' She sets down a tray, hands coffee across.

'Preconceptions are difficult to resist,' says Staffe. 'It's good for us to have it reaffirmed, once in a while — that everything is not what it seems.'

She hitches her trousers up at the knee, the way a man would, and sits on the edge of the wingback chair, leans forward with her forearms on her knees, slightly apart. 'What did you expect? Peroxide? Bad skin? Split ends and leggings?'

'I'm not talking about appearances, Mrs Watkins.' As he says the name, Linda flinches. 'My mistake. I assumed you had kept your daughter's surname.'

'The surname is my husband's.'

'And Sally's too, of course.'

'She's not in trouble, is she?'

'You know what she's doing, don't you, Linda?'

She looks out of the window, keeps her head held high.

'It's none of my business, of course,' says Staffe.

'Except it is, Inspector Wagstaffe.' She looks at him. 'It's illegal. Or are you too busy with your speed traps?'

The hairs on Staffe's hands prickle. He thinks of the latest photograph and its caption.

'I had a female officer speak with her, about safety. Precautions.'

'So she has been in trouble? It's an awfully long way for you to come, Inspector.'

Staffe tries to see beneath the surface. He tries to imagine a younger Linda somehow getting knocked up by a young Tyrone. Then doing all the right things and having it thrown back in her face.

She stares out of the window as if she is trying

161

to muster more strength, then says, 'Sally has only got one life and she has to make the most of it. I couldn't teach her that. You know we can only ever be truly responsible for the life we lead ourselves. We have to do right by ourselves. I learned too late.'

To rescue at least one life from this mess, it's almost enough to make Staffe ashamed to be human. 'Could you ever forgive Guy Montefiore, Linda?'

'Has he had his dirty middle-class fingers in the pants of some other poor estate girl? Is it finally time the bastard got what was coming to him?'

'I'm going to have to ask you where you were on Tuesday — between ten p.m. and six the next morning.'

She gets up and takes a diary from a reproduction writing desk in the alcove by the window. She opens it up and hands it to Staffe. 'There. I had dinner at Leoni's on the Tuesday night in Newcastle and I got the 7.40 train on Wednesday morning down to Leeds for a ten o'clock meeting. The telephone numbers are there. If that would make you feel as though you are doing your job.'

'It would,' says Staffe, making a note of the numbers.

As Staffe and Pulford leave, Linda says, 'You probably think I'm a bad person, but you know if I had stayed, I would have been buried alive. They'd have come for me in fifty years or so and put me in a box and nobody would ever have known I had been there.'

Josie gasps as she takes the photograph from Janine: the frozen look of horror on Montefiore's face. His mouth is bound with gauze and his eyes are wide and wild — two streaks of mascara running from the corner of his eyes. But she knows it's not mascara. His silent screams so loud the pain transformed itself into bursting vessels of blood. They say that pain is simply fear leaving the body. In Montefiore's case it is leaving through the most unlikely conduit.

The caption at the bottom of the top photograph says *Road Safety: is that all you're good for? Look left, look right. Look ahead, look back.* Janine's notes are attached to the photograph, as are blown-up sections of parts of the image.

'The image is digital, probably captured from a video stream.' Janine rests her bottom on the edge of Josie's desk, plays with her hair. She looks Josie up and down, says, 'The pixelation is inferior to a silver image and it would have been impossible to capture the moment . . . '

'The moment it went into him, you mean,' says Josie. She studies Janine, narrows her eyes and makes a thin smile.

'The wood wasn't chamfered. It intruded between 55 and 60 millimetres. I've extrapolated from a CAD model of the room and the measurements from the wood to the walls and ceiling, that he was still falling. There's no blurring.'

'It's a funny angle,' says Josie.

163

'The camera was pointing upwards, probably propped up on a chair or coffee table.'

'So it could have been done by a single person.'

'There was no alien DNA or prints at the scene.'

'Just like Colquhoun.'

'You're with Staffe, then?' says Janine.

Josie's mouth falls open. 'What . . . ?'

'His theory, I mean. The quality of the print is identical to the photograph we received of Karl Colquhoun. It is printed on identical paper.'

'Looks like he's right, then.'

'He doesn't always get it right,' says Janine.

'I heard you and him used to see each other.'

'I wouldn't have called it that, and the club isn't that select.'

'He plays his cards close, doesn't he?'

Janine stands up, brushes a piece of cotton from the thigh of her skirt. 'You don't want to be in that club, do you, Sergeant Chancellor?'

'Who's Sylvie?'

'You'd better ask him that.' Janine opens the door, turns. 'He won't tell you, of course.'

'What happened to his parents?'

Janine leans against the door frame, puts her head to the back of her hand and talks to the floor. 'I studied Jung at med school and he reckoned that to understand a man you have to know what his grandfather lacked. Staffe's parents died before he was a man. He doesn't really know what made him.' She looks up. 'But what do I know?'

'Did he hurt you?'

'He only hurts himself. At least that's his aim.' The phone rings. 'You'd better take that, before I say something I might regret,' says Janine, closing the door.

'Chancellor, do you know where the hell DI Wagstaffe is?' says Pennington.

'No, sir. Can I help?'

'You can tell him he's got his way. Tell him I hope it's not enough rope to hang himself. Leanne Colquhoun will be released sometime tonight.'

Josie gathers her things together, including a scrawled message in Staffe's hand: *Why no CPS push for LS's prosecution? Call WW, nil written.* 'LS', Lotte Stensson. 'WW'. DI Will Wagstaffe.

She pulls out the Stensson file that Smethurst sent over from the Met and scans through 'all known contacts', sees that Ruth Merritt was the lawyer representing the CPS on the case. Josie notes that she is different from the Crown's lawyer on the dropped Colquhoun and Montefiore cases. No obvious conspiracy theory to be developed, then.

On her way down the back stairs to the car park, Josie is wondering why the Stensson case isn't on the whiteboard, why Staffe is keeping it close to his chest, then she sees Stanley Buchanan a flight below, making his way up. He's out of breath and has a sheen of sweat on his face, a film of booze all around him. When he talks she gets a draught of freshly sucked mint.

'Staffe in?' he says.

'Out and about, I'm afraid.' His eyes are on

her — like hands. He gives out a lascivious smile. She leans back against the metal handrail, and watches him look away, swapping his papers from one arm to the other.

'Well if he's not here, I may as well come out with you.' When they get to the door to the back car park, Josie swipes her pass and Buchanan holds the door open, says, 'Fancy a drink?'

She looks him in the eye, thinks 'no way'. 'I'd love to,' she purrs, thinking she might save herself an afternoon of reading up on CPS policy on child abuse — vast tomes that twist themselves up in knots of policy speak.

Outside the Griffin, Josie opens the door and lets him go in first. It's pay day tomorrow and she's down to a pound coin and coppers. 'I'll get a table,' she says, smiling. 'Let's split a bottle of white, shall we? I'm off duty.'

When Buchanan gets back with the wine, he sits down heavily and looks around. House music plays up in the wooden eaves, bounces around the exposed brick walls. 'Great place.'

'You'd remember it as a proper pub, I suppose.'

'I'm all in favour of progress.'

'Progress is one thing we're not seeing much of at the moment,' says Josie. 'There's so many departments pulling in different directions.'

'Hey, I'm only doing my job, just the same as you.' Buchanan takes an unhealthy slug of his wine, tries a stoic 'What can I do?' smile. 'It's an adversarial system. That's the way the truth gets squeezed out.'

'I'm not getting at you, Stan. It's the CPS I

can't get my head round.'

'We share the same enemy, then,' he says.

'They seem to drop the most unlikely cases.'

Stan Buchanan leans back, cups his glass on the ledge of his gut. 'They're only flesh and blood. Same as coppers.'

'Success rates are important, I guess.'

'Ahaa. You've nailed it, girl. You've nailed it.' He takes a slug and recharges both glasses. 'You might call it economy of effort.'

'And it could depend on which particular person there is at the CPS?'

'It's only human beings at the end of the day.'

Josie softens her smile, sips from her wine without taking her eyes off him. 'I've come across a woman, Ruth Merritt. What's she like?'

'Ruthie? Straight as they come.' He laughs to himself. 'Too straight for her own good. I always fancied my chances with Ruthie, but I haven't seen her for ages. I assume she's gone off somewhere quieter. Maybe having babies.'

Josie wants Ruth Merritt to be a cold-hearted career woman, playing the percentages and building a glittering career, but this doesn't fit. Surely she would have pressed the Kashell case. 'What else might stop someone like Merritt from pushing for a prosecution?'

'The disclosing officer is the key to the evidence. If the officer doesn't fancy their chances of a successful prosecution, they may stymie the whole thing. Workloads and targets, my girl.'

She gathers up her handbag, drains her glass. 'You're not going?'

'I'm going out for dinner,' lies Josie. 'Shall we split this?'

Stan shakes his head and holds up a hand as Josie pretends to search in her bag. 'Some lucky fella?'

'No. It's a girlfriend, actually.' Josie winks at Buchanan as she stands up, watches him twitch, go red in his fat face. On the street, she looks through the large plate-glass window and sees Buchanan blowing his cheeks. He gestures at the barmaid for another bottle.

# Thursday Evening

Staffe boots the Peugeot down the A1. It is pale dusk and as he sees signs for Cambridge he is tempted to stop for an overnight. An aperitif in a backwater hotel, a stroll along the backs. Spires, young lovers and a leisurely dinner. Pulford is asleep and Staffe drives on, beyond tired now. He has pictures to hang back at Queens Terrace, and records to unpack. He should call Pepe Muñoz if he gets home before ten. He will phone the Thai Garden for a takeaway and he may also make another call. Sylvie.

Pulford grunts and Staffe turns the CD player up a notch. The loud swell of Charles Mingus retells Duke Ellington, and Staffe feels it, guns the Peugeot way, way over the limit down the bottom stretch of the A1, switchbacking across the North Circular, barrelling into London against the law.

Deliberately, Staffe brakes hard, jolting the car to a halt in the neon glow of Golders Green's Tube station front. 'Thanks for the conversation, Sergeant, you're fantastic company, you know.'

Pulford blinks, bleary-eyed as Staffe leans across, pushes the passenger door open and points up at the station lights.

'What? Where . . . ?'

'You've had your beauty sleep. I want that list of everyone released from Wakefield and living in London. Don't go advertising it to Pennington just yet. And I want a list of all unprosecuted molestations in the last three years. Anything the CPS has dropped.'

'Why's that?' says Pulford, rubbing his eyes, stretching.

'Because if there's going to be a next victim, there's every chance an aborted CPS prosecution will be in their descriptor.'

Pulford puts up a sleepy thumb and makes a forced smile, slams the door shut, and Staffe pulls out into traffic. A red Merc stops short in front of him and Staffe block changes, undertakes, sees the driver holding a mobile phone, happy as Larry. But he lets it go. He sees the road three, four moves ahead and within fifteen minutes is pulling up outside his flat. On the street, he looks up at the night sky: starless and orange blue.

'There will be another. There *will* be, but why put me in the picture?' He says it out loud. 'Why call me? Why watch me?'

Staffe needs to slow down. He breathes long and deep, leaning back against the car, crossing his arms over his chest, closing his eyes, saying under his breath 'pacify yourself, pacify yourself'.

Crossing the road, he is stopped in his tracks. The E-Type is parked up a few doors down. It has a parking ticket and when he gets inside, he opens an envelope with the bill from the garage and the keys.

He makes a rooibos tea, whips up some eggs for an omelette and puts some porcini mushrooms on the soak with the final slug of white wine that Josie left last night. He picks up his messages and hears an echo of the way his name sounds in her mouth, telling him Leanne Colquhoun is about to be released on bail.

He calls her straightaway. 'Is she out yet?'

'Some time soon,' says Josie. 'Do you want a tail on her?'

'Get Pulford to wait outside the Limekiln. Tell him to keep close tabs on her. He's had plenty of sleep.'

'I checked up on the CPS and it was a Ruth Merritt that dealt with Stensson.'

'Merritt? I know that name. I'm sure I do.' He runs a hand through his hair, closes his eyes.

'Sir?'

'Good night, Josie.' He hangs up, trying to dredge a story to go with the name. Ruth Merritt. He presses 'messages' again, wanting there to be more but he gets only silence after the long beep. Without thinking, he taps out Sylvie's number. She answers and his heart misses a beat. 'Hello. Hello? Who is that?' she says.

He hangs up and turns his phone off, goes back into the kitchen and puts cling film over the soaking mushrooms. His appetite is gone and he pours the egg mixture into the sink, runs a modicum of hot water. In the lounge, he leafs through his Muñoz file and begins to read about the Extbatteria brothers, goes back through the clippings of their father's pièce de résistance: the Bilbao bombing of 1986.

Old man Extbatteria was hardcore ETA, raised by poverty-stricken grandparents in

Franco's Spain. When the old General died, he soon became a part of the inner sanctum of the rebel Basques, hellbent on independence.

Staffe can understand that in the scheme of things, a little misery inflicted on the few might be justified by a greater good. Liberation from a cruel dictator. But what of the lost and lonely lives of those left behind in the carnage of the bombs deliberately aimed at the innocent, not the enemy.

He leans back in his father's straight-backed Sheraton and hears an ancient creak that whispers of many, many evenings. He didn't tell his parents he loved them that last time at the ferry. All he had wanted was to burn the E-Type up the A3 to a houseful of party. He calls Muñoz but all he gets is a mechanical, foreign voice, presumably telling him that Muñoz is out for the night.

A red light flashes a missed call. It is from Sylvie. She didn't leave a message. Suddenly, blood prickles in his veins. All chance of sleep is gone, so he puts on his suede jacket and picks up the keys for the E-Type, takes a night drive.

★ ★ ★

He remembers the day his father turned up with the E-Type and his mother went up the wall. But young Will also saw the truth beyond his mother's words, saw the smile that lurked: how much she loved his father. Even then, when he was fifteen and not wanting to have anything to do with them, he saw the kind of a man his

172

father was and feared he would never come up to scratch. He made himself come up to scratch, though, and once asked Jessop what he thought of him. 'You'd pass muster,' Jessop had said. It made him want to weep.

Staffe turns the ignition off and looks up at the Barbican. Rosa's curtains are only half shut and he knows she'll be alone. As he presses and waits, he doesn't quite know how he came to be here. When he says who he is, she kind of gasps his name. 'Will,' she says, 'you should have let me know. You should call.'

'Let me in.'

The lock clicks open. He takes the stairs slowly and by the time he gets there the door is open. She's playing Bessie Smith and when he sees her, dressing gown open and a tiny pair of white lace pants through which he can see her shaven pubis, he knows she has been drinking.

'I'll put something else on.'

'Don't.'

'You've come to talk, right?'

'I don't know, Rosa.'

'Let me get you a drink.' She puts a hand on his chest and goes up on tiptoes, kisses him full on the mouth. She tastes of lemon and booze.

He takes off his coat and walks into the bedroom, sits on the edge of the bed and removes his shoes, socks. 'You got some whisky?' he calls, lying back on the bed. He can feel the beat of his heart. The light above turns off and he hears her pad up to the bed.

'What are you saying, Will?'

He looks up at her, kneeling on the bed,

smiling down at him. 'You decide.' He reaches out and puts his hand on her face. She turns her head and takes his forefinger in her mouth. She sucks on it and looks him dead in the eye. He feels her, through her pants. She pulls her mouth away, takes a slug of whisky and kisses him, lets the spirit trickle into his mouth. She probes him deep with her tongue. He can feel her getting wet, feel her blowing the lid off what prostitutes are supposed to do.

★　★　★

'Don't leave it so long next time,' says Rosa. She steps into a pair of jeans and breathes in as she buttons up. 'I'll be fatter and older and then you'll just want to talk.'

'What do we talk about, Rosa?'

'Can't you remember?'

'I ever tell you about my father?'

'Not a word.'

'Maybe next time.'

'Or your girlfriend.'

He puts on his shoes. 'You got anyone coming round later?'

'Why are you so angry, Will?'

'Now?'

'Most of the time.'

'We don't know anything about each other, do we?'

'Maybe that's the beauty.' She comes up to him and kisses him, full. She puts her hand inside his trousers.

'You be careful, Rosa,' he says, not knowing

174

what to do — whether to offer her money. Surely not.

'You go, Will. And don't be a stranger.'

He walks through the living room, closing the door without taking a look back. He takes the stairs two at a time and steps into the street, feeling brisk.

Then he sees it.

'Bastards!' he says, walking towards the E-Type. He studies the meticulously spray-painted, stencilled message.

## WATCH YOUR BACK

'Watch your back,' Staffe repeats, leaning on the E-Type's roof. He closes his eyes, feels his pulse quicken as he realises they have spoken down his phone line, peered through his windows and now they have etched themselves on his father's pride and joy.

⋆　⋆　⋆

Staffe checks the padlock and can't help feeling the vandalising of the E-Type is some kind of back-handed slap from a higher authority. He shouldn't have gone to see Rosa. He shouldn't have done what he did there. He likes her, but could never love her — if he knew what that was. He has never been cruel to her, he tells himself.

He walks away from the lock-up and round to the front of the Kilburn house. He is certain he can hear someone following him, but when he turns around, the streets are empty all the way to

175

Shoot Up Hill. Up above, the lights are on and the house has a warm glow, as if it were a home to someone. Staffe resolves to be civil to Paolo and, as he knocks, he hopes Johnson hasn't left too vile an imprint on the man his sister loves.

When she opens the door, Marie breaks into a smile. Her eyes sparkle — none of it tallies with what Staffe knows of the recent events in her life.

'Is everything OK?' he says.

'Everything is just great, Will. I'm so glad I came to you when I did. So glad.' She stands to one side and welcomes him in with a sweep of her arm. 'We're having supper. Paolo has done saltimbocca. We're having it on our knees.'

Paolo appears in the doorway to the lounge, holding a large plate and a small ream of napkins, as if he is waiting on them with canapés. He takes two long strides up to Staffe and holds out the plate and offers a napkin. His eyes are both black and his pupils glisten from within the slits of the swollen flesh. His smile glints with gold.

'Christ! What happened to you?' says Staffe, taking a slice of the pork. It has a leaf of sage and a smear of prosciutto.

'I cross the wrong people,' he says casually, still smiling.

'It's a sign, Will. It's all a sign. He's away from those people now.' She links an arm through his and rests her head on Paolo's shoulder, looks up at her brother. 'We're together.'

'Here, I keep my head down.' Paolo is six foot and lean. His arms are wiry in a vest top and his jeans are trendy shabby. His hair is black and shiny and long. Even though he is all beat up,

Staffe can see what a sister might see in him. Paolo places a soft hand on Staffe's forearm. 'How's the saltimbocca?'

The pork and ham and sage have melted in Staffe's mouth. 'It jumps in the mouth,' he says.

'You know,' says Paolo, wrapping an arm around Staffe and guiding him into his own living room. Staffe reasserts his preconceptions: that this man is bad; bad for his sister and bad for him.

'Where's Harry?' asks Staffe.

'He's flopped out, listening to his music. He's never without that iPod you got him,' says Marie. 'Go see him later, when you've eaten. You can put him to bed, but don't wake him.'

★ ★ ★

They sit and chat and Staffe lets his mind wander to the vandalising of the E-Type. He looks at Paolo and tries to work out if he knows who did for him. He pictures Paolo being kind to Marie and tries to imagine her driving him berserk, giving him little choice than to take a hold, shake her out of it. He feels his blood heat up and he stands, shakes his arms down. As he does, he thinks he hears something outside, but the curtains are drawn.

'Stay, Will. You and Paolo need to get to know each other.'

'I won't be long.'

'She told me all about you, Will,' says Paolo. 'The man who has it all. Her big brother.'

'I haven't got it all. Far from it.'

177

'I'm sorry about what happened,' says Paolo.

'Sorry?'

'Go see Harry. See your nephew.'

When he goes upstairs, Staffe looks out of the landing window. Two street lights are out and the double-glazing is too good to let any sound in. He's sure somebody is out there, but there's no evidence.

Harry has fallen asleep in the space that was intended to be Staffe's music room. The alcoves either side of the Arts and Crafts fireplace are shelved at thirteen-inch intervals to accommodate his vinyl. Sylvie picked out the fireplace a couple of years ago on a weekend that re-established them as friends. That soon faltered. But the room is a success and as if to prove its purpose, young Harry has music piping through his Apple white buds as he sleeps.

Staffe wonders what his mother's grandson is listening to, but daren't disturb the flow. He gets gooseflesh when he thinks what his dead parents would have given to hold their grandson.

Harry is lighter than Staffe expects, like marshmallow. Staffe smells the clammy crook of his neck. He hopes he will be big when he grows up, not take any shit. But he questions this and revises his wish. He says a quick prayer that Harry is everything his mother's mother would want him to be. As they stand in the half light, tears run down Staffe's stubbled jaw and fall on his nephew's hair. He has no clue what his mother would wish for her grandson. He doesn't dare think how wide of that mark his own life has been.

He carries Harry out of the room and sits on the stairs. He rocks gently back and forth and whispers a story. He makes it up as he goes along and in the end young Harry saves a princess who didn't ever know who Harry was. She lived happily ever after.

'What the fuck!'

Staffe jolts from his repose.

It is a woman's voice.

'I'll kill the fucker. I'll kill the fucker!' shouts Paolo, running to the front door. He is holding a baseball bat, flicking it expertly from the wrist.

Harry's eyelids flicker and Staffe holds him closer, hears the fizz of the tune being piped in. He watches downstairs as Marie rants into the letter box. Paolo is behind, readying himself.

'Open the door, Marie. Open it!'

'No!'

'I can't take this no more. They kill me. They kill me.'

Marie turns round, looks up at Paolo and Staffe sees the pale horror in her face. He puts his hands over Harry's ears and shouts down, 'No! Wait.' He rushes to the music room, lays Harry down gently and throws himself at the stairs, touching the tread three times the whole way down. He crashes into the door surround.

'Give me the bat. Give me the bastard bat, Paolo!'

Staffe takes a grip of the bat, takes in a lungful of the air and shouts 'Let's have you!' and pulls open the door. He swings the bat as he launches himself out of the door and he trips, commando-rolls down the steps and into the front garden. He waits for the punches — and worse — but nothing comes. As he blinks up towards the house, he can't believe his eyes.

There, sitting cross-legged and weeping, is the only ginger-haired Indian he knows.

'Sohan?' says Staffe. 'Sohan Kelly? What the hell are you doing here?'

'They are going to kill me, Mister Staffe. And your promises aren't helping. No way your promises good for what you say.'

'What made you come here?'

'They're going to kill me. They said so.'

'Where are they?'

'You know I can't change what I say. You have to tell your Pennington.'

'You tell him.'

Sohan Kelly looks up at Staffe, rocking to and fro and shaking his head. 'I can't go back to him. Not him. I can't.'

And it is clear to Staffe that Kelly is more afraid of Pennington than the e.Gang. It is also clear that Kelly won't tell him why this is, or what hold Pennington has over him. It is enough, in the warm balm of the hot summer night, to make Staffe's blood turn cold.

He looks back at the house and beyond the distraught Sohan Kelly, Paolo wraps his arms around Marie. She is weeping tears of joy. Behind them, young Harry, earphones in, comes downstairs slowly, singing a syncopated 'My Heart Belongs to Daddy', which makes Staffe think the child's mother might be doing something right.

# Friday Morning

Pulford has been sitting in his unmarked car at the entrance to the Limekiln estate since 6 a.m. From here he can see up to the fifth floor where Leanne Colquhoun will soon be reunited with her two children. He clocks everyone going into the estate, watches for them appearing on the fifth-floor deck.

A bashed-up Mondeo parks opposite and a horribly familiar face appears. Nick Absolom is one of Fleet Street's worst, climbing over bodies to get to the top at the *News*. Leanne Colquhoun has been free for twelve hours and the vultures are already descending.

Pulford is torn. If he gets out and tells Absolom to scratch his poisonous pen across some other poor soul's life, his cover would be blown. If he stays put, Absolom will sink his teeth into Leanne and spread her story all across the front pages. He waits until Absolom appears on the fifth deck and calls Staffe.

'That slimy bastard,' says Staffe when Pulford calls him. 'Jesus, this is all we need.'

'What can we do?'

'Pennington will go berserk. I'll have to ask him to have a word with the editor at the *News*. He didn't want her released in the first place.' Staffe thinks of that other conversation he has to have with Pennington about Sohan Kelly.

181

'What can Leanne tell Absolom that's not already out there?'

'We questioned her about Montefiore. The press would have a field day putting the two cases together.'

'Hang on,' says Pulford. A shiny purple Clio pulls up and Carly Kellerman gets out. She has a document case under her arm.

'What is it?' says Staffe.

Carly Kellerman ushers two children out of the back of the car. The boy has a zigzag pattern shaved into his hair and the girl has a high-up ponytail.

'It's the Colquhoun children.' The kids look around, nervous, not sure whether to smile or snarl. They look up at the high decks of the tower. 'It's Absolom's lucky day.'

'No luck involved, Pulford. This was set up,' says Staffe. 'You stay put and don't let Absolom see you. I'll send a uniformed WPC round with a counsellor. They'll get Absolom to scarper and hopefully Leanne won't find out we're watching her.' He slams the phone down, curses Pennington, Nick Absolom and the day he came back for this case.

\* \* \*

'I knew we shouldn't have released her till you had another viable suspect,' booms Pennington, not even bothering to look at Staffe. 'Jesus! This is going to be all over the press now. It's day three of your seven and you've got nothing. Where are you going with this?' He glares.

Staffe considers telling him about Kashell. 'We're chasing up Colquhoun's first wife and Montefiore's previous victims.'

Pennington's glare morphs into an incredulous stare as he looks his DI up and down, sees the state he is in. 'Are you all right, Staffe? You look like shit.'

'I had a visit from Sohan Kelly last night.'

'He's taken care of.'

Staffe recalls the horrified look on Kelly's face when he uttered Pennington's name. 'How exactly did you take care of him, sir? He didn't seem 'taken care of'.'

'You know what that scumbag is capable of. He's a grass for crying out loud. He'll find a way to disappear. He certainly won't turn crook's evidence. Don't you worry about that.'

There is a knock on the door and Josie comes in and Staffe can tell straight away it's not good news.

'Sorry, sir.' She looks at Pennington, then Staffe, as if for permission to drop him further in it. Staffe nods at her. 'The WPC couldn't get into Leanne Colquhoun's flat. There was nobody home. No answer at the door. No sound, no lights or anything.'

'She got the right place?'

'I spoke to her myself. We checked and double-checked. It was the right door on the right floor.'

'This is a disaster,' says Pennington, making his way out of Staffe's office. 'Absolom's got something up his sleeve. What if she tells them you interviewed her about Montefiore? You need to get a grip on this.'

Staffe waits for him to leave. 'There's another visit I want you to make, Josie. A mother and daughter down in Raynes Park.'

'The Kashells?'

'Keep it to yourself. And when you go, I want you to . . . ' He softens his voice, ' . . . I want you to suss the place out. See what sort of keys there are to the doors.'

'Staffe . . . '

'I need to be able to get in. Check for bolts. See if there's a dog or neighbours overlooking.'

'Why are you going out on such a limb, sir?'

He pulls on his suede jacket, feels the stubble on his face, almost a beard now. He looks at cloudless London, the towers of the City's eastern sprawl scratching at the Docklands sky. He gives Josie the Kashells' address and makes his way through the thick air of the hot narrow corridors to the incident room. He knows he can't put it off any more. He has to see Jessop.

When Jessop first left Leadengate, Staffe couldn't bear to visit his friend. Then there was a big case, then another and before he knew it, he'd left it too long and when he did call, Jessop's bile was up. Even so, Staffe knows he should have made the effort. But he had his own problems. Sylvie was gone.

Still, he is going to see him now, but it's because Jessop has something to offer him. These are the wrong circumstances in which to call on a friend. And say what you like, they are friends. More than friends.

'You could have done something, Staffe.

184

Nobody said anything. They just stood aside and let me go,' Jessop had said, carrying a small box with his personal effects down the back stairs to the car park.

A voice says, 'You look like you've seen a ghost.' Staffe twitches, looks across and sees Jombaugh. 'Shit, Jom, I didn't see you there.'

'What's troubling you, Will?'

Staffe checks behind him, as though talking about an old friend might damage him. 'You remember Jessop.'

'He thought the world of you. You not seen him in a while, right?'

'Not in a while, no.'

'You give him my best, Will.'

Staffe leaves Jombaugh to it and goes to the toilet but he notices the light switches outside are off. They're never off. He opens the door gently and hears a sigh from the gloom. It's coming from inside a cubicle and he crouches down, sees the feet are pointed towards the pan. Dull light comes in through the high frosted window. Another sigh, an ecstatic sigh and he recognises the voice.

He goes back out and eases the door closed, waits. The toilet flushes and he stands ready, to make as though he is just going in. When Johnson opens the door, he walks into him.

'Sorry, Rick.'

Johnson looks dead in the eyes, says, 'No matter, sir.'

'How come the lights are off?'

'Some prick trying to save the world.'

He watches Johnson go, slow, and once he's

out of sight, Staffe turns on the lights and goes into the toilet, inspects the cubicle. No smell, lid down. There is nothing unusual, anywhere, just a copy of the *Mirror* on top of the bin. He removes it, takes the top off the bin, and prods at a pile of blue paper towels. He puts his hand in, as if it was a barrel of goodies in a grotto, looking up at the tube light for some reason and he feels something sharp, as if he has been nipped by an animal. He tips the bin up, kicks the towels so they scatter and then he sees what bit him. A syringe.

★   ★   ★

Josie follows Greta Kashell into the small kitchen at the back of the house, says 'yes' she'd love a cup of tea. Greta puts the kettle on and continues to make small talk about the summer.

'Is your daughter in?' says Josie.

'Nicoletta? She goes to her grandparents for the holidays. They're down in Hastings. She likes it there.' Greta stops fiddling with the mugs and the sugar bowl and gives Josie a short, stern look. 'Nobody down there knows what happened. When she first comes back here, she's almost like she used to be. Then it's back to the way it was. School's the worst. It happened at school. I was late picking her up. I work, see. If I didn't work I'd have been on time, maybe . . . Can you believe it — a classroom assistant. How could that happen?'

'You know none of that was anything to do with you, Greta.'

'She goes to high school in September. She's a nervous wreck about it. I want to teach her at home but the experts say she has to relearn to be sociable. Sociable! She was the friendliest girl you'd ever meet. What good does that do you in this world?'

'Does she visit her father?'

'No. She loves him. She loves him more than me.' Greta Kashell looks away when she says this, and Josie slips her hand into her pocket, feels for the mobile phone. She is ashamed of what she is about to do but does it anyway. Before she came in, she had put Greta's landline number into her mobile.

She makes sure she's talking as she presses 'call'. 'There's often a strong bond between father and daughter. I know from . . . '

The phone rings and Greta Kashell flinches, lets it ring. 'She won't let me hold her, you know. It was a woman, see. A woman that did it.'

'You'd better get that,' says Josie.

Greta Kashell goes into the hall, head down, and Josie moves to the back door as quick as a flash, takes the key out of the lock and presses it into the tablet of plasticine she has brought with her. The ringing stops and she hears Greta saying, 'Who is it? Who is it!'

Josie hurriedly takes the key from the plasticine and replaces it in the lock. She makes sure there are no bolts on the back door. No signs of an alarm. She hears Greta slam the phone down and she flicks off her mobile, starts busying herself in the making of tea. 'So, Greta, you say you work . . . '

Before she has even finished her tea, Josie makes her apologies and leaves, knowing exactly when and for how long the house will be empty, allowing Staffe to snoop for God knows what.

*   *   *

Staffe parks the Peugeot just off Kilburn High Road, his head pounding. He needs to change his clothes, and traces of last night come back at him, strangely reminding him of Sylvie, not Rosa. Why did she return his call so quickly? The fact that she is in his phone makes his pulse quicken.

He locks the car and makes his way up to the main entrance of Jessop's dishevelled four-storey terraced house and even though this is a different urban backwater, a new postcode, he feels a refrain from those days when he felt like shit most of the time — going into Leadengate on two or three hours' sleep, having to gargle with Listermint and spray himself down with Right Guard before the DCI clocked him.

His finger hovers over the buzzer to flat four. Funny that Jessop lives so close to Staffe's Kilburn house. Funny, they never see each other around but maybe Jessop has seen *him*, has chosen to look the other way.

What ravages might retirement have wrought on Jessop? Jessop who loved the Force more than it loved him. He wonders whether Delores will have stuck by him. Delores who was younger and had a twinkle in her eye. He takes a deep breath, presses the buzzer. Perhaps he will be out.

'Who's that?' The voice rattles in the cracked aluminium intercom grille: deep, belligerent.

'It's Will, sir. Will Wagstaffe.' Staffe knows it's stupid to call him 'sir', but can't help himself.

'What the hell do you want?'

'Do I need a reason?'

'It's been too long for there not to be a reason.' There is an electronic whirr and the latch clunks open. Staffe pushes the door and hears Jessop bark an instruction through the grille as though time has been rewound. 'All the way to the top and take it slow, I need some time.'

Staffe laughs to himself and makes his way past a dismantled motorbike in the hallway. The place smells damp and he guesses it's tenanted. The carpets are shiny and the walls are grubby. When he gets to the top of the final flight, Jessop is standing in the open doorway, practically filling the frame. He has aged more than three years; he's wearing an old cardigan and hasn't shaved for a couple of days. His hair has thinned and his eyes are dark; his trousers bag, and while he is well built in the shoulders and chest, the gut has dropped and the legs have gone spindly, like a drinker's. 'You could have called.' A tight smile betrays him.

'It didn't seem right. So I left it. Then I called and you bawled me out. Remember?'

'I always bawled you out. It never put you off before.' Jessop smiles, like a roguish uncle as he remembers older days.

'And you moved.' Staffe looks around the place, trying not to turn his nose up.

189

'You're supposed to be a detective. Did I teach you nothing?'

'You don't snoop on friends.'

'Aaah. I've got friends now? Lucky me.' He turns his back.

Staffe follows him into what appears to be the lounge and sees that his arse has all but gone to nothing. His mother used to say, 'His arse has gone to gin.' She never swore, but she said that when his father's worst friends came and went.

A duvet has been tossed in one corner, a pile of clothes in another. A thick pall of cigarette smoke hangs even though both sash windows are pulled right open. Outside, North London's rooftops go on for miles under the cloudless sky.

'You working that Colquhoun case, hey?' says Jessop. 'Got nothing?' Jessop flops down into a threadbare chair, gestures for Staffe to sit on a piano stool at a junkshop desk and lights a cigarette. He tosses the pack to Staffe. 'Off the booze? You've lost that boozer's jowl. Doesn't look like it's doing you any good. Christ, I'm better off out of the fucking Force if that's what things are coming to.'

'What do you make of the case?' Staffe tosses the cigarettes back. 'Does it remind you of something?' Staffe flicks through a magazine that was on the chair he's sitting on. When he looks up, Jessop is making a tight smile.

'She was still warm when I got there. You could almost hear her scream when we took the gauze from out of her mouth.'

'Gauze?' says Staffe.

'They use gauze on Colquhoun?'

'Why did the CPS drop the Stensson case?' says Staffe.

'Four hundred hours on a forty/sixty case when they've got seventy/thirties they can put away in half a day? And the perverts always do it again, so you'll get a quickie in the end. It's numbers, Staffe. Numbers everywhere.'

He goes quiet and Staffe looks around the place. Jessop's got a couple of nice things — a decent stereo in its day and a Sévres vase, plenty of silver frames with different versions of the same pretty face.

'How's Delores?' says Staffe, looking around as if she might be in an adjoining room.

'Think she'd live like this? In this shithole?'

'I'm sorry.'

'So you did come round because of Lotte Stensson.' Jessop looks sad. 'You know we got the man who did for her.'

'Nico Kashell,' says Staffe. 'He confessed.'

Jessop stubs his cigarette out, reaches down and pulls a bottle of Scotch from next to his chair. He pours an unhealthy measure into a coffee mug and lights another cigarette. 'Poor bastard,' he says.

'Did you always reckon Kashell definitely did it?'

''Poor bastard.' Is that what they say about me? 'Poor bastard never got his pension brought forward.'' Jessop takes all the whisky back and grimaces.

'It wasn't right, the way they did it.'

'You still work for them. And now you're here.'

'Jombaugh sends his regards.'

191

'Why are you here, Will?'

Staffe thinks about breaching security, telling Jessop about Montefiore. But he ponders too long and Jessop sees part of the truth.

'There's been another?' says Jessop.

'An unprosecuted child abuse. It was torture, again. You don't have any doubts about Nico Kashell?'

'He's doing life. Why would he do that if he didn't kill Lotte Stensson?'

'Because he can't bear not to have killed her? That's what a decent father would do to someone who had pushed their fingers up his little girl. Who'd . . . '

'I know! I fucking know, all right!' Jessop gazes into his empty coffee mug, looking as though he'd prefer to forget.

'Ruth Merritt was the woman at the CPS. We can't find her.'

'Ruthie was a good woman.'

'Was?'

'I haven't seen her since that case.'

'She seems to have disappeared.'

'That doesn't make her a bad person,' says Jessop.

They sit in silence and Jessop smokes another cigarette, takes another mugful of whisky. This is nothing like what Staffe had wanted. He plays with the syringe inside his pocket. As he's reminding himself to send it off to Janine, he catches Jessop's eye. He smiles.

Jessop smiles back, not so tight.

'It's good to see you, Will. It really is, and I hope you get your man.'

'We should have been better friends to each other, Bob. Don't you think?' Staffe stands up, begins the process of leaving.

'We were as good as we could have been.'

'Did I ever thank you, for taking care of me? I'd never have lasted . . . '

'No you didn't. And don't burden me with your police career. I won't be responsible for that.' He laughs and it turns into a splutter. Staffe moves across and pats Jessop's back. He lets his hand rest between his friend's shoulders. Jessop's eyes are cloudy.

'How's Sylvie?'

'She left.'

'That's what happens, Will. I told you that all along.'

Making his way down the stairs, Staffe feels the low thudding bass of a gangsta rap beat, can smell something that's not cigarettes or weed being smoked, and he makes a call. He gets through to Jombaugh and knows something isn't quite right when he's put straight on to Pennington.

'He's recovered consciousness, Staffe.'

'Montefiore?'

'And the first thing he says when he comes round is he's got to see you. He says you can save him. Is that right, Staffe?'

'Save him?'

'What the hell's going on!'

★   ★   ★

'You look terrible,' says Josie. 'Are you growing a beard? I'm not sure I like it.'

193

He wants to stay here all afternoon and into the evening but knows he can't. They are in The Steeles down the bottom end of Belsize Park. He used to come here on his own. He'd sit right here on the corner of the curving bar, watching the sun stream in, lighting up the specks of dust; watching it turn his glass a burning amber.

She takes hold of the rim of his glass with her thumb and middle finger, twirls the Jameson's round. It forms legs down the sides of the glass. She leans towards him.

'I didn't know you knew Montefiore.'

'I don't!' He takes the glass and their fingers touch. He drinks it down and then finishes the water. 'How did you get on with Greta Kashell?'

'He says you can save him.' Josie takes the plasticine out of her bag and lays it on the bar. Straight away Staffe knows which master will get him into Greta Kashell's home. 'She goes to the restaurant every night from six until eight. It was their restaurant until Nico went down. Her brother-in-law runs it for them now and she helps out with the books.'

'I went to see Jessop.' He tries to catch the barmaid's eye but fails. The Jameson's burns his throat and he wants more. 'He used to be a top man, and now he's fucked.' He looks her in the eye. 'Totally fucked.'

The barmaid comes across and Josie says 'Sorry, I think we're going' to the barmaid. She hands Staffe the plasticine imprint and says, 'You've got what you wanted,' and gets up from the bar stool.

Staffe looks across to the barmaid and she

smiles. Her eyes shine, glassy.

He goes to the toilets and runs the water as cold as he can get it, packs the basin's plughole with paper towels and fills it to the rim. He takes a deep breath then dunks his head in the cold water. He looks at himself in the cracked mirror and says, aloud, 'Come on, you prick.'

★　★　★

According to the nurse, Montefiore hasn't eaten since the assault, on account of the lacerations, bruising and haemorrhaging. As the nurse goes matter-of-factly through the details, Staffe looks into Montefiore's sad, dark eyes. The pain has taken its toll on his grey face, but a glimmer of fear shines through. Only in the eyes is he alive. Kept alive with the threat that all this will happen to him again, just as soon as he is fit enough to take it.

Staffe sits alongside and can't imagine this man stalking, catching and violating Sally Watkins, trying to do the same to Tanya Ford. After all the years in the job, it's still sometimes impossible to equate people to the things they do. Apparently, Montefiore used a sex toy on Sally. How much disclosure does the CPS want?

'Who fucked with *you*, Guy?'

'They had a balaclava on.'

'How many of them were there?'

'One. Only one that I saw.' He gulps air after every few words.

'And they said they'd come back, finish the job?'

195

He nods again.

Staffe remembers what Nico Kashell said to him, about wanting Lotte Stensson back. To do it again? Like this? 'They told you to get in touch with me, did they? Well tell me: who really fucked with you, Guy? Who made you think it was all right to do those things to Sally Watkins? Was it a teacher? Was it your father? Maybe your mum or just some bad bastard you didn't know from Adam.'

Guy Montefiore looks afraid but he won't look away. 'There's hate in your voice. I don't hate anybody.' He looks done in, but he musters himself, reaches out and puts a hand on the back of Staffe's neck, pulls him closer. Gasping for air between phrases, he says, 'Love makes the bad things happen. Not hate. Sometimes . . . we love too much.'

'Tell that to Sally Watkins and her father.' Staffe wonders why he omits the mother, realises how high the bar has been raised in this case — to call yourself a victim.

Montefiore raises his arm towards the nurse and Staffe adjusts his tack. He takes hold of Montefiore's arm and pulls it down, says, 'No matter what I think of you, you're my only witness.'

Montefiore raises his eyes, his mouth breaking into a half smile.

'I'm on your side, whether I like it or not.' The nurse comes up, tells Staffe his time is up. 'You make sure nobody comes in here. Nobody!' She flinches and he checks her name badge. He smiles. 'It's really important, Judy. Life and death.' As he goes, he says, 'How would they know me?' turning to Montefiore. But his eyes are closed.

★ ★ ★

Staffe waits for Carly Kellerman outside Parsons Green tube. He calls Johnson and as it rings, his temperature rises. He puts his hand in his pocket and feels the syringe, wants to ask what the hell is going on. What the hell it is that Johnson's on. No wonder he can't afford anything better for his family. But he knows he has to wait. He is down to the bare bones on this case. Perhaps he'll do something when Janine has the findings on the syringe.

'It's good news bad news, sir. We think we know where Ruth Merritt is,' says Johnson.

'What's the bad news?'

'She's in India. Down in the south, according to her sister but she hasn't heard a word for six months. Hasn't got a clue how we'd get hold of her.'

'Send me a transcript of the conversation. I'm in Fulham . . . ' Carly Kellerman comes up the steps and Staffe waves to her. ' . . . just going to see Tanya Ford. You want to come along? We can wait.'

'I can't sir, I . . . '

Staffe hangs up and he and Carly walk down towards Tanya Ford's house, a new block of houses crammed in between the railway sidings and the Purbeck council estate.

'Her parents are absolutely adamant they

197

don't want her to even see the accused, let alone press charges,' says Carly.

'If the Watkinses had followed it through when Montefiore raped Sally, we wouldn't be having to do this. Nothing would have happened to Tanya Ford.'

'It's for the victim to decide, Staffe. Not us. And anyway . . . ' Suddenly, Carly looks sad, kind of ashamed.

'What is it?' says Staffe.

'He'd have been released by now. We just have to do what's right, don't we, Staffe? Do our jobs.'

'That's all we can do, Carly.'

At the house, Tanya Ford's mother answers the door. It leads straight into a small lounge where Tanya is curled into a ball in an armchair. She has the corner of an old, crocheted blanket in her mouth. Tanya's father, Tony Ford, stands against a radiator under the window, arms crossed over his chest and thunder on his brow. He looks as though he can handle himself.

'We want this done with, soon as,' says the father.

'I do need to speak to Tanya, Mr Ford,' says Staffe. 'We think we know who attacked her.'

'Tell me his name and where he lives, then. We don't need you no more.'

'I'd like Tanya to come with me, to identify him.'

'She saw nothing,' says her mother.

'This man, if we're right, might have done this before. He might do it again.'

'Do what? He didn't touch her. My Tanya's . . . '

His wife shoots him a glare.

'I'm fed up of you people. Fed up to here.' He puts his hand way above his head, almost touches the ceiling.

Staffe goes across to where Tanya is curled up, goes down on his haunches, keeping half a yard between them. 'Did you see him, Tanya?'

She shakes her head.

'Did he have something over his head? There were two of them.'

She nods her head.

'Is there anything you remember? The aftershave? Their eyes? The voice?'

She shakes her head.

'Tell me who he is and get the fuck out of here,' says Tony Ford.

Staffe stands up. He thinks of Sally Watkins turning tricks in her bedroom while *her* father watches TV. He tries to calm himself, faces Ford.

'This man used chloroform on Tanya. He did the same thing to another girl three years ago. But he only uses enough to knock them out for a while. He has smelling salts too. He likes them to come round, if you get my drift.'

'Shut up,' says Ford, taking a step towards Staffe.

'Maybe we should go,' says Carly.

'He likes them to be awake when he's . . . '

Ford lunges at Staffe and tries to get him in a headlock, but Staffe dips his shoulder. He uses the father's own mass against him, drops him to the floor and as he falls, Staffe twists him, makes sure he lands on his stomach. Hating himself for it, he kneels between Ford's broad shoulders, twists his arm up his back. Between breaths he says, 'I'm sorry. I'm sorry. We're going.' Then he leans down and whispers to Ford. 'If you want, I can tell you exactly what he did. And because you won't help me, I've got to nurse this fucking pervert and get him back to health and I've got to make sure nobody ever lays a finger on him. You want me to do that?'

'Fuck off,' says the father. 'I've got you, you bastard. I've got you.'

Carly Kellerman takes a hold of Staffe and ushers him towards the door. On the way out he glimpses Tanya Ford crying in the arms of her mother.

# Friday Evening

Staffe sits alone on Parsons Green platform. Carly Kellerman has left him be, not knowing quite what to say about his confrontation with Tony Ford, but saying that she would have to make mention of it in her report.

Trains are announced and 'Wimbledon' stands out. He gets slowly to his feet and follows an instinct — as if the station announcer is some warbling Pied Piper. Greta Kashell and Raynes Park is down that neck of the woods anyway but meantime he has a notion of going further out. Further back.

There was a time, not long after his parents died and in the early days at Queens Terrace, when Staffe would run out west to Putney Bridge where the river curves to meet you. He would do it at night when the moon was full and the river was silver. A couple of times, awash with nervous energy, he would carry on and veer to and through Richmond Deer Park. The deer would sit and stand in groups on the fringe of the woods and watch him all the way down to Kingston Gate. There, he would stop and contemplate a meeting with the river again, a short run along its path to where he used to live. But he always refrained from following it further, towards its source. Back in time.

\* \* \*

Thames Ditton railway station is thirteen miles from Westminster, but alighting now, ahead of the weekend rush, it could be a million miles from that bustle. Here, people disappear down narrow paths between hedged fields. Oaks sprawl. The clapperboard station house has its original burgundy livery. This is England: of Lord Peter Wimsey or Wooster's fearsome aunts. This was once home to Staffe.

He walks slowly, leaning backwards down the gentle hill from the sidings to the village and can see his old house nestling up to the George Inn. He wishes he wasn't here and he also wishes he had never left.

When Staffe's parents died, his grandfather came from his place in France to stay for a while. He was the opposite of his father, as happy-go-lucky as his father was earnest. Staffe wonders now what his grandfather might have made of the life his father carved out for himself. When the old man left, the last time, he said to young Will, 'You must do what's right for you, Will. Nobody else.'

His grandfather declined quickly, was dead within two years and it didn't occur to Will until too late, the toll it must have taken: to survive his son. Now, Staffe's blood flows fast as he conjures what he could do to Santi Extbatteria, the man who killed his parents. He walks on with an extra clip, past the church where he and Marie were christened, and he tries to swallow away thoughts of vengeance.

On the corner of the high street, where an estate agent's and deli stand in the stead of the bakers and the butchers, he takes pause. A 4 × 4 Porsche pulls up into his parents' gravelled driveway and out steps a career mum, Chanel shades perch in her punk-posh coiffure. She is Prada all the way down to her Seychelles thighs and calls her children out of the car with a King's Road husk. He should be happy a family is making a home from his old house. He wonders if the children see more of their father than he saw of his.

The children stare down at their hands as they go, as if reading prayers. But these are the gospels according to Nintendo. They don't talk to each other or even notice that the garden is beautiful. His mother planted the trees — for a better time. She would be so happy the way they have prospered. He turns, goes back to the railway station, and this life.

★ ★ ★

Staffe rubs his thumb along the curved spine of the brass key inside his pocket. He watches Greta Kashell come out of her house and make her way towards Raynes Park Tube. He follows her, to make sure she is going to the restaurant. From behind — when you can't see the bags under the eyes, the clutch of skin at her neck — she looks ten years younger. She is a tall, thin woman with coat-hanger shoulders and black hair that shimmers in the low, early evening sun. She walks with her back straight and chin held high, cuts a sad figure as she disappears through the Delphi's front door.

Staffe slips down the side of the house to the back door, slides in the key, and makes his way through the Kashell home. The only signs of family here are the photographs of a man who doesn't live here any more. Nico Kashell is in every room: laughing with a turquoise sea behind him; laughing with a raised glass in his hand; laughing with his arm wrapped around Greta and little Nicoletta pushing her head between Mum and Dad, trying to get in on the picture; Nico stood between Micky and Minnie Mouse, laughing.

There is nothing of note in the kitchen drawers, or in the sideboard in the lounge. There is no junk mail, no prison letters from Wakefield, no bills waiting to be paid, no school-books or casual reading, just a TV guide on top of the DVD player under the modestly wide TV.

Upstairs, Greta's bedroom is like a hotel room and Nicoletta's is surprisingly tidy for a teenage girl. He goes through her wardrobe. There should be some pink, somewhere in the room — but there isn't.

There's one room left, a box room by the bathroom and when he pushes open the door, Staffe's heart rate goes up a notch. There is a desk under the window and no bookshelves or cabinets, but clearly this is where Greta comes to run the house. There is a neat stack of wicker boxes, each half full of paid bills and bank statements, invoices and school reports. In one box there is a huge pile of correspondence with a solicitor concerning her husband's case and in another more papers for the restaurant.

Staffe checks the drawer to the desk and finds nothing but biros. He switches the computer on and takes out his memory stick. The screen fires up with a screensaver of the whole family dressed in togas in front of a painted Acropolis backdrop.

*My Recent Documents* is all spreadsheets and Nicoletta's school assignments, a couple of downloaded iTunes and a letter to the accountant saying the restaurant's books are ready for inspection for the June year end.

A quick flick through the Word folders reveals nothing and Staffe is about to close down and call it a day when he sees an icon on the desktop called *Contacts*. He double clicks and sees an Excel address book. He closes the file down and drags the icon to his own memory stick icon and watches the information scoot across. Outside a car parps its horn and he jumps up, sees a girl in Brownies regalia run down the path and hug her friend. A mother drives them away.

Checking the time, Staffe grants himself a quick pry into Greta's contacts and reopens the address file. There is nothing to strike a chord under B for Bowker, or C for Colquhoun or M for Montefiore or S for Stensson or W for Watkins.

But something is amiss. His mind is fuzzy and he wonders if it is the lunchtime booze or the spat with Tony Ford, the visit to his old house or the heat. He scrolls back through the file thinking he is missing something and when he gets to the Vs, he sees it — something vaguely familiar. VABBA. A London number.

It's nine thirty on Friday night and back at Leadengate the uniforms have returned to file their findings and quickly drift off towards the weekend. Half of them are coming in tomorrow to finish the data matching. All the names have been inputted and now it's time to see if the same people appear from more than one source. This is relationships reduced to numbers.

Staffe has plugged in his memory stick and is calling VABBA. Victims Against Being Buried Alive. It's a Kennington number and doesn't answer.

He hauls himself over coals for pushing Tony Ford too hard, but considers whether Tanya's father has his own simmering agenda. He certainly displayed the traits of a man able to inflict damage on Guy Montefiore or any of that ilk. But two things count against him as a live possibility: the method of the assault on Montefiore (being premeditated and showing the perpetrator must have been on Montefiore's case for some time); and the lack of evidence that Tanya had been stalked before — that is to say, how would Tony Ford have known his daughter was under threat, unless he was himself stalking her or keeping an unusually vigilant eye?

There are stories, and Staffe recalls a particular instance in Holland, of parent paedophile rings. They tout their children to the criminals. Some even have children specifically to pay that kind of rent. Staffe rubs his face, knows he has to draw a line somewhere. Tony

Ford couldn't be that kind of man.

He clicks into Pulford's transcript of the Linda Watkins interview and allows himself a smile. On the screen: *You probably think I'm a bad person, but you know if I had stayed I would have been buried alive. They'd have come for me in fifty years or so and put me in a box and nobody would ever have known I had been there.*

'Buried alive,' he says out loud and alone, recalling the leaflet in Tyrone Watkins's kitchen drawer. *Victims Against Being Buried Alive.* 'VABBA.'

He checks on the internet for VABBA but the search engine fails to come up with a pure match, which strikes him as being strange. Support groups are normally charities and the funders invariably require public recognition of their philanthropy, a dissemination of their good work. Nor does VABBA appear in the Yellow Pages or in the UK Register of Charities. He switches back into Greta Kashell's Excel file.

Outside, he can hear a group going from one pub to the next and he looks out of the window, sees it is a gang of girls. More flesh than clothes on the streets tonight, but it brings a smile to his face and he thinks it's a wonder that sometimes there is not more trouble on the city streets. Now the girls are clustering around a tramp in the Ritedrug doorway. They kneel beside him and give him cigarettes, push money at him. One of them gives him a kiss on the cheek. For a second, Staffe thinks they might be taking the piss, but they're not. They pull the tramp to his feet and link their arms through his and walk him to the pub. They flirt with the doorman and persuade him to let the tramp in. He's got a smile all the way into next week.

Greta Kashell's grid of contacts seems unfathomable. If you can't predict a random act of kindness in a small corner of the city, how can you hope to make sense of people's motivations? The rows and columns of Greta Kashell's spreadsheet address book look like a Magic Eye painting you have to stare at without focusing to see a hidden image. The columns are so ordered, all the same.

Except one.

A number pushes itself sideways. He counts out his own telephone number on the fingers of his hands. Eleven digits. He tests another number. Eleven again.

He presses '9' on his phone to get an outside line and dials the thirteen digit number. He looks at the name the number is ascribed to and can't think what *Dennis Brown* has got to do with anything.

A female voice answers in a broken foreign tongue. She sounds English. Staffe hangs up and as he checks for the city dialling code, Dennis Brown begins to make sense to him. DB. The code is Santa Cruz, Tenerife.

DB is Debra Bowker.

Greta Kashell knows Debra Bowker. Lotte Stensson and Karl Colquhoun connect. Linda Watkins talked about being buried alive.

Tyrone Watkins had a leaflet for the same support group as Greta Kashell. Lotte Stensson and Guy Montefiore connect.

Now, if that's not a cause for celebration . . .

＊ ＊ ＊

The Boss Clef is an old-school jazz club just off the Old Street roundabout and although Stan Tracey's lad is playing downstairs with his latest band, Staffe takes a position at the upstairs bar. He's only there five minutes before Smethurst arrives.

'So, the wagon sees another one topple off the back. Must be a rocky old road, Staffe,' says Smethurst.

'A healthy balance, Smet, that's all I want.'

'And what's wrong with an unhealthy balance?'

'I'll drink to that.'

They clink glasses and each takes a swig from his bottle of Beck's. Smethurst shouts up a couple of shots of Scotch and Staffe tells the girl to put it on his tab, begins to tell Smethurst about the connections between Debra Bowker and Greta Kashell, and between Greta Kashell and Tyrone Watkins.

'Shame you didn't get a search warrant. If the Kashell woman gets wind you've found something and erases her address file, that evidence is inadmissible.'

Staffe questions whether he has told Smethurst too much. Can he trust him? If he can't, then who can he trust?

'How would she get wind?'

'Why not get a search warrant? You afraid Pennington would think you were wasting your time? His money?'

Staffe looks Smethurst in the eye, smiles. 'I'd appreciate it if you'd keep it to yourself, just till I get my ducks in a row.'

'You really think Greta Kashell could have something to do with Colquhoun or Montefiore? It's her husband that's supposed to be Lotte Stensson's killer, not her.'

'There's no SOC evidence for Colquhoun or Montefiore,' says Staffe. 'Just like the Lotte Stensson case. Clean as a whistle. We'd have got nothing if Nico Kashell hadn't walked in and sung up his confession. I went to see Jessop earlier on.'

'Jessop!'

'He took Nico Kashell's confession.'

'They reckon that's what finally did for the poor sod — sending down a father for looking after his little girl when the police stood by and did nothing.'

'He wasn't looking after Nicoletta, Smet. He was looking after himself. He couldn't live with himself so he murdered someone.'

'And I suppose it's a crime to take revenge on someone who rapes your child.'

'Which side of the law are you on?' He shouts up another round and listens to Smethurst sing the song of sad Bob Jessop with the strains of a soaring sax and a fast-bop rhythm section coming up from the room below. It's a melancholic take on 'I've Got You Under My Skin' and Staffe tries to get his head around Cole Porter being hooked on heroin, in spite of that warning voice in the night. Staffe thinks of Johnson; repeating and repeating in his ear.

Smethurst continues, 'Poor bloody Jessop was on the edge from the first damn day he walked back into the Met. His heart and soul was in Leadengate and he knew we didn't want him. Didn't get his pension, you know. No enhancements and he's got to wait till sixty now.'

Each mention of Jessop takes him back three years. He thinks of Sylvie, too, curled up in his phone, waiting to be called. He tries to forget that and takes a drink. 'I wonder how he gets by, financially?'

'Bit of security work here and there? I don't know.' Smethurst raises his glass to the barmaid, wiggles it.

'Delores left him.'

'Shouldn't marry, too good for you.' He leans towards Staffe breathing ethanol, says, 'Did you ever . . . ?'

'No I didn't. He's a friend.'

'He's a friend, but . . . ' Smethurst goes serious, looks Staffe in the eye, ' . . . but you're snooping on him. You're snooping on him in the middle of a murder inquiry. Makes me glad to be a friend of yours, Will. Truly, it does.'

He waits for Smethurst to laugh, to make a joke of it, and eventually he does. He slaps Staffe on the shoulder and says, 'Gotcha.' But the truth remains, long after the next few drinks have come and gone; long after Stan Tracey's lad has said 'Thank you' for the last time in the room below.

Staffe settles the tab and punches in his PIN, takes the credit card back, leaving a healthy tip. He refuses a contribution from Smethurst who says, 'Why d'you do it, Staffe? If I didn't need the money — if I had your money — I'd be out of here.'

211

'No, you wouldn't.'

'Believe me, I would.' Smethurst downs the last mouthful and stands down from his bar stool, hitches his trousers up on to his low-slung beer belly. 'Come on, Staffe. What's it all about? What kind of kick do you get out of doing this?'

'Kicks? Mere alcohol doesn't thrill me at all.'

'You what?'

'Cole Porter, Smet. I just get the same as we all do.'

Smethurst shakes his head. 'Say what you like, but it's different for you, Staffe.'

'Can you imagine not doing this?'

Smethurst suddenly looks serious, as if a joke is inappropriate. They make their way downstairs and Smethurst pauses by the entrance. 'You don't do it just because there's nothing else to do. You've got a fire in the belly.' He makes a playful swipe at Staffe's midriff and Staffe pretends to double up, as if he's hit.

They push open the door and make their way out of the club. It is coming a pale, pale light and even in the City's dirty eastern crannies, you can hear the birdsong. Walking down towards Moorgate, the Limekiln tower looms, dark. Smethurst flags down a newspaper van and shows his warrant card. The driver looks daggers at him but lobs a paper to Smethurst anyway. Staffe wonders how much like Smethurst he may become, and whether one day he'll be in Jessop's boat.

'Fuck me!' shouts Smethurst.

Staffe says nothing, just feels his heart plummet as he reads the front page that

Smethurst holds out in front of him.

A photo of Leanne Colquhoun dolled up in bra and panties, takes up half the front page of the News. Above the picture is the headline COVER UP. Below the picture is a strapline, WHO IS THE VENGEANCE MAN?

Leanne Colquhoun is quoted as having told Nick Absolom that not only was she wrongly held as a suspect for her husband's killing, but she was denied her rights as a grieving victim. The pouting Leanne had gone on to say how her sister's house was broken into by a plain-clothes officer without a warrant and she continued to be held in custody after another man, Guy Montefiore, was attacked as part of a serial vengeance wave while she was held.

Then Nick Absolom takes up the reins, postulating that Montefiore's attack was hushed up by the police because they were worried about the consequences of a vigilante superhero doing their job for them.

Staffe feels sick to the pit of his guts as he reads on. He gets a personal mention from Leanne who refers to him as . . . *a bit of a hunk but he's got no clue what he's doing. None of them have got any idea who did for my Karl or this other bloke.*

Smethurst says, 'Pennington's going to have your bollocks for wallets this time. Why didn't you keep her from talking to the press?'

'Give me a cigarette.'

'You're going to need a suspect and quick. This will catch and I reckon London's just about ready for some home-cooked justice.'

Staffe lights the cigarette and drags on it long and hard, goes light-headed. He waits for the nicotine wooze to pass and thinks about the messages he's been sent. 'There will be another, too.'

'What?' says Smethurst.

'Trouble is, they've hit the nail on the head. It is a vengeance thing.'

'One murder and one assault, does not a superhero make.'

'I'll see you, Smet. Thanks for the paper.'

'You won't hold on to this one now, Will. Let it go. She's going to blow-up in your face if you don't watch it.'

★　★　★

The man watches Smethurst stagger off down Moorgate and follows Staffe as he makes his way towards Finsbury Circus, sitting down on one of the many empty benches by the bowling green. The odd stripe of early sun makes it through the office canyons and licks the bowling surface a golden green. Staffe sits forward with his head in his hands for five, ten, fifteen minutes. Then he stands, throws the News into the bin next to the bench. He claps his hands together and says something aloud, striding off, chin up. He looks as though he might be late for an appointment.

The man reaches inside his lightweight cream raincoat and takes out the reinforced 10 × 8 envelope. On it, he has written STRICTLY PRIVATE, FAO NEWS EDITOR.

# Saturday Morning

Staffe has called Tony Ford in. All morning he has been searching for a connection between Ford and Debra Bowker or Leanne Colquhoun, or Nico Kashell, or the Watkinses. Tony has a couple of minor charges from his teens but nothing since Tanya was born. He's not in any political organisations and there's no way of finding out if he has any link with VABBA. Why would he? There has never been any report of Tanya being attacked before. The electoral records come through online and he gets a call that Tony Ford is here and is saying he doesn't want a brief, that he has nothing to defend. Staffe tells them he'll be straight down and runs the filter on the register.

Tony Ford's housing DNA flickers up and shows everywhere he has ever been officially resident. A cursory glance shows he has hauled himself up the chain. From one estate to the next, until he presumably bought one, made a killing and moved into a flat in the Elephant, then made the leap west to his townhouse. But Staffe sees a glitch. For six months, before he moved to the Elephant, Tony Ford, his wife and a young Tanya lived on the Limekiln estate.

* * *

'You've got some fuckin' nerve, you lot.' Tony Ford sits back with his arms folded across his chest and his legs stretched out. Even though he has been trawling the data since early morning, even though he is desperate for a break, Staffe doesn't really want Tony to bite. He wants whoever is doing this to be somebody else — not Greta Kashell or Linda Watkins or Tony Ford.

'You haven't said whether you know them.'

'I don't remember everyone I've ever met.'

'Run me through where you've lived before.'

'Then can I go?'

'Then you can go.'

'Stratford. Dalston. Elephant. Fulham.'

'Moving up in the world, Tony,' says Staffe. 'Moving west.'

'It's what my wife wanted. What's best for Tanya.'

'You wouldn't want to stay on a rough old estate, not with a young child. A young child you'd do anything to protect. Or avenge.'

'The fuck you talkin' about? I never lived nowhere rough. Just 'cause they're out east or . . .'

'I'd say the Limekiln was pretty rough.'

'The Limekiln?'

'Just before you bought your place in the Elephant. You don't remember everything, do you, Tony?'

'It was years ago.'

'You ashamed, Tony?'

He stands up, says, 'You said I could go.'

'I'll ask you once again. Have you ever heard of or met Leanne and Karl Colquhoun, Debra

Bowker, Ross Denness . . . '

'No!'

'Then you can go.'

'What?'

'I've got what I wanted, Tony. I'm sorry.'

'Sorry?'

'To have dragged you away from your family.'

Tony Ford gives Staffe a quizzical sideways glance as he leaves, thinking Staffe might be taking the mick. But he sees straight off that he's not.

'I'm going to find the bastard who did that to your Tanya, Tony. But let us do it. Don't do it yourself. There's enough lives ruined in all this.'

Tony Ford nods at him, looks as if he might be thinking something through.

\* \* \*

Gibbets Lane is a mid-nineteenth-century terrace in the shadow of the Limekiln tower. At six o'clock Errol Regis puts his head out of the front door of number eighteen. He looks left and right down the empty street and ventures out, pulls the door gently behind him. He looks up at the clear, milky-blue sky and walks down towards the petrol station on Old Street. Errol looks older than he is with flecks of grey in the temples of his growing-out prison cut. Even though his father was born in Nigeria and met his mother in Jamaica, three years inside has made Errol's skin go pale. He doesn't even look black any more — to himself. As Theresa said when he came home. 'Ell, you look like you seen a ghost.'

He plays with the keys in his pocket, unaccustomed to the simple privilege of being able to secure the opening of his own door. After three years in Belmarsh, Errol prefers the early mornings, shying away from the tumult of cars and lorries and people whirring through his corner of the city. It's what cons find hardest: the lightning speed of life on the out.

Regis makes his way, nervously, across the forecourt of the petrol station and picks a copy of the News from the plastic shelves outside the kiosk. He looks over each shoulder as he scans the story of a London in the grip of vigilantes. Regis is afraid, skulks into the kiosk to pay.

Three years ago, Errol was convicted of raping Martha Spears, a twelve-year-old girl, in Victoria Park. The girl identified Errol and his DNA was found at the scene. He was already on licence for supplying ecstasy and coke to teenagers in the park. It was a conviction that everybody but Regis wanted and the judge gave him six years. Even though Errol has always maintained his innocence, he knows there are plenty of people who think he'd be better off dead.

★　★　★

'We have to be prepared for another attack.' Staffe is addressing his team. The incident room is packed. 'They've threatened to come back and finish Montefiore off, so we know their appetite's not sated.'

It's ten o'clock on Saturday morning and half the team have families. Most people in the room wouldn't want to be in, ordinarily. But this isn't ordinary. This is front page and hotting up.

'Two attacks, sir?' says Johnson, looking like death warmed up. 'It's hardly a serial killing spree.'

Staffe wants to tell Johnson to 'shut up' but he knows it is time to disclose the Stensson case. He's got an appointment with Pennington in half an hour, when he'll tell the DCI about the Kashell connection.

He takes a deep breath, scans the room as he says, 'There was another case three years ago. It was handled by the Met and a woman called Lotte Stensson allegedly abused a ten-year-old girl called Nicoletta Kashell. The CPS didn't push it and Nico Kashell, the girl's father, got hold of Lotte Stensson in her own home. He broke her fingers, one by one, then her forearms and her shins. The pain killed her.' Everybody in the room has shifted forward in their seats. Some whisper to each other. There is something special in the air.

'Some victim,' says Johnson.

'Call Lotte Stensson what you like. She was attacked, just like Colquhoun and Montefiore. We're here to catch up with the perpetrator, stop them from doing it again.'

'It's kicking off already, sir,' says Johnson. 'We've had a couple of attacks on sex offenders out east. Whoever's doing this is going to be a hero to some people.'

'That's why I want you to get on to every case

219

of sexual abuse the CPS has dropped in the last three years. I want you to get in touch with the defendants and tell them to exercise caution. And I want you to contact all sex abuse cons who've been released on to our patch in the last three months.'

'And what about getting on to the CPS, telling them to reopen some of the cases?' says Johnson.

'We're here to uphold the law, Johnson, not practise it. Chancellor is checking out why the Stensson, Colquhoun and Montefiore cases weren't pursued.'

'The CPS want it on a plate,' says Johnson. 'We bust our bollocks and . . . '

'Thanks, Johnson. We'll just have to keep busting our bollocks, I'm afraid. That's why this job is so bloody rewarding.'

Everyone laughs but they know it's time to knuckle down. For some, this will be the biggest case of their careers. Staffe points them to the coded charts that indicate individual and group tasks.

The team disperses and Staffe waits for the call from Pennington. He reads the potted biographies of Karl and Leanne Colquhoun in the newspaper, so hurriedly woven into a jumbled tale of lost love and heavy-handed policing. Buried in the text is the news that Karl Colquhoun's funeral is on Monday. He makes a note to attend and sees a smeared reflection of himself in his window. He should have shaved, should have a comb to run through his hair.

The buzzer goes and Staffe takes a swig from the Listermint in his drawer and sprays Right

Guard inside his jacket. He slaps himself on each cheek, harder than you'd think you could. It makes his eyes water.

He strides up to the fifth floor, knocks on Pennington's door and turns the handle before he gets a response. Pennington is caught unawares and closes a file quickly. A copy of the *News* is on his desk, covered in lime-green highlighter pen. Staffe takes a seat without being asked and says, 'We've had a break-through, sir. Do you remember Lotte Stensson?' And as he says 'Stensson' he fixes a look on Pennington.

More slowly, he continues, 'There's a connection between Greta Kashell, the wife of the man who killed Lotte Stensson, and Tyrone Watkins. And there's a connection between the same woman and Debra Bowker. I need a warrant to search the houses of Greta Kashell and Tyrone Watkins and I want to pull Debra Bowker in for questioning. We need to fly her over from Tenerife.' He tries a smile but Pennington doesn't let it work.

Pennington picks up the newspaper and shakes it in the air. 'How in God's name did you allow this to happen? We're already a laughing stock and what you're telling me now points to there actually being a vigilante killer out there. We've already had attacks on registered offenders. I want to be quashing these rumours, not confirming them.'

'I'm getting close, sir. They're going to do it again, I know they are.'

'Jesus, Staffe. Is that supposed to be a good thing?'

'The victim will be someone the CPS has failed to convict for a sex offence, and the avenger will be someone from a group called VABBA, Victims Against Being Buried Alive.'

'What!'

'I need a warrant to search their premises.'

'We have one murder and one assault. As far as I know, they're not connected. The second one might be a copycat of the first. That's it! The Stensson case was years ago.'

'Greta Kashell, the mother of the girl that Stensson attacked, is a member of VABBA. Debra Bowker is in her damned address book.'

'Because they've got something in common. Their children were the victims of sexual abuse.'

'Victims the CPS failed to protect.'

'The CPS don't follow through on more than half of their cases, you know that.'

'And Tyrone Watkins was in VABBA too.'

'It's a support group, Staffe. Of course people in similar situations are going to know each other. How do you know about her address book? You've already been into the Kashell house, haven't you?'

'The Kashells are at the heart of all this. I know it. Nico Kashell is doing life for killing Lotte Stensson and there's not a shred of evidence, just the confession he coughed up to Jessop.'

'Jessop! Jesus, man. I thought we'd seen the back of him.' Pennington twiddles with a pen, swivels on his seat and looks out of the window. 'This is a mess, Staffe. A right bloody mess. I thought you'd have learned after the way you brought Leanne Colquhoun in. You're making us

222

look like idiots. You're making me look like an idiot.'

'I've made the connection, sir. These three cases are linked and I'm sure there will be another attack. It will be the biggest case of the year. Not just here in the City, but anywhere in the country. If we give it up, we *will* look like idiots. Give me the resources and the rest of the time you said I could have. That's all I want.'

'You fuck this up, Staffe, and you'll be in the same boat as bloody Jessop, believe me.'

Staffe stands up, says, 'So can I have the warrants?'

'What choice do I have?'

'And the overtime?'

'You can have the team you've already got on full overtime, and a code black on the uniforms.'

'And I'll get Debra Bowker flown over.'

'What if she won't come?'

'I'll just have to persuade her.'

'You still got that golden touch with the ladies, Staffe? I'd heard your powers are on the wane.'

'What do you mean?'

'You call her, Staffe. A tenner says she's not here by Monday. That'll be too late for you.'

Staffe extends his hand and takes a firm grip as the two men shake on the bet, each pretending they're not trying too hard to get the upper hand.

★ ★ ★

'What do you want? I told you everything I know,' says Debra Bowker down the phone.

'There's no point me coming all the way over there.'

'That's not for you to say, Mrs Bowker. Or should I say Mrs Colquhoun?'

'Don't call me that! Are you harassing me?'

'That's an easy card to play, for someone who's got something to worry about.'

'Why would I be worried?'

'I don't know, Debra, but this case is hotting up over here. It'd be interesting to see what the press over there made of an expat's past.'

'I'm calling my lawyer.'

'You do that, Mrs Colquhoun.'

'Stop calling me that!'

Staffe lets a silence develop. He doesn't want to tell Debra Bowker he knows that only a couple of months ago, she travelled to England on her supposedly lost passport, as Mrs Debra Colquhoun.

'You still there?' snaps Debra Bowker.

Staffe softens his voice and brings the mouthpiece right up close. 'Debra, this is something we have to do. We know exactly where you were when Karl was murdered and of course you couldn't have done it, but I'm under pressure to interview you. I haven't really got the time to come to you and I don't want to stir things up with the authorities over there. But I would.'

'When would you want me?'

'The sooner the better. Do you want to bring the children?'

'No. Absolutely not.'

Staffe has the cursor hovering over the 'book

224

now' box on the Albion Airways website. 'I could have a car pick you up tomorrow morning, after your breakfast. I could get you into first class.'

'How long will I be there?'

'Three, four nights? There's a nice hotel in Mayfair we use sometimes.'

'You can't buy me, Inspector.'

'I wouldn't try, Debra. And that's the truth.' He clicks, can't wait to collect his winnings from Pennington.

★ ★ ★

Josie skips down the Leadengate steps, looking excited as she slides into the Peugeot's passenger seat. She smells cool, clean, but there's a smudge of the night to her.

'You look pleased with yourself,' he says, firing up the car, driving them away.

'Pulford told me you've got an E-Type. Why can't we go in that?'

'It's older than me for Christ's sake.'

'You're not looking for sympathy, are you, sir?'

'What do you know about these attacks on the Limekiln?'

'You know there's seven people living there on the sex offenders' register. Seven!'

'How did you get on with the CPS?'

Josie twists to face him, hooks her foot so it's under her bottom. 'The Watkins case was a couple of months after Kashell and according to the CPS, Sally Watkins was all set to go through full disclosure. She had positive psychiatric reports and all the forensics stacked up against

Montefiore. Then she withdrew. Montefiore was charged but released on bail. A trial date was set and all the documentation was ready to go, but the CPS had to let it go because Sally's mother said she wasn't up to it, said the disclosure was acquired against their will. There was an interview directly with Sally. Some caseworker had gone round and not waited for her mum to get home from work.'

'It's procedure getting in the way of justice.'

'The point is, it was the Watkins family that didn't put Montefiore in the dock, not the CPS. And it was the same with Nicoletta Kashell. It was only a few weeks earlier that Greta Kashell stopped the CPS from interviewing Nicoletta. It was Nico Kashell that reported the assault by Lotte Stensson, not the mother. Don't you find that funny?'

'There's such a thing as being in denial. And I suppose it fits. The father takes her in, gets the case prosecuted. The mother steps in, protects her daughter the only way she knows how, by stopping the assault from being raked over and over by the likes of Stan Buchanan. And the father can't cope. He needs his vengeance, so he goes out and gets it.'

'But he gets caught and he's banged up. That means he can't be connected to Montefiore or Colquhoun,' says Josie.

'Greta Kashell joins VABBA and hooks up with Tyrone Watkins and Debra Bowker, maybe even Leanne Colquhoun.'

'Who would feel strongly enough to string these people together?' says Josie.

'Maybe it's not a case of which one of them is behind it. Maybe it's all of them. I bet Debra Bowker pulled the disclosure on what Karl Colquhoun was doing to his kids. She had no faith in us. Then she met someone who could show her a way. Let's go and see Greta Kashell. She was the first.'

★  ★  ★

Errol Regis wipes his mouth and looks into the toilet. He pulls the chain and his vomit spirals away. This time last week he was conducting his ablutions in the presence of another man, on Belmarsh's vulnerable wing, 'Fraggle Rock' to the rest of the prison population. Errol had no choice but to 'go vulnerable', put himself in with the kiddie fiddlers and the rapists. He was doing a six-year for raping Martha Spears, but he was also claiming he was innocent. Cons can't stand that, pretending you're better than them, so Errol had to do his time as an innocent man amongst the lowest of the jail's lowest scum.

Now, the week he gets out, the radio prickles with vengeance. There have been more vigilante attacks this morning, some of them up on the Limekiln, and as he takes his copy of the News into his damp Victorian parlour from where he can look up at the Limekiln tower, he practically hears the hot breath of the righteous on his neck. He is on the Register. Anyone who cares could find him. And he can't just move away, start again. If he misses his probation meetings, his licence will breach and he'll be back inside for the other half of his six-year tariff. It might be the safest place, but innocent men don't walk back into jail.

Theresa Regis comes downstairs in her dressing gown and sits on the edge of the threadbare sofa. She looks up at her husband and Errol can see she doesn't believe he didn't do it. She says she does, but he knows her too well.

Most men, when they get out of jail, are like dogs with two dicks. Errol hasn't laid a hand on Theresa yet. The first night, when she rolled over and hooked her leg over his, she rubbed herself up on him. She put her hand on him. There wasn't so much as a twitch.

Poor Theresa started to cry, and so did Errol. He asked if she wanted some cocoa and she said, 'Is it 'cos I'm too old, Ell?'

When he saw Martha Spears all beaten up and cowering in the dock as she testified against him, something inside Errol died. The man who did it to her is out there and doing it still. We all need someone to blame but Errol can't blame young Martha.

'Can I make you a cup of cocoa, love?' he says.

Theresa picks up the paper. She reads about Leanne Colquhoun and Guy Montefiore and someone out there who can't take any more rough justice and is taking matters into their own hands. She says, 'Make yourself one, love.' As she says it, tears run down her cheeks. They cut dark, crooked lines on her smooth, dry, black skin and as she looks up at Errol with sad, wide eyes he knows that she's going to leave him. Who can blame her?

★ ★ ★

From the caff opposite the petrol station at the end of Gibbets Lane, the man watches Theresa Regis close the gate behind her. Sirens warp in the Saturday traffic and Errol Regis waves his wife goodbye but her head is down, chin tucked into her chest. She pulls a garishly green, moulded plastic suitcase. The man feels sorry for her and he knows that she will be better off without Regis. The world will be a better place without him and if someone had done this three years ago, Martha Spears would be more than a basket case.

This might be the last of his obligations. He doesn't know her Errol's movements yet, hasn't pieced together that repeating pattern of behaviour, but he will cut the fourth rope. Sooner than he'd like, but we don't live in an ideal world.

Theresa Regis has barely got on the bus before a police car turns into Gibbets Lane. It stops outside Errol Regis's house and a uniformed officer makes his way up the path. If only they protected the innocent with such vigilance.

★ ★ ★

Greta Kashell asks to see Staffe's ID, apologising that she hasn't had the best experiences with the police. She reads the search warrant thoroughly before letting the DI and Josie into her Raynes Park home.

They work their way through the house and Staffe reminds himself to ask which room is which. In the box room, Staffe fires up the computer and Greta watches as he makes his way through the directories. He goes back and forth from the desktop, into Works and out of it. There is no address book, no *Contacts* icon. 'We'll have to take this away, I'm afraid. I'll try and get it back to you by the end of the week.'

'I need it for my work.'

'Don't you have a memory stick you can use?' he says.

'Yes,' and as soon as she says it, Greta Kashell diverts her eyes, from Staffe. He nods to Josie and she moves across to the door, to make sure Greta Kashell can't get out, can't follow Staffe as he goes to find the device. She calls out after him, 'It's in my handbag. Don't go tipping the place upside down.'

When he returns and plugs it into the USB port, she looks for all the world as if she has nothing to fear.

Staffe goes into the *Contacts* file.

'What's VABBA, Greta?' says Staffe.

'I've forgotten.'

'And DB? This is a Spanish number.'

'Why disguise her name?' says Josie.

'I did it when I heard about Colquhoun.'

Staffe lets the cursor drift over the file icon and sees when it was last amended: the day Karl Colquhoun was murdered. Not the day after, nor

230

the day it was reported in the press. Somehow, Greta Kashell knew Karl Colquhoun was dead within an hour of him taking his last, fear-sucking breath.

'I can understand that, Greta. And when was the last time you spoke to Debra?' He can practically hear the calculations whirring as Greta thinks about telephone records — and what will Debra Bowker's version be?

'Three years ago? Something like that?'

'When you were grieving.'

'The grief doesn't go away, Inspector.'

Staffe waits for Greta to look away, gives Josie the nod to step in.

'Where did VABBA used to meet, Greta?' says Josie.

'Somewhere out in Surrey, I don't know.'

Staffe knows she's lying. Now, he's not so much interested in the information she provides as how tangled her lies become. He tries to forget that Greta Kashell is the mother of a raped daughter, the wife of an incarcerated husband.

'And who else went to VABBA, Greta?'

'I've been in and out of therapy having my head churned up twice a week and you expect me to . . . '

'Don't worry, Greta. Don't worry.' Josie explains that she will have to go with them to Leadengate.

And as Greta tries not to fall apart, Staffe calculates when he might spring the question as to whether she knows Tyrone Watkins. Information is everything and when they don't know you know what they know — you wait.

Josie hooks her arm through Greta's and leads her down the stairs, out of her own front door. Staffe tries to convince himself that he's a good guy.

*　*　*

At Leadengate, Greta refuses tea, says she can't wait for the duty solicitor. 'I have nothing to fear from the truth. I need to get back. Saturday night is our busiest night.'

'You heard what happened to Debra Bowker's ex-husband?'

'Don't ask me to mourn him.'

'Do you read the *News*?'

'Why would I waste my time?'

'When was the last time you saw Tyrone Watkins?'

Greta Kashell looks in her lap and plays with the clasp of her handbag. 'He was already broken when I met him. He wouldn't do it.'

'Do what, Mrs Kashell?'

She looks up, her eyes narrow to fierce slits. Ice cold. 'Do what's right, Inspector. If only he could have.' She opens her handbag, takes out a small red diary and asks Josie for a pen and a piece of paper. 'Tell me the times, Inspector, and I'll tell you where I was.'

*Times*, thinks Staffe. 'Where were you when Lotte Stensson was killed, Mrs Kashell?'

'I was on the psychiatric ward of St Thomas's Hospital.' She gives him a priest's look. 'Some might say I'm mad, still.' Then she checks the dates that Josie gives her and accounts for where

232

she was when Karl Colquhoun was killed and Guy Montefiore tortured.

* * *

Jessop welcomes Staffe and Josie in. Staffe wishes he could be anywhere else, but he has to dig deeper into Jessop's involvement with Greta Kashell and VABBA, and possibly Guy Montefiore. Jessop looks wasted, as if he's been drinking steadily, forever. Bizarrely enough, he is clean-shaven and doesn't smell like a tramp.

'Sorry about the smoke. Sorry it's a shithole, I suppose,' says Jessop to Josie as he chucks a couple of old *Racing Posts* off the only armchair in the room and ushers her to sit. Once she is settled, Jessop sits on a large, intricately carved wooden box that looks as if it hails from North Africa — doubtlessly one of Delores's purchases. It saddens Staffe to think that it must have some kind of sentimental value — for Jessop to have negotiated its retention. Jessop lights up. 'I'd offer you tea but I don't do hot drinks.' He looks at Staffe. 'Not a whisper for three years and now twice in two days. You're spoiling me.'

'It's the Kashell case,' says Staffe.

'You don't say.'

'Nico Kashell took Nicoletta in to press charges. He started the disclosure.'

Jessop nods, furrows his brow. 'The mother didn't want the child to be traumatised, if I recall correctly.' He sucks hard on his cigarette and coughs out a thin spray of smoke. He punches

233

his chest and smiles at Josie. 'His life ended the day Lotte Stensson did what she did. If you can accept that, everything makes sense.'

'What were the two of them like, together, Nico and Greta Kashell?' asks Josie.

'I can't say I remember seeing the two of them together.'

'Did he blame her, for withdrawing Nicoletta from pursuing the case?'

'I'm pretty sure he thought our idea of punishment wouldn't have helped him or his wife, let alone the daughter. A couple of years in jail for Stensson, then a lifetime on the social.'

Staffe says, 'People who do what Lotte Stensson did — allegedly did — are damaged. They need help, regardless of what harm they inflict. Most sex offenders have . . .'

'I know, I know. The cycle of abuse. Try telling that to Nico Kashell.' With his heckles up, life comes back into Jessop's eyes. 'The Kashells did what they did out of love. Not hate.' Jessop runs his fingers along the tight curves of the box's carved filigree pattern. He has a faraway look again and his words reprise what Montefiore said to Staffe just yesterday.

Jessop raises his eyes, makes a thin-lipped smile and Staffe wonders what Jessop thinks of him — the person he has become. He tries to conceive what might be left of the young man Jessop took in all those years ago.

'Whoever is doing this has called me, at home. They've been at my car, too. There's been messages.'

'Looks like you're all sucked in, Will. And

giving them what they want?'

Staffe stands up, knowing he isn't going to get what he came for. Josie follows suit, waits by the door and watches Staffe and Jessop shake hands, awkwardly. She says to Jessop, 'You know, Greta Kashell said a strange thing to me. She said that for her it was like being buried alive. She said for victims it was always the same, they are always being buried alive.'

Jessop scratches his jaw and life glimmers in his watery eyes. 'There was a group, if I remember it right. She might have been a member of it. Victims Buried Alive. Something like that.'

'You don't know where it was, do you? Where the group met?'

He smiles at Josie, as if he has seen something he likes, shakes his head. 'It's not a time I like to remember. I don't know if Staffe has told you?'

She looks quizzically at him, shakes her head to try to preserve his self-respect.

'It was my last case. I didn't leave on the best of terms.'

'He's told me a lot about you, sir,' says Josie. She lowers her voice, says conspiratorially, 'You've a lot to answer for.'

Jessop laughs and Staffe shoots a look of mock disparagement at Josie.

'There's lots we could all be called to answer for. Will's not one I'd be ashamed of.' He looks at Staffe. 'Not when I knew him, anyway.'

'What do you mean?' says Staffe.

'I hear things. Like that last case.'

'Golding? He's guilty,' says Staffe, indignant.

235

'I'm sure he is, Will. I'm sure he is.' Jessop smiles and reaches out, places a big hand on Staffe's shoulder and squeezes it. 'We have to uphold the law. That's all we have to do.'

'We have to go,' says Staffe and as they make their way down the stairs, through the blare and aroma of ragga and crackpipes, Staffe says, 'Nice move. Catching him about VABBA, like that.'

'Deception is nothing to be proud of,' she says.

Staffe's phone goes and he sees it is Leadengate.

'I've checked out Greta Kashell's alibis,' says Pulford. 'She's clean as a whistle.'

'Good,' says Staffe.

'It's weird, isn't it, sir. A case where you don't want to catch a break.'

★  ★  ★

When they get to the Villiers estate, Josie looks around, says, 'You can never know what goes on in these estates. So many doors and windows and secrets.'

Staffe reaches on the back seat for the Tesco Metro bag — fast goodies he picked up en route.

'What is all that stuff?'

'Just repaying a favour.'

'You really think Tyrone could have done for Montefiore?'

'He's a better prospect than Sally. I can't see her thinking up how to rig those ropes.'

Sally lets them in. She looks wasted and slopes off into her bedroom, doesn't even look at the warrant that Staffe shows her. Tyrone is propped up with cushions in front of the widescreen.

There's a tin of corned beef on the coffee table in front of him, half eaten with a fork sticking out of the pink and brown meat.

He looks up at Staffe and Josie as if he's never seen them before and flicks from one channel to another, to another.

'We've come to have a look round,' says Staffe. He shows the warrant but Tyrone doesn't look away from the screen.

Staffe knows what he's looking for and goes straight to the kitchen drawers. There, exactly where it was, is the dog-eared leaflet. There's no address, no meeting time, no contact name, just the same 0207 telephone number as on Greta Kashell's database. He takes out a plastic bag and tags the leaflet. While Josie looks in the cabinets in the lounge and goes in to have a look round Sally's bedroom, Staffe unpacks the Tesco bag and finds a bowl. He combines two table-spoons of mayo, a squirt of ketchup and the king prawns, then butters four rounds of the wholemeal bread. He constructs the sandwich and cuts the crusts off, slices them into triangles and arranges them neatly on a plate before washing up after him. When he throws the packaging away, he sees a syringe in the bin under the sink and it makes his heart shrink.

* * *

It is Saturday afternoon and London has come out to play. The 4 × 4s are cruising up and down Clapham High Street and the tables outside the cafés and bars are teeming. It seems for all the world as though there is nothing to get hung about. Debra Bowker will be touching down at Heathrow soon. She is being met by Pulford and will be available for interview within a couple of hours. As he weaves his way to Leadengate, Staffe's phone goes again.

'Staffe?' says Jombaugh.

'What is it?'

'I'm afraid there's some bad news. Gloucester Road nick have been on. Your flat has been broken into. They've not taken anything, but I think you should take a look. There's some . . . they've written something. It's on the walls and the officers who went round say they reckon it's been written in blood.'

Staffe punches the steering wheel and switches lanes, takes the first left he can back towards the north side of the Common. As he drives as fast as he can to Queens Terrace, he thinks about what Jessop said about upholding the law, about Sohan Kelly being 'taken care of' by Pennington.

The main door is undamaged and the uniformed officer tells him that access into the building was gained by someone who must have a key. He's spoken to all the other residents and one of them had a briefcase stolen on Wednesday. There might have been a spare key in the case.

When he gets to the door to his flat, the frame is splintered all around the lock and the officer sucks his teeth as if to say 'You should know better, sir. You should at least have a double lock.' Going into the lounge, there is no sign of a break-in and it's the same in the kitchen. The only evidence of an intruder is saved for the bedroom wall. There, above the bed, is written in red:

**done soon. over to you**

★ ★ ★

Errol Regis sits at the small, Formica-topped table in his kitchen. Out the back he can see the cloudless blue of the City sky. The willow tree in the yard somehow flourishes. It has dusty trumpets of dirty white bloom and he can't remember it being there before he was sent down, can't remember much of how it used to be before the police came knocking that day, accusing him of interfering with poor Martha Spears. And then came the evidence — from God knows where.

A pile of letters are on the table. Most are from his various solicitors. Theresa's letters petered out soon after her visits did. She made her last visit the day after he wrote to tell her his appeal had been turned down. It seems she had more faith in the law than she did in her husband.

He goes into the cupboard under the stairs and finds an old can of lighter fluid, sticks it into the back of his jeans which are too baggy for him now. He gathers together the letters and slips into the yard, looking left and right as he goes. It feels strange to be living your life in open view of people you don't know. In jail, everyone's in the same boat. Here, it seems so random, the people you rub your life against. He makes a pile of the letters in the grid by the back door, figures that if it makes too much smoke he can always pour water on it. He squirts the lighter fluid on the papers, strikes a match and drops it, watches it go with a whoosh!

Errol feels a lump inside him melt. It rises up from his belly into his throat. It spreads into his lungs. He struggles to catch his breath and then he begins to wail. He cries like a child who doesn't really know what it's screaming for, just that something it desperately needs is missing from its life.

The sun has dropped below the high fence and somebody in one of the neighbouring yards calls through to ask what's wrong. Soon after, someone from an upstairs window shouts for him to shut the fuck up and Errol Regis, as has become his wont, does as he is told and takes it inside.

★   ★   ★

'This sounds like an accusation, sir,' says Staffe.

Pennington is sitting in Staffe's chair. Staffe stands, hands in his pockets, like an errant schoolboy.

'You're tied up in all this more than is healthy for any of us. First, they call you at home when they've tortured Montefiore. You shouldn't have gone in on your own, but you did. And there's the cryptic messages on those photographs. You started grubbing around in the Stensson case and checking up on Jessop. And now your flat is broken into with a message daubed in blood. And there was your car, too.'

'How did you know about that?'

'Who exactly is this case about, Staffe?'

'It was sheep's blood, sir.'

'So bloody what? Whether you like it or not, you're involved. You're personally involved.'

'I'm leading the investigation. This is all about the investigation. It goes back to when Lotte Stensson was killed. That was when Karl Colquhoun was accused of messing with his kids. It was when Guy Montefiore assaulted Sally Watkins. And I'll wager that it was when VABBA was set up.'

'I've had over a dozen cases of people on the sex offenders' register being hounded out of their homes. I've got two of the thugs downstairs. And Karl Colquhoun was killed this week, not three years ago, if it's slipped your mind.'

'I'm right, sir! I'd stake my . . . '

'Your reputation, Staffe? I hope you've got more than you're telling me. I'm glad it's not my reputation.'

'I've tracked down the property that VABBA used to operate from. And Debra Bowker's in the country. She's on her way from Heathrow.'

'She was out of the country when her husband was murdered, for God's sake.'

'You said I could have a week. You gave me your word.'

Pennington leans back in the captain's chair, puts his hands behind his head. 'There's something else, Will.' He gives Staffe a doleful smile.

'What is it?' Staffe feels tight in the stomach.

241

'The Police Complaints Authority have opened a file on that young scrote's allegation the other night.'

'The e.Gang? You know that's a load of crap.'

'We have to go through due process.' Pennington stands up.

'Because of Sohan Kelly.'

He walks past Staffe. 'Three days, Will. I gave the commissioner my word. You want me to keep my word, don't you?' As he leaves the room, he hands Staffe a ten-pound note. 'That's for getting Debra Bowker over here. Don't say I'm not a man of my word.'

Pennington has left his residue on and around the chair. Not unpleasant, just the smell of another. Staffe opens the window and rings through to Johnson for the trace on the VABBA number. 'The line was disconnected two and a half years ago, sir.'

'Find out who the freeholder is and check the tenancies in that building over the last three years.' He's about to ask Johnson how he is faring when the buzzer goes.

Pulford says, 'We're back, sir. I've got Debra Bowker here. Just giving her a sandwich and a cup of tea.'

Staffe clicks Johnson off and says to Pulford, 'Take her to interview room three when I say so. Get Josie to stay with her in the meantime, and make sure everyone's got their kid gloves on.'

'Stan Buchanan's the duty solicitor.'

'He's got a conflict of interest. He represented Leanne Colquhoun.'

'He says the charges against Leanne have been

dropped. He's not budging, sir.'

'I'm coming down.' As he makes his way downstairs, Staffe visualises Debra Bowker and the things she might be capable of.

He has to go into reception and out the other side to get to the interview suites. As he does so, he clocks the familiar shape of a man being processed by Jombaugh. The man sneaks a peek at him, pretending to scratch his ear and the instant he turns away, the penny drops.

It is Ross Denness, the very man who, in the Ragamuffin pub, told Staffe that Colquhoun had got what was coming. And now, Debra Bowker — who had left the country because of Karl's derelictions against her kids — and Ross Denness are in Leadengate nick at the same time.

Staffe goes straight on through to room 3, which is empty, and he calls Jombaugh. 'Don't say my name, Jom. Just tell me what charge code you've got on those two in reception.'

'It's a section 43, sir.'

'On a sex offender, just say yes or no.'

'Yes.'

'Under no circumstances whatsoever is Ross Denness to be released. And get him out of reception. Quick!'

★  ★  ★

'Debra? Take a seat,' says Staffe, taken aback by Debra Bowker. She has the permatan he expected, but almost everything else disarms him. She is wearing a smart cream suit with a

243

mid-thigh skirt and her hair is shiny and straight — a hundred quid cut is his guess. She has perfect teeth and her skin looks in good nick, despite the sun. 'This is my colleague, DC Josie Chancellor.' The women nod and exchange thin smiles.

'I've seen the *News*. Looks like that alley cat hasn't changed her spots. Leanne always would turn a trick for a couple of quid,' says Debra Bowker, her East End accent stretched to the breaking point of how posh it can go.

'Let them ask the questions, Mrs Bowker,' says Stanley Buchanan. 'And refer to me before you answer.'

She turns, slowly, to face Buchanan. 'I have nothing to hide, Mr Buchanan. I volunteered to come here and if it is all right with you, I'll tell the truth.'

'Of course we tell the truth, Mrs Bowker.'

'It's 'Miss'.'

'Of course,' says Buchanan.

'When did you drop the Colquhoun name, Debra?' says Staffe.

'The day I kicked him out.'

'And you got a new passport, I dare say.'

She takes out her passport and shows it to Staffe. He takes it and smiles, flicks to the back page and notes that the passport replaced a stolen one. He makes a written note of the missing passport's number. As he hands it back, he sees Stanley Buchanan beginning to fret, so he hits them with it. 'Your other passport wasn't stolen, was it, Debra?'

'I never said it was.'

'Aah. Never mind.'

'Never mind what?'

'That you just said you were here to tell the truth and that you told the passport officials your Colquhoun passport was stolen. And you told us you hadn't been back to England since you left. Yet Budjet Air had a Debra Colquhoun on one of their flights this April. And she stayed ten days.'

Debra Bowker smiles at Staffe. 'I found the passport and never thought anything of it but then I got the chance of a cheap flight. I keep all my valuables in a safety deposit box over there and it was a Sunday. I couldn't get to my new passport.' She doesn't blink, she doesn't look away. Her voice is calm and unwavering. 'I'm sure you can check that it was booked on a Sunday.'

'You seemed to loathe the name so much, though, Miss Bowker.'

'I loathe *him* enough for a name to mean nothing. I changed the name for my children.'

'Why lie to us when we asked you if you had been back to England.'

'Because I knew it would bring you back snooping. I soon realised it was naive of me to imagine you wouldn't get your nails in a little deeper. It was an error.'

'Do you drink, Debra?' says Josie.

'A little too much, probably.'

'And did that cause you any problems, when you and Karl were together?'

'He caused me enough problems. A few too many glasses of vodka doesn't count when you

245

look at what he did to my children.'

'Did you drink to get at him, to damage him?'

Debra Bowker looks at Stanley then quickly away. Stanley says, 'I hardly see why you're wasting my client's time with this.'

'You know about Karl, the way his father used to beat him. The other things he did to Karl.'

'You're not going to get me to feel sorry for him.'

'The things he did to your children, who can blame you if you tortured him.'

'Torture?'

'You said you took the children away as soon as you found out, Debra,' says Staffe.

'Of course. And you lot did nothing. Nothing!'

Josie says, 'But that wasn't the start of the bad times between you two? Not if you were drinking and he hated it so much.'

'It's no mystery that if I hadn't got pregnant, me and him would never have been together. It was a mistake.'

'Two mistakes.'

'I tried to make us a family. I tried to make the best of a bad job.'

Staffe scribbles a note and slips it to Josie. *Get Denness and sit him outside.* He waits for her to go and says, 'We're nearly done, Debra. I know you weren't happy with the way the allegations against Karl were dealt with by the police and the CPS. However, we're trying to do our jobs as well as we can and there have been other incidents drawn to our attention.'

'That poor Watkins girl. I read it in the *News* on the way over here. Let's hope that bastard

Montefiore gets what's coming properly this time.'

'Tell me about VABBA, Debra.'

Without the faintest hesitation or flicker, Debra Bowker says, 'It didn't work. For me, it made things worse, getting together with people who just wanted to keep going over and over the worst thing that's ever happened to you. They were hooked, some of them. They let the grieving replace what they loved. That's no way to carry on.'

'Can you remember who went to VABBA?'

'A whole bunch of people who got more and more into that victim 'thing'.' She makes speech marks in the air and shrugs.

'Specific people, Debra.'

'It was a while ago. There were only one or two I ever got on with. One was a man, funnily enough. Tyrone. That's Sally Watkins's dad. He was in bits, poor soul. Like me, he was trying to put it behind him.'

'Anyone else?'

'A woman called Delilah. I forget her surname but she was a black lady. A real lady.'

'Why was she there? How had she suffered?'

'Her daughter was raped. Poor Delilah. She wanted to go out and kill the bastards. That's why I left, truth be known. I'd've ended up doing time when it should have been him.'

'But you couldn't have killed Karl, could you, Debra?'

She smiles. 'If only I could have been there.'

Staffe thinks, *If only someone had videoed it!* 'Would you have paid someone to kill him, Debra?'

'Maybe,' says Debra.

'Miss Bowker!' says Stanley.

'To stop him doing it again?'

'That was Leanne's problem. I told her, what more could I do?'

'Why do you hate her so much?'

'He'd been seeing her for two years while he was still with me. He was lining up her kids while mine were getting bigger. When I found out about, you know, what he did to Kimberley, I told Leanne and she told me to 'piss off'.'

'You must have dreamt of getting back at him,' says Staffe as there is a tap on the door and Josie sidles in.

'And ruin my children's lives more? I've found better things to do than having that dirty bastard get his comeuppance.'

'Thanks, Debra. We might want another word while you're here. We really appreciate you coming in.'

'That's it?'

Stanley looks at Staffe as if to say 'Was that it?' and as soon as Debra Bowker gathers her handbag up and makes her way to the door, he says, 'I forgot. What about a woman called Greta? Greta Kashell? Did you ever meet her at the group meetings?'

'Greta? I didn't like her one bit. But you didn't need to ask me that, did you, Inspector? She calls me every so often. You wouldn't be doing your job if you didn't know that, would you?' And she winks at Staffe.

'Why don't you like her?'

'She gives me the creeps, that's all. If you take

my bastard husband as the exception, I'm not a bad judge of character.' As she says it, she smiles. Then she opens the door and sees Ross Denness. The smile disappears. His too.

'Do you two know each other?' says Staffe.

'Never seen her,' says Denness.

'How about you, Debra?'

'I've seen him, when I lived on the Limekiln. He's that bitch's cousin.'

'You're Leanne Colquhoun's cousin?' says Staffe, looking at Denness, recalling that he claimed not to know her.

\* \* \*

As she slides into the car, Debra Bowker lifts her feet in the footwell of the Peugeot's passenger seat and looks down at the drinks cartons and discarded newspapers. Staffe says, 'Don't worry, there's nothing important down there.'

'I didn't want to dirty my shoes,' says Debra Bowker and she gives him a mischievous wink. 'I take it you're single,' she says, looking across at him. She casts her eyes down and back up. 'It's nothing to be ashamed of.'

'How's your room?' says Staffe, looking over his shoulder and pulling out into traffic.

'It makes me feel like a tourist.'

Staffe thinks that she's a cool customer, whether or not she has anything to feel guilty about. For most people, simply visiting a police station makes them feel as though they are a criminal. Most wouldn't feel like jaunting around to see the sights.

'I might even go up the Trocadero later,' she says.

Staffe laughs out loud, says, 'I could drop you.'

'Come with me, Inspector. You look as if you need to loosen up.'

'I don't do 'loose',' he says, looking across at her, smiling.

She leans forward in her seat, frees up the back of her hair and her scent wafts through the front of the car. Staffe can't imagine her and Karl Colquhoun together. He can't imagine Linda and Tyrone Watkins together. He wonders at mothers like them fashioning some kind of improvement from the terrible things that happened to their daughters.

'You've not always been single, Inspector?'

Staffe brakes and eases himself forward, takes a peek down at how the traffic is on Queensway. 'I've always . . . ' He looks in the wing mirror, pulls into the bus lane, gets bad looks and V-signs from the stationary drivers.

'Always?' she says.

He looks across at her, watches her expression soften. Suddenly, she looks as if she could be easily hurt. 'Always preferred to ask the questions. It's my job, Miss Bowker.'

'A man can get too much of his own way.'

Staffe pulls up outside the Grafton and leans across, pushes open Debra Bowker's door. 'Like I said, we'll need to speak with you again.'

'It's his service on Monday. Are you going?'

'Are *you* going?' he asks.

'I wouldn't miss it for the world.'

'Have you seen his mother yet? Maureen.'

'I've got nothing against her.'

'It's just that she didn't even know you'd moved away. I think she'd like to hear how the children are. I could get my colleague to take you.'

'I know the way.' Bowker gets out of the car and reaches back in for her handbag. 'Thanks for the lift. And for not being a bastard.'

'I wouldn't know how,' says Staffe.

'Don't spoil it by lying, Staffe.'

'Staffe?' he says, but she shuts the door, walks through the Grafton's revolving front door; he moves off and parks up in the underground car park. There's only one way out of the Grafton and the Alma Café is straight opposite. He takes his accounts out of the glove compartment and decides to spy on Debra Bowker for an hour or so.

★   ★   ★

Staffe's accountant sent him the papers three weeks ago. It only takes an hour to check them over, but there are always more important things to do. He orders a double espresso and a slice of Dutch apple pie and looks across to the Grafton's entrance, then down at the profit and loss account. The figures look extraordinary. The rental income is twice his salary but everything is not what it seems. Deductions take their toll: interest payments; sinking funds for repairs, renovations and rental voids; management company's fees; accountants' fees; bank charges; and a provision for the taxman.

He looks back out at the Grafton with the

figures swimming around in his head and takes a sip of the coffee. It is scalding and bitter and a much-needed slap to the system. It makes him crave a cigarette. He looks back down to the next page, sees a breakdown of the monthly income and makes a note to let the accountant know not to expect anything from the Kilburn flat now Marie is staying there.

He turns to the balance sheet and sees how much this part of him is worth, after the building societies have been taken care of. The noughts look absurd, make him feel alone.

In the corner of his eye, the shape of Debra Bowker shimmers. She doesn't look out of place. Somehow she has managed to narrow the gap between the Limekiln and Mayfair. Staffe tips out all the change he has and swigs back the rest of the espresso, follows Bowker up towards Piccadilly.

She turns the occasional head as she clips her way up Grafton Street on stiletto heels. Turning on to Albemarle Street, Bowker disappears from view and Staffe has to break into a trot, stepping off the kerb to widen his angle of view and as a taxi comes towards him, he sees her disappear into the Albemarle pub. Staffe remembers the place from years ago when he had a night on the tiles with Georgie Best. Not exactly a collector's item, but one to remember.

There is a snug on the left as you go in and a large back room through a small corridor. Staffe waits a few minutes to make sure Bowker has not just gone in to use the toilet. It is a strange place for a woman to come. He glances into the snug and sees her at the end of the bar, his pulse quickening on the way through to the back room as he glimpses Debra talking to another woman, younger than her and blonde. At first, he thinks she is Sally Watkins. Surely not.

In the back room, Staffe gets himself a spot at the bar and angles himself away from the small gap that shows through to the snug. The same staff serve both bars and from here he can see the back of Debra Bowker, a three-quarter profile of Sally Watkins. Except it's not Sally Watkins. Is it Leanne Colquhoun? He's sure of it. Or is he going mad?

He orders a pint of Carling so as to fit in and risks another look. Debra Bowker is neither smiling nor frowning. If it is Leanne Colquhoun, surely there would be some kind of a row going on. He takes a slug of the beer and steals another look through to the snug.

Leanne has spent some of Nick Absolom's thirty pieces of silver on a new look. Her hair is cut on to her shoulders and the blotches on her face have been vanished.

Two things concern Staffe: firstly, Debra Bowker and Leanne Colquhoun are in earnest conversation with no sign of a fight brewing; secondly, he mistook Leanne for Sally Watkins — Leanne being the woman he first thought might be the figure behind the hood in the photograph of the butchered Karl Colquhoun.

He takes a second and final swig of the lager and leaves, quitting for now while he is ahead.

★ ★ ★

'He's not here,' says Becky Johnson, down the phone.

In the background, Staffe thinks he can hear Johnson calling out to see who it is. 'Funny, the station said he left. Never mind. Do you mind if I pop round, Becky?'

'There's no point.'

'How are things?'

'Don't you know how things are, Will? Things are crap.'

Staffe wants to ask if she knows all about her husband, but knows he can't. There's a muted kerfuffle on the other end of the phone and he says, 'I'm only round the corner.' And he hangs up.

When he gets to Milford Street, at the wrong end of the Holloway Road, Staffe braces himself for crossfire. He's known Becky since before Johnson came across from the Met but in the last few years, since Charlie was born it would seem, she has become increasingly resentful and cold. Maybe it's because the London allowance doesn't scratch the surface of their outgoings and the pension is a speck on the horizon. Up front and large, Becky Johnson represents the frustrations of a CID widow.

'I told you not to come round,' says Becky, standing in the doorway with Charlie clasped to her hip. His Teletubby sweats are clearly handed down and smeared with God-knows how many meals.

'I just need a quick word with Rick.'

'I told you.'

'It's all right, Becky. Show him in,' says

Johnson from behind her. He is wearing a T-shirt and boxers, has a duvet draped over his shoulders.

'He's done in, Will. Can't you see?'

In truth, there's little to deny. Johnson looks like death warmed up.

'Just a quick word, about Sally Watkins,' says Staffe.

Becky calls the children through from the lounge, to take them into the bedroom. The lounge is open-plan to the kitchen and a decent size, but there is a cot in the corner and it's easy to see that the place isn't big enough for a family of five.

Young Ricky leads the way. He is six and runs at Staffe, head-butts him in the stomach and throws his arms around the waist. It is an act of affection disguised as aggression. Staffe ruffles his hair and throws a few play air-punches.

'Don't wind him up, Staffe!' calls Becky.

Sian follows — the oldest. It is all too juvenile for Sian who has an adult's face. She walks past, head down and glum; Staffe can remember when she was a happy-go-lucky little thing.

'Are you OK, Sian?' He beams a smile at her.

She says nothing. Staffe looks at Johnson who looks at the carpet.

'You look terrible, man,' says Staffe once Becky has closed the bedroom door on the mayhem.

'Thanks,' says Johnson.

'You corroborated Sally Watkins's alibi, didn't you?'

'I wrote it up.'

'Just tell me if you didn't follow it up.' Staffe

listens to the commotion in the next room. 'We can change the paperwork.'

'She was with some bloke off the estate. He's married. I didn't want to go busting his family apart but it stacked up. What's the problem anyway? You can't finger her for the Montefiore case, surely.'

'No. Colquhoun.'

'Colquhoun! Why'd she do anything to him? She never knew him.'

'Tyrone Watkins knows Debra Bowker.'

'I don't get it.' Johnson sits down on the edge of a threadbare sofa and pulls the duvet tight around him. He's shivering.

'We can manage without you for a day or so. I'll see you Monday, Rick.'

'A whole day off, why thank you,' says Becky Johnson, leading the children out of the bedroom.

Staffe tries a stoic smile out on Becky as he walks towards the door but gets nothing back. He wants to ask how the Chinese was the other night, but says nothing. Just as soon as Janine gets back to him about the syringe, Staffe will have words with Rick. He daren't think about the action he will have to take.

As he leaves, young Ricky is trying to wrestle Sian to the floor. She fends him off, disinterestedly. Tiny Charlie hits Ricky on the back of the legs with a fish slice and Becky Johnson starts up on her husband before Staffe can close the door behind him. As he does, Sian looks at him with wide, sad eyes, as if to say she can't live like this much longer.

# Saturday Night

Ross Denness has been brought in for assaulting one of his neighbours, a five-feet-four 'rag-head' who was supposedly on the sex offenders' register. Josie has checked it out and the victim is not, nor has ever been, on the register. As if Saturday nights in the station weren't bad enough anyway.

'The fuckin' register's wrong, innit,' says Denness. 'Everyone knows what goes on with them Moslem bastards.'

Staffe raises his eyes to the duty solicitor who shrugs as if to say, 'Don't blame me. I don't get to choose my clients any more than you do.'

'Even if he was on the register, assaulting him is still a criminal offence.'

'You sayin' the law protects him more than me.'

'You tell me how you know Debra Bowker. Tell me why you never told me you are related to Leanne Colquhoun and then we'll see what the law's got in store for you.'

'I've been here hours. You charging me, or what?'

'Did she tell you what he was doing to her kids? Ask you to sharpen him up, did she?'

'You know where I was when that happened,' says Denness with a smug smile. He leans back, puts his hands behind his head.

'You knew Karl when he was with Debra

Bowker and you never liked him then. Debra told you he was more interested in her kids than he was in her. That's right, isn't it, Ross? Were you giving her one?'

'Inspector, please,' says the solicitor.

'Well?'

'Might of,' says Denness, unable to resist.

'Who'd blame you', says Staffe, 'for getting involved.'

'Involved?'

'Maybe you can sleep on it, Ross.' Staffe stands up, makes to leave.

'You can't just hold me here like this.'

'An officer will be in soon, to charge you with actual bodily harm and inciting racial hatred. For starters.'

'You bastard.'

'Mr Denness,' says his lawyer.

'Keep it coming, Ross. Keep it coming,' says Staffe. 'It's all good for business.'

Denness's smug grin falters; he looks as though he can tell Staffe isn't interested in the ABH.

Staffe pauses by the door. 'Should be right enough for a two-to three-year sentence. You ask your friend here,' says Staffe, nodding at the duty solicitor. 'With your history.'

'It was self-defence,' says Denness. 'I've got a dozen witnesses.'

'Just like for when Karl Colquhoun was killed. Best we let the courts make sense of it, eh?' And Staffe turns his back on Ross Denness for a final time tonight. He's had as much as he can take for one day and decides to kill two birds with one bottle: in the Steeles with Smethurst for a bit of R&R and Met networking.

On his way out, he calls Pulford, tells him to chase up the Sally Watkins alibi and get it re-corroborated. Pulford sounds down, but Staffe lets it slide. He can't afford to get sucked into being another man short, so he says he's breaking up and clicks his DS dead.

*   *   *

Errol Regis has spent sixteen hours sitting in his mother's old rocking chair in the window of his front room, praying for Theresa to walk down the street. He doesn't think he can bear a life all on his own.

At three o'clock some men came to fix the porch roof of the house next door, except nobody lives there any more. Errol opened the top window of his front room to let in the smell of the burning tar. He likes the smell but in the end he had to shut the window because it reminded him of Theresa. She couldn't bear the smell. At four, he made tea: two mugs instead of one and he put out ginger biscuits even though he doesn't like them. He's been eating them fifteen years and never said a word.

The men went away but they left the tar burning in a small tin drum over a Calor ring. Just half an hour ago, a man in a donkey jacket came along to check everything. He went away and left the ring burning, still. Errol wanted to ask him why, but he didn't have the nerve. He thinks something might be afoot so he turns off the lights and gets a blanket to spread over his legs. He turns the radio right down and dials the number for Leadengate Station. He lets it ring once then hangs up, rests his finger lightly on the redial button.

Later, drifting in and out of a troubled sleep, Errol wakes. Thinking he can hear somebody knocking on his front door, he draws his knees up to his chest, feels his body tighten. His head pounds and he thinks he hears steps, fading away. He waits, musters the courage to go to the window and peers through the gap in the curtains. He sees two people disappearing and thinks they are police but he's not sure. He checks the doors are locked, front and back, and resumes his position in the chair.

On the hour, Capital Radio tells him that the attacks on sex offenders on and around the Limekiln have abated. Men have been apprehended and order is, for now, being restored.

\* \* \*

Smethurst is already in the Steeles when Staffe gets there and before he can say what he wants, Smethurst gives the barmaid a wink and puts up two fingers. Two halves of bitter arrive together with two large Jameson's. She is the same barmaid who served Staffe and Josie the other day. She fixes her hair, puts a hand on her hip and smiles.

'You get it in the neck from Pennington about the Leanne Colquhoun story?' says Smethurst.

'I can handle it.'

'And what about the complaint, from that gang. I heard the PCA are involved.'

'That's my business.'

'Word is, the Montefiore and Colquhoun cases will be with AMIP before the weekend's out.'

'No chance. I'm getting there.' The AMIP rumour, the Area Major Investigation Pool, is news to Staffe. He downs his Scotch in one.

'How d'you make that out? Some victim support group and a bunch of people with rock solid alibis.'

'Everybody knows each other. Even Ross Denness, Karl Colquhoun's workmate, is Leanne Colquhoun's cousin. And we've had him in for beating up a supposed sex offender.'

'He's got an alibi right?'

Staffe thinks about Sally Watkins and Johnson's cock-up over the corroboration of her alibi. He doesn't want her to become a real suspect.

'How's Johnson bearing up?' asks Smethurst.

'Why d'you ask?'

'He's got mates at the Met. I hear he's got problems at home. Word is, he's struggling. And that young pup, too.'

'There's nothing wrong with Pulford.'

'You can be *too* loyal, you know, Staffe.'

'I'm not *too* anything,' says Staffe.

'Course not.' Smethurst clinks glasses, says 'Chin chin', drains his beer and throws his head back, laughing. 'I'll drink to moderation.'

'Bastard,' says Staffe, following suit, trying not to think about the PCA and AMIP.

'You're a different man since you split up with that Sylvie. All uptight.' Smethurst laughs again.

'Maybe being single doesn't suit you.'

The barmaid sets down another brace of braces. She smiles at Staffe. Ever since he went to see Jessop, this case has taken him back. Towards Sylvie? If he was to see her, just once and for old time's sake, it might somehow help the case.

'Staffe?' Smethurst is looking straight at him, obviously talking to a deaf ear.

'Sorry,' says Staffe.

'Hit a nerve, did I?'

'I've just got to make a call,' says Staffe, getting up from the bar stool and making his way outside. It's coming up to last orders but it's still warm out — revellers spilling round the bench tables.

He scrolls down through *Calls Received*. Sylvie comes up and his thumb makes contact with the green *Call* button but just as he applies the telling degree of pressure, the handset vibrates in his hand and he gets the incoming call, hears his sister's voice.

'What's wrong, Marie?'

'Nothing. Nothing at all is wrong. It's exactly the opposite.'

'What is it?'

'I wish Mum and Dad could be here.'

'Have you been drinking?'

'I've had a couple, but . . . '

'What do you want?'

'Paolo's asked me to marry him.'

'Are you mad?'

'I think I am. I just wanted to say thanks, for letting us have your place.'

Staffe clicks the phone dead and curses into the hot night. As he turns to go back into the pub he thinks he hears someone shout his name. He spins round and looks up and down Haverstock Hill. There're some youths in a bus shelter on the other side of the road, but a bus pulls up. Staffe thinks they might be the e.Gang. Then he thinks he's being paranoid. When the bus pulls away, the youths aren't there.

He marches back into the pub, barging into a couple of youths by the door. They're holding bottles as if they are weapons and say something he can't make out as he passes them. 'Fuck yourselves!' he says, turning on them. They take a step back, in formation. One of them looks familiar, but Staffe can't place him. When he gets back to the bar, Smethurst says, 'Jesus. Looks like we're going to need a couple more.'

'Get them in,' says Staffe, looking towards the youths at the door — who have disappeared.

★　★　★

When the Steeles won't serve them any more, Staffe and Smethurst make their way out. They're the last by a long chalk and in the middle stages of disrepair. As she makes the way to her minicab, the barmaid gives Staffe a friendly pat on the back. 'Look after yourself, sweetheart,' she says.

'I can look after you, too,' he says. 'I'm a policeman, see.'

'I don't think you mean that,' she says, smiling. She gets in the minicab and it pulls

263

away, past a group of youths hanging around in the car park. Even though he's half cut, Staffe recognises two of them from the pub. They smirk and another youth appears from the back of the group — the one who claims Staffe stabbed him outside the Ragamuffin.

'Shit,' says Staffe, instinctively feeling the cut on his wrist.

'What's going on?' says Smethurst.

'It's that shitbag who's got me up on that PCA. Leave this to me.' Staffe takes a step towards the gang, shrugs off Smethurst's attempt to restrain him. 'What the hell do you want with me? And how do you want it? Two or three of you will get it. You know that.' He looks them each in the eye, one by one and when a bottle gets thrown from the back, smashing at his feet, he knows he has a chance. That's a coward's move, a gang mindset. He plants his feet, shakes his arms down and turns his palms to face them, as if to say 'Come on'.

The gang mumble to each other and Smethurst moves alongside Staffe, says, 'And the rest of you we'll bang up. I've seen you. All I need is to call up your file and your girlfriends'll be in line, too. It's an offence to pimp your girlfriends, boys.'

'Wo! You can't say that. No way, man. This is harassment.'

'Who threw the bottle?'

The youth from the other night is smirking. He says, 'We not causing no trouble, man. When we bring you trouble, you won't see or hear us, pussy.'

Staffe takes a step forward and the youth doesn't flinch. The gang gathers tight around him and Staffe thinks he hears the metallic shift and lock of a gun being braced. His heart misses a beat and his legs go weak. Smethurst must have heard it too because he whispers, 'Fuck off out of here. Now!'

The youth smiles as he sees police bravado turn to mush. The law just hasn't got the weaponry these days and he takes a step forward. 'Don't think Jadus gonna lie down and take your white justice. We know about Kelly, man. Don't matter if it's from his brief or his bredren — things will come level.'

The gang take a step up and Staffe feels Smethurst tug at his jacket. Beyond the gang, a car swerves across the road. Its lights come straight at them and Staffe holds his breath, not knowing which way to jump. The youth looks round and the gang follow suit.

'Fuck, man!'

The car's brakes screech and it mounts the kerb between the gang and Staffe. He recognises the MR2 and although Pulford calls for them to 'Get in. Bloody get in!' the gang have begun their retreat. Staffe squeezes in behind the front seats and Smethurst gets in the front. As they tear off in the cram-packed Toyota, a missile hits the boot. 'Shit,' says Pulford, 'I hope that's covered on police insurance?'

'Isn't it Mummy's car?' says Smethurst.

'Do you want to walk?' says Pulford. Then under his breath, 'You fat bastard.'

'What the hell were you doing there?' says Staffe.

'There's something I need you to see,' says Pulford.

'But how did you know I'd be there?'

'I'm supposed to be a detective, remember?'

* * *

They dropped Smethurst at the Boss Clef and carried on up to Pulford's flat in Southgate with Staffe recounting the run-in with the e.Gang.

'If you don't mind me saying, sir, maybe you'd be better off not drinking, with everything that's going on.' He pulls the car up sharp, pulls into a parking space.

Staffe looks up at the grey-rendered, inter-war semi with its red-tiled, half-hexagon bay window on a long curving street, all the same, and says, 'You live *here*. I just mean, I thought you'd live somewhere . . . else, I suppose.'

'Somewhere hip?' Pulford locks the car up and ushers Staffe towards his front door. 'There's plenty you don't know. Wait till you see this.'

Inside, Pulford shows Staffe up the stairs and into his first-floor flat. In the small living room there is a blue-grey glow from a computer screen, but Pulford heads straight to the tiny galley kitchen and puts the kettle on. He makes the coffee strong and hands it to Staffe.

'I don't need to sober up, you know.'

'I didn't say you did.' He logs on to the Internet.

Staffe picks up his coffee and sits alongside Pulford, watching the web make itself available. 'Every four seconds, someone hits a child-porn site. Did you know that?'

'I told you,' says Pulford, busy with the mouse, taking the cursor round the screen double-quick, with the speed of youth. Staffe blinks, trying to keep up. The coffee makes him grimace. 'Now, look at this.' Pulford leans back in his chair, blows out his cheeks. 'Just look at this.'

'Jesus!' says Staffe. 'What is it?' The screen is cut into four segments. Top right is the photograph of Karl Colquhoun. Bottom left is Montefiore. Bottom right is a blur that Staffe can't make sense of but in the top-left quadrant is an image which Staffe has never seen before. It is a face he feels he should know, but doesn't.

'You don't recognise her? Top left?' says Pulford.

'I do and I don't.'

The woman's face is hard and pale. Her hair is blonde, the skin grey. Her eyes are closed but pain is written all over her still features. 'I'm pretty sure this is an autopsy photograph. See the slab in the background?'

'It's not . . . '

'It's Lotte Stensson, sir.'

'What the hell is this site?'

'Look,' says Pulford, pointing to the web address at the top of the page. *vengeancevictims.com*

'Victims?' says Staffe.

'VABBA?' says Pulford.

'What's going on in this bottom right section?'

'I can't make sense of it but I think that's the point. It's not decided yet.'

'Oh my God,' says Staffe.

'They want us to see it here first, sir. It's going to be a live execution.'

'Can you find out where this site is coming from?'

'I've got a techie working on it, but I didn't know if you wanted it to get back to Pennington.'

Staffe's pocket vibrates. The telephone screen tells him he has missed calls: Sylvie and Pennington. He curses under his breath and calls Pennington. Even though it's nearly midnight, his boss sounds bright as a button.

'Aah, Staffe! You've got one hell of a sense of timing.'

'I'm sorry it's so late, sir.'

'No. I was about to call you. I need to see you at the station. We've got a problem. Quite a problem.'

'There's something I need to tell you, sir. About a website.'

'Vengeance something dot com?'

'What!'

'We've got the News to thank, Will. I've got Nicholas Absolom here with me now. They're being civilised about the whole thing, Will. Very civilised. But I would like you to get here as soon as you can. Absolutely as soon as you can.'

Pennington hangs up and Staffe can imagine him showing a brave face to Absolom, the forced smile straining to break into a snarl. Suddenly, Staffe feels the booze catching up.

\* \* \*

Nick Absolom is heroin thin in a skinny-fit Paul Smith suit: legs crossed in the manner of a faux intellectual and his hooded eyes slightly shut. He talks through a pursed, superior smile and regularly reinstates the centre parting of his fop's hair with a slow sweep of his left hand. He says, 'I have to tell you, Inspector Wagstaffe, I think this should be our front page.' He reaches into the pocket of his suit jacket and unfolds a tabloid-sized piece of paper with a photograph of the website and a headline:

## MURDER
## WHILE YOU WATCH

Underneath the image of the website is the strapline:

## BRITAIN'S FIRST SNUFF-CAST?

Staffe takes the sample page from Absolom and scrutinises it. He swallows his pride, says to Absolom, 'It's good of you to pull it. In the public interest.'

'It's not in the public interest,' says Absolom.

Pennington sighs.

'You know how incendiary it is out there. How did you get hold of this anyway?'

'I'm an investigator, just as much as you.'

'Don't flatter yourself, Absolom.'

'Staffe!' shouts Pennington.

Staffe scans the front page mock-up.

**Child rapists drop like flies as vigilantes cut and crucify their way through London's long, hot summer. But what should the police do? If you**

**were a copper, in a world where the guilty
are set free and the innocent are left to a
slow, slow death, what would you do?
Just ask yourself.**

He looks long and hard at Absolom, who stares
him down in turn. Neither man gives an inch.
Neither blinks. Pennington sucks hard on a
plastic cigarette. Eventually, the silence snaps.

Absolom says, 'Say what you like, the public
have a right to know. I'm only representing
conventional wisdom.'

'Isn't it convenient that it just happens to be
raising your profile. Climbing over dead bodies
to get yourself on to the ladder. How gallant of
you.'

'Are you talking about the bodies of child
molesters set free by the state? Well I do
apologise. Maybe we should do more to protect
the likes of Karl Colquhoun and Guy Montefiore and Lotte Stensson.'

'Lotte Stensson! How do you know about
her?'

'I don't doubt that you're probably quite good
at your job, Inspector Wagstaffe. But that's not to
say I can't be too. She's right there in the top-left
corner of the web page. It's not rocket science.'

'How exactly did you get hold of that web
address?'

'We're a long way from me having to tell you
that. And you'd have to disprove that I happened
to simply stumble across it.'

Staffe looks back at the front page, reads again
about the slow death of the victims and wonders

270

how much Absolom might know about VABBA.

'You should thank Mr Absolom, Will,' says Pennington. 'This has bought us some time to regroup.'

*Regroup?* thinks Staffe, fearing the worst.

'Will you be reassigning the case, Chief Inspector?' says Absolom. 'You did say we could have first run with the next big break on the case. This would be a start.'

'You're nothing but a muckraker,' says Staffe.

'I am simply establishing a debate about the nature of guilt and innocence.'

'You're inciting anarchy.'

'And the release of known sex offenders into the community, simply because the pursuit of justice doesn't meet your budget, doesn't contribute to anarchy?' Absolom snatches the front page off Staffe and stands up. He's not smug. He looks genuinely angry and slowly folds the page back, sliding it into his pocket. 'You were lucky this time.' He looks at Pennington. 'If this had anything to do with justice, anything at all, you'd be choking on my words over your cornflakes tomorrow morning. Now, can I assume that this case is being reassigned?'

Pennington nods. He gives Staffe a resigned look. 'Detective Inspector Wagstaffe will remain attached to the case but it is now under the control of AMIP.'

'The Area Major Investigation Pool? Who will be in charge?'

'DI Smethurst.'

'Of the Met? And where will it be based?'

'Hammersmith.'

'What would you like to say to my readers, should they ask why it took so long for the Met to take the lead on this case?'

'Synergy,' interrupts Staffe. 'Evidence has emerged connecting the murder of Karl Colquhoun to a case which the Met allowed to lapse. Three years ago. You can ask Smethurst if you want any more.' Staffe watches Absolom shake Pennington's hand and leave. 'So I'm off the case, then?'

'Like I said, Smethurst will run the AMIP squad.'

'I've just had another run-in with the e.Gang. I told you they know all about Sohan Kelly.'

'He's untouchable.'

'Untouchable?'

'Don't fuck with me, Staffe. You can go.'

Staffe makes his way down through the building into the night. As he goes, he looks through the windows. Outside it is black, pinpricked with bits of life going on all over the city.

# Sunday Morning

'Did you sleep in those clothes, sir?' says Josie in the entrance to the Queens Terrace flat. She is holding a brown paper bag and a copy of the *Sunday News*.

Staffe rubs the sleep from his eyes and goes back into the flat, calls out, 'Don't just stand there. Come in!' In the kitchen, he puts mound after mound of coffee beans into his grinder. The machine roars and Staffe rubs his temples with his free hand then takes a slug of water from a Guinness pint pot.

'Do you want one?' he says, holding a white china mug up.

Josie nods and gives him a curious look, as if to say, 'You're supposed to be pissed off.' 'What will you do now Smethurst is in charge?'

'It's not about being in charge. It's about catching this person before they get to whoever is in the bottom right-hand corner of that web page.' He jabs his finger at the *News*' front page. 'What have the photoanalysts said about the images?'

'Anybody could set the website up. It's a ten-quid, standard web-camera lens. But get this. The original location where the domain address was bought, was Guy Montefiore's computer. It was his landline.'

'And they used his credit cards, too?' says Staffe.

'Yes.'

'Where's the transmission coming from?'

'The image is too blurred. They reckon they've got some kind of gauze over the lens. But the techies think it might be a building, an outside shot. And it's in our time zone. It came light the same time as London.'

'Gauze?' Staffe downs the rest of the pint of water, pours himself another. 'What are you up to today?'

'It's Sunday, but I don't suppose I have any say in the matter.'

'How do you fancy breaking and entering?' Staffe taps the back of a chair at the kitchen table, inviting Josie to sit down. 'I'm going to grab a quick shower then we'll get off.'

'What are you going to do about Montefiore?'

'Montefiore? Why would I do anything about him?'

'Aah,' says Josie. She looks at her feet, clearly embarrassed.

'What's happened? Josie?'

'Last night, just after eleven, he was attacked, in his bed at the hospital. A porter disturbed them but they got away.'

'The bastards! Pennington didn't say a bloody word. I was with him last night. Sod them! Sod them all!'

As he goes into his bedroom, Josie can hear him banging and cursing, then a mobile phone rings and the place falls silent. Staffe speaks and closes a door and Josie is left to drink her coffee in a resounding lull.

Staffe's heart beats double time. 'I don't really know,' he says. His stomach turns, slowly, super-slo-mo. He sits on the edge of the bath and takes a deep breath, feet tapping sixteen beats to the bar.

'What made you call me?' says Sylvie.

He stares blankly at the wall and sees the tiles as if for a first time. They are cheap and white but the border course is handmade, from Cordoba. He bought it from a shop in Acton when he first got the flat. When Sylvie saw the tiles she asked if they were his choice and said he had taste. 'That's obvious,' he had said, running his hand up her back, pulling her towards him.

'The Cordoban tiles are still here.'

'What?'

'I'm in the bathroom, Vee.'

'Will, you're being weird.'

'You said you liked the tiles and I said . . . '

'Have you been drinking? You're not drinking again, are you, Will?'

'I haven't had a drink all day.'

'Will!'

'I'm joking.'

The line goes quiet and he thinks he can hear her sniff. She says, 'I said you had taste and you said that was obvious. You touched me. I have to go, Will.'

'I need to see you, that's all.'

'Will . . . '

The phone goes quiet. Just hearing her voice transports him back through the years. His words stick, like a nervous kiss. 'What is it?' he says.

'If you wanted to see me, you should have just said.' She says the time and place and the phone goes quiet again.

Staffe summons the courage, takes a deep breath, and says, 'Sometimes, I really miss you, Vee.' But the line is dead. He can't fathom whether she heard him or not.

★   ★   ★

Staffe and Josie drive east along Embankment. The sun is low and golden, casts long shadows down the road to Westminster. It could make you believe in a yellow-brick road; the queues for the Tate are already snaking down towards the river promenade. Staffe wishes that just once he could have an ordinary Sunday morning that took in the papers and a gallery; a late, long lunch in a dark pub on the river and then a fifties film or the cricket highlights.

Instead, he hangs a right at the Albert Bridge and winds his way against the traffic, on to Kennington Lane.

Josie says, 'It's over there. Above the estate agent's. Take a right after the pizza place. It leads up to Cleaver Square. I used to have a boyfriend who lived there. We can get in the back way.'

Staffe wants to know about the boyfriend. Why they split up. Was he good to her? Maybe she cheated on him.

'Here. Just here,' she says.

Staffe parks, peruses his catch-all ring of keys.

The back way in is easy enough. The entrance to a block of flats juts out and he obscures himself in its nook while he heaves himself up, scuffing his shoes as he clambers. He scrapes his shin on the ridge bricks but with a final effort he is over. The padlock on the gate is standard and Staffe soon finds a key on the ring that unlocks it. He lets Josie in and slides back the bolt.

Steel stairs lead to the first floor and as they climb, Cleaver Square comes into view. People walking dogs or sitting on the benches, lolling in pairs at the tables of the pub that's not open yet. The higher they get, the more Staffe and Josie are exposed. Staffe knows if he's caught, he'll not just be off the case. Suddenly, he feels weak.

The first key he tries doesn't get close, so he has to bend down, look into the aperture of the lock then inspect the keys.

'Staffe!' hisses Josie.

He puts the key to the lock and it goes all the way in, but it's too late. Below, a man with a dog on the other side of the road has stopped while his dog takes a shit. He calls up, 'Breaking in, are we? I should call the police.' He's smiling.

Staffe calls out, 'We are police. And if you don't clear that shit up, I'll have you doing community service.'

The man's smile goes and he looks down, forlorn, at the pile his dog has just produced. Staffe turns the key and pushes the door open. He looks down, watches the man scurry away, leaving the dog's mess for somebody else to cope with.

Inside, three doors lead off the dark corridor

with its threadbare brown carpet. The place is musty and Staffe opens the doors as he goes. There is a small kitchenette with two bugs in the washing-up bowl, then a toilet, and finally a large room with two floor-to-ceiling windows looking down on Kennington Lane.

'This place hasn't been used for months,' says Josie.

'Let's hope it's not been used since VABBA were here.' He looks through the drawers of a cheaply veneered reproduction desk. 'You check the filing cabinet.' The drawers of the desk are empty, save a few paper clips and some dog-eared menus to the local takeaways.

'I've got a bad feeling, sir.' Josie drapes her short suede jacket on the back of a velour wingback. It slips off, unnoticed.

Staffe picks up the phone and gets a dead line. There is an old fax machine on a low table but it has no papers, in or out.

'There's nothing at all in these,' says Josie.

'What a waste of time,' he says, looking at the desk. In its left pedestal are three drawers; he crouches down, pulls the empty drawer out completely and sets it down on the floor.

'What are you doing?'

Staffe gets down on his knees and reaches into the drawer's void with his outstretched hand, dragging his cupped palm back towards him. He feels scraps of paper on the rough plywood. The detritus will have fallen down the back of the drawer when it was once overloaded and he scoops it out. As he sifts, cross-legged on the floor, Josie stands by the window, pulls the dirty nets to one side and looks down for danger.

The pile of papers comprise yet more menus and an A5 VABBA flyer, a Tube map of London and a child's picture of their school with matchstick figures waving and big yellow smiles on their faces. There is also a telephone bill, from 2006. He flips through the pages quickly and sees that the bill is itemised. He smiles to himself and slides it into the inside pocket of his jacket. Finally, there is the torn wedge of cheque-book stubs. He puts the stubs into his hip pocket and stands up, slides the drawer back into its void and says, 'Nothing. Let's go.'

They leave quickly, closing all the doors as they go. Josie peers through the narrow gap of the cagily opened outside door. Down below, standing outside the gate are two men in suits, looking up. They see Josie and she gasps.

'What is it?'

'There's two men down there. They saw me. I think they're waiting for us.'

'Shit!' He sighs and opens the door, shows Josie through. He follows her down the iron steps, raising a hand to the waiting men and sussing out who they are. He slides the bolt of the gate and goes on to the street, extending a hand to the older of the two men. 'Wonderful day.' The man takes his hand but before he can say anything, Staffe says, 'You're from the estate agency.' He looks the man right in the eye and smiles. 'You don't remember me? We used to be the tenants. Just looking for a copy of the old lease.'

'Ah. Right,' says the older man.

'We thought we'd better check,' says the younger one, looking Josie up and down, fidgeting with his tie.

'Better safe than sorry,' says Staffe, thinking how desperate for business these poor souls must be, working on Sunday.

'I thought we had all the keys,' says the older man.

Staffe taps his pocket. 'The lawyers said to give them back to them. They need to do an inventory.' He crosses the street and waves a hand at them as he goes, walking past his car. He keeps going towards the square, touching the cheque stubs, and considers a good thing he could do.

\*  \*  \*

'Will!' says Marie, standing back from the Kilburn doorway and opening her arms, inviting him to hug her. She is beaming all over her face and for a moment, as she wraps her arms around him, he surrenders to the softness of her small body. Her head nestles in the crook of his neck and shoulder as she squeezes him.

'I can't say how glad I am, how pleased I am about you letting us use your place.' She stands back and holds him, still, by the hips. 'Come and say hello to Paolo.'

'Marie, there's something I need to do.' He puts a hand in his jacket, fingers the fat cheque he has come to give her.

'Me too.' She holds his hand and leads him into the lounge. He can smell drink in her wake,

280

even though it's not yet midday. The sun streams into the lounge. Takeaway cartons litter the coffee table and there is a bottle of vodka on the floor by Paolo's chair. Which is Staffe's chair. The man who once beat his sister is sitting, one leg draped casually over the other and rolling a cigarette, in Staffe's chair. It is an American-style spoonback he paid two hundred for, fifteen years ago.

'Hi, Paolo.' Staffe tries not to stare at the yellowing bruises.

'Dude,' says Paolo without getting up.

Staffe wants to tell him to be careful with his cigarettes on the chair but he thinks twice. Then he says, 'Watch those cigarettes on the chair.'

'Will!'

'It's valuable.'

'Don't be like this,' says Marie.

'No worries, man,' says Paolo. His yellowed eyes hood down, heavy, and even though he is clearly southern European, he has an affected New World, upwards intonation to his speech.

'I'm not being like anything, Marie.'

Marie retreats towards the door and beckons Staffe to follow her. 'Can't you see we're happy!' she hisses. 'Can't you be happy for us?'

'I'd like nothing more,' says Staffe. He takes hold of her hands with his and squeezes them softly. 'Really. Believe me. I just worry about you.'

'It sounds like you're worrying about your furniture.'

He takes hold of the cuff of her loose-fitting, bright and swirly, long-sleeved hippy blouse and

281

runs his hand up along her arm. The sleeve of the blouse ruches up, shows her pale, naked arm. He holds the sleeve up with his left arm and with the right he touches the yellowing bruise. 'These didn't come from the good fairy,' he says.

'I don't know what you're trying to say, Will, but he loves me and I love him. If you don't want us here, we'll go.'

'I didn't say that.'

'Sometimes, Will . . . '

His mobile rings. It's Josie and he decides to ignore it.

'I'm happy for you, Marie. Honestly I am. I just know what . . . '

'And I know what you're like, Will. You're not exactly a role model when it comes to relationships, are you?'

He wants to tell her that he wishes he'd done more to help her when their parents were killed. He wants to have someone else to blame for the way she has turned out. 'Marie . . . ' He hears a *whoosh!* And something hits him on the head. Something soft. At the top of the stairs, Harry is standing with his hands above his head as if he has scored the winning goal at Wembley.

Staffe holds out his arms and as Harry runs down the stairs, he drops to his knees. Harry launches himself from the fifth step and Staffe catches him. He holds his nephew tight and hears his own words vibrate on the boy's head as he says into his ear, 'You look after your mummy, Harry. Look after your mummy.'

He knows that if he gives her the money, Paolo will blow some of it. But he also knows that some of it will make things better for her and Harry. He cradles Harry in one arm and stands up, pulls out the cheque. 'I want you to have this, Marie. Here, take it. Please.'

She looks at it, trying to be casual, but her eyes go wide. She narrows them as soon as she can. 'It's too much, Will.'

'It's for you and Harry.'

'But not Paolo?'

'I'd better go.'

'I'm trying to make us a family, Will. Say goodbye to Paolo.'

Staffe looks back into the room, sees Paolo burning a corner of his hash resin. 'He's got other things on his mind,' says Staffe and as he lets himself out he can hear Marie sounding off at Paolo. He chastises himself for stirring things up, then chastises himself for not stirring things up more. He makes a quick prayer that his sister comes to no harm and clicks open the car but before he can get in, his mobile goes off again. He answers without looking. 'Hi Josie.'

'It's not Josie,' says Pulford. 'We've had some bad news. Nico Kashell tried to top himself last night. They've been asking what we said to him, saying we should have told them to put him on suicide alert.'

Staffe looks back up at the flat and wonders what damage he might be leaving in his wake. He gets in the car.

'How did you find out?'

'The governor rang me. We're on Kashell's visits list.'

'Nobody else knows?'

'Not yet.'

'I'll tell Pennington. You say nothing.' He shuts down his mobile phone and turns off his police radio, leans back in the Peugeot's driving seat and rests his head. He closes his eyes and breathes deep, in, out. Deeper. In, out. He pictures the air in his lungs burning clean, burning to a shining silver and his pulse slows, slows further until he opens his eyes, looks at the VABBA phone bill. The only number he recognises is Debra Bowker's. The call was made eighteen months ago. Not necessarily sinister.

As he drives, he takes out the cheque stubs, flicks through, wondering if he needs a trace putting on the account. Pulling on to the High Road, with the winos and Sunday shoppers stumbling and milling, he puts the brakes on, pulls in. The car behind blares its horn, swerves and gives him the V's. But Staffe doesn't care. He's looking at the blue-black fountain ink figure of 50,000 on one of the cheque stubs. Underneath is a single letter, '*J*'. The date is 20 September 2005 — a week before Nico Kashell reputedly killed Lotte Stensson.

★   ★   ★

'You look like shit, Rick,' says Josie.

Johnson holds the mug of tea in both hands. He looks like death warmed up. They are in a cafe opposite Smithfield market, just round the corner from Leadengate. It's old school, from the days before the media and City types took

284

the area over with their offal eateries and gastro shacks.

'Thanks, Josie. I feel a lot better for that.'

'How are the kids? Still keeping you on your toes?'

'Smethurst gave me a ring, says he wants me on board the AMIP ship. You too?'

Josie nods.

'And what about Staffe?'

Josie studies her empty cup of coffee. Bites her lip.

'What is it, Josie? What's he done now?'

'I need to get hold of him. I think I might have dropped a bollock.'

'Tell me.'

She takes a deep breath. 'We broke into some premises and I left my jacket there.'

'Which premises?'

'You've heard him talk about VABBA?'

'He's still barking up that tree, is he?'

'We didn't find anything. You won't tell Pennington, will you? Or Smethurst.'

For a moment he has a devilish glint in his eye, then the tiredness bites back. 'You know, Josie, you can tell me if he's dragging you deeper than you want to go. I can help.'

'It's not dragging me deeper that worries me. I think he might be going out on his own.'

'Upriver?' says Johnson, mainly to himself. He looks outside and a slow cloud rolls a shadow over the market. He can't remember the last time he saw a cloud in this stifling summer. He shivers, pulls the jacket across his chest and calls for the bill.

★ ★ ★

Prison Sundays are bad news. It is twenty-three-hour bang-up for everybody bar Christians and as he is shown across the yard to the new healthcare wing, Staffe sees a gaggle of the prison faithful slouching towards the chapel, all smoking, all with an effortless profanity on the tips of their tongues. Surprising, how popular God can be.

'Thank God for his next-door. He could have been a lot worse,' says the duty governor.

Staffe feels a pang of guilt for the prints he left on Nico Kashell's desperate prison life. 'I'd like to speak to his next-door.'

'Wedlock?' The governor shoots a wry smile. 'It doesn't quite work like that, Inspector. Maybe we can arrange an interview some other time.'

The governor flicks the keys from his pocket and catches them in mid-air. He selects one from a ring of many and twists as he puts it to the lock and kicks open the heavy steel door. He does the whole thing without breaking his stride. Staffe wonders how many tens of thousands of times a year he does the same thing.

'He's up and with it,' says the governor, 'but I can't let you have more than ten minutes. He's weak.'

'How did he do it?'

'Hang and slash. He meant it all right. The inmates call it double bubble. You hitch up to the top of the window, plaited sheet around the neck and then you slash up along the wrists with two safety blades wedged in a toothbrush and kick the chair away. Bleed as you swing. Luckily for Kashell, Wedlock was listening out, heard him saying a prayer. We reckon he must have sounded the alarm even before Kashell slashed up.'

'Not exactly a cry for help, you'd say.'

'Oh no,' says the governor, striding into the hospital reception, picking up the visitors book and scanning down as he shows Staffe to Kashell's bedside with a slow sweep of the arm. He hands Staffe a pen and indicates where to sign the book. 'Ten minutes. There's an alarm bell above each bed and an officer back on reception.' And he's gone.

Kashell has dark rings around his eyes and dressings on each of his wrists. 'Can't you leave me in peace?'

'Didn't your blessed revenge bring you the peace you thought it would, Nico?'

'You wouldn't know the half.'

'Or is that it, Nico? Is it only half the story, when you take someone's life. Once they've gone, you can't forgive them, can you? Is that what you really want, to forgive, to let the hate go?'

'Quite the philosopher, aren't you?' Kashell is propped up in bed, his head on plumped pillows and a half-drunk glass of blackcurrant juice on the bedside table. A CCTV camera is fixed to the ceiling.

'Or maybe I should be asking these questions of the person who actually killed Lotte Stensson.'

'You are.'

'Last time we talked you wished you could bring her back.'

Kashell has a picture of Nicoletta next to the

287

glass of juice. She smiles out at them. Looking at the picture, he says, 'It can't be right — to make yourselves as bad as the people who do the bad things.'

'You're not a bad man, Nico. And that's the problem.' Staffe thinks about what he has heard. 'Yourselves.' Not 'yourself'.

Kashell looks down at his bandaged wrists. His jaw goes weak and his bottom lip trembles. It seems as though he has to summon a last drop to raise his eyes. His voice is weak. 'If there is a loving God, he must love the badness in us, just as much as the goodness. How can we live in such a world?'

'Who is J, Nico?'

'What you talking about?'

'Someone you might have paid, to help you.'

'I don't know.'

'There were no signs of a forced entry to Stensson's house. It was a professional job, or someone she knew, someone she trusted. You didn't know her, did you, Nico? How did you restrain her?'

'She's a woman.'

'Did you tie her up?'

'It was a long time ago.'

'Where did you get the chloroform from, Nico?'

'Shut up!'

'And the hammer? Which hand did you start on?'

'Nurse!'

'It's OK, Nico.' A nurse appears in the doorway and Staffe stands up. 'It's OK,' he says to the nurse. He waits for her to come forward, to stop him upsetting her patient any more, but she doesn't. Instead she crosses her arms under her breasts and nods her head, mouths the words, 'Go on.'

'It doesn't make you a bad man, to have not killed her. It doesn't make you a better man to be in here, doing someone else's time. You have to be with your daughter. Don't you think she needs you?' Kashell drags the back of his bandaged arm across his face, wipes away some of the tears. As he does it, Staffe sees smears of blood where the wound has leaked. 'If there's anything you want to tell me, Nico, anything at all, you call me. Don't hesitate. It can't be any worse than this.'

'That shows how much you don't know. I'd like you to go, Inspector.'

The nurse shows Staffe towards a small waiting room with a steel door. She is in her early twenties and has a mop of auburn hair twisted into a trendy confection with long strands curling down to frame her face. She has the greenest eyes. 'There's something I feel I have to tell you,' she says, looking up and down the corridor before closing the door, locking them in. She plays with the strands of her hair and wraps an arm across her own waist. 'Inmates all have a story about how they've been abused by the system. Some are stitched up by the police or grassed by a friend. Some say they're innocent. But he's the first I've come across who swears he's guilty. You can see he's lying just the same.' She goes to the window and nods to another nurse. 'There's someone you should talk to. It'll have to be quick.'

She works the magic with her keys and opens the door, takes a step back to let in a fearsome bulk of pasty white menace. 'This is Wedlock. Billy Wedlock.'

Wedlock is about the same age as Nurse Louisa, but as far from her in every other respect. He has prison tatts all up his arms and even one on his forehead — done with needles and burning matches and biro ink. Staffe's guess is he's been jailbirding all his life.

One step ahead, Wedlock laughs at Staffe. 'You checking the tatts, man? Got me for a jaily, yeah? But you be wrong, man. This just where I belong now. That's what society wants, that's what society gets. They want me down the gym and beefing up and mixing with these evil fuckers teaching me the business for when I get out? That's what Billy's doing, man. I'm learning the language, I'm graduating.' He looks at the nurse and says, 'Miss? You not told him what I done, miss?'

She shakes her head.

'Just cleaning the streets, just like Nico wants. 'Cept I know he's not cleaned no streets. He's just fucked himself over, man. He done nothing. For real.'

'He told you?'

'Like the cat sat on the fuckin' mat, man. He told me straight up.'

'And you'll testify to that?'

'No way, man! What do you think I am?'

'But he told you. Maybe he wants to be discovered.'

'Wasn't like that. He just had to get it out of his mind — like a priest thing in the what you say?'

'Confessional. So why are you telling me?'

'Kashell has to do any more time, he'll die, man. And he's a good man. A proper good man.'

'What exactly did he say to you, Billy, to make you believe him?'

Wedlock looks at the nurse and she nods for him to go ahead. She looks anxiously through the reinforced glass, up and down the corridor. 'I mashed some man proper. He was fiddlin' some kids of a woman I knew. Just a neighbour but I'd heard her crying. I couldn't get it out my head. She was marrying him. Fucksakes!' Wedlock is pacing up and down the small room, pressing up to the glass and looking left and right. He turns on Staffe and gives him a look to kill. 'He's not putting his dirty prick near no one, man. You get me.'

'And you told all this to Kashell.'

'I heard he was in for the same beef. But he wouldn't talk, man. Over and over he'd listen to me tell what I served that perv.'

'And what else did he tell you, Billy?'

Wedlock shakes his head and punches one open palm with the fist of the other. 'I swore down I wouldn't tell.'

'He told you he didn't do it, Billy?'

'I'm saying nothing, man.' He shoots the nurse a look, as if she has betrayed him. But she's having none of it.

She takes a step towards him and plants her feet, puts her hands on her hips. 'It was you that came to me, Billy. It's me who's sticking her stupid neck out here.'

Wedlock hangs his head, says, quiet as a church mouse, 'Sorry, miss.'

'You don't always have to blame, Billy.'

'Did he tell you who did it, Billy? Who killed Lotte Stensson?'

Wedlock shakes his head, sadly defiant, without looking up.

'I'm not asking you to tell me who, just did he tell *you* who killed Stensson?'

He shakes his head again and the nurse works her key magic, pulls open the door and shows Wedlock out, reaching up to give him a pat on his shoulder as he goes.

⋆　⋆　⋆

Pulford watches Staffe on his video-entry phone. He looks all washed out: bags under his eyes, unshaved, grey-skinned. He lets him in and kicks a pizza box under the sofa, puts all the newspapers into one pile. He turns off the game, even though he's got too much on Ashton for the first goal. He boots his computer and opens the door.

'How can you live like this,' says Staffe, striding into the room.

'You want a coffee or something?'

'I might catch something.'

Pulford shrugs and flops into his armchair, lets his arms dangle to the floor and stretches his legs out, waving a hand casually towards the sofa. He smiles to himself as Staffe sits down, leaning forward with his elbows on his knees, unable to relax. From where he is, he can see the debris of too many weekends on the floor, less than a foot below Staffe's backside. He nods at the computer. 'Just keeping track of the victim site.'

'Any change to the fourth quadrant?'

'No.'

'You're not going across to AMIP?'

'Smethurst doesn't want me.'

'I'll have a word.'

'It doesn't matter.'

'It does and I will.'

Pulford hands Staffe a sheet with those names appearing on both the case's database and the VABBA telephone bill.

'Any key names?'

Pulford smiles and begins to read the highlighted names from the sheets. 'Debra Bowker.'

'We knew that.'

'Tyrone Watkins.'

'You'd expect that.'

'Delilah Spears.'

'Spears? Isn't that . . . ?' Staffe rubs his face, hard.

'The match comes from the transcript of Debra Bowker's interview.'

'That's it! Bowker thought she was a bit strange.'

' 'Poor Delilah',' remembers Pulford. He flicks through the transcript. ' 'Her daughter was raped. Poor Delilah. She wanted to go out and kill the bastards. That's why I left, truth be known. I'd of ended up doing time when it should have been him.' '

'Have we interviewed Delilah?'

'Johnson cleared her.'

Staffe looks at the dead TV. 'You not watching the game?'

'I might later.'

Pulford takes a deep breath and studies Staffe's face for the next reaction. 'Jessop was on the list, sir.'

'Jessop!'

'There's one call to Leadengate and two later ones to his home number.'

'Jessop?' Staffe's face tightens and his bottom lip whorls. 'He never mentioned he had spoken to VABBA.'

'They called him.'

'Maybe it was when they were dropping the charges. When Ruth Merritt let the case lapse.'

'I checked the dates. The second two, yes. The first — to Leadengate — was a couple of days before the CPS wound the case back in.'

'J?' says Staffe, as much to himself as Pulford.

'Sir?'

Staffe looks at him, as though he is a doorman deciding whether he is good enough to be allowed in. He makes a tight smile and shakes his head. 'Nothing. Maybe I will have that coffee.'

'We are honoured.' Pulford puts the kettle on and while it boils, he tidies up a mess of poker chips on the small, circular dining table.

'It's all the rage now,' says Staffe.

'I've been playing for years.'

'Playing for money, too?'

'The way you play football with a ball.' He can

294

feel Staffe weighing him up, so he adopts a casual air. 'You should join us for a game one night.'

'Maybe when this case is done and dusted.'

'You can have a life and a job, sir.'

'I beg to differ. You're young.'

'And I don't care enough?'

'I didn't say that.'

Pulford puts a dessert spoon of own-brand coffee granules into the chipped mug. 'You know, sometimes I think it was a godsend, me working for you. You're . . . ' He busies himself putting the milk in, stirring the coffee.

'Carry on, Sergeant.'

'Sometimes, it's like you're the antidote, an extreme. A lesson in how to go too far. You're so wound up . . . all the time.' Staffe is gazing into nowhere.

Eventually, Staffe takes a sip from his coffee and looks at the papers, says, 'Thanks for doing this. Don't think it's not appreciated. I'll have that word with Smethurst. He's way out of line.'

'It's only a case, sir.'

Staffe gives him a rueful look and drops his gaze. He stares at Pulford's feet then gets up, shows himself out without saying another word. When he has gone, Pulford bends forward, sees one of his bank statements on the floor under his chair. Bottom line, eleven and a half grand overdrawn.

\* \* \*

Staffe sits behind the wheel, closes his eyes and sees the numbers on Pulford's bank statement, the look on his DS's face when he spoke of his poker.

He turns the ignition. Jessop once told him that we are defined by our faults. 'No problem, no person,' he said. 'Bloody Jessop,' says Staffe, aloud, and he swings the car round in the direction of his old boss's home. He tries desperately to remember if his father had ever supplied him with such maxims for life. But he can't.

At a red light, Staffe checks the stub again, making sure the *J* couldn't be another letter — a twitchy *T*, a lazy *l*, a straight *S*. There's no mistake. He rehearses the questions he will ask Jessop, but he can't make them sound casual, unthreatening, or remotely respectful: do you think Nico Kashell didn't kill Lotte Stensson; why *did* the CPS really drop the case; why were VABBA calling you before and after Lotte Stensson was killed — at the station and at home; who is the *J* on the VABBA cheque stub; can I see your bank statements; what were you doing on the night of the Lotte Stensson murder; and what were you doing on the night Karl Colquhoun was murdered, and the night Guy Montefiore was tortured? And can you prove it?

Staffe parks up the road from Jessop's flat. He leans back against the car and squints up at his ex-boss's squalid abode. What has he done to the gods to deserve this case?

If he doesn't ask these questions of Jessop, will Smethurst? Staffe knows he has no choice — there is already an innocent man serving life and there is, Staffe is certain, another victim about to be added to the list of the dead and tortured. Jessop brought him up to do precisely this. He locks down the Peugeot and walks slowly up to the front door. He presses the top buzzer, still hoping a plausible and alternative truth will hit him with a rabbit punch. He takes a deep breath, closes his eyes, tries to see his way through to a brighter end.

There is no answer so Staffe stands back, looks up to the top flat and sees the curtains are half closed. He feels the bunch of keys, still in his hip pocket from the VABBA sortie.

And suddenly, he feels sick. He is meeting Sylvie soon — as if for a first time. He should go home, shower and get ready. It will be the first time they have been out for dinner since he and Jessop were still friends; when Lotte Stensson was alive and Nico Kashell was a free man; when Karl Colquhoun and Guy Montefiore were leaving indelible prints all over the ruined lives of Tyrone, Linda and poor Sally Watkins.

He looks up into the sun and says 'Come on!' aloud, then goes back up to the door and presses all the buzzers, continuously until someone berates him.

'The fuck you playin' at!'

'Police! Now let me in or I'll have you for . . . '

The buzzer sounds and the latch whirrs itself unlocked. Staffe pushes it open and takes the ring of keys from his pocket, strides up the stairs. He smells the same old illegal smells, and notices that the rubbish bags outside the doors on the landings are piling up.

When he gets to the top floor he pounds the door. If only he could let himself in, rifle through his friend's possessions and find out what he needs to without having to ask. 'Ask?' You may as well say 'accuse'.

Staffe waits, weighs up the locks on the door. There are three. To triple lock a top-floor flat in such a dismal block is abnormal. He looks closely at the wood around the middle lock and runs his finger around the pale, routed subsurface where the lock was fitted. It rubs rough on his finger and he catches a splinter. It's a new fitting. Very new by the look and feel of it.

He holds up the ring of keys and realises — as he offers them to the new lock one by one — that none match. His heart sinks and he knows Jessop must have something to hide. He knows, too, that he must get to Jessop before Smethurst. The least he can do for his old friend is hear it first — then react accordingly.

Staffe knows he should go straight home and get ready for dinner with Sylvie — after all this time. But first, there is just enough time for another trip down Memory Lane.

★ ★ ★

Approaching the Scotsman's Pack, Staffe remembers the rollickings he used to get from Sylvie for the Sunday lunches he spent here with Jessop. Sunday dinner was the only meal she ever cooked. A bottle of Aligoté for him, a Brouilly for her. The wrong way round, some might say.

Staffe opens the Scotsman's door and goes

into the dark. The door slams violently behind him. As soon as you walk in through the panelled, narrow corridor, you can feel the appeal. A handful of diehards still slope up against the bar, pulling on pinches of snuff between sips of their halves and house doubles, with trips outside to smoke in the fresh air.

Jessop and he used to sit in one of the tiny snugs — little more than booths — so they could discuss cases without being overheard. But today, Staffe maintains a spot at the bar with a pint of Adnams. The landlord, Rod, looks as if he half recognises Staffe but he doesn't say anything, even when Staffe offers him 'your own'. When the change comes, Staffe sees he took for one anyway.

He bides his time, looks around with a scratch of the ear, a readjustment of the trousers, a trip to the paper rack. There is no sign of Jessop and Staffe finishes his drink and orders a Laphroaig. It's the reason they made a habit of coming here. Jessop introduced Staffe to the Islay malt and he couldn't get enough. Not everywhere has it.

Staffe surrenders to the slow wash of nostalgia. The old times seem happier than they were, now, in the beer's sepia as the slow roast of the malt takes him right the way back.

He says to Rod, as casually as he can muster, 'I don't suppose you remember, but I used to come in here. Used to come in with a friend of mine.'

'I remember all right. You're a copper.'

The old soaks down the bar turn, look him up and down and take a drink before they each take a half step away.

'Bob Jessop. I don't suppose he still comes in?'

The landlord shrugs and the soaks say nothing. If he didn't still come in, they'd have said. They know Jessop all right.

'Not been in today? He used to love his Sunday lunches,' says Staffe.

Rod turns his back and bends down, comes up with a packet of scratchings from a box and puts it in the one empty clip in the rack beneath the optics.

'Never mind.' Staffe drains his Laphroaig. 'See you again.' He goes into the dark, narrow corridor that leads outside and opens the door. The brilliant day floods in. Staffe lets the door swing its violent slam, shut. But he remains in the corridor, his back to the panelled wall. He holds his breath and listens hard. After a minute, maybe more, Staffe begins to feel foolish, makes to leave. But then, just a few feet away, he gets what he wants. Rod starts to talk, telephone loud.

'He's been in. Longish hair, yeah. He asked after you, straight out. No. Not a dicky bird.'

Having heard enough, Staffe opens the door and walks into the light, closing the door ever so gently behind him.

He has to meet Sylvie in San Giorgio, round the back of Leicester Square, in less than an hour. He can't be late, not after all this time. Instead, he goes west, to Hammersmith.

★ ★ ★

The Viva room is on AMIP's sixth floor. Viva is the case's code word. Victimvengeance. *Viva*. In

300

some places 'Viva' means 'life'.

'Ahaa,' calls Smethurst across the room as Staffe enters. 'You grace us with your presence.' Everyone in the room sees the funny side. Even Johnson joins in the craic of Smethurst's laughing policemen.

'Just thought I might be able to help.'

'We're getting on just fine, Inspector. But it's nice of you to pop in.'

Smethurst walks right up to Staffe and puts a hand on his back, ushering him to a quieter place. If the officers in the room didn't already know, it shows them exactly who's boss. Staffe wants to shrug him away, but he fights his instincts and simply flexes his shoulders, walks with Smethurst into a small meeting room.

'We're pushing ahead with this now, Will. Say what you like but we've already got our killer for Lotte Stensson and with a bit of luck, if he doesn't top himself, he'll get his parole in a few years.'

Staffe tries to work out whether Smethurst has tied Jessop into the case. And if he has, what is he doing about it? 'I wanted a word with Johnson.'

'Maybe you can persuade him to go home. He's a good man, but he's done in. Most of the continuity work is finished. I'll send him in.' Smethurst turns at the door. 'Oh, and Will.'

'Yes.'

'I understand if you don't want to be involved. I wouldn't want to — if I was you.'

Staffe says nothing. As he waits for Johnson, he smells drink on himself. It reminds him of younger days in smoky pubs that supposedly smelled of Wormwood Scrubs. 'And too many right-wing meetings . . . ' he says, aloud.

'Talking to yourself, boss?' says Johnson.

'It's a song.'

'The Jam.' Johnson looks as if he's been kept awake every night for a month.

'How's the case going?'

'This website should blast it open. The techies are working on it now.' Johnson looks around, uncomfortable. Staffe thinks about the needle and makes a mental note to check with Janine precisely which narcotic his DS has been injecting himself with.

'Any fresh leads?'

'I heard you went to see Kashell.'

Staffe nods.

'We're not going down that road,' says Johnson.

'What about Delilah Spears?' As he asks the question, Staffe studies Johnson for his response.

His face flickers then breaks into a grimace, then a coughing fit.

'Sorry, sir.'

'You taking something for that? Or is that the problem?'

'I don't have a problem, sir.'

'She's on the VABBA list. A bloke called Errol Regis raped her daughter, Martha Spears.'

'What makes you ask about her?' says Johnson.

Staffe shrugs, says, 'Her name cropped up, in the Bowker transcript.'

'Like I said, DI Smethurst is going his own way.'

★ ★ ★

It feels like a first date. Walking down Gerrard Street. Staffe pictures Sylvie the last time they were together. Her hair was short in a French bob, shiny black and fashioned into sharp curves that came together on her pale, pale neck. Her eyes — green as new shoots in spring — were dewy wet from him being too much of a bastard once too often. He had a reason, but like she said, he always had a reason.

He is shown towards their table by the maître d' who seems to recognise Staffe. Sylvie is sitting by the window, looking out and twirling the ice in her Campari and soda. He should have got here first, but then he wouldn't have seen her this way, the sun flitting across her, through her flimsy cotton dress.

'I'm sorry,' he says, sitting. 'So sorry.' A waiter hovers, asks him what he would like to drink. 'A Bloody Mary, please,' he says.

'You look as though you've had a few.'

'It's the weekend,' he says. 'You've changed.' And she has. Her hair is long, wavy and full, resting on her shoulders, shiny. She looks happier than he remembers.

'I haven't.'

'Have you chosen?' he says, opening the menu.

'I don't need to. I know what I'm having.'

'It was work. That's why I'm late.'

'Don't apologise.'

He looks down at the menu, even though he knows what he will have. He takes a breath, 'You're happy, now?'

303

'I always was.'

'Sometimes, a lot of the time . . . '

'Nobody died, Will. At least we didn't get stuck.'

The waiter brings his drink. 'Chin chin.'

They clink glasses and she says 'Chin chin' laughing. 'At least I made some kind of a mark on you.' The sun catches her hair, the side of her face. She shimmers, her eyes shine. 'I know there's a good reason you're late. And I know you might start to tell me but I know that you'll stop.'

'I can't tell you *exactly* why.'

'Exactly.' She smiles fondly. 'You always did the right thing, Will. For better or worse.'

'What do you mean?'

She takes a drink. 'You do the right thing, but it's not a good thing. You do the right thing because you can't do anything else.' She puts a hand across the table and takes hold of his, squeezes it. 'I'm glad you called.'

The waiter reappears, holding his black leather notebook, folded open for their order. Staffe says, 'The lady will have the marisco soup, then the turbot and I'll have the smoked salmon, then the skate. And we'll have a bottle of Aligoté and the Brouilly. Together.'

The waiter nods approvingly and Sylvie shakes her head, says, 'I might have changed my mind.'

'You said you hadn't changed,' says Staffe, finishing his Bloody Mary.

'Do you still have your friends?' she says.

'I never had many friends.' He looks into her eyes and she smiles. 'Never that many.'

'Whatever happened to that old rogue, Jessop?'

'Jessop? Why do you ask?' Staffe feels his breath go short.

'Don't look at me like that, Will.'

'Why ask about him?'

'It's a perfectly innocent question.'

Innocent. A strange word to use. The waiter brings the starters and they both lean back. A different waiter brings the wine. He holds out a bottle in each hand, offers the red to Staffe who indicates that the lady is to taste. As he readjusts, Sylvie looks daggers at Staffe who watches the wine being poured.

'It will be fine. Just pour it,' says Sylvie and leans forward, hisses, 'Don't be suspicious with me, Will. I only asked how he was.'

'I saw him the other day. Funny, isn't it — us being here, me seeing Jessop.'

'Is that why you called me?'

'No! It's just one of those life tricks.'

'Course it is.' She pulls a face then takes a good slug of her Brouilly and as she swallows it down, her features relax, almost into a smile. 'Hmm. That's *good*. So how is he?'

'You know he got kicked out of the Met.'

'We were still together.'

'And Delores left him.'

'That was on the cards.'

'What do you mean?'

'They were dead in the water. She told me.'

'She *told* you?'

'If you remember, we were both alone at the same times. She'd call me. I can't believe you didn't know.'

'Know what?'

'He was having an affair. With that woman in the CPR. Is that right?' She takes another slug of her wine, leans back and wipes her mouth with the starched linen napkin.

'CPR?'

'You were always saying they got in your way.'

'CPS? You mean CPS! What was her name?' The drink has got to her eyes and they sparkle. 'Can you remember her name?'

'Yes.'

'And what was it?'

'Can't we talk about us?'

'Of course we can. What was her name?'

Sylvie looks sad. 'Ruthie. Ruthie something. I had an aunt called Ruth. She was my favourite.'

'I remember. Does she still live down in Rye?'

Which makes Sylvie smile.

\* \* \*

Sylvie stands with her arms crossed in the window of the Queens Terrace flat, looking out.

'Do you want me to draw the curtains?' says Staffe.

'It's still light. Why would you want the curtains drawn?' She turns, eyes glistening and her mouth soft from drink. She tilts her head and reaches out, takes the glass of wine from him. She draws her fingers across his as she does it. 'You've got big fingers, Will.'

'Big fingers? Why would you say that?'

'I always liked them.' She takes a slug from her wine, puts the glass down and goes up to him. She stands so their legs dovetail, clasps her hands behind her back and leans back from the hip. 'Why shouldn't I say it?' She laughs.

'No reason.' He can smell drink on her as she speaks. He watches her tongue as she speaks, feels her against his thigh.

'You know I never had the measure of you, Will. Most girls would never say that of a man they love.'

'Love?'

'I loved you, Will.' She reaches up on tiptoes, hooks a finger in the top of his jeans and pulls herself up against him. With her mouth an inch from his, she says, soft as you like, 'And you l . . . loved me.' With the 'l' of loved she flicks his lip with her tongue. She puts a hand on the back of his neck, kisses him, slow, soft, and with her eyes wide open. He feels as if he doesn't know her at all. She slips a second finger down the top of his jeans, brings her thumb up against the top button.

'I'll draw the curtains,' he says.

'After all these years, you finally learn,' she says.

He draws the curtains and when he turns round she is pulling the flimsy cotton dress over her head. She stands there naked, bar her strappy sandals. She puts her hands on her hips and smiles.

'You coming?' she says.

'I don't know,' he says. He wants to hold her. He wants to tell her he loves her. He wants a life he never had.

She picks up her dress from the floor and holds it over her, walking backwards out of the room.

# Sunday Evening

Staffe pays the cab and feels for the pavement beneath his outstretched foot. He rubs his face and squints up at Leadengate, the evening sun still bright in the western sky. He walks up the steps and hears his name in a familiar voice. He struggles to place it, then his heart sinks as he turns. Nick Absolom has his pad and pen at the ready.

'You said I could have first run on any breaks in the case,' says Absolom.

'I'll let our press officer know.' Staffe turns, takes another step.

'I'd say that you being investigated by the Police Complaints Authority is pretty newsworthy.'

'Who told you!'

'You can give us your version, or we'll speculate.'

'I haven't got time for this.'

'At the moment, I've only got one headline for this case and, unfortunately, it's you.'

'Go to hell.' Staffe takes the steps two at a time and kicks open the front door.

Jombaugh looks at him disapprovingly, says, 'DC Chancellor has been asking for you. She wants you to call her.'

Staffe watches Absolom leaning against a pillar, making notes. As he does, a thin smile shows in the corners of the journalist's mouth.

'I hear you've been back in touch with Jessop,' says Jombaugh. 'Give him my best.'

'He was a good friend, wasn't he, Jom?'

'He thought the world of you, Will.'

Staffe makes his way up to his office, feeling for his mobile phone. He checks all his pockets, trying to remember where he has left it and making a mental note to call Josie.

As the computer boots up, he stretches out his legs, crosses his arms across his chest, closes his eyes and, breathing deep, incants 'pass-if-eye-your-self'. He measures out his breathing, waits for his pulse to calm, tries to fathom why he turned Sylvie away.

When he opens his eyes, he leans forward, slowly moves the cursor to the web address box. He clicks *victimvengeance.com* and tries to imagine Jessop doing the things that were done to Lotte Stensson, Karl Colquhoun and Guy Montefiore. He pictures him with the hammer, the scalpel, the ropes. He tries to kindle the bitterness he must have felt, the slow death of faith in the law. He can't see Jessop being unfaithful to Delores, either. How can you think you know someone so well? The quadrants on the website are unchanged and in the bottom-right corner the image is still unfathomable.

He goes into *Authorised Searches* and activates *Financial*. A textbox appears and he fills in all the compulsory fields: All Names, Address, DOB, Occupation, and clicks *All Accounts, All Clearing Houses*, and *Search: last five years*, then *Amounts in Excess of £10,000*, then says a prayer against coming up with the evidence he needs. The machine whirrs and comes up with the *Protected Data* script boxes. He shouldn't know the password, but he does. He takes a breath and types it in. He presses 'Send' a last time. Aloud, he says, 'Sorry.'

Staffe makes his way through the almost empty building. It is late Sunday evening and now the case is transferred to AMIP, Leadengate echoes with old, shoved-aside crimes. He looks up and down the stairwell, remembers good times. More good than bad, it seems, now. He doesn't want to go back for Jessop, but knows it has to be him who does this.

First, though, he has to discover one last thing about his friend.

★　★　★

'What you doing here?' says Sally Watkins, crossing her arms and not budging from the doorway. In the background, Staffe can hear the TV turned up too loud. He wonders what sounds Tyrone must have been trying to obscure.

'Can I have a quick word?'

'Fire away.'

Staffe looks over her shoulder, nods to be invited in.

'I've got company,' says Sally, unashamed.

'You gave an alibi to my colleague, DS Johnson.'

'You know what I do.'

'And I know you're underage.'

'So report me.' She sneers, a completely different cup of tea from the girl who made him

310

a tuna Marie Rose sandwich less than a week ago. 'You could've before, but you didn't. Why not? You feel sorry for me? Jails are all full?'

Staffe feels out of control.

'What is it you really want?'

'I want you to think back to when, you know, Montefiore attacked you.'

'If you know he attacked me, do something about it.'

'I'm trying to, for God's sake! Can't you see that?'

Sally takes a pace back. A flicker of warm blood comes to her face and her eyes soften. She uncrosses her arms and clasps them together on her narrow, child's hips.

He says, 'Before the case was withdrawn, the police interviewed you, right?'

She nods, looks over her shoulder and back again.

'There was a senior officer, a bit older than me. His name was Jessop. DI Jessop.'

She looks at the floor and shakes her head.

'Come on, Sally. This is important. Please.'

'What's going on!' An angry male voice cuts through the sound of the TV. It sounds familiar.

'I've got to go,' she says, taking a hold of the door.

'Sally! Jessop did talk to you, didn't he? Please! If he didn't, I need to know.'

'Never heard of him.' She closes the door and Staffe jams it with his foot. 'You ain't got no warrant. You can't force your way in.'

'Oi! Sally!' comes the man's voice.

'I'm sorry, Sally, for what happened. But

'there's other people suffering here.'

'Anybody wants to swap with me, they're welcome.'

'You shouldn't be doing this,' says Staffe, looking over her shoulder towards the man's voice.

'He's a friend.' She looks hurt.

Staffe withdraws his foot but holds the door ajar with his outstretched arm.

'If you tell me, it will help bring Montefiore to justice.'

She smiles at him, as if he is a fool. 'And how would *you* do that?' She pushes the door harder and Staffe lets it go. In the instant that it slams in his face, Staffe gets a snapshot slice of Sally Watkins's face: she looks disappointed in him — way beyond her years.

'You know him all right,' Staffe calls out. As he walks along the concrete walkway to the stairwell, he mutters, 'Bloody Jessop. Bloody fool.'

He leans against the wall in the stairwell. It takes half an hour, but when it comes, it's worth it. Ross Denness emerges from the Watkinses' flat with his head down, hands stuffed deep in his pockets and looking for all the world as if he didn't get what he went for.

\* \* \*

Staffe drops in at Queens Terrace before going to see Jessop; when the cab draws up, he sees the curtains are still drawn and the stupid argument from years ago reprises — the second time in as

312

many days. Then he double takes. On the steps to his front door is a familiar-looking figure. She looks downcast, staring into the distance, chewing her nails — something he has never seen her do before. As soon as he slams the cab door behind him, she stands up, looking nervous.

'Where have you been?' says Josie. 'I've been calling you.'

'I must have left my phone inside.' He nods up at his flat.

'Didn't the station say to call me?'

'I've been busy.'

'We've cocked up. Remember when we went to the VABBA office? I left my jacket there. I knew we shouldn't have gone.'

'Shit,' says Staffe, looking up and down the street as he walks up the path. 'Come in.'

He opens the place up and goes into the kitchen.

'My Tube pass is in the pocket.'

'We'll go and get it tomorrow.'

'Can't you do it tonight?'

'There's something I have to do, on my own.'

'You shouldn't be doing things on your own.'

Staffe picks his mobile phone up off the dresser. Is he letting things slide? The phone tells him he has six missed calls: four from Josie and two from Smethurst. He goes into the *view* details and sees Smethurst has only just called him. 'Why don't you make us some coffee? I've just got to get this. I won't be a minute,' he says, pressing 'Call' as he goes into the living room. He draws the curtains back, stands in the

313

window, looking out as he waits for Smethurst to pick up. Opposite, a taxi stops. Its light goes off and an old lady emerges. She smiles at the cabbie and looks up at Staffe, waves.

'Where the hell have you been, Staffe,' says Smethurst, clearly unhappy.

'Getting a bite to eat.'

'We've got a problem here. Montefiore has discharged himself from hospital.'

'Why would he do that?'

'He says he was threatened. We've had a uniform on his door but he reckons he was asleep and someone came in and held a chloroform rag to his mouth and a knife to his throat. It's bullshit!'

'He'd know all about chloroform.'

'It makes us look like muppets. It's bad enough that we have to guard a child molester without him trumping up some dereliction theory.'

'It's your case, Smet.'

'He's asking for you, Staffe. He won't talk to anyone else and he says if he can't talk to you, he'll go to the press.'

'Asking for me?'

'He says you can save him. Says you're the only one.'

Smethurst hangs up. Another taxi pulls up across the road. This time, the light stays on.

When he turns round, Josie is standing in front of the sofa, a hand on her hip, waiting. Exactly where Sylvie was.

'I've got to go to Montefiore's,' he says.

'Do you want me to come?'

314

'I could do with your help.'

She wiggles a finger in her ear. 'Am I hearing things?'

'You heard right,' says Staffe, allowing himself a smile.

It's getting dark. He looks up and down the road as they walk to his car. As they pass the cab, the light is off but there is nobody in the back.

\* \* \*

It seems weeks since Staffe was last at 48 Billingham Street. Now, with evening the sky streaked like rainbow trout, it is a less sinister place, save the uniformed officer on the front door. He checks Staffe's warrant card, opens the door and smiles at Josie, looking her up and down.

'Were you on duty at the hospital when they got in and threatened him?' says Staffe.

The officer looks sheepish, says, 'Yes, sir. I don't know how they got in. Honestly I don't.'

'Nip off for a cup of tea, did you?'

'No. I've given a statement. It's the truth.'

Staffe can tell what the constable is thinking: what a waste of time, protecting a child molester? No wonder the police get a bad press.

Montefiore sits in a reproduction library chair with a rug over his lap. His eyes are dark and he is gaunt, like someone from a different economy. Staffe can smell soup — probably the only thing Montefiore can take. He is holding a mobile phone in both hands, as if his life depended on it.

Staffe pulls up a framed Louis XV chair, another reproduction, and sits a couple of feet away from Montefiore. He looks into his eyes and tries to forget what he did to Sally Watkins, what he tried to do to Tanya Ford. 'Tell me what happened, Guy.'

'He just appeared, in that balaclava, again. He came from nowhere.'

'You're sure it was a man?'

'The same as the first time, you know, when he did what he did.' Montefiore looks as if he might be sick.

'And what did he say this time? Exactly.'

Josie is looking out of the window, trying not to be conspicuous.

'I don't want her here. He said it was you who could help me. Only you.'

Staffe nods for Josie to leave them alone. 'I'll have a coffee. Do you want anything?' he says to Montefiore.

Montefiore shakes his head, slowly, and as Josie leaves, he leans forward, beckons Staffe to come closer. As he does, Montefiore smiles at him. It is a look of fondness and makes Staffe look at his shoes.

'He said you're a good man.' Montefiore's smile cracks. 'He said, 'I'll be back. This is to show I can get to you any time I want.' He said 'You'll see me coming and nothing will save you. Only Wagstaffe can save you. Keep him close, I warn you.''

Staffe looks up, determined to find some kind of perspective.

Montefiore has tears in his eyes and he leans

forward more, lets the mobile phone drop into his lap and reaches out to take a hold of Staffe's hands. He clasps them the way you would a lover who was trying to leave you. 'You can save me, Inspector.' He looks at Staffe as if it is the last blast of love to someone you know doesn't feel the same. 'You will, won't you? You will save me?'

'Why don't you confess, Guy. Let Sally Watkins move on. It's the right thing. You can save yourself.'

'You don't care. I can tell.' Montefiore lets go of Staffe's hands. 'Why do they say you can save me when you don't even care?'

Staffe thinks about this and tries to make sense of the warnings he has received, the messages too. 'Why do you think he would say that, Guy?'

'Because you're the only one with a real faith in the law.'

'The things you've done, that's quite a compliment.'

'What, precisely, does the law say I have done?'

'Tell me why you did it, Guy. Tell me that and I can help you. Who hurt you, Guy?'

'You wouldn't believe it.'

'And why did you marry? You never loved her.'

'You don't have to love them.' Montefiore looks back up at Staffe. He doesn't quite smile.

Staffe dearly wants to spurn this sick and damaged man, but knows he can't. He wants to be anywhere but here, yet here he is — stretched to breaking point. He stands, says, 'I will save you, Guy. Tell him that next time.'

317

'Next time?'

Staffe makes his way down the hall to the kitchen and what he sees through the glass panes of the door stops him in his tracks. He can feel his pulse quicken, the colour come to his face, a thin trail of sweat at the nape of his neck. He feels so far removed from the younger self that joined the Force.

Josie is sitting at Guy Montefiore's kitchen table, her hands interlocked around a mug of tea, looking studiously down, avoiding Staffe. Standing beside her is DCI Pennington, shaking his head, slowly.

'What the hell is going on!'

Pennington frowns, tight-lipped, and Staffe hears a mechanical cough. It comes from neither Josie nor Pennington. He looks around and realises it is piped in from elsewhere. It was Montefiore coughing. There is a loudspeaker on the dresser.

'You bugged us? You bastards. You can't trust me to tell you what he said?'

Josie looks up, pleadingly, as if to say she had nothing to do with it, but she says nothing.

'You haven't exactly been straight with us, have you? And quite frankly, I'm glad I heard what I did. It's all pretty disturbing, Staffe. Pretty disturbing.'

'What is?'

'Your relationship with Montefiore.'

'What!'

'Hardly regular, is it?'

'I am trying to get him to confess to a crime.'

'He seems to think you're on his side.'

'I wasn't the one who let him off the hook.'

'Why didn't you tell me you were going to see Kashell? Or were you afraid you were barking up the wrong tree, causing a vulnerable prisoner to make an attempt on his own life?'

'He didn't kill Lotte Stensson. I know for a fact.'

'Which fact? Go on! Show me the fact.'

Staffe looks down, tries to slow his fast-beating heart. He takes a step back from Pennington who suddenly seems like the enemy.

'And I know about the break-in — to the office on Kennington Lane. I don't know why you couldn't just use a warrant like anybody else. And why you had to drag DC Chancellor into it, I . . .'

'He didn't drag me, sir. I went of my own volition.'

'That's not exactly true, sir,' says Staffe.

Pennington plunges his hands into his pockets and sighs. He looks out of the window. 'We've had a complaint from the parents of Tanya Ford, too. They say you attacked the father.'

'That's nonsense.'

'There was a careworker there. She doesn't contradict their claims.'

'He came at me. I was just trying to get some justice for their daughter! They call it disclosure, sir.'

Pennington turns, puts his hands behind his back, as if he was at a scene of crime — protecting evidence. He takes a step towards Staffe. 'Meting out justice, regardless of procedure. Where have we heard that before?'

319

'It's not like that!'

'It doesn't look good, Staffe.'

Staffe looks into Pennington's cold grey eyes. 'What exactly are you saying?'

'The PCA are following through on the e.Gang's accusations. The spotlight's on.' He takes another step closer. Staffe can smell the clean lemon of his aftershave, as though the long hot day has taken no toll. Suddenly, Staffe feels tired, outgunned. 'I have to be seen to be white on this one. Whiter than white. I hope you'll play ball, Staffe.'

'Ball?' Staffe loses his breath. He fears the worst and his jaw is so slack it feels like stage fright. But he knows this isn't make-believe. This is his life.

'I'm going to have to ask where you were when Karl Colquhoun was murdered and when Guy Montefiore was attacked.'

'I can't believe this!' Staffe sits at the kitchen table. He feels dizzy.

'You were at the scene. You were here when it happened, Staffe! You opened the door that did for him. Believe me, I want the right answers. For your sake and mine.'

'Are you arresting me?'

'I'm warning you, DI Wagstaffe. This is a formal warning, in the presence of DC Chancellor. I want a full explanation of all your movements during the past week. I want alibis and witnesses. And I don't want you within a country mile of this bloody case! Do you understand me?'

'Yes, sir.'

'On my desk tomorrow.'

'Are you suspending me, sir?'

'I'm afraid I have no choice, Inspector.'

⋆ ⋆ ⋆

Darkness descends and the Limekiln tower looms over Gibbets Lane like a blue-black giant. Errol Regis looks out of his living-room window to see the flame burning beneath the drum of tar in the pathway to the unoccupied house next door. The pink-streaked sky is low tonight.

Errol had called the council to see what is going on but received only the answering service. They don't open for business until 9 a.m. tomorrow morning. In the meantime, he looks up and down the street and paces from room to room. He makes pots of tea that don't get drunk. He flicks from channel to channel, stopping on the weather even though he has heard it before. As soon as the news comes on, he switches away.

He takes a sleeping pill and checks the bolts on all the doors and says a prayer that Theresa makes some kind of return, even if it is just to collect more of her things. Like he always does, he says a prayer for Martha Spears, and finally he asks God to one day let the truth arise — that he may be forgiven for something he never did. And as usual, he curls up like a foetus, listening to the deep resound of his own heart.

⋆ ⋆ ⋆

As he drives home, Staffe designs a route towards what seems an improbable sleep. He will run himself a deep Radox bath and open a decent bottle of red, then he will watch the cricket highlights in bed and hopefully drift away. Then he will rise early and document his whereabouts ever since the afternoon Karl Colquhoun was murdered. He has never been able to turn a blind eye to a problem.

Outside the V & A, he sees a news-stand touting the *News* and he feels a bubble of bile. He tries to swallow it away, begins to sing a song in his head. For some reason, the opening refrain of 'Love For Sale' announces itself. He indicates away from home, turning away from all the things he has prescribed. Staffe can't get Jessop out of his mind. Why the hell would he do the things Staffe thinks he has done?

Montefiore's recanted words resound: 'Only Wagstaffe can save you. Keep him close, I warn you. But there will be a time when he won't be there.' Were they Jessop's words? Staffe can't help feeling his old friend might have played him like a fiddle.

When he gets to Jessop's place, Staffe sees lights on all the way up the building, until you get to Jessop's windows that jut from the sloping, slate roof. He isn't surprised to get no response from the intercom and feels the ring of keys in his pocket. He thinks about the alibis he must produce, the hearing he will have to face. What else can he do, but uncover the truth.

He picks out a key and puts it to the lock, slips inside and takes the stairs one at a time in the dark. At the top, he knocks lightly on Jessop's door — just enough to raise him, not enough to draw attention from the flats below. When he gets no response, he removes his diary and pen, takes off his leather jacket and drapes it on the floor in the corner of the small landing. He checks that Jessop won't see him as he comes up the stairs, and he begins to jot down his precise movements at the times in question.

When Karl Colquhoun was being delicately butchered, he had cooked a meal for Josie, was packing for Spain. And as for Montefiore, that night he had gone for a run and asked Johnson to 'take care' of Marie's bullying boyfriend. He had gone to bed, found an imperfect sleep — a good match for his imperfect alibi.

He snugs down into the corner of the landing where the walls and the floor meet. He pulls his jacket up around him and smells the leather and pubs and too much hurry. He feels so, so weary but knows he cannot allow himself the luxury of sleep. His eyes lid down and he blinks himself awake, feels himself drifting again. He thinks of dinner with Sylvie, can see her standing naked. He remembers the cut of her hair and the deep green of her eyes, the way she spoke as she ate, spearing the turbot flesh with her fork. On the back of his eyelids he pictures the way she looked when she spoke of her favourite aunt — as though she had never left him, as though the last three years had been a dream. A long, long dream.

★ ★ ★

A searing light wakes Staffe. He blinks into the fierce white. He smells meat on a man's breath, can feel the dull weight of something blunt on his throat. He struggles to breathe and squints into the light, trying to see what is beyond. Right up against his face is the leather sole of a boot, the frayed edge of trouser bottoms. He tries to lever himself up, but can't.

'Do yourself a favour, Staffe. You think you're doing good, but you're not. Believe me,' says Jessop. He talks calm and slow, as if he has nothing to fear from his friend.

Staffe tries to work out where he is and how long he has been asleep. He stretches out with his right hand, feels wood and the coarse fabric of worn carpet, the soft leather of his own jacket. Even though he can see nothing beyond the torchlight, up close and shining straight into his eyes, he starts to remember.

Jessop says, 'Believe me, there are forces of good at play here. More than you might imagine.'

Staffe fancies his chances to overcome Jessop but doesn't want to hurt him. 'Let me up. We're friends, for God's sake.'

'Some friends we've turned out to be.'

'I could have handed you to Smethurst and AMIP, but I want to be wrong. Tell me I'm wrong.' He drags his legs round, prepares to spring up, but one of his legs snags. Something bites into his ankle and he realises he is tethered.

'What exactly is it that you think I've done?' Jessop takes his foot away and lowers the torchlight. 'Keep your voice down. I've got neighbours you know.'

Staffe takes his chance and makes to spring up off his free leg, but he falls back to the floor, bangs his head against the wall and sees that his ankles are tied together. 'What the hell?'

Jessop slowly places a heel on Staffe's chest. 'Go on. Tell me what you've got.'

'Nico Kashell didn't kill Lotte Stensson and you know it. And you pulled the Sally Watkins prosecution, you and Ruth Merritt between you.'

'Why would I do such a thing, friend?'

'You were pissed off with the law, fed up with the way you were treated, the way people got off.'

'And your evidence?'

'There's no interviews. There are massive gaps in the filed evidence on that case. Only one interview with the defendant. There's no sign whatsoever that you saw Sally Watkins. But I know you did.'

'I hope that's not your idea of evidence. Do you have a statement from Sally?'

'Tell me I'm wrong. Deny it!'

'You know a lot for a man who's been suspended.'

'How do you know I've been suspended?'

'Let it go, Will.'

'How can you let Kashell do his time?'

'You should leave well alone. He was all right until you upset his apple cart.'

'You killed Stensson, didn't you? And you're letting an innocent man serve your time.' And as he says this, Staffe has the hollow feeling he has underestimated Jessop.

Jessop lifts his foot off Staffe's chest and turns off the torch. In the dark, Staffe can discern the crouching figure of Jessop. The smell of meat on his breath is stifling now. 'I went to see Stensson to get a confession out of her. We had other accusations but nobody would disclose. There would have been others, too, if we hadn't . . . ' Jessop sighs and his speech slows right down. 'You should have seen the way she looked at me. As if she was better than me. I could have killed her there and then, wiped that smug look off her face. She saw it and she screamed the place down, accused me of trying to beat her. So I went back to see Nico.'

'You killed her?'

'He wasn't supposed to confess. Everybody had alibis.'

'Everybody in VABBA?'

'It's not what you think.'

'What about the fifty grand?'

In the half light, Staffe sees Jessop's mouth goes slack. His eyes turn from angry to sad. 'What fifty grand?' he says.

'The fifty grand VABBA paid you to do all this, to live out their fantasies of revenge and record it all. You recorded it all for them, didn't you?'

Jessop stands up again, rests his boot on Staffe's chest and puts all his weight on it, supporting himself on the banister. 'You think this is for money? Do you, my friend? Do you!'

Staffe can't get his breath. He thinks he will pass out, thinks his breastbone is about to crack, breaking into pieces and piercing his lungs.

'Please,' he wheezes, his eyes filling with water. Life draining away.

Jessop bends down towards him. Staffe has adjusted to the dark now and through the glaze of his own watery eyes, Jessop's sad face comes bigger and bigger. He smells a chemical.

'You know, Will, if you could see yourself the way you were when you first came to Leadengate — you were washed up. You had nowhere to go. But I saw a spark. Nobody else did, just me. I took you on and it was the right thing to do. If only we could see ourselves as others do, eh, Will? That would be something.'

The smell gets closer, stronger. It's a smell Staffe has come to recognise. And with the last blots of sensory perceptions running into each other, he feels the damp rub of gauze around his mouth and nose. He tries to hold what little breath remains, but he can't and as he breathes in, he slips away.

# Monday Morning

Pulford minimises *victimvengeance.com* and the 'snuffcast', as Nick Absolom calls it, disappears into its icon at the bottom of the screen to reveal the homepage of *Poker-Rich*. Pulford rubs his face, the way you would rub a whiteboard clean. He leans back in his chair and takes the mouse. The cursor hovers over *Join Game*. He looks down at the financial statements on the floor and blows his cheeks out. He leaves the cursor where it is and goes into his tiny kitchen, makes himself a black coffee because there is no milk. He tries Staffe's mobile again and gets the answering service, doesn't bother to leave another message. He curses Staffe and goes back to his workstation.

You're only ever one game from a change of luck. One more punt might turn the tide that got him into this predicament. He raises the mug to his mouth and it burns his lips. He takes it as a sign and says, 'Fuck it. Fuck you!' and closes the site down, turns the computer off. He looks at the pile of statements and sits cross-legged on the floor, making separate piles of HSBC, Ladbrokes, Paypal and Barclaycard, putting the most recent bills on the top. He rounds the totals down to the nearest hundred and tots up in his head, adds on another seven hundred for last month's unpaid rent. He might get two and a half for the MR2 but he still owes the finance company three grand. All in all, he's looking at twenty-two grand. Eight months' salary. His parents keep asking him when he's going to buy a place of his own, get a foot on that ladder. They don't know he's sliding down snakes.

A black suit hangs on the back of the door, ready to be worn to Karl Colquhoun's funeral. Even though he's not on the AMIP team, he will go, thinking it might rule a line under the case before he throws himself back into his backlog of car-ringing gangs, DVD smugglers, extortionists and immigrant sweatshops.

He goes back to the kitchen and pours the coffee into the sink, takes a pair of scissors from the second drawer down and returns to the lounge, cuts his credit cards, one by one, into tiny pieces. Halfway through, he rubs his eyes and punches the pedestal of his desk. 'Idiot!' he says to himself. 'Bloody idiot!'

★ ★ ★

The ceiling is dirty and a paper lantern hangs from the cracked, off-centre ceiling rose. Staffe rubs his eyes, wipes his mouth. He can tell they have fashioned this entire flat from a single old room, probably for a servant in a moderately well-to-do family. He remembers what happened last night. Was it last night? And he waits for the anger to surge at him, but it doesn't. He feels calm, kind of distant from himself: separate from the space he is in.

He considers the quality of the refurbishment, sitting up and looking around at the bare room.

329

No books, no ornaments. The sun streams in, showing the window smears. He stretches and yawns. He feels fresh, kind of brand new.

'Jessop,' he says, softly, standing slowly. He paces sedately around the room, opening drawers and crouching to look under furniture. The place has been packed up and shipped out. There is a pile of dirty clothes in the corner by the kitchenette and junk mail in the paper basket, but apart from that no sign of life, except . . . except a single sheet of paper Blu-tacked to the microwave in the kitchenette. Staffe squints until it gradually comes into focus. It is handwritten.

*Please, my friend. In the name of whatever friendship we had or will ever have, let this go. Don't follow. This will be resolved soon. Trust me.*
   *J.*

He ambles across to the window in the slope of the roof and bends to take in the view across North London's rooftops, remembering some of what his old friend had said last night.

Staffe feels a vague compunction to call Smethurst but considers that Jessop has left him untethered and unharmed. Thus, he is disinclined to snitch on his old friend — even though the man did, after all, assault him. He begins to recall that he is suspended from the case. Yes, he is definitely suspended from the case. But he feels less miserable about this than he ought.

As he makes coffee, the ceramic of the mug

feels soft and he thinks that his fingertips might not be entirely his own. He tries to pick his way though the conversations he had last night, remembering what Jessop told him about Lotte Stensson and Nico Kashell. Jessop has now fled far, of that he feels certain. He has probably gone to meet up with the woman. He can't quite remember her name.

If he called Smethurst and put him on to Jessop, would it lead to Nico Kashell being released? Probably not. In the absence of a confession from Jessop, nothing has changed. And what does Staffe really know about Nico Kashell; what that poor, broken man wants for his life.

What good has come of this long, protracted case of vengeances? Would good come from the incarceration of Bob Jessop? Only if he is to kill again; or if the law must always be an end in itself. He resolves to consider this.

Staffe lets himself out and slips into the long, blue day. His tread feels light, as though his feet barely touch ground. He walks briskly, not really knowing where he should go. He has a notion that he will be watched, or followed, and switches sides of the road, looking around as he goes.

Looking at the papers on the news-stand tells him it is Monday and the position of the sun in the sky implies it is late morning. In the Sainsbury's on Kilburn High Road, they are queuing at the checkouts already. Perhaps people queue all day every day.

They always say, 'Why do you bother, Staffe?

You don't have to work.' Every day could be like this — nothing behind him, nothing ahead and God knows what new people he will meet, what joys and hardships he might encounter without having to do something about them.

What has Jessop done to him?

He wonders where his friend is now. On a plane or a boat. Has he found a kind of peace? Or love?

Staffe cuts off the High Road, not far now from his own house. He will call on his sister. That is what he will do.

★ ★ ★

Marie opens the door to the Kilburn house and she beams a broad smile when she sees him, throws her arms open wide and takes him in. She smells of something green, he thinks. Turquoise, perhaps. The house is spick and there are fresh flowers on the coffee table — lilies. He knows he might tell her to be careful the stamens don't fall on his fabrics. They stain. But he thinks she will probably know this for herself. Paolo gets up from his knees. He has a rag in his hand and there is a smell of lacquer. Has he been cleaning the hearth? He too is smiling and he extends a hand, shakes Staffe's firmly. The swelling around the bridge of his nose is down and the bruises on his eyes are fading.

'Sprucing the place up, Will. I hope it's all right,' says Paolo.

Staffe sniffs up, can't smell tobacco smoke.

Behind him, he hears a scream and a whoop

and something crashes into the backs of his legs, hard enough to knock him off balance. Paolo stops him from falling to the floor.

'Harry! Be careful,' shouts Marie.

'He's fine,' says Staffe. 'Just fine.' He reaches down for Harry, picks him up and presses the infant's head hard to his cheek.

'Take me park, Uncle Will,' says Harry. 'Take me park.'

'He's been doing my head in all morning,' says Marie. 'Strange you've come now.'

'Can I take him?'

'Paolo and I have got to see about a car. We're getting a van, a small van with some of the money. Paolo's going to start on the restaurants again. He has such green fingers you know, for the herbs. We're going to lease a place out Surrey way. He's going to show Harry how to grow.'

'Take me to the park!' screams Harry.

'Can I?' says Staffe.

'Of course you can. It's meant to be,' says Marie.

★   ★   ★

Pulford looks at the jagged plastic snippets of the hole he is in. He scoops the credit-card cuttings together with a cupped palm and puts them in the bin, then showers, gets into his black suit and tries Staffe a final time, but gets no response. He trousers his mobile and picks up his keys, warrant card and notebook and takes a look around the room, hoping he has put something behind him.

Just as he is about to lock up, his mobile

vibrates, then breaks into his ringtone — the chorus of the Clash's 'I Fought the Law'. Staffe gives him stick for it, says it might advertise what he is. Josie thinks it's funny. Johnson thinks it's sad. Everyone has an opinion, which is why he keeps it. He looks at the screen, sees it is Leadengate.

As he raises it to his ear, he feels afraid.

'Thank God somebody's answering me,' says Pennington. 'Where the hell is Staffe?'

'What is it, sir? Can I help?'

'Tell him to get in touch with me. Tout suite!'

'Can I tell him what it's about?'

Pennington pauses, eventually says, 'You tell him there's been a major breakthrough. Smethurst has cracked it, no thanks to you and your so-called boss.'

'Cracked it, sir?'

'Don't come the innocent with me, Sergeant, and don't think that you can always hide behind people like Staffe. You should have told me you knew it was Jessop. Nobody's bigger than the law, Sergeant, and you can tell Staffe that. Nobody!'

★ ★ ★

Staffe watches Harry from the park bench. He goes up to the other children and joins in even though they are strangers. The mothers and fathers smile into next week at him and twiddle their fingers at Staffe as if to say what a good job he is doing. He will take Harry to Hamleys later in the week and maybe buy him a rugby ball. He

334

will teach him to pass and kick, take him to see a game when the new season starts.

Harry is on the roundabout now, playing nicely with younger and older children. Staffe feels a warm glow, and stares off into infinity. There will be something of Staffe's mother and father in the boy. There may be something of Staffe in the boy, but will it ever show itself? Could it possibly transcend the difference between him and Marie? He tries to get his head round where her free-spiritedness comes from. Could it be the same place as Staffe got his — before it died?

He reaches down into his pocket and pulls out his dead phone. He tries turning it on and can't recall if he turned it off or if the battery is dead. It sparks up and sings its jingle. He will call Sylvie. She said he could. She said not to be a stranger. Didn't she?

A jangle of unread text messages. Six missed calls, all from Pulford and Pennington. He highlights the most recent and presses 'Call'.

'*Staffe!* Thank God, where the hell have you been?' says Pulford.

The case comes to him, like many segments from different dreams. 'I'm due some leave, Pulford. I'm going to take it.'

'Pennington's been on. He says Smethurst has got Jessop for the Colquhoun murder.'

'*Got* him?'

'Did you know it was Jessop? Pennington thinks you did. He reckons you were protecting him. Why didn't you tell me, sir? He thinks I am in on it.'

'Nobody knows anything, Sergeant,' says Staffe. He crosses one leg over the other and leans right back into the bench, watching the top of the trees sway against the wide, blue, unclouded sky.

'You sound strange, sir. You're coming to the funeral?'

'Funeral?' He can hear the children shouting and squealing. They sound further away.

'Karl Colquhoun's funeral is at two o'clock.'

Staffe looks for the sun, tries to work out what time it might be.

'I'll come and get you,' says Pulford.

'When you say they've got Jessop, what do you mean? Have they *got* him?'

'I reckon Pennington thinks you know where he is.'

'He'd be wrong.' Staffe looks down, away from the sky and across to the swings and slide. There is nobody there. The children have gone. The parents have gone. He stands, looks all around him.

'Sir?'

'How would I know where he is?'

'You went to see him. You're friends.'

Staffe looks at the playground. He knows something is wrong. 'Harry!' he shouts. 'Harry!'

'Who's Harry? Sir, are you all right?'

He clicks off the phone and walks towards the swings and slide, calling 'Harry, Harry!' as he goes. He climbs the steps of the slide, feels his pulse booming inside his head. He looks to the four corners of the park. There are several couples, strolling. A handful of people are

336

starting picnics or having a snatched lunch on the benches. But no Harry. He calls his name again, louder. Far away, a woman pulls her child close to her and scurries away.

There is a copse of trees fifty yards away and Staffe jumps down the steps, runs across the grass to the trees. Halfway, he stops dead in his tracks. He thinks of Tanya Ford and the rag he found in that copse. He is suddenly struck, like a leather cosh across the back of the neck, by how real the world is. 'Harry!' he calls, sprinting hard for the trees. He ducks his head and calls Harry's name, time and again inside the copse. The twigs scratch at his face as he crashes all the way through and out the other side. A lump forms in his throat and his stomach is tight. Suddenly, all the blood seems to drain from the muscles in his legs. He sinks to the ground and rests up against the trunk of a tree. In the distance are railings and, beyond, a pond. He sees a boy being led away by a man.

'Harry,' he calls. 'Harry!'

The two of them turn around. Harry pulls away from the man's grip. The man looks up. He is smiling. Harry runs towards Staffe and the man jogs after him. Staffe gets to his feet, clenches his fists as he runs towards the pond. Halfway, Harry runs into his midriff, knocks all the wind out of him. He bends double, holds Harry tight. The man's jog peters to a walk and he says, 'I hope you don't think I'm being funny, but are you his dad?'

★  ★  ★

Marie is out and Staffe isn't carrying a key to his Kilburn house so he tells Pulford to get hold of Josie and meet him outside the Scotsman's Pack and hangs up. As he puts the phone in his pocket, he feels something sharp. He pulls out a torn foil blisterpack of pills, empty. He studies the name of the medication Jessop must have forced on him but it makes no sense. Wellbutrin. He slips the foil pack back into his pocket and takes a tight hold of Harry's hand. 'Let's go and play with some of my friends, shall we?' As he says it, he feels dreadfully sad and he can't help but hope that Jessop is safe and sound.

In the Scotsman's, a few old boys have their elbows on the bar, looking at the racing pages and pinching snuff whilst they grumble about jockeys and how the whole game is a fix. They don't know why they bother. But they do.

Staffe is sitting in the snug at a table by the window, teaching Harry to play pontoon. It's not a kids' pub, but Staffe had reminded the landlord, Rod, of who he was and what happens to people who withhold evidence. Harry has a J2O with a straw and Staffe has a large malt.

As he approaches uncle and nephew, Pulford sees there is further cause for concern: Staffe is smiling, looks thoroughly relaxed, and appears to be at peace with the world.

'Get yourself a drink, Sergeant,' says Staffe.

'We're already late. The funeral started five minutes ago.'

'These things go on forever.'

'Smethurst is there.'

'Bully for Smet.'

'I think you'll need to get your story straight.'

'Story? I'll rely on the truth, thank you very much, Sergeant.'

Staffe's eyes look heavy, but his glint is bright. An easy smile curls in one corner of his mouth. He looks as if he hasn't had a shower in a week. 'You need to do what you can, say what you can to protect yourself, sir.'

'Thanks for the advice.'

'Sir, I don't like to say, but . . . what's wrong? You seem different.' Pulford looks at the glass, the sun lighting up its golden barley. 'How many of these have you had?'

Staffe reaches into his pocket and tosses the empty sleeve of pills on the table. 'I reckon I've had a few too many of these. Where's Josie?'

Pulford picks up the blisterpack. 'Shit.'

'Good shit,' says Staffe.

'Where did you get these? They're not yours, surely?'

'A parting gift, from an old friend.'

Pulford squints at the small print, says, 'This is full of buproprion. It's a serious anti-depressant. Jesus.' And he presses his way through the menu of his phone, tracking a route to Janine in Forensics. He gets the answering machine and leaves a message for her to call back asap. Sooner, if she can.

'Josie's outside. She'll take the boy home and wait with him. Come on,' he says to Staffe, standing. He extends a hand but Staffe shrugs him away and downs the rest of his whisky in one. Slowly, he gets up from his chair, cajoling young Harry. The boy beams up at his uncle, clearly trusting that there will be many more where these good times come from.

'Show the way, Sergeant. Show the way.' And he takes Harry by the hand and leads him to his temporary childminder. For a split second, his altered state is darkened by a snapshot tirade of what Marie will say when she sees Harry sitting in a patrol car, outside the house, in the custody of DC Josie Chancellor.

\* \* \*

By the time they get to the funeral, the service in the tiny chapel has finished and the small gathering is forming a line towards the grave. The gravedigger leans on a long shovel, looking disinterested. Leanne Colquhoun is at the front with Calvin and Lee-Angelique — done up like gelled poodles. Debra Bowker is there, too, keeping her distance and looking good in tight black.

Pulford picks out Smethurst and Johnson at the back of the line and they catch his eye. Johnson mouths something to the effect of 'What are *you* doing here?' They start to come across and Pulford leads Staffe to a large yew tree with a bench around its base. 'You sit here. Leave the talking to me, eh, sir?'

'Let's see how you go.'

'Staffe, Pulford,' says Smethurst. Johnson loiters, a few paces away, kicking at the ground, hands in pockets and looking as though he needs some of what Staffe has had.

'I believe congratulations are in order, sir,' says

Pulford, trying to muster a smile.

'That depends.' Smethurst looks at Staffe, his eyebrows pinching together, the tip of his tongue peeking from the corner of his mouth.

'What put you on to Jessop?'

'I'm sure Inspector Wagstaffe knows. Hey, Staffe.'

'All ears, Inspector Smethurst. All ears.'

Smethurst hands a folded note to Pulford, says, 'It's a copy. You can keep it, for old time's sake. Seems Jessop has a knack with confessions. Except this one's his own.'

'Have you got him?'

Smethurst shakes his head. 'It came registered, posted yesterday from Central London at one in the afternoon. We're checking all the flight lists but I reckon he's gone. If he can do what he did to Colquhoun and Montefiore, plotting it ahead all these years, he can bloody well get out of the country — on a dodgy passport is my guess, amount of grasses he's had down the years.'

Pulford reads the note aloud.

'*If you've got this I suppose you might think you've got me. But you haven't. It's too late now and all I can say is things got out of hand, turned on their head. You couldn't know what it was like but if you'd known Stensson, you might have done what was done. Someone showed how and I had to follow, but don't follow me, there's nothing to be achieved. What's done is done. The law is an ass but you won't pin a tail on this old donkey. J.*'

He hands it to Staffe and says, 'Short and sweet.'

341

Staffe reads it through, but the words don't quite make sense to him. He watches the graveside scene take shape. Even from fifty yards away, he can see that Leanne Colquhoun is shaking. Her head is dipped and her children are clutching at her legs, hiding their faces. Ross Denness comes across and puts his big arms around them. He looks around, not comfortable with what he is doing — but doing it nonetheless. It makes Staffe want to respect him, just for now. But as he is looking around, Denness clocks Staffe. He double takes and his face goes hard, as if he could kill. His lip curls and he doesn't blink. Staffe smiles and Denness mouths something that might be 'stay away'. He looks different and Staffe feels that he could somehow trust him. But he quickly reminds himself that his mind has been altered; that he shouldn't entirely trust himself.

To Denness's left, Debra Bowker walks up to Leanne. She walks with her back straight in short, stiletto steps. She is wearing a tailored frock coat and a matching black miniskirt. Her hair shines and her nyloned legs shimmer. She crouches, back still straight and puts her arms around the children. They respond, wrapping their arms around her. Leanne Colquhoun moves her hand towards Debra Bowker and takes a hold of her shoulder. She rubs Debra's neck and Debra looks up at her. They smile, sadly, at each other. Tears smudge Leanne's mascara. Still, Denness looks at Staffe, beseeching him to go away.

Staffe considers the possibility that the world

is a better place for Jessop having betrayed his law. These poor people are now somehow coming together in a safer world. In the shade of the yew, he says an instant prayer for Sally and Tyrone Watkins, for Nico and Greta Kashell, and thanks God that Jessop got to Tanya Ford in time — so many steps ahead of the wheels of justice.

But can it be right? And if it is right, then what does he do with his own life?

Smethurst and Pulford have been talking. 'We're still holding her,' says Smethurst.

'Holding who?' says Staffe.

'Greta Kashell,' says Smethurst. 'I checked up on Nicoletta's counselling history. She only went for a few weeks, then Greta signed her off so I sent someone to interview her down in Hastings at her grandparents' place but she wasn't there. They said she went missing over two and a half years ago, not long after Nico went down. Greta lied.'

'Oh Christ,' says Pulford.

'She held Jessop responsible, for getting that confession out of Kashell and when Nicoletta disappears, she gets hooked on revenge. Lotte Stensson was already dead, so she uses VABBA.'

'She uses VABBA to source the victims?' says Pulford. 'And Jessop's motives?'

'The bloody fool, he didn't know how much he'd bitten off. My guess is that when he got Stensson's charges dropped he knew what Nico would do. But Nico can't bring himself to do it, so they come up with that mad pact. When Kashell gets sent down and Greta finds out about Jessop, she starts to blackmail him, says

343

she'll tell the authorities unless he does more, for VABBA.'

'You put them on to Jessop, Rick.' Staffe looks Johnson straight in the eye. He doesn't sound angry. He says it as if he is saying 'Canberra is the capital of Australia'. Johnson looks at the ground, chews at his lip.

Smethurst looks at Staffe as if he doesn't really know him. 'You should hear Greta Kashell when she talks about what happened to Colquhoun and Montefiore. She gets high on it. You heard what Debra Bowker said about her.'

'It's all consistent with a different truth.'

'What?' Smethurst turns to Pulford, says, 'What's he on?'

Pulford says, 'We should go, sir.'

'What does Greta say about the fourth quadrant?' says Staffe.

'What?'

'The website.'

'Aah.' Smethurst looks at Staffe as though he is ailing for something.

Staffe scratches at his head, and talks as if someone behind the scenes is feeding him lines. 'If your man has slipped the country and still a fourth one dies, that wouldn't be good.'

Staffe recalls someone telling him the website was set up in Guy's name, from his address. He feels light, his feet still not quite touching the sun-parched golden grass beneath. Debra Bowker and Leanne Colquhoun walk away from Karl's grave, linking arms.

Smethurst is saying something else now. He's getting irate, thinks Staffe. He knows it would probably be better to get his head straight, but he beckons Smethurst for a private word, walks away, from under the yew shade.

'Something will happen to Montefiore and there will be a fourth victim,' says Staffe, turning round to make sure Pulford and Johnson can't hear what he is saying to Smethurst.

'Look, Will! I don't know what you're on, but take it from me. You let this sleeping dog lie.'

'You know Jessop didn't do it.'

Smethurst looks round. 'I know nothing of the sort. You need to watch what you're saying, Will. Take some rest.'

'Did you help him get away?'

'You should go home. He was your friend, for Christ's sake!'

'All I want is the truth.'

Smethurst leans forward, hisses into Staffe's ear. 'There's no such thing. There's just the stuff that people tell you. That's all there is. Now, I don't know what you think the game is here, but we've got our man.'

'What if there's another killing?'

'We can't be sure Jessop's not still around. And anyway, it's gone crazy out there. Who's to say what people might do — to copy him?'

'There's a fourth quadrant. You've seen the website.'

'That could be Jessop. It could be anybody. Those images of Colquhoun and Montefiore have been published. Anybody could use them.'

Staffe turns his back, beckons Pulford towards him.

'Watch yourself, Will,' calls Smethurst.

345

'What was that name, Sergeant?' he says to Pulford. 'The young black girl. It was a Tom Jones song.'

'Spears? Martha Spears was the girl. The mother was Delilah.'

Staffe looks back at Smethurst. He's talking to Johnson and losing his rag. Johnson looks as if he can't take much more. 'Did you say Janine is coming?' says Staffe. As he says her name, he remembers she has Johnson's syringe.

'We're meeting her at my flat.'

Staffe looks all around, back at the graveyard, across to the flats behind and the broad hint of London spreading itself out to the blue horizon. So many lives.

Walking back to Pulford's MR2, Staffe stops, turns to see the young sergeant, stock still, by a news-stand.

The guy pushing the news looks at his own gear and then at Staffe, back to the paper. On the front page is a photograph of Staffe: looking worse for wear.

The headline says:

## EX-STAFFE

Beneath, the strapline is:

## FIDDLING COP OFF THE CASE
### Arrests Will Now Follow

Pulford comes towards him, newspaper in hand, and wraps an arm around and turns him to face the MR2. The lights flash on and off, the car makes a beeping noise. Pulford shows Staffe the passenger side and once Staffe has bent his frame into the low seat, the DS shuts the door gently.

Staffe tries to work out when and where the photograph was taken. The hanging baskets in the background are from the Steeles. The jacket is the one he's wearing now. The stubble is a day behind.

'Bastards?' He says it quizzically, as if he is unsure whether he is right. The story dissects everything that has gone wrong with the case. It suggests Staffe had been protecting a suspect. He looks up at Pulford. 'Fiddling? What do they mean?'

Pulford says, 'Like Nero. While London burns.'

'Nero,' says Staffe. He stares out of the window, as if in a trance, at people, shops, building sites, schools, offices. Some trees beyond.

★  ★  ★

Staffe says, 'Do you have to stick me?'

'It will be faster this way,' says Janine, tapping at Staffe's bare upper arm with the second and third fingers of her left hand. She holds the syringe between her teeth, as if it might be a rose.

'What is it?' says Pulford.

'An ampakine, kind of like Modafinil, but industrial strength.'

Staffe sits on a dining chair in Pulford's flat,

his face riven with fear. His shirt is pulled off, draped at his feet. 'I hate needles.'

Janine takes the syringe from between her teeth. 'Be a brave boy,' she says. She holds the needle aloft, gets some liquid out and eyes Staffe's upper body. He looks after himself but you'd still have him at forty, plus. He could do with a haircut. It suits him long but the layers have grown out. His body goes tense as she takes aim at the reddened skin she has been softening up and as she slides the needle in, his whole body quivers, as if he's in the last throes of something. She pulls it out and his body goes slack.

'I gave you a needle,' says Staffe.

She says to Pulford, 'It will take hold very quick. Get a glass of water and mix it up with a tablespoon of sugar and a teaspoon of salt. You'll need to be vigorous.'

Staffe gets up from the chair and looks around the room as if he is clocking it for the first time. His legs go weak and he reaches out for the sofa, flops on to it. His chest rises and falls, high and deep and he starts to blink. Janine pulls up a chair and crosses her legs, clasps her hands together in front. 'It was morphine — the syringe you gave me. You thought it was smack but it was only morphine.'

'Only?' He looks up at her. 'I'm thirsty.'

Janine takes the glass from Pulford and holds it for him as he guzzles it back in one. He leans forward, elbows on his knees, fingers pulling at his hair. After a minute or so, he looks up, wide-eyed, jaw set.

'I'm not buying that confession. No way,' he says.

'But you were on to Jessop yourself, sir.'

'It's written in his hand,' says Janine. 'And the ink matches a sample from his flat. There was a DNA fit on a hair we found on the gum of the envelope. Jessop wrote it, Staffe.'

'That's not what I'm saying. He's lying.'

'Fitting himself up for a murder he didn't commit. Just like Nico Kashell,' says Pulford.

'Yes!' Staffe stands up, starts pacing around the room. Janine and Pulford find a corner each and wait for him to knock into something, but his movement is lucid. 'Just like Kashell.'

'Sir, could it be? I don't know . . . ' Pulford can't bear to look his DI in the eye.

'Spit it out.'

'Well, Smethurst has pinned it on Jessop but he has got away by the looks of things. It was your case and now it looks like it won't be cracked. I'm sorry, sir, but maybe you just don't want to let it go.'

Staffe smiles at Pulford. 'But it's not cracked. Give me that note. And you get yourself off to see what's her name. What's her name?'

'Delilah. Delilah Spears.'

Staffe nods, already deep in the text of Jessop's note. His eyes flit, rapidly, from side to side.

'Or perhaps you just can't bear for it to be your friend,' says Janine. 'I remember you two when I first joined Forensics.' She looks at Pulford and winks. 'He was only a young pup.'

'Of course I don't want it to be him. That's not rocket science.'

'No, it's semi-professional psychology. And you'd be to blame, wouldn't you, Staffe? A bit more blood on your hands, eh?'

'What do you mean?'

'What Nico Kashell tried the other night. It seems like all the wrong people are suffering, doesn't it?' She looks at him, waits for him to look back. When he does, she softens her face, makes the slightest smile and says, 'Putting yourself in the mix won't help anyone, Will. Cut yourself some slack. You're in deep enough by withholding what you had on Jessop.'

'They suspended me! And anyway, he didn't do it. Here's the proof.' He holds up Jessop's note. 'Here's the bloody proof!' Staffe waves the note and starts to pace the room again, reading extracts from the note aloud. '' . . . you've got me. But you haven't.' See. Nothing's what it seems. That's what he's saying, I know it.'

'He's just saying he's got away. That's all.' Pulford looks at Janine, raises his eyebrows.

'It's a riddle. ' . . . all I can say is things got out of hand, turned on their head.' Don't you see? 'Turned on their head.' Don't believe what you see. Kashell didn't kill Stensson, but he confessed and now Jessop's repeating history. 'The law is an ass but you won't pin a tail on this old donkey.' He's even written it as a riddle.'

'If he didn't kill Colquhoun and torture Montefiore, who did? And what about the website?' says Pulford.

'Exactly! He could never set up a website. He doesn't even have a computer, never did. He refused to have an email address.'

350

'He had an accomplice — Greta Kashell, according to Smethurst.'

'They've let Jessop get away and he'll cop for the lot. Except he never will. Case closed.' Staffe switches out of the conversation, sits on the edge of the sofa and stares deep into the note. 'Did you get that read on his bank account? It said '*J*' on the stub.'

'Josie's coming over with it when your sister gets back,' says Pulford.

'Did you see the way Leanne Colquhoun and Debra Bowker and Ross Denness were at the graveside? Like happy families. But they'd have us believe they can't stand each other.'

'It's a funeral, Staffe. People don't fall out at funerals.'

'A fat lot you know, then,' says Staffe. 'Give Josie another ring, tell her to get her skates on.' He puts his shirt back on.

'I'm going to get to the bottom of all this. It's my job for crying out loud.' He runs his hands through his hair and goes to the window, looks out. 'My job,' he says to himself, wondering . . . what would be left of him if they took that away.

# Monday Night

Earlier, before his re-medication at the hands of Janine, Staffe was calm as a tripped-out hippy. Now, he is up to the window and back again every couple of minutes, waiting for Josie to arrive at Pulford's flat. Far away, it looks as though someone has smeared black across the sky — all along the horizon, like a primitive painting.

Down in the street, Josie parks up. 'She's here,' says Staffe, striding across to the door, buzzing her in.

'Sir!' calls Pulford, sitting at his computer. 'You've got to see this.' Pulford pushes his chair back so Staffe can get to the screen.

Staffe goes across, kneels down and rests his forearms on the desk. He leans right up to the screen. 'Sweet Jesus,' he says. 'It's getting clearer.'

'Sorry to interrupt your porn, boys. But I thought it was urgent,' says Josie, standing in the doorway.

'Come and have a look at this,' says Staffe.

On the screen, the bottom-right quadrant is demisting. Beneath the picture of the prostrate and butchered Karl Colquhoun and to the right of the crucified Guy Montefiore, the outline shape of a house can just be discerned.

'What's that in the background? A hill?' says Staffe.

'Or a shadow?' says Pulford.

Staffe leans back, puts his hands on the back of his head and sighs, exasperated. 'It could be anywhere.'

'Why would they make it less obscure?' says Pulford. 'Is it a sign that something is about to happen?'

'Or a red herring. They're in the driving seat. We're just guessing,' says Staffe, standing up, going to the window again. 'What was the upshot of that trace on Jessop's account, Josie?'

Josie is peering into the computer screen, squinting. 'I'm not so sure? It could be a building.'

'I asked about Jessop's bank account.'

'If Jessop is our man,' says Pulford. 'Maybe they are using the website to distract us, buy him some extra time.'

'It reminds me of somewhere,' says Josie, still staring at the screen.

Staffe goes back to the desk, looks over her shoulder. 'Come on, it could be anywhere.'

'I've got a feeling,' says Josie. 'A feeling I've been there. That dark area is a building, I'm sure of it.'

'It's too big, compared to the one in the foreground.'

'If it's nearby,' says Pulford, 'we could go down there and see if we can see the camera.'

'If I'm right, it's close.' But Josie shies away from Staffe, stares out of the window.

'You have to tell me,' says Staffe. 'If it's relevant to the case I need to know. I *have* to know. We're a team for God's sake.' Staffe goes up to Josie and she hangs her head. 'Oh. I see.'

'You don't know what trouble I got into for going to VABBA with you. Pennington threatened to pull me off CID.'

'We're in this together.'

'In what, sir?' says Pulford. 'It's a case that's solved.'

Lightly, Staffe puts his hands on Josie's shoulders. 'I'm asking you, Josie. Anything you can tell me, *anything* — I'll only damage myself, I promise you.'

'They're barking up the wrong tree.' She leans in, peers and the men gather round her. 'If I'm right, the building in the foreground is empty.'

'What is the shadow?' says Staffe.

'I think it might be the Limekiln tower.' Josie stands up, backs away from the screen, narrowing her eyes. 'And . . . ' she tilts her head, unable to take her eyes off the computer, ' . . . remember the Martha Spears case? That's why I went.' She reaches out, taps the screen. 'This is the street where the guy who raped her used to live. He was released last week. His name is Errol Regis. And there's no point rushing over there. Johnson came with me. We knocked on the door but the house is empty.'

'Why did you go with Johnson? That seems like overkill,' says Staffe.

Josie is dialling the station. 'The neighbours said Regis has gone. They saw the wife leaving. She had suitcases. There were no lights on, no sign of life and the curtains were drawn shut. He missed a probation appointment, too.'

Jombaugh picks up at Leadengate and she

says, 'Sergeant, can you find out the address of an Errol Regis. He's a recent release on a rape — the victim was Martha Spears. Me and Johnson visited a few days ago. Thanks.'

Pulford says, 'This one's going to be live. It's like Absolom said, it'll be filmed on the web this time — for everyone to see.'

'Nobody's there, though,' says Josie.

'There will be,' says Staffe.

'Unless like you said, it's a red herring,' says Pulford.

'It's a swansong,' says Staffe.

'But Jessop's out of the country.'

'Here's his statements,' says Josie, pulling a wad of papers from her bag.

Staffe quickly scans each page. 'There's nothing here.'

'That's all there is — going back three years.'

'No payments in over a grand, apart from his last salary.' Staffe closes his eyes, says 'J'.

'Sir?'

'Where's Jessop's confession? Read the last paragraph.'

Pulford unfolds the copy that Smethurst gave him. '*Someone showed how and I had to follow, but don't follow me, there's nothing to be achieved. What's done is done.* That's it. What's that got to do with anything?'

'Jessop didn't follow. He showed the way. He's written this note for someone else. He's protecting someone.'

'Ruthie Merritt?' says Josie.

'Or Greta Kashell,' says Pulford.

Staffe picks up his coat. 'You monitor that

screen, Pulford. Call me the second, and I *mean* the *second*, anything changes on that website.'

'Who's going to tell Smethurst what's going on?' says Pulford.

'Nobody.'

'I'm not sure about that, sir,' says Josie, but her phone rings and Jombaugh gives her the address. 'Gibbets Lane,' she says. '18 Gibbets Lane.'

'Let's go,' says Staffe, more his normal self. 'And keep schtum, for now. Schtum, I say.'

★ ★ ★

The curtains are three-quarter closed, the way they have been for two days and a night — ever since they came knocking. Three-quarters shut, and with the lights all off, it means he can see out but they can't see in. Even though he doesn't know who 'they' are, Errol knows he can't afford to show any signs of life.

It is beginning to go dark, but surely it's too early. He looks at the clock on the mantelpiece, which says seven thirty. Theresa used to wind it religiously. He peers through the gap in the curtains into the gloom. The sky is dark; he can't see any stars in the sky. He pulls the chair up to the window, looks out on the angle so he can't be seen. Pulling the blanket up around his neck, he watches the fire next door. He feels sick in the empty pocket under his belly.

The tar has been going non-stop even though the council said there's no work down to be done on Gibbets Lane. Not now, not in the future, they said — as if he was mad for asking. And he asked them if his wife had been in to get on the housing list. 'Theresa Regis,' he had said.

'I'm afraid that's our business — and hers. Not yours,' they replied.

'She's my wife.'

'Then ask her.'

Soon — when he's sure Theresa isn't going to come back, ever — he will move on. Tonight, he will stay awake with the phone in his lap until dawn breaks. Leadengate is still on redial. Just in case. Probation will be round before long and he'll be sent back to serve the rest of his licence for the breach. At Belmarsh, the POs hadn't been happy to see him go. Not because they liked him, but because they thought a three-stretch was insufficient for a sicko, a frag, a fiddler. As he had walked through reception, on his way out and carrying all his worldly in a clear, plastic, prison bag, they said, 'See yer, fiddler. You'll be back for more, you fucking frag.'

The strangest thing about jail is the way they let you leave. One morning — and even though you know it's coming, it's like a kick to the balls when it finally does — you are taken to a small room and they give you the one prison bag. You get into the clothes you arrived in — all that time ago. In Errol's case they hung off him. You even get your belt back, as if you're no longer a danger to yourself; you walk out across the yard without having to hitch your trousers and you go into reception where all the normal people come in and out. And someone opens a door and the world is on the other side. Down the road, there are buses and trees. Somewhere among the raging streets is a train station. You can go left or right or straight ahead. The air is all around.

He knows he can't go back, can't do another day.

Even though the windows are shut tight, he can smell the tar. He used to like the smell, but he's learned to adjust.

★ ★ ★

'Thanks for looking after Harry,' Staffe says to Josie. 'What did my sister say when she collected him?' He stares straight ahead, not even blinking. From here, behind the petrol station's condemned outside toilet at the top of Gibbets Lane, and with the jacket of his collar pulled up against a long forgotten chill, he can just see the windows of number 18. The curtains are drawn almost closed. The house is sandwiched between two derelict units.

'She's got a temper is all I'd say. I'd get her some flowers if I was you.'

'You explained. You told her it was to do with Jessop.'

'That didn't seem to help. She said . . . ' Josie bites her lip, can't help a smile slide into the corners of her mouth.

'What did she say?'

'She said you always had an excuse to make bad behaviour seem good.'

'Fine. That's just fine.'

'The boyfriend's kind of cool, isn't he? Is she younger than you?'

'A year. And they're reasons. Not excuses.'

'Hmm.' Josie looks to the sky. 'Did you feel that?' She holds her hand out, as if to catch a falling droplet.

Staffe looks above him then up and down the street. 'I can't work out where the camera would be — if this is the right place.'

Josie looks up and down the street then up at the lamp posts. She blinks as the rain begins to come down hard. Staffe doesn't stir, stares straight ahead. The sky is suddenly black and even though this is the broken heart of the city, in the shadow of the Limekiln you can hear seagulls above. Their squawk gets louder and a feather drops, slow, to earth. 'Let's go to the café,' she says.

'You go,' says Staffe.

'It's just there, on the corner. We'll be able to see who comes and goes.'

'OK.' He doesn't move.

'You coming?'

He shakes his head, slowly, without diverting his attention from the windows of number 18. Before the sky went black and the rain came you could see the wall of the house next door warbling behind the heat generated by the flame, keeping the tar liquid — ready to go.

Up and down the street, people come to their doors. They peek their heads out and look to the sky, hold out their hands. Staffe can't help himself from taking in the scene: a community coming together in the face of the elements, brought together by a crazy storm. Some of them are in their stocking feet — on tiptoes against the

359

wet or only wearing a thin shirt, crossing their arms across their chests against the sudden chill. People shout across their fences to neighbours with broad smiles on their faces. It is over a month since it last rained. Good for the gardens, good for the water companies. But Staffe can't help thinking it will be bad for someone.

He looks back to number 18. There is a car outside. He narrows his eyes, sees it is a small van. It wasn't there before. Damn it! Through the rain, he can't see if anyone is in the car. Have they gone up the path?

Staffe doesn't know whether to go to the café and tell Josie or down to the house to see what's going on. He decides a middle way — to call her and stay put. If it's nothing and he races down there, his cover is blown. He feels the clock tick against him, but before he can make the call, his mobile rings.

He lifts the handset to his ear, feels the wet metal cold on his ear and hears Josie's crackling voice. She sounds distressed but the line cuts dead. He calls her back but now the line is engaged. Is she calling him back? He looks to the skies and the rain runs down inside his collar.

Maybe the van outside number 18 is the workmen coming to load up their kit because they'll be rained off tomorrow. He peers into the stair-rod rain and a fork of lightning flashes in the sky. He counts the seconds to the thunder. On four, the ground shakes with deep wrath. The storm is sweeping fast into the city.

The mobile rings again and Staffe has to shout

to even hear himself through the storm. 'Someone's come!'

'I need you here,' says Josie.

'What!'

'Come here!'

'No! You come here!'

'Staffe! Montefiore's missing.'

He can't help feeling he is doing the wrong
thing, but Staffe ducks his head and walks into
the rain, away from whatever is going on in the
abandoned house of Theresa and Errol Regis.
When he looks back, a last time, the van is gone.

★　★　★

The knock at the door makes Errol's heart stop
for one, two beats. He looks at his mobile phone,
unsure whether to press *Leadengate*. Having
stopped, his heart races to catch up. The pulse
thuds in his eardrums. His fingers tremble. He
stands, weak at the knees, and peers out between
the curtains. The rain teems down, bouncing
back up to knee height. A small, thin girl with a
pretty face is standing by his gate. She is young
and smiles straight at him. Then she disappears.
There is another knock at the door.

The young girl isn't what he was expecting at
all and he doesn't know what to do, now she
knows he is in. *Leadengate* is illuminated on
the screen. He puts the pad of his thumb on the
green button, ready to call, and makes his way to
the front door. Errol suddenly feels less gloomy
than of late. This will be the first conversation he
has had since Theresa left, the first face he has

seen. He feels nervous, knows that is ridiculous.

In the hall, Errol can see her waif torso outlined in the frosted glass of the door. He takes a deep breath and says a quick prayer that the visit might have something to do with Theresa. With one hand holding the mobile, Errol unbolts at the top and turns the key for the lock. When he opens the door, he can smell the rain washing the summer clean.

The girl is smiling still. She has a collection box in one hand and extends it towards him. She shivers as she does it and says, 'All right for cats and dogs.'

'Cats and dogs?' Now he smells sweet, roasting tar.

'The rain. I don't suppose I could step inside, just for a minute.' She shakes her head and her high-up ponytail sends water spouting in a wide arc. Errol stands back, away from the wet and she takes that as an invitation to come in, makes a stride on to the threshold.

'No!' says Errol. He holds out his hand and looks at the mobile. He watches as his thumb presses green.

The girl's smile disappears in an instant and she too raises a hand — not the one with the collection box. In it, she holds a tiny canister.

Errol looks at the screen, waits for the call to engage. 'This is the police,' he says to the girl, pleading. 'I'm calling the police. Now go. Go away! Please!'

The girl shakes her head, looks angry now and says, 'I don't think so.'

'Hello!' he shouts into the phone.

The girl laughs a sneer and reaches out, points the canister at Errol's face.

'Hello!' he shouts into the phone but looking up at the girl. 'Who are you? What do you want?' Errol is walking backwards now. He can't stop her coming in, such a tiny girl. How could he raise a hand to her?

He is backed up against the understairs cupboard and wants to sink to the floor, curl into a ball and let the hurt come so it can go again. Her frown disappears and as she smiles he hears a hissing sound and a fine spray comes towards him. It stings around his eyes, burns his nostrils. He can't breathe and when he gulps at the air, the acid burn gets into his mouth and throat. He can't see and he throws himself on the ground, screws his eyes tight shut, fills his lungs and holds his breath. His head jolts and a sharp pain shudders down into his spine. Then another. And another. He curls into a ball, tries to make himself small. The pain gets duller, cruel in his kidneys. He tries to hold on to his breath but as the pain registers, he can't help himself. He wails. He tries to keep it quiet, trap it inside himself to preserve some dignity, but he fails.

After what might have been seconds or minutes, she stops kicking him. His eyes still sting from the spray and his throat burns. There is blood on his hall carpet. He bought the carpet with Theresa. They almost had an argument about it, but Errol reined himself in.

Errol squints up and sees the girl bent double, exhausted. Her hands are on her bare knees. She has a short skirt on, even though she is wearing heavy walking boots — built for the job. He looks further up and sees fat streaks of mascara all down her thin, white face. In the newspaper, she had worn a white hood and a cloak. When he makes this connection, he can't help himself, feels the wet spread of urine warm in his groin.

She sees him looking and summons an effort to stand up straight. She spits down at him and he closes his eyes again. He feels nothing, just hears the girl say, 'Fuck me. Fuck me? Fuck *you!*' And she stamps on him, this time in the midriff. It knocks all the wind out of him. The last thing he hears, before the darkness takes him, is the girl say, 'I am Sally and this is from Martha.'

★  ★  ★

'What do you mean, Montefiore's missing?' says Staffe.

Josie is sitting at a table in the window of the café. 'He insisted on going for a walk, told the officer on his door that he was only going round the block. That was three hours ago.'

Staffe looks out of the window and down the street. He can't see Regis's house for the rain. 'I've an idea where he might be.'

'Where?'

'I can't say, in case I'm wrong.'

'What happened to us being a team?'

He wants to tell her, to see if she might immediately come up with an argument to prove him wrong — something so obvious he can't see it. 'I promised you, I'll only damage myself.' He pulls up the collar of his jacket, buttons it all the way and makes to leave. 'I'll be an hour.'

'What about Regis's house?'

'Keep an eye on it. Call me if anything happens. For God's sake don't go in.'

'I'm going to call Smethurst. Tell him where I am.'

'No. You can't do that.'

'It's his case, sir.' Josie stares out of the window, down Gibbets Lane — into the darkness and rain. 'He's on our side.'

'He doesn't believe there will be a fourth — it goes against everything he's saying about this case. He doesn't want it. He'll go storming in and ruin everything. They're working to a different agenda.'

'Maybe it's you that's got the different agenda, sir.'

'Think what you like.'

'At least tell me where you're going.'

'Will you hold off from telling Smethurst?'

'Where are you going?'

'To Jessop's flat.'

'But he's gone. That's what you said.' Josie looks at her watch, says, 'I'm calling Smethurst in an hour. Sooner, if anything happens.'

'Thanks,' says Staffe, taking out his car keys.

Outside, he ducks his head to the rain and runs full pelt for his car, wondering if the lie he has just told Josie may come to haunt him. He quickly calculates that it could cost him dear.

The traffic is terrible, the way it always is when the rain comes. Nobody is walking and taxis are everywhere. Staffe switches into pursuit mode.

He overtakes and undertakes, constantly switching lanes and mounting the kerb or going the wrong side of bollards. He switches on his hazards and all the way along Holborn he drives through red lights with the heel of his hand pressed full to the horn.

As he drives like a maniac, Staffe questions whether this could all prove to be a horrible misjudgement — a jump, feet first, into a pool full of mistaken conclusions.

J, the recipient of the fifty thousand from VABBA.

J signing off the note that says he was 'showed how and I had to follow'.

Turn everything on its head, perhaps. 'Don't follow me', Jessop had written.

The traffic slows to a dead halt, nose to tail with three lanes cramming into two, so Staffe turns left down a no-entry street, switchbacking north of Oxford Street and through the embassy squares to the sound and vision of blaring horns and abusive fingers. Then he's on the taxi-cuts up towards Marble Arch and across Hyde Park towards his own place.

He leans back, relaxes his hold on the wheel, begins to re-rack the evidence that led him to a final hunch that brings him snooping on himself: wanting to be right but praying he is wrong.

Staffe parks round the corner from his Queens Terrace flat and breathes in, deep. He calls Helena Montefiore. Why would Guy go walk-about when he knows the venger is waiting to catch up with him? Staffe can think of only one type of wild horse that would drag him outside.

'Mrs Montefiore, it's DI Wagstaffe, Leadengate.'

'Oh.'

'Can I speak to Thomasina?'

There is no response.

'Please.'

'She's out.'

He can hear Helena's breath catch on the edge of her words. 'They told you not to speak to the police, did they?'

'Are you involved?' she says.

'She'll be all right. I have a feeling. They're just using her to get to Guy.' He looks down along his street. His curtains are drawn shut. He knows he left them open and his heart leaps. Then sinks. A bright light glows beyond the curtains. 'I'm sure she's fine.' He walks slowly towards his flat, heavy footed.

'Are you there?' he says, stopping, listening hard. He is sure he can hear her breathing: slow, even.

'You're not always right, are you, Inspector?'

The light within his flat seems unnaturally bright — or is it simply that the storm's black sky makes it seem so?

'I have to go,' he says, hanging up and putting his key in the door, urging himself to slow down but his head is pounding, hands shaking. He can't make sense of what Helena Montefiore has said.

The lock slides across and he slowly presses open the door, goes into the communal hallway and leans back against the wall, cups his hands around his mouth and nose, taking back his own carbon dioxide.

Staffe eases the door shut. The hallway is dark but he doesn't want to use the lights so he feels his way along, treading as lightly as he can. The closer he gets to his own oak door, the thinner the oxygen seems to be. He presses his ear to the oak, can hear something happening inside. He is sure there are low, measured voices. He can feel the rhythm of an earnest exchange. Or can he?

He uses his Yale key and eases open the door to his flat. A bright band of white light shows under the closed door to the lounge and he questions what his eyes tell him. The light seems ridiculously bright. He holds his breath, the better to hear what is going on inside. At least two people are talking: one man, one woman. Maybe more. Staffe feels his thigh vibrate. 'Shit,' he hisses under his breath. His phone is about to burst into ringtone and he fumbles it from his pocket, retreating towards his kitchen. As he goes, the sound from the lounge diminishes and he opens the door to the dark kitchen, goes inside quickly and closes it silently behind him, looking at the screen. Pulford is calling and he holds the handset tight to his ear, cups his hand around the mouthpiece, and whispers quickly, 'I can't talk.' He wonders what the hell he can do now — trapped in his own home.

'The website's on the move,' says Pulford. 'It's switched to indoors. There's a body laid out on a table and a figure in a cloak — just like the Karl Colquhoun photograph.'

Staffe's mind races. He wants to tell Pulford to get himself down to Gibbets Lane straight away and to alert Smethurst, but he daren't say anything. Figuring whoever is in the lounge will hear anything he says, he stays quiet, nudges inch by inch, round the kitchen that is fed only by the storm's dark twilight. He reaches for his knife block but it is empty. He opens the cutlery drawer, peers in. It is empty. 'No knives,' he says to himself. Someone has made it a safe house.

Pulford says, 'I feel like I should go down there. Jesus! . . . What shall I do? Where are you?'

Staffe cups his hand back round the phone and whispers, 'I can't talk.' A sound appears from somewhere in the flat. Low and human. He presses himself to the wall, behind the door.

'I'm going down to meet Josie,' says Pulford. 'If you don't want me to, don't hang up. If you hang up, I'm going.'

Staffe closes his phone down and lets his arm drop to his side. All he can hear is the thud of his own pulse, the roar of his own tight breathing. He tries to fathom what to do for the best. He knows he cannot stay here, skulking in his own disarmed kitchen, waiting for the situation to come to him. So he steels himself, stands tall and opens the kitchen door, walks steadily towards the bright seam of light underlining the door to the lounge. It sounds as if the conversation is becoming more heated and he pauses with his palm wrapped on the brass handle.

He twists the handle and pushes, walks quickly into the room, his arms taut, flexing at the knees ready to swerve or rush his adversary, but he is blinded by a fierce light. The room is floodlit and Staffe has to blink his eyes open-and-shut to adjust. He squints and holds a hand up to shield the direct glare. His heart races to catch up and he suddenly feels weak, slightly absurd. All he can see, when he has adjusted to the glare sufficiently, is history repeating itself.

Strung up and gagged, Montefiore is lashed to a steel cross, a piece of wood jutting from the floor and his trousers ruched around his ankles — his legs bound up and tied to his chest like trussed fowl. His mouth is stuffed with gauze and his eyes bulge, pleadingly. His cheeks are streaked with dried blood, the shape of blades, like the last time.

Staffe wants to look away but he makes himself watch as fresh blood trickles from Montefiore's eyes, down his face. He can't help think that the man has had enough. He wants to die. They have finally got him to the point they wanted. A fate worse than death. Staffe turns quickly on his heel, checking behind him, but nobody is there.

On the floor, by the fireplace, his portable TV broadcasts an unravelling drama. These are the voices he heard earlier. He feels a fool. 'Who's here? Who did this!' He strides to Montefiore, reaches up to untie the gauze and when he gets up close, he smells faeces. He looks down, sees it on his floor; sees also that the jutting wood is inside Montefiore — God knows how far.

Staffe can't believe that he could have got in here so easily. This makes him afraid — as though anything might be possible. What else has he overlooked or underestimated? What horrors might simply lie outside of his own abilities? He can't work out why Montefiore has been left like this, alone. Why do this? He weighs up the options, but he thinks he hears something shift, behind him. He freezes. Before Staffe can turn around, Guy Montefiore convulses. He open and closes his wild, bleeding eyes, and he shakes his head. Staffe's heart sinks. Montefiore is trying to tell him something.

But Staffe knows already. He didn't check the bedroom. He senses a presence behind him coming closer in the same instant that he hears the voice.

'Don't touch him. Don't help him,' says the voice.

Staffe recognises it immediately.

He turns, sees Johnson — as if he is seeing him for a first time, the fatigue replaced by a bright-eyed zeal. His sleeves are rolled up, as if he has been getting stuck into a job of work. He has thick forearms, big hands, dappled with freckles. Johnson puts on a pair of black sunglasses and smiles at Staffe, watching the light hurt his eyes.

'Sergeant,' says Staffe.

'You shouldn't have come,' says Johnson.

'You wanted me to, though. Didn't you?'

Johnson shrugs. He reaches behind his back. He pulls out a short tubular length of steel from the back of his trousers. It gleams, looks freshly machined. Johnson lets the steel hang loosely, down by his side. He taps the side of his knee with it.

'I said, you wanted me to catch up with you. Why the messages — on my car, in my flat.'

'It wasn't me, that's for sure,' he says. 'Sounds more like Jessop.'

'You were in it together.'

Johnson laughs, sneeringly. 'That couldn't be further from the truth.'

'You can't do this, Rick.' Staffe turns to look at Montefiore, shielding his eyes from the photofloodlights as he takes in the sight of a human reduced to its barest bones.

'Don't for one minute think he deserves any better. The lives he has ruined. The things he did — to Sally — and how many others have there been? To just kill him isn't enough.'

'Sally?' says Staffe. 'What have you done, Johnson?'

\* \* \*

'OK, I'll wait for you,' says Josie to Pulford, closing down her phone. But he could be twenty minutes, maybe more, and — judging by what Pulford has described as going on in number 18 — that might be more time than they have, so she puts on her coat and leaves a two-pound coin for the coffee. As she walks through the storm to Errol Regis's house, she palpitates, feels weak. She knows she should call Smethurst, but she promised Staffe she would wait an hour and he still has half of that. Even so, she knows she should call.

As she walks quickly down Gibbets Lane, head down, the rain running inside her clothes, Josie takes out her phone and calls AMIP. Someone she doesn't know tells her Smethurst is out.

'Unavailable,' they say.

'I need back-up, number 18 Gibbets Lane, just behind the Limekiln.'

'What's the call-out?'

'Suspected break and enter.'

'That's not a CID call.'

'I've reason to believe a suspect for the Karl Colquhoun murder is on the premises.'

'That case is closed.'

'Speak to Smethurst! This is urgent.'

'I told you, he's not here.'

'It could be another attack.'

'Look,' the AMIP officer sounds uninterested, 'I'll send a local unit round. Number 18, you say?'

'Tell them to be quick.' Josie ends the call and turns the phone to vibrate. She takes a deep breath and walks quickly, almost overshooting the house she last visited with Johnson. At Regis's gate, she sees that the bucket of tar has gone from next door. The butane flame is extinguished, too. She goes up to his window, curtains now completely drawn, backlit by a strong light and she immediately knows the house is occupied. As she draws back to knock on the door, she sees her hand shaking. She knocks, takes a half-step back and feels for her warrant card. The number 18 is cheap and askew.

There is no sound of life from within, so she leans forward and peers through the mottled window panel. She knocks again and a slender shape appears through the frosted glass. Whoever it is pauses and adjusts their clothes then comes right up, sliding the lock across. The door opens slowly and a small voice says, 'Come in.'

Josie takes a step closer and crooks her head to see who has answered, but nobody seems to be there. 'Who is that?' she says, her words cracking at the edges.

'Come on in. You must be soaking.'

Josie doesn't recognise the voice but she guesses it is a young girl, possibly in her teens. She relaxes a little and says, 'Is your father in?'

'Oh yes. He's in,' says the girl.

She takes another step forward, into the dark, placing a foot in the doorway and pushing the door further open. Something stops it from opening all the way.

'Don't let the rain in,' says the girl.

Josie steps right into the house and the door moves sharply, knocking into her shoulder and slamming shut behind her. Josie shouts: 'What the . . . ' And then she sees the girl, smiling. It's a face she knows. The girl holds up a small canister and Josie hears the 'sshhhh' of the spray at the same time as the jet of mist hits her eyes. It stings her nostrils and tastes acrid in her mouth. She begins to choke and falls to her knees. The last thing she feels, as she prays for the back-up unit to arrive, is a rough fabric being pressed to her face.

★ ★ ★

Staffe clenches and unclenches his fists. He could try to get out and to his car. But, as if he knows his superior too well, Johnson smiles, says,

'You know there's nowhere to go. Even if you could get out.' He taps the length of steel against the palm of his hand. It slaps. 'Pennington doesn't know what to think about your relationship with *him*.' He jabs his head in the direction of the impaled Montefiore. 'Very odd, wouldn't you say? And I'm guessing the alibis he asked you for don't quite come up to scratch.'

'You bastard.'

'I don't have to be. Not if you do the right thing, Staffe. Just let me get on with things.'

'And Jessop takes the rap.'

'Him? You? As long as this gets done.'

'And what about you, Rick?'

'I'm sorted,' says Johnson. He clutches his chest, coughs hard and dry. 'But before you go, I've got something you'll want to see.'

Staffe takes his phone out of his pocket. 'One call from me and a squad car will be here before you know it.'

'Try it. And, anyway, what will they find?' Johnson sneers again, crossing his arms. The steel glistens bright in the white light.

'Why in God's name are you doing this?'

'Same reason you do what you do. Exactly the same, so don't kid yourself you're good and I'm bad. Nothing is black and white — you know that. We have no choice in what we do.'

'But it is black and white. It has to be.'

'Don't waste your breath, Staffe. And don't waste my time. I don't have much.'

'What do you mean?'

'And don't do anything rash. If you do, I'll give the word.'

'Give the word? Who to?'

Johnson coughs again, holding his chest. When he is done, his face is more gaunt, his lips more pale — as if he's suddenly got the wrong kind of blood running through him. 'This bastard is going to pay!' Johnson takes a stride towards Montefiore and hits him across the shins with the steel.

Staffe is certain he can hear the thin crack of bone. He is frozen, has to watch as Montefiore whimpers. His head hangs.

'Where does this come from, Rick? How can you do this?'

'Somebody has to. Somebody fucking has to when bastards like him shit on people, shit on them and rub it into what's left of the lives that are left behind. And people like you do nothing. Nothing! There has to be people like us.'

'Us?'

'Empty your pockets, on that table. Everything.' Johnson reaches down and takes something from under the sofa. When he straightens up, he is holding a machete. He rubs the face of the blade up and down along the one rope which suspends Montefiore. 'Go on!'

'Where's Thomasina?' asks Staffe.

'She's safe.'

'Is her mother involved?'

'I said empty your pockets. Now!' He presses the machete blade to the rope again.

Staffe does as he is told. Wallet, warrant card, keys, change, all going on to the coffee table in the middle of the room.

'And the phone.'

Reluctantly, he takes hold of the phone. He looks at Johnson, knows that if he were to press green he would get Pulford, but in the time he took to respond, what would Johnson do? And where is Josie?

It begins to dawn on Staffe that he has missed his chance, so he pulls out the phone and looks towards the door but Johnson immediately takes a step to his right and reaches out with the machete, touching the rope again. Staffe slowly places the mobile on the Cobb table that Karl Colquhoun had restored with such love.

Johnson takes a step towards him. 'Stand by the window. Go on!' As soon as he retreats, Johnson raises the steel high, brings it down on the phone, smashing it to pieces. The battery drops to the floor and the marquetry on the table cracks, like a smashed windscreen.

Staffe slows himself down: clenches, un-clenches his fists. 'What's the morphine for, Rick? You said you haven't got long.'

'Don't pretend you're interested.'

'There isn't just you to think about.'

'Don't you think I know that. I'm not selfish, Staffe. That's the whole fucking point! Who'll look over my children, who'll stand up for any of the children — if I don't do this . . . ' Johnson struggles for breath.

'You said there's something I'd want to see,' says Staffe.

Johnson nods to the kitchen and as Staffe makes his way, he follows. As they go into the kitchen, he says, 'You know there's nothing in here, no knives or anything you can use. Open that.' He points at the fridge with the tip of the machete.

Staffe opens it and inside sees the strangest thing. A laptop.

'Take it out. Open it up.' Johnson struggles for breath. 'It's turned on. Just click.'

Staffe taps the mouse panel and the *victimvengeance* homepage glows alive. He doesn't know where the wireless is coming from and clearly Johnson knows his neighbours better than Staffe himself — their passwords and their movements. He remembers the break-in, the sheer volume of time and energy and imagination that Johnson has devoted to this cause.

The second quadrant is blank. The bottom right is now an interior with a black man laid out on a table. His arms and legs have been lashed to the legs of the table and he is bleeding from his face and legs. His trousers have been cut right up to the tops of his thighs. Lying next to him is an axe and on the floor is a bucket. 'The tar,' says Staffe. 'Is this Errol Regis?'

'You do know your stuff. Jessop was right about you.' Johnson's voice sounds different, muffled, and when Staffe looks up from the screen, he can see the DS is wearing a hood. He has taken off the sunglasses and through the slits, his dark, dead eyes show through — barely open. He puts lipstick on his mouth and throws the steel to the floor.

'Take it through, to the other room. Go on!' Johnson prods Staffe with the tip of the machete and he carries the laptop through, as if he is a butler with a tray. Once he is in the lounge, he looks closer at the fourth quadrant. In the corner of the room, a hunched figure is curled up on the floor under the window. Staffe leans closer to the screen, says, as if he can't believe his own words. 'Josie? Is that Josie?'

'She's been working with you too long, Staffe.'

'You bastard!'

'You should have done the right thing, Staffe. You should have shown more faith in justice than your precious law.'

'What do you want me to do?'

'Put the laptop down.'

Staffe turns on Johnson who takes a step back, holds the machete out in front of him. He takes two more paces and takes a hold of the aluminium cross. Montefiore makes a muffled whimper and a trail of urine spurts on to the floor. 'You sick bastard,' says Staffe.

'You don't know the half of it,' says Johnson, coughing. 'You don't know anything,' he splutters. He points the machete at Montefiore. 'You want sick?'

Staffe looks at Johnson, caught up in short convulsions. On his hood, where his chin would be, a thick seam of red begins to spread.

'What's wrong with you? That's blood you're coughing.'

'You didn't notice, did you? All the years we worked together. Who's the bastard, Staffe?'

'You should have said something!'

'I can leave this world in peace.'

'Leave? But what about Sally? What's her way out?'

'You don't know . . . what she was like

. . . without this. She's found peace.'

'You're deluding yourself — and her too,' says Staffe.

'She came to me.'

'Why you?'

'He wouldn't help.'

'Jessop?'

'I knew what he did . . . to that bitch. Stensson. But he wouldn't do anything for Sally. I had to help her, you can see that, can't you, Staffe? What were we to do when Jessop lost his bottle?'

'This hasn't got anything to do with bottle.'

'What would you know?'

'A damn sight more than you think, Johnson.'

'You lost your parents. Imagine if that was your kids. But you haven't got kids. What if someone messed with your kids?' Johnson reaches down, behind the sofa, looking at Staffe all the time. He tosses a white cloth at Staffe's feet. 'Put that on.'

Staffe unfolds the white sheet which turns out to be a cloak just like Johnson's. And a hood. He puts them over his head and inhales the fabric conditioner. It reminds him of when Sylvie was in this place. It reminds him that he is not ready to die and he thinks about the line that connects us all. In this mad instant he looks at Montefiore and Johnson and thinks of the line that runs through them to their children. The lines that are cut when we die.

'What happened to you, Rick?' Staffe remembers poor Sian, the dead look in her eyes.

'Don't you think it's a bit late for you to get

interested,' says Johnson, reaching into his pocket. He pulls out a remote control. He presses it.

'I need to understand.'

'This isn't about you. Look,' he says nodding at the laptop. The second quadrant flickers to life and Staffe can see a cross hanging from the ceiling of a brightly lit room, Montefiore's limp body strapped to it. The backs of two men, similar build, in white cloaks and hoods. You can't tell them apart.

'You're not going to get away with this.'

'I don't need to.'

'But what about your family?'

'Don't talk to me about that. I've done the right things. Don't waste any prayers on me.'

'And Sally?'

Johnson's body tightens up. Through the slits in his hood, his eyes blink, fast. 'When I first met her she wanted to kill herself. You know how long it took . . . after he stuck her . . . till she started fucking her way round that estate? Do you! I'll tell you. A month.' Johnson bends down, hands on knees, struggling for air. 'She was a star, a bloody star at that shit school. I spoke to her mother. Linda.'

Staffe remembers the gaps in the paperwork on the first Montefiore case. 'You stole the interviews, destroyed the evidence?'

'She died the night he stuck her. You know what he did? He waited. He waited till she woke up. Then he stuck her. He stuck her everywhere. He used a toy on her. And when he was done . . . he called her a whore. He said she was a filthy tart. Then he pissed on her.'

Staffe can't help himself from looking up at Montefiore. He tries to think of him as simply meat.

Johnson says, 'But then she found me. And I found her. We've made things better. You have to believe that.' He stoops again, gulping for air and wheezing badly. When he stands back up straight, he points with the machete at Montefiore. 'Well, look at him now. Look at the bastard now.'

Staffe looks Montefiore up and down. He tries to forget what Johnson has just said and imagines what Montefiore has suffered, what chances there are of finding some sort of treatment to remedy him, what chance to fashion some kind of justice.

Johnson draws back the machete and sizes up the rope. Another spurt of urine falls on Montefiore's thigh and Johnson laughs. Staffe holds his breath and thinks of Josie trapped in Gibbets Lane; his parents in body bags in the hold of an aeroplane.

Staffe holds the breath, still. He holds it and imagines his blood turning silver. He closes his eyes, summons all his strength and in one movement he stoops down, pulls a plug from the wall, grabs hold of the TV and launches it at Johnson. In the same instant, he screams, making Johnson look away from his target and as the TV hits him full in the chest, Staffe takes one, two, three strides and throws himself at Johnson. They fall to the ground and he hears the metallic clang of the machete's steel, loud, close by his head.

Johnson is underneath him, the hood all askew

and he looks up. His arms are spreadeagled and he still has hold of the machete. He brings it up sharply. Staffe sees it coming and ducks his head, as sharp and fast as he can, full in the face of Johnson. He hears the slap of flesh and the cracking of bone. Johnson groans weakly and the machete drops from his hand. Staffe leaps to his feet and kicks the machete away, puts his boot on Johnson's throat, but there is no need. He is all done in.

He looks down at Johnson, pulls off the hood. Up close and amidst the subsiding panic he can see now just how grey his skin is, and everything begins to make a little more sense. 'What *exactly* is wrong with you, Rick?' says Staffe, lifting his boot from Johnson's throat.

His gums and the inside of his mouth are brilliant red. 'As if you care.' He coughs again and spits out blood. He turns on his side and draws his knees to his chest.

'Are you in pain?'

He nods and puts a hand in his pocket. Staffe watches him closely, picks up the length of steel and readies himself. Johnson pulls out a small medicine bottle.

'It's terminal?'

Johnson nods.

'And you're close to the end?'

'This would be a good time . . . you reckon?'

Staffe reaches down and grabs the bottle off Johnson.

'Let me ease the pain.'

'You'll want to say goodbye properly,' says Staffe, knowing Josie's well-being hangs on the slender whim of Sally Watkins.

'Call Sally off and you'll get the goodbye you'd want.'

'Go to hell.'

'The goodbye Becky would want.'

'She's taken care of, don't you worry.'

'Is that what the fifty grand was for?'

Johnson looks up, a last blast of adrenalin feeding his shock.

'Fifty grand won't get her and the kids very far. I bet you invested that money — was it an insurance policy, Rick? Was it?'

'That's none of your business.'

'It won't be valid.'

Johnson sneers up at Staffe. 'It is. Trust me.'

*Trust me.*

'Is it a life policy? Even if you weren't diagnosed when you took it out, they won't pay if you commit suicide.'

'What?' says Johnson.

'And believe me, if you don't call Sally Watkins now, I'll make sure the world thinks you committed suicide.'

'You wouldn't do that.'

'Try me.'

'You couldn't.'

Staffe thinks of Josie, curled up in the corner down at Gibbets Lane; thinks of Errol Regis, too, and the terrible fate that awaits him, lying prostrate alongside the axe and the tar — a long, drawn-out death, another cycle of suffering and healing. A fate that is worse than death.

He bends down, goes through Johnson's pockets and finds what he is looking for: a syringe. 'There's more than enough morphine here. Maybe you just couldn't take the pain any more, or the humiliation of being caught.' He puts his boot on Johnson's chest and takes the top off the morphine and depresses the syringe, making sure all the air is expelled. He puts the needle into the liquid and draws it up into the barrel of the syringe. 'There was only you here, Rick. I can remove myself from a scene just as well as you. I'll do it. Believe me, I'll do it. They'll find you all alone and pumped full of all this.' He thrusts the hundred-mill bottle of morphine into Johnson's face.

'Leave her alone. Leave Sally. Please. You don't know.'

'Call her!' Staffe bends down, his knee on Johnson's chest, pushing out a rattling wheeze.

Johnson shakes his head, closes his eyes.

★ ★ ★

Josie comes round, slowly. A dull pain comes from her ankle but when she tries to straighten up, it sears up her leg like a series of stabs. Now she is conscious, it is an effort to breathe. She slumps back to the floor, her face on the rough carpet. She can see Sally Watkins's heavy boots on the other side of the table. She can't see Errol Regis, but she knows he is there. It is his incessant, muffled moaning that awakened her.

She inches herself on to her back, so she can lift her head, straining to see what is happening. Errol is still laid out, stock still on the table. Sally is in a white robe and hood and she is tightening the lashes that pin Errol to the table. As she makes her way around the table she curses and spits at him. He is crying.

Josie says, 'Let him have his say, Sally.' She tries to struggle to a sitting position in the corner under the window. Her arms are tied behind her back and her legs are bound at the thigh and ankle. She thinks her right ankle might be broken. Her skirt has ridden up around her waist and she feels exposed. Strange, in these circumstances, but she is embarrassed.

'He had his say in court. Don't you believe in justice? And he had his say when he done what he done to Martha. You seen Martha, have you? She's fucked, man. Fucked.' Sally picks up the axe from the table and lets it swing by her leg. She moves round the table, picks up a saw.

'What will you do, Sally?'

'Cut him off at the knee.' As she says it, Sally shakes her arms and the heavy weaponry flails. The axe and the saw seem too heavy for her to wield. 'I know how. Then put the tar on. Stop the bleeding, see. So he gets it long and slow. Long and slow, man.' She paces round the table, wired, and Josie wonders what the girl might be on.

'But what will *you* do? When it's done,' says Josie. She reckons that if she can keep Sally talking, the local response might get here in time.

'I got somewhere to go, don't you worry.'

'Will you meet Jessop? In India?'

Sally laughs. 'You people are just shooting in the dark, right?' She swings the axe and saw to punctuate her words.

'You can't kill him, Sally. I have back-up coming. I called in before I came here.'

'You should of waited for them.'

'Go now, Sally, while you can.'

'I've got time, more time than you think.'

Sally puts the saw down and places a hand on Errol's leg, just above the knee. She holds the axe high. He squeals through his gag and his body convulses — as much as it can. Sally slowly removes her hand from his leg and holds the axe high with both hands. She plants her feet, square and bends at the knee, setting herself like a boxer or a gymnast. Her breasts rise and fall against the robe.

'No!' shouts Josie.

In the distance, a police siren warps, gets louder. Josie curses AMIP — giving the all-clear for the locals to use a siren to cut through traffic, shaving a few minutes or so off their journey time.

'I told you, they're coming.'

Sally slowly lowers the axe and hisses at Regis, 'Don't worry, it's gonna happen. I'm gonna cut you up and stop the blood. You'll live for days, man. It'll kill you. The pain.' She takes the saw and swings it through the air, as if it is a toy. Then she uses it to cut into the curtain and tears a strip off. She reaches inside the robe and pulls out a ball of gauze.

Josie says, 'We're on to you. We know Jessop's got Montefiore. DI Wagstaffe's gone to get him.'

Sally laughs again and leans down, takes hold of Josie's face. 'You know fuck all.' She squeezes

Josie's mouth, forces the gauze roughly into her mouth and secures it by tying the strip of curtain tight around Josie's head. 'Now! We'll have some quiet while they come and go.' She switches off the lights and goes out of the room. The front door opens and closes and when Sally comes back into Errol Regis's front room, she throws a number 18 on the floor. Then she tightens the gag around Errol's mouth and sits cross-legged on the floor, her head dipped, as if she might be in a primary school assembly.

No sooner is she sitting comfortably than the police-car doors slam. The footfall is steady. She hears the police knock, but it's too far away. There are voices, raised in argument, then falling in a calmer trail of resolution.

'Silly police, they've gone to the wrong house. Someone must have got the number wrong.'

Josie tries to work this out. She thinks back to how she came to know the house. She came with Johnson. But even if they had a bogus number, or even if the numbers on the houses have been switched, surely the police will check the houses either side. She tries to recall exactly what she had said when calling for back-up. A break and enter, is what she said; a connection to the Colquhoun murder but no mention of Errol Regis. She should have referred to him by name and she silently chastises herself, holding her breath, praying for the knock to come on Errol's door.

A glimmer of torchlight shines across the window. She can hear the police talking, a few feet away on the other side of thin glass. It seems the storm might have abated. And Josie thinks that maybe this could be what God wants. She considers how it might be: that what Sally is about to do, might be for a greater good.

'What did they say?' says one policeman.

'A break and enter.'

'You sure you got the number right?'

'Course I have. It's derelict by the look of things. There's no one in here. We can check back with the station.'

The voices fade and the car doors open and slam shut.

In the dim quarter light, Josie watches the headlights beam and curl away.

Sally resumes her preparations. She says to Regis, 'See, you got plenty time to suffer. Suffer like the children.'

★ ★ ★

Staffe puts the syringe between his teeth and takes hold of Johnson's arm. 'You're going to call Sally, Rick.' He slaps Johnson's arm with the back of his fingers. He inspects the red flesh for an emergent vein, and slaps again. He takes aim. Can he kill a dying man?

He feels sick, that he might be able to do this to a man he'd call a friend. Many times in their shared lives, Johnson had stepped in and saved Staffe — on the street and in station politics. You have to trust — that's how it works.

Staffe moves the syringe quickly to the raised vein on Johnson's white arm and closes his eyes. Time seems to stand still. He feels resistance, feels the needle go slowly into the flesh and Johnson's body goes stiff. Staffe's thumb begins to press the plunger and Johnson wheezes, 'Stop! Stop, you bastard.'

★ ★ ★

Becky Johnson sits at the dining table, young Charlie on her lap and Sian and Ricky at her feet: battling each other in a handheld, virtual world. Ricky whoops and Sian says nothing — as if there is no pleasure in it at all for her.

And all the time, their mother stares at the computer screen with tears running down her face. She can see Montefiore trussed up and lashed to the aluminium cross, but wonders where Rick is, wonders when the man she loves will kill the child rapist. She prays with all her might for that salvation. She reaches down, runs her fingers through Sian's hair and feels her daughter flinch, go stiff.

When he makes it back to her, she will nurse Rick to death. God willing, they'll be granted the time to do that together. She hopes that everything he planned comes to fruition.

'Oh, Rick,' she says, full of fear. Full of pride. 'Why did it have to be you?' On the table by the side of the laptop is a pile of documents from the insurance company. She has been re-reading them. Now the time is near, she can't believe there isn't some kind of loophole. But it is clear. Even should he be convicted and die in prison, the policy will still bite. It will reach out and comfort them — the family of a murderer. A serial killer, is what he said it would be. How sweet the law can be, sometimes. She remembers the way Rick smiled when he worked it all out — even though it was his life that was ending.

She begins to sob and Ricky reaches out to her. He does it instinctively, doesn't stop playing his *Call of Duty* with his free hand.

'Don't mind me,' she says to her children. 'Just being silly again.'

'Is Daddy coming home?' says Ricky.

She can't bear to answer. She doesn't want to lie more than she has to, which makes her wonder about the lies Rick might have told her. He swore that he got the diagnosis as soon as he could, that he didn't wait until the policy took hold. But how could that be true? She holds the baby tight and she looks down at her eldest. Poor Sian. She looks at Sian and she hugs young Charlie so tight that he begins to cry. She wants to hold Sian this tight but she knows she can't.

'You're hurting him, Mummy,' says Sian. 'Stop it, Mummy. You're hurting him.'

Becky Johnson looks back to the screen, where Guy Montefiore hangs like a Scorsese Christ, and she wills her husband to stick it to him. For the children.

★ ★ ★

'Will you call her?' pleads Staffe. 'Call Sally. Call it off.' The needle is in Johnson's arm and Staffe's thumb is on the barrel.

Johnson's eyes well with tears. He nods his head.

391

Staffe takes his thumb off the barrel and says, 'Give me your phone.' He leaves the needle in Johnson's arm while he twists his torso, reaches round the robe and into his trouser pocket. He tosses the phone on the floor.

Staffe removes the needle, stands up. He picks up the phone and scrolls down through the numbers, is amazed that she is there, under *Sally*. He presses 'Speaker', then 'Call', and listens as the number beeps through the handset. They look at each other, listening as the phone rings and Sally Watkins answers.

'Who is this?' she says, sounding like a child who might have been caught off guard in an empty house.

Staffe hands the phone to Johnson, 'It's Rick. Have you started yet?'

'I was just going to.'

'Don't, Sal. You can't.'

'But I have to. There's a copper here, too. That woman.'

'Get out, Sally. Go where I said. Remember?'

'I've got everything sorted, Rick. I've got time. The police have been but they went to the wrong house, just like you said. I'm almost there.'

'They're here, Sally. They've got me.'

'But what about Becky? What about everybody? You said . . . '

'Careful what you say, Sal. People are listening.'

'You said . . . '

'I know. We've done what we could.'

'What will I do, Rick? This isn't what you said. I trusted you.'

Rick Johnson's eyes glaze. Tears form quickly and fall heavy. 'I'm sorry you trusted me. I'm so sorry.'

'What shall I do?' She sounds lost, alone.

'Do what I said. *Exactly* what I said. And don't touch the policewoman.'

'Or Regis,' says Staffe.

'And leave Regis. Please, Sally.'

'You're dying, Rick.' Sally starts to cry.

'You be careful, Sal. Remember what we said.'

Staffe takes the phone from Johnson and steps away from him. 'There had to be a better way, Rick.'

Johnson looks up at Staffe. 'You don't know the half of it. You might think you do, but you don't.'

'Where will she go, Rick?' Staffe picks up the syringe again, looks at it quizzically, as if it could still administer some good.

'That wasn't part of the deal. No fucking way, Staffe. You can do what you like but I won't tell you that. Sally comes to no harm. She's done no harm.'

'You've got to be joking.'

'It was all me. All me and you can't prove otherwise.'

'She's assaulted Regis and Josie.'

'That's assault. She had nothing to do with the others.'

Staffe looks at the screen, tries to see what is going on down at Gibbets Lane but the camera is on Regis. He can just make out Josie in the corner, and the back of Sally, crouching nearby. 'What if she does it again?'

'Does what again? And anyway, she's among friends.'

'What friends, Rick?'

Johnson's eyes lid down and Staffe checks his pulse. It is slow. He calls Leadengate and tells them to get an ambulance here, double quick. 'It's one of our own. I've got a DS dying here. One of ours.'

Johnson looks up. He tries to smile but it collapses under its own weight. 'I trust you, Staffe. I do.' His eyes close and his great chest rises and falls in shallow, stolen breaths.

Staffe taps the laptop's cursor pad and the screen comes to life. He watches the Gibbets Lane room. Josie is struggling to sit up on the floor beneath the window, her face is wrought with pain. Errol Regis is still laid out on the table. By his bare legs rest an axe and a saw. At his feet is the bucket of tar.

There is no sign of Sally Watkins.

# Wednesday

Staffe watches Josie through the safety-glass panel of her private hospital room. She turns, catches his eye, and appears to reset her mood, smiling weakly and batting her eyes. But as Staffe opens the door, making a magician's sweep with the flowers he had been holding behind his back, he can see that she has been damaged.

'I'm out tomorrow. I said not to come.'

'You look great,' says Staffe.

'Liar.'

'When did I ever lie to you?'

'How's Errol?'

'Just fine.'

Her smile fades and she looks down at the scrunched-up blankets. 'He's never been fine. He didn't do it, you know. He never laid a finger on Martha Spears. He swore that to me and I believe him.'

'You should concentrate on getting yourself right.' Staffe worries that after her ordeal she might never be quite the same.

'I promised him I would track down his wife. I said I would help. Have you had any joy?'

'We've got our hands full looking for Sally Watkins.'

'Do you have to, Staffe?'

'She did this to you.'

'There's nothing wrong with me.'

'She drugged you and beat you. She tied you

up and threatened to kill you. You're traumatised, for crying out loud.'

'She's a child.'

'We're not in the business of letting people get away, Josie.' He thinks about what might have happened if he had brought Sally in for being under age and on the game.

'How is Montefiore?'

'He's not regained consciousness. They don't think he'll make it.'

Josie looks as if she wants to say something, but decides against it. Her eyes are heavy. She sits forward and reaches behind her. Staffe rushes to her side and leans across, plumps the pillows. Her hair needs doing and she has no kohl around her eyes but she smells fresh and cool. He puts a hand on her shoulder, feels her slide through him and back to the pillows. Her flesh is warm and soft.

'Thanks,' says Josie. She takes Staffe's hand, holds it with both hers. 'Helena came to see me. Montefiore's wife. She asked me to do anything I could, to help Sally. She said if there was anything I knew about where she had gone, would I keep it to myself?'

'You told me Sally said nothing to you.'

'Is Helena Montefiore involved?'

Staffe hooks his leg around a chair by the uncoupled intravenous trolley and drags it towards the bed. He sits down without taking his hand away from Josie's and looks deep into her eyes. 'Sally has got more friends than she knows.'

'But she said she was alone in the world. All alone.'

'They were looking after her. When I thought they were all tied into it, they were just doing their best to stop her.'

'You mean Debra Bowker and Greta Kashell?'

'Not so much Greta, but Ross Denness, too.'

'You got him wrong, then?'

'One act of kindness does not an angel make.'

'Is that why he was round at Sally's that time you went?'

Staffe nods. On a cabinet by the window, he sees a Manila envelope, marked by a fountain-penned 'S'. Josie catches his eye.

'That's not you. It's a different 'S',' she says.

'Would that be Helena Montefiore's handwriting?'

'It is a personal letter, sir. And like I said, it's not for you.'

'You know, it's a crime to protect a witness.'

'How's Johnson bearing up?'

'Did you know he was so ill?'

Josie shakes her head. Her eyes film over and she takes her hands away from Staffe, draws her sleeve across her nose and puts her head right back, stares at the ceiling. 'Some friends we were.'

'But what kind of a friend was he to us?' Staffe stands up, wondering quite what sort of friend Johnson is to Jessop. He shakes his head, puts his hand into his pocket, touches the letter that came yesterday. 'Johnson is saying he killed Lotte Stensson, too. His statement is very convincing.'

'And what about Nico Kashell?' Josie's eyes flutter. Her lids are heavy.

'My guess is, he's going to have to cope with a

life on the outside.'

'And Rick takes the rap for the lot.'

'And then dies a natural death. It looks as though he'll get to take the truth to his grave,' says Staffe, looking out of the window. Planes make criss-crossed white powder trails above the London roofline. His heart bleeds for Sally, running away. Ever since Montefiore raped her, she has only really been able to function when she was running *at* her enemy, plotting revenge. What will she do now? He checks his watch, sees he is running late for the flight.

He puts on a smile and turns to Josie, but she is asleep. Her eyelids are dark grey, her lips pale and downturned like a sad clown. She doesn't look anything like herself. He looks at the Manila envelope, marked 'S', and makes his way quietly round the bed, checking over his shoulder that nobody is looking through the safety-glass panel. He picks up the envelope and looks closely at the 'S'. He turns it over, to see if there is any telltale sign — a crest or embossment, but all he gets is a waft of scent. He runs his thumb along the gummed flap and as he does, something outside in the corridor crashes to the floor, makes a metallic sound. His heart stops for a beat and Josie's head lolls to one side. Her eyes don't open but his mind is made up. Staffe places the envelope back on the bedside table and leaves the room, empty-handed, but somewhat the wiser.

Making his way down the stairwell at the back of the hospital, Staffe walks through vast slanting columns of light from the eastern sun. Way down

398

in the car park, he picks out his E-Type and the waiting Debra Bowker. She leans against the bonnet and blows out plumes of sun-dusted cigarette smoke. She looks up, shielding her eyes. It seems impossible that she might see him from all that way but she waves an arm, slowly.

He will drive her to the airport, just as he promised, and he will try to prise from her the likely whereabouts of Sally Watkins. A part of him hopes she will not yield, but the bigger part thinks that he has no business in letting Sally off the hook.

As he reaches ground level, Staffe pauses to let a cortège of wheelchairs pass. They are led outside by a nurse who has her Embassy Regals at the ready. Amidst the absurdity of the smoking cripples, he thinks of Jessop and takes out the letter that arrived that morning.

*Will,*

*I truly hope there is no need for this. For my part, I am long gone and hope to find some kind of peace. But I need your help, friend. Please believe everything Johnson says. Take him at his word — which will be close enough to the truth for most people. The more you believe him, the less harm will be done.*

*I'm home clear, but you're not, Will, and there will come a time when you won't be able to live with yourself if you don't do the right things now. Suffer the Children.*

*Your friend,*

*J.*

Staffe still can't quite make sense of it and nor will he, he suspects, until he sees Johnson, who is across town in St Thomas's Hospital. Word is, he will die within hours rather than days, and Staffe knows that unless he goes soon, it is unlikely that he will get to speak to his sergeant ever again. The hospital said they will call if they consider Johnson strong enough, but they said not to hold his breath. That's exactly what the young doctor said as he handed across Johnson's confession: to everything, from Lotte Stensson right the way through to Errol Regis. The doctor had smiled, as if he knew the note was a granted wish, a thing of beauty.

'Don't take it all on your shoulders, Staffe,' says Debra Bowker, twisting the sole of her kitten shoe on the cigarette dimp and pinching the corners of her mouth with finger and thumb. 'There's a whole legal system out there to make sure you don't fuck up.'

He laughs and goes round her side.

'It's the V12,' she says, looking the Jag up and down.

'You're into cars?'

'Karl was. He'd have killed for one of these.'

Staffe puts the key to the door and lets her in. 'I would have picked you up from the hotel.'

'That young pup dropped me off.'

'Pulford?'

She slides in and fixes her skirt as she wiggles to some kind of comfort. She pulls at the seat belt, but it doesn't work.

Staffe leans across and his cheek brushes against her hair. It tickles him as he jiggles the webbing of the seat belt, unsnagging it. He leans away and their eyes clash as he clicks her in. 'I've seen your testimony, you saying Johnson admitted to you about doing for Colquhoun and Montefiore?'

'Don't forget Stensson. He did for her, too.'

'And how would you know this? What connects you and Johnson?' He manoeuvres the car out of the car park, sets them on a course for Heathrow.

'How do any of us know each other? It's only through VABBA. As innocent as that,' she says in a light tone but with a serious face. Her thin, pencilled eyebrows crease together.

'VABBA? How can I be sure you're not directly involved?'

'If that's a threat, it's not a very good one. You know damn well where I'm coming from.' She turns to face him, crosses her legs at the calf. She makes a downturned prayer of her hands and slides them between her thighs. She lifts up her chin. 'I made a new life for my children after what my ex-husband did. It was what I had to do. They needed a new future, not me going over the past, getting myself sucked in. I have to believe that good is stronger than evil and good doesn't get to be stronger than evil by killing people. I come from the same place as you, Will. There's no place for revenge in my world. My children's world.' She stares straight ahead, all the way to infinity, as if she is tuning out of what she is saying, thinking ahead to something else. 'You don't have to believe me when I say I'm not involved. I know I'm not. You believe in the law.

401

I believe in the power of good.'

'So why confuse the two,' says Staffe. 'Help the law. Tell me where Sally is.'

'Good things can come out of this. All I can do is look after my children.'

'And Sally?'

'Sally is a child.'

'When did you last speak to Helena Montefiore?'

'What makes you think I ever did?'

'Or Ross Denness.'

'You might think Ross is a thug.' She looks into her lap. 'And he might be. But he cares. He's not everything you think.'

'If I don't catch up with Sally Watkins, she could do this again.'

'She won't.'

'She was hooked on it, Debra. That's why you got the call to come over — to try and help talk her out of it. Am I right?'

'No. We tried to show her some love. That's not a bad thing, and it's certainly not a crime.'

'Sally has been filled with hate for three years. Since Montefiore, it has governed her. That's not going to change overnight.'

'You can't put her in prison, is all I know. You can't.'

'So it's all right to take the law into your own hands?'

'She won't do it again.'

'You know you have to tell me where she is.'

'I don't have to do anything.' The words catch in her throat.

He looks across, sees that her lip is quivering.

'Did you know that Errol Regis never touched Martha Spears? He did three years because of people lying to the law and he nearly died because of Johnson and Sally. Sally needs help, Debra.'

'I can't play God like this.'

'It's just the law. It's the closest we have to good over bad.'

'You've no right . . . ' Debra Bowker presses her belt release, and says, 'I've had enough.' The belt is stuck.

'I said I'd take you. I'll stop with the questions.'

'I don't believe you can.' Debra dabs at the corners of her eyes with the cuff of her blouse. Two smears of black make dark gashes on the white silk.

'She's still in London, isn't she?'

'I'm not saying,' says Debra, sniffing.

'She's with Helena Montefiore.'

'Let me out!'

When Debra Bowker gets out of the car, she busies herself adjusting her skirt and the sleeves of her blouse. Then she does her hair. Staffe pulls away but has to stop at a red light. He checks Debra in the wing mirror and watches her shoulders shake, dark tears streaming down her cheeks.

As he drives away from her, Staffe is smothered by feelings of regret. All through this case, he has been amazed by the kindnesses and atrocities that people are capable of bestowing and inflicting on each other. He thinks, now, that he knows how this is going to pan out. But as he drives his father's car towards that end, he fears the worst — for the victims and for himself.

Officially, Staffe is still suspended from the investigation and, although he made the connection to Johnson, Smethurst and Pennington are still fuming that he kept the cards so close to his chest. But what else could he do? What can he do now, to make sure he is doing the right thing: by the victims. For justice.

The cats are pretty much all out of the bags and the endgame is being played out in public — with more than one eye on the politics. This is Nick Absolom's domain. After everything that has happened in this case, why not go into the den, offer his head up to the mouth and see what happens?

'I can't believe Kashell is still insisting he killed Lotte Stensson,' says Nick Absolom, running his long fingers through his hair and sucking on a cigarette in his seat by the open window on the sixth-floor offices of the *News* in Ravencourt House.

A part of Staffe feels compelled to respect a part of Absolom — his devil-may-care.

'What angle are you taking?' asks Staffe.

'I think you know. But that's not to say I believe your DS Johnson did all this on his lonesome.' Absolom flicks his cigarette out of the window, not caring how it falls to earth.

'Sometimes you've got to follow the party line, hey, Nick?'

Absolom lights another cigarette and swivels on his chair to face Staffe. 'We're not so different, you and me. We get our hands dirty, but it's nothing like the grime at the top. Same in news, same in law, same in politics. It's a mad, mad food chain, hey, Will?' He laughs, but cuts it dead and leans forward, fixes a look you could hook a fish with. 'You and me both know it's all shit. I can't follow the line any more than you can and it's killing me like it's killing you. We believe it'll be different when we get to the top.' He leans back. 'But will it?' He looks at his cigarette, inhales deep, blows the smoke into the room. 'You can't help yourself, can you, Will? Even though you're suspended from the case, you're going after Sally Watkins, aren't you? And you know where Jessop is.'

'I haven't a clue.'

'That's only half an answer.'

'She could be anywhere.'

'You could just let her live in peace,' says Absolom.

'And if she does it again?'

'You know as well as I do that if you put her inside, she's more likely to do it again. She's nearly sixteen. In three months she'll be padded down with proper crims twenty-four seven. It will become her land of opportunity and she'll be a hero in jail for doing what she's done. Does that make a better society? It would be law for law's sake.'

'Is that your headline?'

'As you well know — I don't have freedom of expression on this case. If I did, maybe I'd direct myself to ex DI Jessop for my headlines.'

'You haven't had any new messages?' says Staffe.

'You reckon they were coming from Jessop, not Johnson?'

'I know nothing.'

'We'd have printed them.'

'Isn't there a party line, though?'

'If there was, do you think I'd be telling a suspended detective?'

Staffe stands up and turns his back on Absolom, deciding he has no information regarding Sally Watkins.

'Straight down the middle, hey, Inspector? You can't help yourself.'

Staffe spins round on his heel. He wants to absolve himself but he knows that if you reduce everything down, Karl Colquhoun and Guy Montefiore have caused all this. Without them, the crimes would not have dominoed. They should be the ones he is bringing to justice. He spits out the last of what he has to say. 'I believe that Sally Watkins is a danger to herself and a danger to the world around her. I believe that if we catch her, we can give her help. She will be better off this way than left to her own devices — running scared, dragging herself up like some feral creature. I try to make the world more civilised, Absolom. That's where we differ.'

'We're both involved in the truth. Don't forget that. And don't ever underestimate how much truth I've got stashed. I know it all.'

Staffe shoots out a hand and grabs Absolom's throat. He watches the journo's eyes bulge and he thrusts his other hand deep into the inside pocket of Absolom's Paul Smith suit, pulls out a clear plastic bag. Two, three grams, he reckons. He smiles at Absolom and tosses the bag out of the window.

'You can't do that!'

Staffe walks away, treating himself to a smile as he waits for the lift to come. He has just two more calls to make before his final visit: to Helena Montefiore, up in her grand confection of stylish living, high on Harrow's hill. Suspended or not, he will see Johnson. They can't stop him doing that.

★   ★   ★

Looking up at St Thomas's, Staffe tries to predict the reception he will get inside. He makes his way past the squad cars, showing his warrant card to the uniforms on the main door and outside the lifts. It's the press they're guarding against, but just as he thinks he is home clear to the third floor, a uniformed constable holds out a hand. Staffe had shown him the warrant card but the officer smiles, patronising. Before he can say anything, Staffe snarls through his gritted teeth and spits out the words, 'That's my man in there. My sergeant! He's dying and I have to make my peace with him. Now what kind of a bloody man are you? Hey!'

'I can't . . .'

Staffe presses his face right up to the constable and whispers, 'Sometimes, just sometimes, being a decent copper is about what people can do, not what people can't do. Remember that. Now get the hell out of my way.'

The constable stands aside, and as he walks on Staffe can hear the rustle and rattle of a radio being pulled out and used. But he puts that right to the back of his mind.

Just about everything he believes in tells him that Sally Watkins must be brought to justice — in the same way Nico Kashell must be released and Guy Montefiore protected. Even Debra Bowker told him as much — even though it broke her heart to do so. And Helena Montefiore, too, must have figured out what he was likely to do. Why else would she visit Josie? Why else set down so red a herring as the letter to Sally?

It all points him towards Harrow on the Hill, but he figures that, somehow, being with Johnson will give him the strength, show him a final sign. Johnson will point him the opposite way. He is the antidote. If Staffe is wrong, Johnson must in some way be right. He must prove Johnson wrong. Absolutely.

Johnson was in VABBA and Staffe rewinds all the visits he has made to Johnson's house, puts together everything he knows about that family. The faraway look in Sian's eyes; Becky locking herself away from her career and the world. He tries to work out how old Sian would have been when it happened, but he soon swallows that calculation away. He feels sick, wants to weep for his sergeant, wants to be punished for every break he ever denied him.

He recognises a couple of Smethurst's men on the door to the ward. They look glum, as if they would rather be anywhere else. Staffe nods at them and they nod back, bring together their feet as they do it — too formal. One of them steps forward, as if to stop him. 'I was his friend, for crying out loud.' And, outside Johnson's private room, Staffe sees Pennington, surrounded by a bevy of uniforms. He fears the worst.

One of the uniforms nods and Pennington turns round. He is not glum, and nor would he be. The second he opens his mouth, with his superior and faux grave words, Staffe knows that Johnson is on his way out.

'I'm sorry, Will. They're stopping the medication. He's too bad to take the chemo and without that, it's too big to operate on.'

'Where's Becky?' says Staffe.

'She didn't want to bring the children.' Pennington beckons Staffe, sends the officers away. He whispers, 'She's said her goodbyes, is what she said. I said we'd let her be. I've got a WPC over there, on the door. If she wants anything, we'll know.'

'Has he said anything else?'

'He doesn't want to see you, Will.'

'Did he say anything about Jessop? About Nico Kashell?'

'Can't you just treat him like a friend? A colleague.'

'And leave you to control all the information?'

'Be careful, Will,' says Pennington. 'You've got a career to think of. I know you're upset, but . . . '

'Don't patronise me, sir.' Staffe takes a step towards the door to Johnson's room and Smethurst flexes, looks to Pennington for a sign, but the DCI must think there is no more damage left for Staffe to inflict. It spells out how near the end Johnson must be.

'We've got all our statements,' says Pennington. 'Let him make his peace.'

Staffe feels the bile surge up, from his belly up into his throat, and before he can help himself, he rounds on his superior. 'I'm not the coward piling all the blame on to a dead man's shoulders. You . . . '

Smethurst steps in between the two detectives and leans on Staffe, his considerable bulk easing him towards the door to Johnson's room. 'Come on, Will,' he whispers, 'this is between you and Rick now. Don't ruin it.' He takes Staffe by the shoulders, fixes him a deep and penetrating stare. 'Tell him you forgive him, Will. Let him have his peace.'

Staffe nods and reaches out, pushes open the door. He sees his sergeant's eyes close as he enters the room and he sits down between the feed station and the pinpricked Johnson — three different goodnesses going into him.

He takes a hold of Johnson's hand, careful not to disturb the intravenous tubes. He waits for his sergeant to look him in the eye and he leans forward, says in a soft voice, 'I want to say sorry, Rick.' His voice begins to crack. 'I should have been a friend. You should have been able to come to me.'

'It's not . . . ' Johnson can barely speak.

'I know about VABBA, Rick. It was Sian, wasn't it?'

He nods and tears fill up his sad pale eyes. He sets his jaw.

'And you never found out who did it?'

He shakes his head, one way then the other, just the once. 'I took her shopping. It was Christmas. So packed, so many people. I had her and Ricky.' He begins to sob and Staffe squeezes his hand as much as he dare. 'We were having another. Becky was at the hospital.'

Staffe can't hold it back. His jaw goes slack and he feels his lips lose form. His eyes become wet and he leans forward, puts his head on Johnson's chest, feels Johnson's hand on the back of his head. He tries to find the words that would offer the forgiveness that Smethurst talked about.

'We had Charlie. But I lost my life. I couldn't love my baby.'

Staffe waits until he thinks he can speak without breaking down. He wants to ask Johnson if he really did kill Stensson, but he thinks he knows the answer. He will find out by checking Becky's hospital visits but he's sure the records will show it was after Stensson died. Johnson already said it was Christmas. Without looking up, he says, 'You got your life back when you met Sally. That's right, isn't it, Rick? For a while you got it back.'

Johnson doesn't reply.

Staffe looks up and sees his sergeant staring, wide-eyed into the light. He runs the palm of his hand over Johnson's face, checks to see his eyes have closed, and he leaves.

★ ★ ★

Two squad cars are parked up at the bottom of the block of flats off the Holloway Road and Staffe shows his warrant card to gain access to the tenement. He feels ashamed that this

411

cramped and tatty flat is the best a detective sergeant can do for his family in this day and age. As he climbs the stairs to Becky Johnson's floor, he tries to formulate a first sentence he might say to her. He comes up blank.

Outside the door, one of the Met's WPCs stands guard. She pushes a palm out at Staffe and says she knows who he is and she doesn't give a toss, he's not going in. 'No way, sir. I'm sorry.'

Staffe turns his back on the WPC and looks down at the Holloway Road. If he leans out, he can almost make out the line it cuts north up towards Archway. Harrow-on-the-Hill is way beyond but he needs to know what to do when he gets there. He turns back to the WPC and feels the muscles in his face become weak. His voice sounds soft and low. And as he speaks, he believes every word.

'You know, I worked with this woman's husband for three years. I could have been a lot kinder to him and to her. I could have given him more time. His wife in there' — Staffe jabs a finger at the door to the flat — 'and those children, have suffered for what the Force has made them do. And now I need to say these things to Becky Johnson. I have to explain what happened so she can understand that what her husband did has a purpose. It still has a purpose.'

'I don't really know what you're saying, sir,' says the WPC.

'She is a mother. She has to bring those children up in this world. I need to tell her what will happen next. She needs to know. And I need to hear from her what she wants to do next. What she says to me has a bearing on what I do with this case. If that was you, would you want me to hear you or to plough on regardless? What do you think she deserves?'

The WPC nods, says, 'I'd love to let you in, but . . .'

'Thanks,' says Staffe. He wraps the palm of his hand around her elbow and squeezes, gently. He looks her deep in the eyes. 'Just give me five minutes. You can trust me. I promise,' and he opens the door, makes his way into the flat, holding his breath as he goes. It is deathly quiet.

He presses open the door to the lounge as quietly as he can. The curtains are drawn and there is a blue-white wash to the room from the TV screen. He can't see the picture because of the angle, but the sound is turned down and Staffe looks around for signs of life. He makes his way in, so slowly, and sees the back of Becky Johnson's head peeking up from an armchair in front of the TV.

'Becky,' he whispers.

There is no response. As he moves around, his eyes pinned to her chair, he sees that she has Sian on her knee. There is no sign of the two boys. Sian is asleep and has white music buds in her ears. She has an arm wrapped around her mother's neck. Her face is squashed and he can't discern whether she is at peace or perturbed in her slumber.

Becky also seems to be asleep, at first sight. But when he looks closer, he can see her eyes are

413

half open. Her face has a fixed expression — of mild amusement. He moves closer, and crouches, slowly. He takes her wrist in his hand and watches her face for signs of life. As he touches her, there is no change to her expression. Yet the pulse is strong.

He looks into her eyes and there is the faintest registration of life. He looks deep into them and follows what they are fixed upon.

And there . . . there, on the moderately sized LCD television screen, are the moving images of Karl Colquhoun writhing in agony. Staffe can't take his eyes off the screen — until Becky's husband takes out the scalpel, goes to work on Karl's testicles. He scrunches his eyes tight shut when it gets to the part when Johnson had turned the blade to Karl's eyes.

By the time Staffe opens his eyes, the subject has changed. Guy Montefiore is strung up, bleeding from his eyes.

Staffe looks at Becky and gasps. She is looking straight at him now and smiling. She says nothing. Staffe looks down at young Sian and sees that her mother has the wherewithal to rest the palm of her hand over her daughter's eyes — in case she should wake.

'Becky?' he says.

She says nothing. Ever so slowly, she turns her head to the screen, and as Guy Montefiore jags down on to the wood, her smile becomes infinitesimally wider.

Staffe goes across, leans slowly over the wing arm of the chair and kisses Becky Johnson on the forehead. He hopes to God that she will tire of reliving her husband's work, and as he makes his way out of the flat, he makes a prayer that he is just a little bit wiser.

★ ★ ★

Staffe feels sure that he knows what to do. He wishes he wasn't quite so alone, but knows that this is no kind of decision for Pulford to take, and Smethurst and Pennington's interests are too vested. They have their man. It's not the one either of them would have wanted, but he is dead now and they can begin to pile on the guilt, like earth to a coffin. He feels alone. Dreadfully alone.

But not for long.

Sitting on the bonnet of his E-Type and swinging a set of keys around on his forefinger — as if they might be a revolver — is Ross Denness. He looks sharper, cleaner, and somehow more capable than when Staffe first came across him in the Rag. Denness is wearing a suit jacket and twisted jeans. His hair is waxed and he looks handy, smiling at Staffe as if he has nothing in the world to fear from this officer of the law.

'Get off my car!' calls Staffe.

Denness doesn't shift an inch. He says, calm as you like, 'There's no need. You're not going anywhere. Not till we've had a chat.'

'I'll go where I want and when. It's nothing to do with you. I could still have that racial incitement pressed, you prick.'

Denness laughs. 'I'm no prick, and you're no

415

fucking hero. And that's why I'm here — to make sure you've got that straight.' He stands up, probably measures a couple of inches taller than Staffe a good ten years younger. His scars are more pink and Staffe can't work out if this is a good or a bad thing. For sure, Denness has enough violent form, most of it gratuitous, and he would be a firm favourite in anybody's book.

'Move away from my car. I need to go somewhere.'

Denness moves to one side, sweeps his arm like Walter Raleigh and says, 'Making the children suffer just a little bit more, hey?' and as he registers the look of shock on Staffe's face, he slowly spreads his arms, like an Angel of the North, and kicks out with his winklepicking foot — straight to Staffe's groin.

Staffe bends double and sinks to his knees. The rough tar of the road cuts his knuckles as he falls and he gulps for air.

'You must be very proud of yourself, Inspector.'

He looks up at Denness and sees him smile down at him, crossing his arms across his chest as he stamps down on Staffe's torso.

'I've got the measure of you, Denness.' A sharp pain jags into Staffe's lungs as he talks and he thinks Denness might have cracked a rib with the heel of his winklepicker. 'You think you're some kind of vigilante, cleaning up the streets, hey? But you're a thug. Just a thug.'

'Doing your job for you, is what we're doing.'

'We?'

Denness furrows his brow and kicks out at Staffe's head but he manages to roll away and

416

takes a blow on the shoulder. He scuttles away, on his backside, up against the tyre of the E-Type and Denness walks casually after him, still towering above. 'She's a good kid, Sally. Only thing she done wrong was get in the way of that dirty fuckin' nonce. An' you want to send her down. You fuckin' muppet.'

Staffe looks into Denness's eyes as he talks. He believes that he believes what he is saying. There might be some greater cause to be fought behind the common violence. But Staffe sees something else. It is something he sees ten times a day — on a good day. He tries to take in lungfuls of air, readying himself for the next blow, but each pocket of air pushes his lung into the cracked rib. He feels as if he might faint. 'You hate me, don't you, Ross?'

'Why should I?'

'I'm police. I'm a pig. I bang the good people up. Let the nonces get away. I'm on your case, aren't I?' The words wipe the smile off Denness's face. 'And I'll get you, Ross. I'll send you down.'

Staffe watches Denness plant a sharp-toed shoe, ready to swing the other at his head. He wills him to do it. 'You prick,' he says, readying himself for the contact and focusing all his energy on the whoosh that precedes the instant that the material of Denness's low weave jean hits his raised arm.

It comes, the Whoosh! And when it does Staffe rotates his arm — hard and fast. He feels a bone crack. But he also sees Denness's standing foot skid upwards. He watches Denness struggle to keep his balance.

Staffe pushes himself up against the Jag and off the ground, and he throws himself at Denness. He knows that if this struggle lasts any time at all, he is done for, so he dives at Denness's face with his head. He feels the *schlock* of bone on flesh and pulls his head back for another go. But he sees Denness smile, as if he might have something up his sleeve. Their faces are close up and he can smell Denness's breath and aftershave: sweet and leather.

Beneath him, Denness's body shifts, as if he is manoeuvring to get to a weapon. A knife? A gun, even, and Staffe knows he has to end this soon, so he opens his mouth as wide as he can and thrusts his face at Denness's, biting hard into Denness's cheek. He brings his teeth together until he can taste a vestige of blood. He watches Denness's eyes go wild with pain and he brings up his hand, rams his big fingers into Denness's eye sockets. He doesn't just hit the eyes, he hits through them — as if his own sight depended on it. And he rolls away.

He rolls away and he stands, slowly, looking down at Denness holding his head, hands over his eyes and wailing, curled up. There is no sign of a weapon, on the ground or in Denness's pockets.

Jessop taught him that trick, taught him that sometimes, you have to distil all the violence you are capable of and pack it tight into a couple of instants — especially as the years roll on by. He takes the E-Type's keys out of his pocket, puts them in the hand at the end of the arm that feels as if it is fractured. Simply making a weak fist to

418

hold the keys brings tears to his eyes, but with the other hand he takes a hold of Denness's hair and he drags him along the rough tar. He knows Denness is a more complex character than he first thought, but there's no time to investigate that now. He needs a clear mind and knows he must neutralise Denness.

Staffe opens the boot and lifts Denness's blinded head one more time, kicks his backside and watches him tumble headlong into the tiny boot. With the heel of his Chelsea boot, Staffe stamps and stamps at Denness's torso until it finds a way to fold itself into the minuscule void, then he slams the boot shut and locks it.

He sits on the boot and looks at his forearm. He needs to go to hospital but is certain that time is against him. Denness was here to stall him for a reason and when Denness doesn't turn up, wherever, they will know to close the door on him. He reaches into his pocket with his good arm and takes out the one hundred mill of Johnson's morphine and plunges the needle into the solution. He presses the syringe's plunger, expelling the air and squirting the solution high into the air. He lets most of the liquid out, just leaves himself a modicum, knowing this is a fine balance. If ever he needed his wits . . .

* * *

Helena's garden is a lovely thing, but it is not made for security. The willows weep so low that Staffe can scuttle along the path, to the sound of birdsong, and out of view of the drawing room

419

without getting within thirty yards of the house. He takes a wide arc around the perimeter of the herb garden and down along the side of the house where there are no windows at all — save the frosted glass of bathrooms. The pain has returned but he swallows and incants a mantra. It does some good, but the morphine is better. However, he doesn't want to impair his judgement.

All being well, just another ten minutes and his work will be done. He will be able to get a cab to the nearest A & E and put in a call to Harrow nick, saying that they should look for an E-Type Jag in the staff car park of the holidaying school. A Ross Denness can be found in the boot. The keys are in the exhaust and under no circumstances should the officers involved use force to gain entry to the car.

This is what he wishes for. Just a few minutes more.

When he gets to the side of the house, he crouches as he makes his way back round the front, below window height. Once he gets to the French windows of the drawing room, where Helena Montefiore had received him and Pulford those few days ago, he takes pause. He can hear voices, even though the doors are closed. The top panels to the side windows are open and he can hear the singsong, cajoling poshness of Helena. He thinks he can hear her say 'Thommi' but that is not the name he came to hear. He suddenly considers how foolish he will seem if Sally Watkins isn't here.

He waits and waits, but still he doesn't hear

Sally's name. Helena talks to Thommi's friend, a girl called Georgie, and Staffe begins to curse.

As a last ditch, he decides to venture further round so he can see into the room and take one final look before he makes good his retreat. He inches forward and peers into the room, hoping that nobody is looking his way.

And he is in luck — in one way.

The three women sit around a coffee table. It seems that they are looking at a map. They all appear to be happy and they smile, look lovingly into each other's eyes. Thommi talks with her hands and Helena answers back, with her hands. They are like a mirror image. Georgie, hair short-cropped and black, just like Thommi, has her back to the window.

Helena stands up and goes across to the sideboard, comes back with purple-covered booklets and the two girls snatch them up, read them from back to front, cocking their heads and rocking to and fro, laughing at each other.

It would seem that Helena Montefiore, rather than harbouring a criminal, is planning to take her daughter away from it all. While her husband lies dying in a London hospital, she is keeping it all from Thomasina. And who can blame her.

Staffe trusts his judgement. He is pleased to have taken an instant liking to Helena Montefiore. He prepares to knock on the window, wish her all the best, when Georgie jumps up and turns to the window.

Georgie looks straight at Staffe and her mouth drops open. What little colour there is in her pale face quickly drains away. Staffe's heart stops and he looks behind him, to see what it is that has spooked Georgie so, but there is nothing there.

When he turns back to face into the room, Helena has an arm around Georgie. Georgie, with her freshly cropped and dyed hair. Georgie with her brand-new name and her new passport and her new life.

Staffe looks into the eyes of Helena. They narrow and she makes the faintest, imploring smile. Then he looks at Sally Watkins. There is a new life, a new brightness in her eyes. He looks at Thomasina Montefiore who is about to burst into tears. And, finally, he looks back at Georgina. She smiles like he has never seen her smile before and in the instant he decides to walk away, she blows him a kiss. As he turns, the three women embrace and make a tight circle. Walking away, he hears them crying. It is a happy sound and by the time he is in the shade of the weeping willow, it merges with the birdsong.

★　★　★

Staffe goes through to his bathroom in Queens Terrace, takes out his running gear from the Adidas bag and runs the shower. The water jets down, hard on his scalp and shoulders and Staffe turns the heat up a notch so it almost scalds him. He scrubs and scrubs, the smell of coal tar getting thicker and thicker, the steam getting more and more dense.

Tonight, he will run west in the dark and the

river will be silver in the moonlight and it will curve to meet him at Putney Bridge. He will leave it to run into the Deer Park but it will find him again, on the other side of Kingston Gate, closer to its source — back in time.

We do hope that you have enjoyed reading this large print book.

Did you know that all of our titles are available for purchase?

We publish a wide range of high quality large print books including:
**Romances, Mysteries, Classics**
**General Fiction**
**Non Fiction and Westerns**

Special interest titles available in large print are:
**The Little Oxford Dictionary**
**Music Book**
**Song Book**
**Hymn Book**
**Service Book**

Also available from us courtesy of Oxford University Press:
**Young Readers' Dictionary**
**(large print edition)**
**Young Readers' Thesaurus**
**(large print edition)**

For further information or a free brochure, please contact us at:
**Ulverscroft Large Print Books Ltd.,**
**The Green, Bradgate Road, Anstey,**
**Leicester, LE7 7FU, England.**
**Tel:** (00 44) 0116 236 4325
**Fax:** (00 44) 0116 234 0205

*Other titles published by*
*The House of Ulverscroft:*

## IF IT BLEEDS

### Duncan Campbell

Infamous gangster Charlie Hook wants someone to write his biography. He chooses crime reporter Laurie Lane as ghost writer. But the next day Hook is dead, his blood and hair on the walls of his north London mansion. Who killed the last of the London Godfathers? Laurie needs to find the killer to keep his job. There are several possible suspects: the Russian businessman with something dodgy in his Hampstead garden, Hook's two sinister public schoolboy sons, and the relatives of men whom Hook had killed decades ago. And what secrets lurk in Hook's empire? Laurie's search for the killer takes him to the bars of Thailand, and the bowels of the Old Bailey — as bizarre and hair-raising a journey as it is potentially lethal . . .

# JUSTICE DENIED

## J. A. Jance

The investigation of LaShawn Tompkins' murder seems straightforward. Just another ex-drug dealer caught up in turf warfare. Seattle investigator J.P. Beaumont is handed the assignment under the strictest confidence. But as Beau starts digging the situation becomes more complicated. It appears that LaShawn really had turned over a new leaf. Someone had targeted the man for death. Meanwhile, Beau's lover and fellow cop, Mel Soames, is given her own hush-hush investigation. A routine check on registered sex offenders has revealed a disturbing pattern of death by unnatural causes. The latest suggests an inside job and Mel isn't letting go. As Mel's investigation becomes entangled with Beau's, the two begin to uncover a nightmarish conspiracy involving people in high places — which could include their own.

# BREAKING POINT

## John Macken

There is a killer loose on the London underground. He kills without leaving any forensic trace, and seemingly without motive. The UK's elite forensic unit is stretched to the limits trying to find one usable clue. And there is another problem. Before he was sacked as head of the unit, Reuben Maitland developed a system to predict future homicidal behaviour from people's DNA. Now rogue elements in the police are employing Reuben's research to hunt down and incite latent psychopaths beyond their breaking point. Reuben must track down whoever is misusing his technology and stop them before more lives are destroyed. But what he cannot know is that his investigation will lead him directly into the path of the underground killer.

# DAISYCHAIN

## G. J. Moffat

Over the course of three days, the paths of three people's lives will intersect and change forever . . . Logan Finch is sitting pretty, with his penthouse apartment and a shot at making partner in Glasgow's largest law firm. Yet he still pines for the woman he thought was 'the one' and who left him with no word of explanation twelve years ago. Alex Cahill is a client and friend of Logan. The American owns a security business, but has a shadowy past. Detective Constable Rebecca Irvine, of Strathclyde Police's CID, is stuck in a failing marriage. On her first day in the new job she is called to a murder scene. The victim is Penny Grant, Logan's former girlfriend. And her eleven-year-old daughter, Ellie, is missing . . .

# RED BONES

## Ann Cleeves

When a young archaeologist studying on a site at Whalsay discovers a set of human remains, the islanders are intrigued. Is it an ancient find — or a more contemporary mystery? Then an elderly woman is shot in a tragic accident and Jimmy Perez is called in to investigate by her grandson — his own colleague, Sandy Wilson. His enquiries uncover two feuding families whose envy, greed and bitterness have divided the community. Jimmy, surrounded by people he doesn't know and in unfamiliar territory, is out of his depth. Then there's another death and, as the spring weather shrouds the island in claustrophobic mists, Jimmy must dig up old secrets to stop a new killer from striking again . . .

# CRY FOR HELP

## Steve Mosby

Dave Lewis is a man with a history. Haunted by his brother's murder when they were children, and drowning his sorrows over his lost love, Tori, he tries to leave the past behind. Dave had made a promise to Tori, which got him into trouble before, but he won't let that happen again. Detective Sam Currie is a man with a past. A shadow of grief lies over his marriage and his career. He's directed his hatred towards the man he sees as responsible, but he has other priorities right now. A killer is stalking the city, abducting girls and sending texts and emails to their families before he kills them. When Dave Lewis appears to connect both investigations, it's an opportunity Currie can't resist . . .